WITH
REGRETS

Also available by Lee Kelly

The Antiquity Affair (with Jennifer Thorne)
A Criminal Magic
City of Savages

WITH REGRETS

A NOVEL

LEE KELLY

CROOKED
LANE

NEW YORK

Published in the United States by Crooked Lane Books, an imprint of The Quick Brown Fox & Company LLC.

Crooked Lane Books and its logo are trademarks of The Quick Brown Fox & Company LLC.

Library of Congress Catalog-in-Publication data available upon request.

ISBN (hardcover): 978-1-63910-467-3
ISBN (ebook): 978-1-63910-468-0

Cover design by Sarah Brody

Printed in the United States.

www.crookedlanebooks.com

Crooked Lane Books
34 West 27th St., 10th Floor
New York, NY 10001

First Edition: September 2023

10 9 8 7 6 5 4 3 2 1

For my mother, Linda. Best friend, role model, momager extraordinaire.

APRIL 3RD WEEKLY UPDATE—INSPIRATION
Search results for <"eerie" and/or "uncanny" and/or "catastrophe" and/or "apocalypse" and/or "widespread problems" and/or "no known cause" . . .>

UNITED KINGDOM STILL "IN THE DARK"
Governments and Civilians Scramble to Establish Contact with Non-Communicative Isles
New York Times

WASHINGTON, DC—Kelly Davenport was speaking to her mother, a retired sociology professor in London, when their connection was abruptly severed Thursday morning. "I tried calling her back for the better part of two hours," Davenport, 42, said, adding that the last sounds she heard over the line were "**eerie** chirps" and whistling wind. "I can't call or message my dad either, or even reach them through Facebook. Their pages are just frozen in time. It's like they've **disappeared**."

Davenport joins thousands of individuals who, over the past twelve hours, have lost all communication with their family, friends, and colleagues in the UK. Officials have confirmed these **widespread** connection **problems** but have **yet to determine** their **cause**. The **uncanny** pervasiveness of the issues has quickly stoked discomfort, **fear**, and speculation . . .

10 SHOWS "SKYFALL" FANS SHOULD WATCH WHILE THEY WAIT FOR SEASON 6

Go Pop! News

HBO's **post-apocalyptic** saga *Skyfall* remains one of the network's biggest hits (we credit the show's stellar cast and showrunner Ben Schreck's **uncanny** vision). But with six months left until season six (*How can we stand not knowing if Everly survives the burning rain?!*), viewers will have to look elsewhere for their weekly dose of **catastrophic** drama . . .

[See More Results] | [Edit this alert]

**

To: Liz Brinkley
From: Padma Khare
Sent: Saturday, April 2, 12:34 PM
Subject: FW: Re: Reminder—SUNDAY SOIREE!

OMG how did I not know you're going to this?! When's the last time we saw each other, back-to-school night? I know, right, silly of me to think that I can pin down such a bigtime author <3!

AHHH we're going to have so much fun! I can really let loose now that I'm a "Falls Elementary retiree" ;)! New drinking game: sip every time Britta Harris-Che mentions Insta? Gulp if she snaps a pic? Drain wine if she starts demanding we make our lives "rise to the challenge"?
GET READY!

[download entire message]

**

To: Liz Brinkley
From: Tom Brinkley
Sent: Friday, April 1, 5:16 PM
Subject: FW: Re: Reminder—SUNDAY SOIREE!

Thank you for doing this. It's good for me, good for Reid, good for *us*.

Just . . . please try. Okay?

It'll be fun, I promise.

——

To: Mabel Young, Spencer Young, Dev Khare, Padma Khare, Tom Brinkley, Liz Brinkley, Gwenyth Russo, Frank Russo
Cc: Joel Che
From: Britta Harris-Che
Sent: Friday, April 1, 4:15 PM
Subject: Re: Reminder—SUNDAY SOIREE!

Darling friends,

The Harris-Che "Sunday Soiree" dinner party is finally around the corner.

I assure you, this will be a night to remember. As you're all aware, Joel's Pilates prowess has granted him access to the most exclusive workout circles in SoHo, where he frequently rubs shoulders with Manhattan's latest and greatest, including the MICHELIN STAR DREAM TEAM behind the so-very-now restaurant, Cash & Moreno. And—wait for it—Romer Moreno will be serving as *our* personal in-home chef right here in The Falls (we CAN have it all in the 'burbs, and I'm committed to proving it! :)

Seven daring avant-garde courses, top-shelf wine pairings, an intimate setting a la the Harris-Che abode . . . I mean, BEYOND.

Kindly arrive at our home on Sunday, April 3rd by SEVEN SHARP—trust me, you don't want to miss a minute. And remember please, no children (you're very welcome ;).

My absolute best,
Britta

Britta Harris-Che
PR Specialist / Lifestyle Influencer

IG Channel: brittasays
Website: www.brittasays.com
"Life Will Rise to the Challenge"

**

1

Liz

"WHAT IF ALIENS snatched your car on the ride over to Avery's house?" Reid asks. "You can't go to a dinner party if you've been abducted!"

Liz shakes her head at her son, then smiles to herself in the bathroom mirror. As they say, the apple doesn't fall far from the tree. And considering all the brain teasers and riddles she gives to Reid, he'll likely be able to run brainstorming circles around her by the time he's ten. Hell, maybe one day *he* can be her co-writer. Reid even looks like Liz's mini-me: dark thick hair, lanky frame, freckles.

She rubs her face with tinted moisturizer. "Bonus points for creativity, but Dad would insist we call and cancel—and wouldn't the aliens take our phones? That leaves Dad struggling to be polite right down to his last moments on the dissection table." She adds in her husband Tom's grainy voice, *"WAIT! I just need to RSVP!"*

Reid doubles over with laughter. She probably shouldn't be encouraging him to cook up excuses for her. She promised Tom she'd attend Britta's "night to remember" (what a stomach-roiling way to refer to a dinner party) smiling, sans writing sweatpants, and eager for seven courses of Britta's insufferable and unsolicited "life advice."

Liz swallows. "What else you got?"

As Reid flicks his eyes to the ceiling, deep in thought, Liz leans forward to apply her eyeliner. She's actually putting on eyeliner for these people. God, does Tom owe her big. All weekend, she's been thinking about how to parlay her grudging acquiescence tonight into some sort of exciting payback: more writing hours out of Tom in exchange? Or an overnight camping trip to the Poconos, with just their family of four? Remuneration for this Stepford soiree must truly be rendered.

Reid sighs. "Aliens are too unbelievable, anyway."

Liz's youngest, Callie, slips into the bathroom and bee-lines for Liz's open makeup container. Callie looks both ways and pockets a lipstick, stealthy as a purse snatcher.

Liz gently takes the weapon of pink destruction away and places it on her cabinet's highest ledge.

"Wait." Reid's eyes light up. "What if instead of aliens—"

"It's monsters!" Callie adds, gleeful to get in on the action. "Monsters trapped us in the kitchen, in the driveway—"

Reid flips his floppy hair out of his eyes, leans down, and scary-wiggles his fingers in front of his sister's face. "What if our new babysitter is a monster?"

All of Callie's bravado promptly falls away. She looks up at Liz with saucer eyes. "I really don't want you to go tonight, Mommy."

Reid drops his creepy jazz hands. "Yeah, why do you have to if you don't even *want* to?"

Where, exactly, to start?

Because your dad framed tonight as a relationship crossroads—invest in our lives here in The Falls or prepare for Brinkley family Armageddon?

Because the suburbs are an ancient cult pledged to the evil god of Conformity, and they might eat us if we don't at least try to "belong"?

Because adults have to do things they don't want to do all the time?

Like a reflex, Liz mumbles, "When you're an adult, you'll understand." Then cringes at herself.

She bends down to meet Callie face to face and stares into her big brown doe eyes. Her five-year-old is already looking more like the "bigger little girl" she's destined to become: her rounder chin more chiseled, her shoulders broad and lean. Liz's chest contracts a little. "I promised Daddy. If I could bring you, I swear I would. Besides, you're going to have way more fun here than I will there. Promise."

Liz's phone, sandwiched between makeup bags, bleeps with an incoming ping. *Please, please let it be Laura.* It would be such a game-changer if her sister Laura's flight landed early. They could send this new sitter home as soon as Laura arrived, or cancel her altogether. Liz could even duck out early from Britta and Joel's. Who'd fault her for wanting to see her sister on her layover?

But it's just another news alert about the UK blackout.

Liz is honestly surprised she hasn't gotten more alarmed about this "blackout" yet, but maybe work and the steady diet of surreal news these past few years have just finally pushed her past a saturation point with the supposed "weird." Even her and Reid's games of *Would You Rather?* on their commutes to school can't always "out-strange" the real world anymore. Or maybe it's because the blackout story was promptly followed by another freaking accolade for *Skyfall*. Seriously, "visionary" Schreck? The man's a tyrant! If Liz reads one more article with the subtext *"Dear Liz: You Missed Your Golden Goose,"* she's going to need to start Zoom therapy again.

A text pings below the news alert:

Britta H-Che

SO GLAD YOU'VE TAKEN MY RECOMMENDATION ON SABINA! TIME TO LOOSEN UP A BIT, YES? >:)

LIFE WILL RISE TO THE CHALLENGE (IF YOU LET IT ;)

-B

"Oh my God, is she nauseating," Liz mumbles.

Recommendation.

Such bullshit. Last week, Britta had "serendipitously crossed paths" with Tom on his commute home. When Tom tried to tell Britta that he and Liz couldn't attend tonight's party since his parents were booked, Britta whipped out her glitter-studded phone and called Sabina on the spot.

What kind of meddling psycho does that?

"Who?" Reid asks at the same time as Tom walks into the bathroom behind them.

"Britta," Liz supplies, while Tom attempts to cover for her with a ruffle of Reid's hair and a "No one, honey."

Through the mirror, Tom shoots Liz one of his "friles."

Trademarked by Reid, Tom's (increasingly used) signature facial expression is a cross between a frown and a smile. As Reid said when he coined the term, *"It's like your eyes are mad, Dad, but your mouth can't decide."*

"You are going to try with the Ches tonight, aren't you?" Tom asks as he smooths his own light brown wavy hair, which is perfectly styled, longish on top but swept back in a way Liz thinks is decidedly debonair. He's freshly shaven, too, which always makes him look younger. Is that a new button-down shirt? And the splurge Prada loafers that Liz got him for Christmas last year?

You look nice, Liz almost says, but stops because of course he does.

Everyone else gets Tom's best.

Liz wrangles on a smile. "This is me trying." Then she angles her phone in front of her face selfie-style, winks her only eye with too much hastily applied eyeliner, and cocks her hips to display her ratty Rutgers sweatshirt. She raises the glass of liquid courage (aka cabernet) beside her. "Sweatshirt chic is seriously BEYOND."

Tom of Two Years Ago would've laughed at the Britta dig. But Suburban Tom just pastes on another *frile*. "You can't alienate these people, Liz; they practically rule The Falls."

"Oh come on, I'm just messing around."

"Yeah, well, your 'messing around' at that Delmonico's get-to-know-you dinner nearly started a war."

"Because Britta has no sense of humor! I didn't mean her life was *literally* a show. Shouldn't that be a major compliment to an 'influencer' anyway?"

Tom turns to Reid. "Wouldn't it be nice if Mommy and Avery's parents were actually friends? Wouldn't it be nice to have more playdates with Avery?"

Reid tosses his shaggy bangs and shrugs. "I don't really care."

Reid's obvious lie pricks her with sharp, almost overwhelming guilt. Avery Harris-Che has been Reid's best friend since he started first grade at The Falls Elementary. But Reid's a smart kid—he's heard Liz and Tom's running arguments about "priorities." Reid eavesdrops on their car rides, weekend bickering, silences. And he would never break allegiance with Liz.

"Hey, Tom, can we just . . ."

"Come on, you two." Tom pinches his nose. "Let's just let Mom get ready."

". . . start over?" Liz whispers.

But they're already gone.

Liz makes an angry monster face at the mirror, then takes a big gulp of wine and leans against the sleek marble counter. The counter that Tom picked out at some point when Liz was passed out in Callie's rocking chair, zonked from round-the-clock nursing and *World Breakers* edits. Tom picked out nearly all the home's finishes, including the "new build" itself. Liz barely even remembers agreeing to the move. Something about a yard for Reid and Callie? A way for the kids to grow up more "well-rounded"? Some days she aches for the city's anonymity—her bubble of four in a sea of millions of strangers. Reid, Callie, and Tom are all Liz needs, all she's *ever* needed.

Which is obviously not the case anymore for Suburban Tom.

Liz grabs her phone, desperate to think about something else, and checks her emails, hoping for an update on the fate of her book series. Still no word from Garrison Cromwell's team about her idea for the ending to the *World Breakers* trilogy.

"Don't worry," she murmurs. "It's a killer plot twist." But now the email silence is conjuring dread. *Stop, you're the writing muscle of this supposed "collaboration." Garrison's just the . . . celebrity sparkle.*

The self-pep talk doesn't help. If her co-writer is a pain in the ass, his agent is a walking hemorrhoid. Neither is going to just give their approval and let it be easy.

It's *never* easy.

"Come on, Cromwell, just surrender," she whispers.

Refresh . . . no emails.

"Liz, a car pulled up," Tom calls from downstairs. "I think Sabina's already here."

"Crap." Liz hurries to her bedroom's curtained window. Sure enough, a white Nissan Altima is creeping into the drive. Gah, she planned on having time to show the new sitter the house, grill her a bit, make sure this college girl has the savvy and wherewithal to keep Reid engaged. And Callie gets scared at night, so Liz needs to explain the Lullaby app and Callie's complicated night-light situation. Tonight is really not the night she wants to train a sitter.

Liz sprints into her closet, throws on her tried-and-true "family dinner out" wardrobe of jeans and a silk blouse, then doubles back to the messy bathroom. Grabbing her eyeliner pencil, she tries to match her left eye to her right—close enough—and dusts bronzer across her freckled cheeks. She coughs from inhaling some of the powder while she twists her long, dark, wet hair into the presentable looking updo she mastered when Reid was a baby.

She gut-checks herself in the mirror. Nothing fancy. But presentable.

By the time the doorbell rings, Liz is already hurrying down the stairs with her leather tote bag slung over her shoulder.

"The MONSTER's here! Mwahaha!" Reid sprints around the stairwell.

Callie careens after him. "Reid, STOP SAYING THAT!"

Reid spins and waggles his eyebrows at Liz. "I heard the only way you can tame a monster is with candy and a movie marathon."

Liz laughs. "Nice try, buddy."

His face falls. "Aw, come on, please? Can't we at least stay up till Aunt Laura gets here?"

Tom bellows from deep inside the pantry: "Are you getting the door? I'm trying to find a nice bottle; Joel's an aficionado. Spencer's texting about Barolo. What do you think?"

Liz thinks she may well break the world record for most eye rolls in a single evening.

She hurries across the cluttered foyer, nearly tripping over the kids' mountain of shoes—Callie now hugging her legs, Reid beside her—and flings the door open.

Liz's jaw locks when she sees who's standing on her doorstep.

Oh. Oh God. *No.*

"My, my, what a *welcome committee*," a middle-aged woman sporting a perfect lob blowout and stylish taupe jogging suit calls from the Nissan's driver's seat. The car's wedged at the top of Liz's driveway, engine still running. The woman waves at Liz—a big fan girl wave: frantic hand, manic smile.

Liz, though, isn't focusing on her. She's mesmerized by the young girl on her stoop.

"Thanks for the ride, Mom, but I've got it from here," the girl calls over her shoulder.

Mom-chauffeur puts her hand over her mouth in an exaggerated *Oops!* "That's right. Pretend you never saw me! You've got a professional on your hands, after all! I'm Mila Ford, Joel and Britta's next-door neighbor. Such a lovely family, the Harris-Ches. If you need anything—it's Liz, right?—I'm right across town. Speaking of, your husband said you have a landline? Sabina doesn't have her own phone yet, which we will remedy as soon as her business gets off the ground . . ."

"Your services will no longer be required, Mom, much obliged!" Sabina says tightly.

The girl spins back around to face Liz, Reid, and Callie and breathes out a slow, yoga-worthy exhale. She slaps on a huge smile and extends her hand to Liz.

"I'm Sabina Ford. *Ford Sitting: Bringing Care to Childcare.*" Sabina says that last line in a tone worthy of an "*in a world . . .*" voiceover. She adds, "That'll be my slogan, anyway, once my cousin has time to design my company website."

Liz still can't seem to speak. Sabina has blunt blonde bangs, a dust of chin acne, and dons a pencil skirt and fully buttoned-up oxford, which somehow only exaggerates the fact that she can't be older than eleven. Maybe twelve, if she's a late bloomer.

College.

Tom promised she was *in college*—and a college-aged stranger was a stretch for Liz anyway. As she's argued with Tom countless times, they do not *need* to go out more than Liz's in-laws can handle. Doesn't anyone other than Liz question modern society's reliance on random "babysitters"? There's no way prehistoric couples were trusting unvetted cavepeople to watch their primeval pride and joy. Just because her counterparts have their priorities messed up doesn't mean Liz has to go along with it!

Reid cocks his head, flashes his mischievous toothless grin at Sabina. "Wait . . . I'm almost as tall as you."

Liz takes a shuddering breath. "Um, hi, Sabina. Yes, are you . . . in middle school? Eighth grade, or . . . ?"

"Seventh," Sabina squeaks out, like a dirty secret. "Ask my mom, though, and I'm nearly twelve going on thirty." She laughs nervously. "And I've already had two years working as a mother's helper."

Liz aches to sprint after Mrs. Ford's car, jump onto her hood *21 Jump Street* style, but the sedan disappears down Old Falls Road.

Sabina says in a rush, "I'm trained in CPR, too. And I've created dozens of original games and activities based on the latest pediatric research. Kids today are so overstimulated by screens, don't you think? That's why Ford Sitting has a passionate commitment to old-fashioned fun, promptness, reliability. And did I mention my time as a mother's helper?"

"Indeed you did."

"It's just so hard to break into the solo sitting market," Sabina says. "*Experience requires experience*, right? So Mrs. Harris-Che says I just need to get out there and claim my experience. Let my life *rise* to the challenge." Sabina huffs from the intensity of that little speech and smiles. "It's really amazing of you and Mr. Brinkley to give me a shot."

Before Liz can correct her, Sabina bends down eye to eye with Callie. "You must be Reid, right?"

Callie looks up at Liz, confused, but gives a tentative giggle.

Sabina nods solemnly at Reid, extending her hand. "And you must be Mr. Brinkley. It's such a pleasure to meet you, sir."

"Are you kidding? I'm *Reid*!" Reid devolves into chuckles, and Callie, seeing that it's safe, gives a big *ah-ha-hah-hah* fake kid-laugh.

But Liz isn't laughing. She is *light-years* from laughing. She's not completely shocked—Britta Harris-Che makes a living telling everyone how they ought to live their lives—but she's gone too damn far, setting up Reid and Callie to be Ford Sitting guinea pigs. Liz can't trust Sabina with them; she's a kid herself! No, as soon as Tom sees how young she is, he'll have to agree. They'll cancel, and it won't be Liz's fault. It's obviously *Britta's* fault.

"Come in a sec, Sabina." Liz opens her door wider. Silver lining: at least this is a legitimate excuse. "I have to talk to my husband, Tom."

Sabina beams. "Oh yes! He was with Mrs. Harris-Che when she booked me."

"Hey, Sabina, you want any candy?" Reid says, then grins bashfully at Liz. "Just kidding, you like Magna-Tiles?"

Callie sidles up beside Sabina. "You've got to see how tall we can build a castle!"

"I would *love* to." Sabina takes off her shoes and follows the kids into the house while Liz beelines to find Tom.

"You ready?" Tom murmurs to his phone as Liz appears beside him in the pantry. "This Neighborhood Watch chain is such a time suck, I swear. Damon Campbell wants a 'street meeting' next weekend about the new stop sign. But all for the good of the community, right—"

"We need to talk." Liz gestures toward the door to their basement stairs. Tom looks suspicious but follows. They pause when they reach the last step, simultaneously wincing at the mound of unopened boxes, trash, and recently and not-so-recently purchased products. They gingerly navigate through what Liz has taken to calling their "staging area."

Liz's writing has led to way too many online purchases—research books and novels, sure, but also more creative, tenuous "necessities." This post-apocalyptic series with Cromwell, and her stint in the *Skyfall* writing room before that, have this uncanny way of worming into Liz's daydreams, nightmares . . . and weekly buy lists of prepper "must-haves." The past year alone, Liz has purchased a monthly subscription plan of astronaut food, water pouches, fold-up cots, and even—after lengthy, frustrating discussions with Tom—an Elephant Safe Room, installed in the basement alcove. *Mental note: they still have to wire that thing.* And, okay, maybe it's all over the top, but she writes it off as a worst-case scenario insurance policy. For tax purposes, too. Anyway, it's not like Tom's a Marie Kondo devotee. His Amazon hoard just consists of recommendations from other people: Lacrosse sticks his brother swore made their nephew a "fourth grade–level player." A set of vinyl kettlebells that "changed Joel's life." A keto starter kit that Dev Khare's company sponsors.

Liz holds her cell to her ear. "Hello, yes?" She keeps up with the fake phone call, adding a pause for effect. She looks

Tom dead in the eye. "Ah. It's *The Babysitter's Club*. They want their kid sister back."

Tom shakes his head. "Liz, what—"

"Sabina, Tom . . . Sabina is prepubescent!" Liz paces. "There's no way we can go."

"What are you talking about?"

"You said Britta said the sitter was *in college*," Liz hisses.

"Yes," Tom says. "She said she was 'in school,' and 'in school' means college!"

"*Seventh grade*. She's never watched kids on her own before. I mean, how did you not know? You talked to her—"

"For a second." Tom at least has the decency to look shocked. "Britta made all the arrangements."

Liz points her finger at him. "I know what I said, but this isn't safe—"

"Aw, Liz, come on, Laura's coming in about an hour—"

"Then you go, tell them I have a stomach bug or a migraine, or that I sprained an ankle."

Tom throws up his hands. "That's not the point. They expect *you* there—"

"I don't care!"

Cartoon cowboy-worthy hollers drown them out as Reid and Callie dash down the basement stairs. Each of them carries a massive mound of blankets, books, Magna-Tiles.

Behind them, Sabina holds a stack of board games—a bowl of popcorn precariously balanced on top—and a bucket of flashlights dangles from the bend in her elbow. She stops short on the bottom step. "Whoa."

Tom leans over to grab the popcorn and games. Meanwhile, Liz's inner tribunal is still on its feet, roaring, decrying injustices.

"Sorry about the mess." Tom's face folds into a *frile*. "We're keeping Amazon in business down here. Tom, by the way."

"Sabina. Nice to meet you in person, Mr. Brinkley." Sabina sidesteps the staging area. "Um, sorry to add more clutter, but we're planning a screen-free party. True play is so important."

She eagerly turns to Liz. "According to the American Association of Pediatrics—"

Reid, with blankets up to his eyes, jumps in front of her. "We're going to tell ghost stories and play games and build forts. Mwahahaha!"

Callie does a little shimmy dance. "Woohoo!"

She and Reid dash into the sitting room beyond the staging area.

Liz stutter-steps back. Are those . . . her kids? It's been minutes, *minutes* since they've met Sabina, and they're already treating her like a long-lost friend?

Liz should be thrilled, she knows this, beyond relieved. But all she feels is a sharp jab of inadequacy.

"Their bedtime's actually around seven thirty, Sabina." Liz swallows. "And they're quite the handful trying to get to sleep. Though speaking of, I'm not really feeling—"

"*Bedtime*," Tom jumps in. "We're thinking it'll be easier if you let them stay up."

Liz stares at him.

"Liz's sister, Laura, is flying in from California tonight and sleeping at our house to break up her travel," Tom says quickly. "Aunt Laura's got bedtime down pat. She can take over when she gets here. When's Laura due in, Liz, around eight?"

Liz's stare becomes a glare.

Still, Tom chugs onward. "I bet Sabina can handle them for a couple of hours until Laura arrives."

Sabina beams. "Absolutely!"

"Oh, and don't worry about the safe room." Tom clears his throat. "It's not wired, so the kids can't lock themselves in. Besides, they know not to play in there."

"I was wondering if it was even *real*," Sabina says.

Tom gives his nervous laugh. "My wife likes to be prepared; sort of comes with the *World Breakers* territory."

"Mr. Che told me about your series, Mrs. Brinkley." Sabina blushes. "The first book is amazing. Do you think they'll make it a TV show like *Skyfall*?"

"Are you guys going to *go*?" Reid calls out. "Sabina, come build with us."

"Sure!" Sabina says. "One second."

"Wait." Liz steps forward. How has she completely lost control of this situation?

"It's amazing how fast they've taken to you," Tom tells Sabina, but his eyes stay locked on Liz. "We were just saying how much we need a real sitter. Reid and Callie are older now, and Mrs. Brinkley and I, well . . . we need to live our lives. Tonight's the perfect night to try. We'll be *right* down the street." He makes another frile. "If we can't try now, I don't know when we will."

Sabina nods sagely—as if she could possibly follow any of that.

Liz, flushed and blindsided, blinks away fury tears, her eyes drifting to the kids again, the pile of games, their fort . . . then to their small French-doored TV room beyond. She can almost see her and Tom in there still—his words from last night hanging there, haunting her. They'd been watching *Walking Dead* reruns after Reid and Callie were in bed, when Liz joked that zombieland was less precarious than high-def suburbia. "At least zombies have the decency to attack you to your face. Stepfords rarely give you that courtesy."

Tom, though, had looked so defeated by her joke. "Isn't it exhausting?"

"Isn't what exhausting?"

"Liz Brinkley against the *world*?"

They'd watched the rest of the show in silence, Tom oblivious, or apathetic, to the fact that she was still reeling from that sucker punch.

It used to be us, Liz had wanted to say so badly. *It used to be us against the world.*

Liz shakes her head. Is she incapable of compromise? Unable to even try with these people that Tom so clearly wants to impress? Is Tom right? Is *she* the problem? Has he been pulling away, or is she pushing him?

Liz slowly pockets her phone. "Your mom asked about our landline?"

Sabina looks at Liz hopefully.

"It's by the stove, if we need to reach each other," Liz says. "I'll leave my number, Tom's, too. My sister Laura's, just in case. Call if you need *anything*. And if you're not comfortable, we can always come home—"

"Thank you so, so much." Sabina glances at Reid and Callie, happy as clams as they stack Magna-Tiles. "Everything's going to be fine. No, *great*. Enjoy yourself!"

Liz and Tom will be a few miles down the road. Five minutes across town. Right in The Falls.

Still. *Enjoyment* is out of the question.

2

Britta

Prepare for the Extraordinary

> [*Instagram post displays a bottle of Duet champagne bordered by lit candles and lush flowers.*]

Brittasays　　　　✔Follow

New Jersey

Lots of people ask me how to start claiming the life they want to live and I always say: buy the saddle before the horse. Curate the home "future you" deserves. Build the set for YOUR story and your life will rise to the challenge. Beauty, elegance, confidence, power, in that order. Now look at this champagne again . . . the lilies, the candles. Do you see how it demands that success, joy, and celebration <u>will</u> follow? #brittasays #risetothechallenge #empowerment #lifestyle #elegance #duetchampagne #birchcandles #mandaflorist #selfcare #wellness #wellbeing

B RITTA CROPS THE photo a tad, adds a Clarendon filter for more high-impact sparkle, and shares the post to her feed. *There. And only 6:43, plenty of time.*

She drops her phone and spins around, taking in the full glamour of her newly renovated home. The dizzying in-vogue chandelier that looks like a glass firework frozen mid-boom above her black-and-white tiled entryway. The custom walnut shelves filled with curated knickknacks and trinkets that run the length of their glittering grand hall. Across the corridor, the crystal-studded serving trolley, the just-handsome-enough-to-not-be-intimidating young server behind it prepping modern old fashioneds (so very now). The arrangements of lilies and dahlias threading the grand hall like lace. Her home screams beauty, elegance, confidence, looks cut from her younger self's dreams.

She smiles. Her own success is sure to follow.

"MOM?!"

Britta's smile wavers. She calls up the steps, "It's not eight eleven, darling!"

"But we need help!"

Britta resists the urge to groan and instead trades knowing smiles with the young sommelier carrying a box of wine bottles into the kitchen. The silk chiffon of Britta's high-neck dress swishes as she takes the stairs, her heels magnificently echoing across her two-story foyer with a satisfying *clock-clock-clock*. She catches herself in the full-length mirror when she reaches the top step and pauses dramatically. Her long blonde hair is all soft waves, thanks to GlowBar; her Dovia foundation and eye shadow pop. Her dress-and-heel combo makes her legs look even more sculpted and spectacular (easy plug maybe for #FallsBarre?).

She grabs her phone, assumes picture pose—left leg slightly in front, right hand on hip, chin set to a dramatic tilt—and snaps an #OOTD selfie to post later. Tagged with something about treating yourself like a queen? Or building your castle, perhaps? This chiffon and tulle dress just looks so *regal* . . . it really does.

A news alert lights up her screen. Wait, why on earth is UK travel suspended?

"Mom!"

Britta snaps at the mirror, "Christ, Avery, where's the fire!"

She swipes away the alert, stomps down the hall and throws open Avery's bedroom door to find her three children in darkness, each encased in a halo of blue light, as if they're all swimming in their own private little lagoons. Britta's oldest, Avery, is tummy-down on her bed. She looks up from her iPad. "Jane can't get YouTube."

Britta says, "So did you reset the Wi-Fi?"

"I forget the password," Avery says.

Britta crosses the room and grabs her five-year-old Jane's device. As she does, she notices Marco is wearing his threadbare Mickey Mouse PJs *again*, instead of the new ones she purchased. Britta silently curses their housekeeper, Maria, for not hiding the Mickey pair this afternoon as Britta asked; by now the pants are so small they're basically capris. She is not tolerating *Disney homeless chic* tonight.

"You've got to change," Britta tells her three-year-old, her eyes still on Jane's screen.

Marco wails. "No, no, Mommy, I don't want to, I love these—"

Britta stares at him. "Then no more *T Is for Trucker* time."

"Christ, FINE!" Marco stomps out of the room.

Britta makes a mental note to watch her language in front of the kids.

She refocuses on Avery. "Okay. Run me down again."

Avery sighs. "For the five jillionth time, we set the alarm for eight-oh-eight." Her oldest sits up straight and locks her eyes on Britta, just like a good soldier. "I'll get Jane and Marco off their iPads and to the breezeway to wave to everybody from the second floor at eight eleven sharp. Marco will rub his eyes and say, *I'm tired*—"

"*I* should get to say it. I'm older," Jane mutters.

Britta raises her hand. "Don't even start—you refused to do a dress rehearsal." She hands Jane back her fully functioning iPad. Jane's pout falls away.

Avery continues. "Then you say, *Be right back, everyone!* But then I say, *Don't worry, I've got it, Mom! I love helping!* Then we come back here and shut down the screens by nine."

The bedroom door creaks, and Britta twirls around.

Joel.

Britta's husband looks around warily. "Everything all right in here, rascals?"

When the kids just stare at him, blankly, Joel fully steps inside, pressing his back to Avery's unicorn wallpaper. Joel wears a perfectly tailored white shirt and undone polka-dot bow tie, his long, thick, dark hair styled back in a look reminiscent of *American Psycho*. He smiles sadly at his children, his tan skin luminous under the tech-blue glow.

Christ, is he beautiful. Which just pisses Britta off all the more. Because she knows—despite how much she sometimes fantasizes about murdering him now, how much he's killing *her*, little by little, each time he comes home late without explanation, passes out drunk in the living room, makes a scene at The Falls Club—there's still no alternative universe where twenty-nine-year-old Britta wouldn't have been compelled to sleep with him on that fateful European "adventure."

"Did you lock the guest room?" Britta asks Joel, then gives a small, meaningful nod toward Avery. "Guest room" obviously being code for Joel's new first-floor "separation quarters."

But Joel is focused on Avery and Jane, both oblivious, lost in separate worlds of neon color and high squeaky voices.

"Joel, did you lock—"

"You're really letting them fall asleep to the iPads?" He shakes his head, his bright eyes narrowing. "Would it have killed you to get a sitter?"

Britta's heart clamors into fight mode. She's explained *this* five jillion times. "That doesn't quite work with doing it all, having it all, now does it, Joel?"

Joel just stares at her incredulously.

"They're fine. They know the drill. Avery can handle everything, can't you, sweetheart?"

Avery says to her screen, "Promise I've got it, Dad."

Britta feels a surge of pride over her daughter's self-sufficiency, then grandly opens her arms, like a welcoming circus conductor. "See? *Everything's* under control."

Joel plops down next to Avery and kisses her head. "I know you've got it," he whispers. "I just want you to get to be a kid."

Avery glances up with pure adoration—"Love you, Dad"—before burrowing back to the iPad.

Joel rests his head in his hands.

"Stop being so dramatic," Britta says. "I handled a lot more when I was a kid."

"I'm just tense." Joel glares up at her. "Aren't I allowed to be tense before 'a show'?"

"You're not ruining tonight for me, you understand?" In fact, this conversation has to end. She refuses to let Joel unwind her. There's too much at stake. All her hard-earned, hard-won victories come down to tonight: Dev Khare, CMO of the cutting-edge wellness and lifestyle brand Clementine, could launch her into macro influencer status. MACRO! "Did you check Romer's canapés like I asked?"

Joel gives a bitter laugh. "He's a Michelin star chef, Britta; I think he can handle it."

"Fine, I'll do it, like everything else." She sidesteps him. "And wipe that scowl off your face. Guests are here in minutes and *you're not a sullen teenager!*"

Britta nearly trips on Avery's dollhouse on her way out the door. *Get ahold of yourself: elegance, confidence, power.* But she's fuming as she stomps down the recently renovated back stairwell into the kitchen. She has a sudden urge to punch a wall—to take one of the back hallway's artfully arranged bowls of floating votive candles and smash it against the slate floor. Joel is intent on dragging her two steps backward every time she takes one forward. He almost derailed this entire night with his "March Madness party" antics. Britta still can't believe she lost two soiree invites to *Gwen and Frank Russo* to shut Gwen up—there were so many other more strategic invites, but no, Joel had to get wasted and make a spectacle in front of *The Falls' biggest gossip*!

As she clomps down the corridor, she can't resist a much-needed detour into the kids' playroom to do some rearranging. Didn't she tell Maria to showcase an eclectic mix of the kids' artwork across the room's clothesline? There's too much finger-painting, a total lack of second-grade realism.

Finally satisfied, she heads into the gleaming breakfast nook. "Are all the appetizers ready for seven fifteen sharp?"

The lithe young sous chef stops stirring the sizzling pan before him, then turns around to face her.

Britta squirms. It's annoying, really, how this man's allure has been completely disarming her, ever since he arrived on their doorstep with his four-person staff. Romer Moreno, the younger, less-accomplished member of the Cash & Moreno culinary duo—with his shock of black hair, decadent tattoo sleeves, and an olive complexion so flawless Britta's dying to ask him if he uses spray services. His charm almost feels like a personal affront. A consolation prize on a night when charm alone won't cut it. She nagged Joel for *months* about locking in tonight's date with Cash & Moreno, to sign a formal catering contract—and when Joel had finally gotten around to it, only Romer was free to attend. No matter that Joel also does Pilates with Romer and head chef Nico Cash, that he practically squats at their restaurant bar after class (she found the pics on Instagram), or that Britta scheduled the dinner on a Sunday so that Moreno *and* Cash could be here with Michelin-starred bells on.

Romer smiles. "Come see for yourself." Of course, charming Romer has an accent to boot. Venezuelan, Joel said, with a voice that reminds Britta of drumbeats, dim lights, the sound of a far-off ocean (#SereneinSouthAmerica).

She slides closer to inspect the rows of ruby-red tuna tartare, the mini clouds of burrata floating on tiny spoons, the assortment of golden-fried empanadas sizzling on the stove.

She's about to admit that everything looks perfect when Romer leans against her counter and adds, "But are *you* ready?"

She straightens. What a silly question.

"I'm really glad you could take advantage of this opportunity," she says carefully. "A pity your boss wasn't available too, but it will be . . . *character-building* to run your own show for a night. To take the reins and show us your flair."

The self-satisfied smile slides from Romer's face. "Nico Cash is not my boss."

"Good for you as well, to get your name around in the 'burbs. And great buzz for Cash & Moreno. Lots of the guests tonight are very important, very well-connected people."

Romer studies his empanadas and bites his lip. "Joel and Nico told me you are—how do they say—Instafamous, yes?" He tosses the pan with a quick flick of his wrist. "You share stories of your home, yourself, your family?"

Instafamous. Britta loathes that word. "Well, Romer, there's quite a lot more to it. I'm in the business of telling people what they *want*."

"I saw. And admit, it is hard to look away. You paint a pretty picture. Very convincing." Romer peers back at her, his tapestry of tattoos gleaming under the kitchen's low lights. "Though it left me curious . . . what do *you* want?" He tosses his hair and smiles again. Smirks, really. If Britta didn't know better, she'd say he was flirting with her.

Or is he poking fun at her?

"Well, that's obvious. I—"

She stops. There's a car pulling up—she can see it on their security tablet resting on the marble kitchen counter. A sleek, black Lexus winding around the small garden island in the center of their long drive.

She clomps around the island to peer closer. The Russos. Damn it, Gwen and Frank are the first to arrive? It's not even seven!

"Joel?" Britta cries. She fluffs her hair, uses her camera's photo app to check her lipstick and hurries down the back hall. "Joel, Gwen's here. I need you by my side looking HAPPY, RIGHT NOW!"

"Very interesting, the suburbs," Romer murmurs.

"Joel," Britta calls again. "I'm not joking!"

She dashes into the family room, peers around at the empty space teeming with gold-tasseled pillows, dimly lit tortoise shell sconces, tasteful art—but no Joel.

Bastard. He promised he'd fix things tonight. He swore he'd explain away his antics at The Club last month, show their friends what they expect to see, remind everyone that they're the family you wish you were; #Brittasays doesn't work without all of it. Really, what does he have to complain about? His gorgeous wife? His beautiful kids? He's a trust-fund baby, for hell's sake, who quit working at his family's fund years ago. A bona fide thirty-eight-year-old man of leisure!

"Joel," she hisses. "Please stop fucking with me!"

She checks the playroom, then pushes against the door to Joel's current bedroom. It's locked, lights off, from what she can tell.

As she pulls away, huffing, her eyes fall on the mudroom. The garage door's been cracked open. The caterers aren't setting up in there, are they? She *just* told them absolutely not.

She stomps toward the door, ready to tear someone a new one, and saunters through it.

"OHMIGOD!" Britta steps back, right heel buckling, and stumbles chiffon forward into the row of trashcans.

"Jesus, Britta!" Joel says from the driver's seat of his new royal blue Westa.

He covers himself with one hand and, with his other, swipes the contents of the passenger's seat to the floor. He's not fast enough, though. Britta already saw it through the window. The tangle of naked arms—or legs?—on his iPad. A mirror. The way Joel's hastily zippering his pants.

He stumbles out of the car door toward her. She tries to back away but slips again, this time careening into the recycling bin.

"Britta—"

"Don't touch me." She rights herself and looks down, horrified. A gash of mud now streaks her lovely, delicate chiffon dress. "What the hell were you doing?"

"What does it look like!"

Britta's head swivels back toward the mudroom. Did anyone see him? Hear them? Could Gwen and Frank already be inside? "*Now?* Are you insane?"

Joel sputters, his face red and blotchy. "Well, you called me a sullen teenager—"

"Are you actually blaming me for this?"

"No, it's . . . this is just me relieving the tension!"

"You're masturbating in a car as our guests arrive!"

Britta wipes her eyes, then quickly stops, remembering she has on enough mascara to paint her entire face Emerald Envy (#Shisiedo #MascaraInk).

"Get your shit together." She swallows a gasp of air. "And meet me in the foyer."

Joel runs his fingers through his hair. "Wait, Britta, what did you see—"

"Ten seconds."

She hurries through the kitchen, past Romer, past the beaming servers now poised in the gallery with trays of canapés and champagne. She can't think, can't hardly breathe.

She looks down at her dress, lets the new mud stain anchor her to the here and now, to something tangible, something she can fix. If she keeps her hand on her hip, she can mask the smudge. Or she can wardrobe change pre-dinner. Brides do it all the time! A new trend, *#7Courses7Changes?*

The doorbell rings shrilly. Britta closes her eyes, wills the lava coursing through her to turn diamond-hard, to let its brightness make her shine. She slows her stomp into a carefree runway stride across their long Persian rug and exhales. So what if they haven't had sex in six months and Joel's whacking off to an iPad? So what if he's chosen to do it the night she needs to close the biggest collaboration of her career? So what if Gwen and Frank Russo are on the other side of that door, hungry for another little nugget of discord and disarray? Clementine's Chief Marketing Officer Dev Khare will be here in *moments. Beauty, elegance, confidence, power.* IN THAT ORDER.

"Britta, wait," Joel says, breathless behind her. "Do not open that door; we need to talk—"

"No, what we *need* is to pull this dinner off." She flings the words over her shoulder. "Do you think you can just do what you're told? Do you think we can just survive tonight?"

She turns and signals to the server, who nods and grandly opens the door.

"Britta!" Gwen Russo coos.

Gwen edges around the server, into the foyer. She looks up, surveying the splendid two-story entrance, the glass chandelier, the beautiful waitstaff closing in to take her and Frank's coats, her gift of wine. Her ruby-red lips pucker—just for a second, but her flash of jealousy stokes Britta's fire with a warm gust of satisfaction.

Gwen pastes on a smile. "Britta, Joel, thank you so much for having us. Your home is perfect, as to be expected." She flips her brown curly hair over her shoulder. She's elevated her usual "Frazzled Carline" look: now fully made up, her mom body flattered by an empire-waist, floor-length dress. "Are we the first ones?" she asks innocently.

Britta nods. "Yes, right on time."

Gwen's such a strategic little weasel. Britta can't prove it, of course, but she's positive *Gwen's* the one who told their mutual friend Lila about Joel's March Madness meltdown (Lila had texted Britta on Monday with a vague, SO SORRY TO BAIL, BILL FORGOT TO TELL ME HE'S GOT A CALL WITH TOKYO!). Gwen got to Club board member Ainsley Braithwaite, too. Suddenly, Ainsley's twins' lacrosse tournament was going to *"eat up the entire weekend."* Britta had to put a stop to Gwen's wildfire; there was simply no choice but to invite her. *Keep your friends close, but your enemies closer* (#RIPMichaelCorleone).

"Such a lost art, punctuality," Britta adds, willing her pulse to slow. She beams at Joel, who steps forward on command and shakes Frank's hand.

"Joel, buddy!" Frank bellows in his loud finance-frat-guy boom. "So glad we got the invite." Frank raises his hands as if to summon the room. "Wow! What's this baby cost you—four mil? Five?"

Joel gives a small laugh. "A gentleman never brags."

Frank claps him on the back. "Never mind, I'll look it up on Zillow."

"It's been too long." Gwen squeezes Britta's forearm. "When was the last time—the March Madness party at The Club?"

Christ is she shameless.

"Speaking of hefty price tags, Joel . . ." Frank pulls his belt an inch higher. "I've got to see the new beaut you've been drivin' around up close and personal. Tell me, what's the occasion for buying a Westa? A regular midlife crisis? Or something juicier?"

"Pretty dress, by the way," Gwen says. Then adds, a stage whisper, "Though I think there's a bit of a stain near your waist."

"Ms. Harris-Che?" the server says. "The Brinkleys have arrived."

Britta sidesteps Gwen, never more relieved to see Liz Brinkley. "Liz, Tom, welcome." She covers her dress stain and gives both Liz and Tom airy kisses, then notices that Liz is wearing *jeans*. Does Liz not know what a soiree is? Britta only shoved Sabina on them because she'd thought Liz could be a social media asset, drum up fresh interest in #Brittasays on her author platform, tap Britta into a new audience. Clearly that was desperate, wishful thinking. Nota bene: *only include Liz in waist-up pictures.*

Tom says, "Your home is lovely."

"Oh, thank you. So glad you could come." Britta winks at him. "And what did I tell you about Sabina? A lifesaver, so much excitement, energy—"

Liz says stiffly, "Well, given that she's *eleven*, I believe that comes with the territory."

Tom shoves a wine bottle at Britta. "I heard you're both fans of Barolo?"

"It's our favorite." Joel steps forward with a hair toss. "Thanks, bro."

Britta adds quickly, "You'll have to see our collection downstairs."

Gwen jumps in, "Oooh, are you going to give a tour of all the work you've done?"

"Soon." There's no way Britta is showcasing the wine cellar and all their recent renovations until Dev Khare is around to take notice. She waves a server forward. "Perhaps after champagne?"

The front door opens again. Mabel and Spencer.

Britta greets her old friend Mabel with an unsolicited, borderline wolfish hug. Neither of them is what you'd call "overtly emotional," so Mabel, naturally startled, takes a step back.

"Thank you," Britta whispers into Mabel's ear. Really, how could Britta have possibly survived tonight without her?

Mabel pulls away, tucks her lobbed, straight auburn hair behind her ear, and hands Britta a beautifully wrapped loaf of banana bread. A huge pink bow is looped on top, with a handwritten *thank you* on an adorable vintage car notecard tucked under the bow.

Britta smiles. It's such a Mabel gesture.

"Sorry we're late." Mabel clutches her simple, gorgeous strand of pearls. "We had a quick errand to run, and Greg, of course, didn't want to say goodbye."

"Your 'Finn Ferrari' bedtime stories didn't help the cause." Mabel's husband Spencer clears his throat as he scrubs his close-cut gray hair. "Greg's nearly eight, Mabes. My mother could've handled it."

Mabel flushes. "It's just our tradition," she explains to Britta. "You know me with tradition."

Joel gives Mabel an airy hug and nods at Spencer. He checks his watch and says, "Perhaps some pre-dinner drinks in the living room?"

Joel leads the crowd forward without waiting for an answer, because they've discussed this. He's finally falling in line, maybe trying to make it up to her—bringing the guests into the living room by seven twenty, where old fashioneds await, freshly mixed on Britta's new crystal-studded serving trolley. But Britta isn't yet ready to leave the foyer. She'd counted on being at the door for Dev's arrival, wants to see him enter, stunned and impressed. She wants to witness the potential she holds for Clementine wash over him in one awesome wave.

"Canapé?" a young server asks her.

Britta shoos him away. "Please, just work the crowd."

It's ten minutes—ten painstaking minutes of smiling and small talk in the living room with Mabel and Spencer, the Brinkleys, the Russos—before the Khares finally make their appearance.

"GAH, sorry to be so late!"

Padma rushes into the living room with their apparent hostess gift tucked under her arm, copies of *Clementine Wellness* and *Clementine Cookbook*—as if Britta hasn't already obsessively studied both. Padma, at least, looks photo-ready—flawless brown skin, bright lips, an emerald feathered bolero wrapped around her narrow shoulders. She'd always looked office chic at The Falls Elementary, but has clearly elevated her new mama game. Though, does Britta detect the smell of champagne? Were Padma and Dev in the foyer drinking alone?

"Darling, so glad you two could make it." Britta tries not to look around too hungrily as they exchange air kisses. "Is Dev using the little boys' room? I hope he didn't get lost."

Padma's forehead crinkles as she hands Britta her gift. "Oh. No, I . . . it's just me." She flashes a conciliatory smile. "He stayed behind with the baby so that I could get out for a night since I'm home all the time now. But I promised we'd switch so he could come say hello . . ." Padma trails off when she meets Britta's eyes. "Oh, Britta, I'm so sorry. I swear Dev said he let you know—"

"He did," Joel says. "He told me." He waves Padma forward. "And no worries, love, it's just dinner. Come in, come in, have a drink."

Padma laughs, relieved. "Thought you'd never ask."

Shocked into silence, Britta watches her dashing husband lead Padma toward the serving trolley. Did he actually say *just dinner?*

Joel has been watching Britta run around like a headless chicken, prepping the house, prepping herself *for Dev*—for proof that she is Clementine-worthy, for this "organic" way to showcase her brand, to parlay tonight's exhausting performance into a definitive social media collaboration—and all along *Joel knew Dev wasn't coming*!?

She hates him. She wasn't 100 percent sure until right now, standing here, watching Joel adjust his bow tie. But her loathing is so intense all she sees are thick, dark, suffocating waves. As if she's drowning. As if she forgets which way to come up for air.

Britta closes her eyes. A cathartic shiver runs through her as she imagines strangling him in the front seat of his royal blue Westa. Maybe documenting it all on that fucking iPad.

"Are we all here?" Gwen says eagerly, dusting off the last of her champagne. She signals to a nearby server for another, then leans forward, as if expecting a show. "Well, Britta? How about that tour!"

3

Liz

Today 1:15 PM

Laura
YES PROMISE! WILL CALL AS SOON AS I LAND!
XO

Today 6:33 PM
Me
YOU'RE NEVER GONNA BELIEVE THIS SITTER. I HAVE OLDER *HANDBAGS.* REMEMBER MY COACH PURSE YOU ALWAYS "BORROWED"? EASILY TEN YEARS HER SENIOR.
SEND HER HOME AS SOON AS YOU ARRIVE, K?

Today 7:17 PM
Me
THOUGHT YOU WERE LANDING AROUND 7?

Today 7:25 PM
Me
YES I'M ANNOYING, SRSLY SHOOT ME A TEXT.

Today 7:37 PM
Me

LAUR ARE YOU THERE?

L IZ TRIES TO refresh her texts. What is this, 1999—why is
service so bad? Is there a dead spot in this magazine-spread-
worthy living room, or has Laura's flight not yet landed? No,
that's impossible. She checked the flight's status before they left.

"We've done so much work on the place, Gwen," Joel says
from beside the trolley. "What do you think, Britta, okay to
show it off a little?"

The silence stretches on so long that Liz looks up from
her phone.

Britta pastes on a cardboard smile. "Yes, of course."

The crowd gives a little festive cheer as Joel waves everyone
toward the gallery. "Please, bring your drinks on the road."

Liz follows the party—phone refresh . . . refresh . . . still
no dice—as Tom sidles up beside her.

"You just had to comment on Sabina, didn't you?" he
whispers.

They pass by the Harris-Ches' fully set dining room, sparkling with patterned chinaware and bouquets of orchids and
dahlias. The room's massive crystal chandelier is dimmed low.
It dusts everything with a coat of glittering polish, reminds Liz
of a time of grand balls, corsets, parlor rooms. A moronic era
when social approval was all a woman could strive for.

She takes a large gulp of the old fashioned. "Of course I
did. She totally overstepped."

"So that *we* could attend *her party*," Tom overenunciates.
"Seriously, Liz, how old are you? Sometimes I feel like I'm
talking to Reid. If people are nice enough to include you, you
don't go insulting them."

"But it's okay to insult *me*? Or wait, are you insulting
Reid? I can't keep track of the many ways you find our family
disappointing."

"Don't turn this around."

Up ahead, Joel says, "And we completely redid the kitchen."

Tom pulls on his suit jacket's lapels, as if ironing himself out, shaking off all their little "imperfections." They leave the low-lit gallery for a bright, modern kitchen. Gray slate floors and sleek white cabinets, marble countertops, and navy backsplash tiles. An almost sinister-looking gentleman—dark, thick eyebrows, arms crawling with tattoos—stands leering at them from the eight-burner stovetop.

Joel smiles. "Ah, can't go by without commending the chef. Please meet tonight's culinary wizard: Romer Moreno of the South American fusion sensation Cash & Moreno."

Chef Romer crosses his arms, conspicuously flexing his muscles (*What do people see in men like this?*), and gives a little nod. "The Harris-Ches have quite a night in store." He has a thick, rich accent that makes Liz think of adventure movies, damsels in distress, devious bad guys. The chef glances at Britta, then adds, too overly flirtatious for Liz's tastes, "They know how to give you what you want."

Britta, though, just keeps absently folding the fabric along her dress's hem. Liz expected her to capitalize on that little endorsement, provide some not-so-humble brag. Is she somehow drunk already?

Joel picks up without a beat. "We also redid the home's original extension and added a conservatory . . ."

The crowd follows, while Padma Khare sandwiches herself between Liz and Tom.

Padma winks, handing Liz an embroidered napkin. "Excuse me, Ms. Brinkley. Could I have your autograph?"

Liz blurts a laugh. She's the opposite of a town celebrity. A no-name in The Falls. A ghost.

"Do you keep your gem of a wife preserved in a closet, Mr. Brinkley?" Padma keeps up with her teasing, leaning toward Tom for an air kiss. "I haven't seen her since back-to-school night."

Liz manages a smile. "I know, it's been too long." She's still surprised the Harris-Ches invited Padma Khare. Are Britta and the school's previous secretary actually friends? If Britta just wanted to butter up to the administration, wouldn't she have invited Padma's replacement, Peggy?

Padma motions for Liz to get on with her drink. "I already had a head start in the car. Champagne in a Yeti. Don't recommend—the bubble situation gets complicated. Thank goodness for Dev. I *needed* to get out. Now that I'm not a *face of education*, we can finally party down." Padma adds to Tom, "OMG, your wife had the funniest commentary on everyone at the back-to-school after-party." She rattles her dwindling drink. "What did you call Britta, the Middle-Aged Queen Bee? Oh no, Insta-Britta!"

Insta-Britta. That's right. Liz had been so out of her element at The Falls Elementary back-to-school after-party she'd pounded two glasses of cabernet, then started typecasting all the parents, and to the school's secretary, apparently. Maybe time to pull out her mental to-do list. *Research small talk icebreakers. Ditch liquid courage. Remember to avoid socializing entirely.*

"And who was Joel? The high school quarterback?"

"Reigning Paddleball King," Liz whispers. "Though, really, same difference."

Padma (Party Principal Padma, Liz now remembers, a title Padma accepted enthusiastically) throws her head back and laughs.

Tom keeps glaring at them.

Up ahead, Joel opens the hallway's first door, sending a waft of cool air into the warm, decadent-smelling corridor. The doorway leads to an expansive terrace bordered by potted topiaries, rows of pink redbud trees in the distance, all framed by a cobalt blue sky.

"We put in the conservatory this winter," Joel explains, "as well as a billiards room."

Liz peers across the courtyard to a twinkling room of glass. Even from here, she can spot the massive fish tank inside, twin white couches flanking a bronze table, floor-to-ceiling book-shelves. She wishes she could dash across the courtyard and hide in there, reading, for the rest of the night. She bets Insta-Britta and Paddleball King Joel have never cracked a single one of those books.

Padma says, "Remind me, who was—"

"It's a silly habit of Liz's, turning people into stock char-acters," Tom interrupts. "We're obviously huge fans of the Harris-Ches." He looks at Liz for confirmation.

Come on, keep it civil, Liz. "He's right. It's just a writer tic."

Gossipmonger Gwen purrs, "Oooh, are we talking *shop*?"

Joel, meanwhile, leads everyone back through the kitchen.

"I'm *fascinated* by your job, Liz," Gwen adds. "You must let us stay-at-home moms live vicariously! Tell me, do you have to make everything up, or can you borrow from real life? Because this town is full of stories. I know you're not in the 'in crowd' or what-not, but if you're ever looking for a consultant."

Padma makes a clandestine gagging gesture as they're led inside a playroom so massive that it looks like a North Pole warehouse. Mabel (Patron Saint of the PTA) and her husband Spencer (Stony-hearted Spencer—really, the man did not crack *one* smile during the entire "Teachers' Improv" sketch on back-to-school night) survey the fully stocked, color-coordinated shelves so seriously you'd think they were Santa's elf inspectors.

Come to think of it, why is Stony-hearted Spencer even here? Liz swore she saw him and Joel fighting at the school's carline a few weeks ago. Yes, she remembers it clearly now: the two men pulled over on East Lane, half obscured by their car doors, and were screaming at each other over the rooftops of their Jeep and Mercedes. Liz had felt a rare, giddy desire to pull over herself and speculate on the brawl with the other moms, trade theories as they sipped on morning coffees. She kept driving, of course, too much to do. Plus, she barely knows any of the parents anyway.

"Kids love the new space," Joel tells the crowd.

Liz does a 360 now, taking in the dollhouses, the trio of professional art easels, the clotheslines of adorable artwork. So how old is the Harris-Ches' other daughter? Four? Five? Would she and Callie get along as well as Reid and Avery?

Liz blinks at the pictures. Maybe she could try a little harder with these people. It won't kill her to smile and sip wine for a few hours if it helps Reid and Callie.

As they leave the playroom, Gwen's husband, Frank, slides between Liz and Tom. "Brinkley, my man! Where've you been hiding?"

The men tap fists.

"Mainly at the office," Tom says. "But I've been scheming the easiest way to get into The Club so you see me around more."

Frank laughs. "Ah, you should have told me! You two need a sponsor?"

Liz's stomach curdles as Tom smiles sheepishly.

"I'll admit," Tom says, "I *had* been hoping to get on the paddleball courts this winter . . ."

Frank raises his glass. "I didn't even realize you played, Tom; The Club is dying for fresh blood. One of our best players relo-ed to San Fran with a new fund . . ."

Liz tries to refocus on Padma and Gwen, on Joel up ahead, on *anyone* really but Tom and Frank. The fucking "Club." "Everyone who's anyone" belongs to The Falls' social club, and every time Tom mentions it, Liz's soul dies a little. Hobnobbing with frenemies about trips to Anguilla? Chardonnay wine tastings in tennis whites as eleven-year-old babysitters "handle" the kids at home? PS, *meanwhile*, Reid still can't ride a bike without training wheels and Tom spends half the weekend buried in work. If they joined, they'd barely have any time for the four of them anymore. That can't be what Tom wants, can it?

Padma says, "Oh, Liz, seriously, join, we'd have such a ball."

"*Everything* happens there." Gwen winks. "For example . . ." She looks both ways, as if crossing a dangerous street. "The Club's March Madness event was one for the ages. Honestly, Liz, right out of a novel. Joel was off his rocker," Gwen whispers. "Frank said he'd celebrated tipoff by ordering the entire bar tequila shots. Toasting, *to nothing left to lose*—"

Ahead, Joel checks his understated (and likely exorbitant) watch. "Britta, do we have a few moments to show them the cellar?"

"—An hour later, I found Joel and Britta cussing each other out in front of the bathrooms," Gwen adds. "Nasty stuff: '*You ruined my life!*' '*I hate you!*' Dropping F-bombs. At. The. Club. I'm not trying to spread it around, others heard, obviously—"

Padma rolls her eyes.

"—But, I mean, *so* many people canceled tonight because of that spectacle." Gwen looks at Liz pointedly. "As a result, tonight's attendee list was . . . ever evolving."

It takes Liz a moment to register Gwen's not-so-subtle subtext: is she suggesting that Liz and Tom were pinch-hitter invites? Oh my God, these women.

". . . tally it up, this mega-mansion, his Jeep," Frank's voice drowns out Liz's inner scream. "A Lamb, and now a Westa. Dying to know what Joel's worth. Some of the funds in Singapore aren't as transparent as those in the States, but I'm trying to find a work-around—"

Tom answers, "At least a Westa's a good investment."

"Understatement of the year, Brinkley. Those things are *rockets*. Six hundred horsepower, biodefense like a tank? The thing's apparently fitted to drive *you* around." Frank hollers up to Joel, "Hey, pal, there better be a stop on this tour for that Westa!"

"Oooh," Mabel coos ahead of them, "I'd love to see the new model, too."

That, of all things, pulls Britta out of her coma.

Britta clip-clops through the crowd and flings herself in front of her garage door. "Sadly, everyone, the Westa is in the shop." She takes a deep breath. "But you're going to be wowed by the cellar."

The crowd files into the basement, but Liz lingers at the top of the stairs.

Still no calls or messages from Laura. What the hell? A few notifications have come through—Twitter updates, what seems to be another news alert on the UK situation . . . it looks like they suspended travel. When did that happen? And why? But Liz can't manage to load the alert to find out more. This bad service is agonizing. She's calling her house line after the tour, checking in with Sabina. Who's she trying to impress with her restraint, anyway? Tom?

The Ches' cellar corridor, lined with crystal-studded sconces, winds past a movie theater with a mammoth projector screen and a dozen reclining chairs. Then a workout room larger than Liz and Tom's primary bedroom. The hall finally abuts into two towering doors of glass.

Joel swings open the doors, turns on the lights. The party funnels inside with a chorus of *oohs* and *aahs*.

It's impossible, even for Liz, not to gape. The wine cellar is a wide, sleek, slate corridor flanked on both sides by floor-to-ceiling wine racks and rotating towers. Interspersed throughout the storage units, on both sides of the long aisle, are small alcoves adorned with armoires and tasting islands.

Liz steps forward, running her hand along the nearest alcove's granite-topped table. The hallway ends in a wall of fully stocked dual-access fridges framing two *more* glass doors, which then lead into a spacious sitting area—one furnished with leather armchairs, a couch, and a coffee table. A long bar spans the room's left side wall.

"Hot damn," Padma marvels. "Better be careful. I might move down here."

Britta beams. "We'll end the evening here with a chocolate and port tasting. Though I suppose that will be with Dev, right, since you need to get home to the baby?" Britta pulls out her phone. "Speaking of, Padma, would you let me snap a quick pic of you and Liz in front of the Bordeaux section? Here, yes. Wait, stand behind the island—from the waist up!"

Gwen moves to follow.

Britta says, "Oooh, Gwen, can't fit you, next time."

Liz asks, "Britta, are you getting service down here?"

"No, just collecting pictures for later." Then Britta adds softly, "You know, to showcase my life?"

Showcase my life. Those words sound oddly familiar . . .

Liz swallows. Oh. Right. Because they're Liz's.

Maybe Tom had a *bit* of a point. Maybe she went a little over the line at their Delmonico's dinner.

"Sadly, our cellar's a true internet black hole," Britta says. "But Total Homes put in ethernet and a landline, which does the trick." She slips her phone into her dress's billowy pocket. "It's getting late," she adds. "Let's not keep Chef Romer waiting."

They file back through the glass doors.

"What do you think this thing cost, two hundo, maybe three?" Frank murmurs to Liz and Tom. "Only cellar I've ever seen bigger is Damon Campbell's bunker."

"How could a bunker be bigger?" Liz says. "What's he got down there, a subterranean artillery? A man spa?"

"Can't put a price on safety." Frank hikes up his belt as they climb the stairs. "You'd never guess it, but Damon's nearly worth ten mil. He was a client, once upon a time."

Tom, of course, serves another safe, vanilla answer. "Damon lives around the corner from us. Seems like a real nice guy."

Frank puts the sprinkles on: "*Great* guy."

Liz bites back a groan. What she would give for a DeLorean to time travel back and show "City Tom" a montage of the way Suburban Tom acts these days. *A good investment. A real nice guy.* They'd roast the hell out of him together.

But she promised she'd play nice. "Guess I don't know Damon very well."

Frank claps his hands and says gleefully, "Nothing a dinner date can't solve! You, Gwen, and Sara Jane can talk PTA drama while your husband and I start wooing Damon . . ."

"Meaning *Damon* could sponsor me?" Tom's eyes go all glassy, like some mind-controlled cartoon. "That would be amazing. A word from him in this town is better than God's."

"Oh, please, he's a know-it-all asshat—you've said it yourself."

Shit. That just slipped out.

Frank arches an eyebrow.

"She's obviously joking," Tom says, "Liz has such a weird sense of humor—"

"Guess it was someone else then, muttering to their phone about Damon turning The Falls into a police state—"

"LIZ!" Tom snaps.

Frank looks back and forth between them. "Fireworks so early in the night, eh?" He hitches up his pants (what a strange nervous tic; she'll have to borrow that) and hurries after the rest of the party.

Tom grabs Liz's hand before they reenter the kitchen. "You need to stop. You're being beyond rude."

She knows that, obviously, and she was going to apologize, but the magnitude of Tom's rage makes her go on the offensive. "*Me?*" she says. "Seriously? I can barely stomach you. You're being so ridiculous."

Then she waits for the vestiges of City Tom to reappear, to laugh with an *Agreed, eff these people and their cult-like exuberance for dinner dates.*

Instead, Tom just shakes his head and walks away from her.

"Angling for The Club when we barely see you as it is?" She hurries after him. "Kissing *Frank Russo's* ass? Why do you care so much what these people think, anyway?"

"Because this is our *life*, Liz." Tom spins around. "How many times can we have this same conversation?"

"Too bad you can't try this hard with your own family."

"You're impossible."

His words slide under her skin like a paper cut. Still, she keeps trailing him, grabbing a champagne from a smug-looking server in the living room. Tom better slow down. They can't sit down to dinner all worked up, they need to download, privately—but her husband's already stormed his way into the dining room.

Liz edges past Gwen, hot on Tom's heels—before noticing the little gold-flecked notecards atop each plate.

Padma waves. "Oh, Liz, over here. We're next to each other!"

Liz looks around. What the—are there *assigned* seats?

Joel's already ushering Tom toward a spot near the table head. "Don't worry, Liz, we'll take good care of him. Have a night with the ladies. Enjoy yourself."

Stunned, Liz lets Padma guide her to her seat.

Padma raises her champagne glass. "Time to get this party started."

Mabel, who's passing by looking for her place card, stops and hovers over them. She gently puts her hand on Padma's shoulder. "Perhaps you should slow down?" she suggests quietly. "Seven courses, after all." She glides away.

Padma mouths to Liz, *"Um? What the fuck?"*

Liz doesn't answer. She's six seats away from Tom, sandwiched between Party Principal Padma and Gossipmonger Gwen for four hours on a freaking Sunday. Of course, the real icing on tonight's cake: she and Tom weren't even wanted by these pseudo-acquaintances. They were third-tier invites to this dumbass soiree!

Beside her, Padma snaps open her napkin. "Did you just hear what Mrs. Young—what Mabel said to me? The nerve. I'm home all day, nursing, changing diapers, cooking, cleaning. I deserve a break, and PS, Dev agrees with me. He knows I've become a completely different person after having Isobel, and I *need* this. I mean, not that I don't enjoy every minute with her."

Liz takes a much-needed swig of champagne.

Padma joins her. "We can't all be these little Martha Stewart clones—I swear, Mabel even drives the same Mercedes.

She's just so damn self-satisfied, used to float into my office holier than thou, as if she was doing more for the school than I was. What's your nickname for her?"

Liz coughs. "Patron Saint of the PTA."

"Hear, hear." Padma takes a large gulp.

"Ooooh, ladies, now *who's* a patron saint?" Gwen asks from Liz's other side.

Liz fishes for her phone, hoping, at least, for catharsis there.

No texts from Laura. Still no calls. There is a local alert, though, from Newark. This one takes a few moments but, thankfully, finally loads.

"Holy hell," Liz whispers.

"What's wrong?" But Padma's voice sounds like it's coming from the bottom of a well.

Holy hell. Holy hell, holy hell.

[PUBLIC SAFETY ALERT:

Hazardous air at dangerous contamination levels. NEWARK AIRPORT quarantined and flights grounded. All persons in vicinity ordered to take indoor shelter immediately.]

4

Britta

Pivot with Intention

> [*Instagram post displays a luxurious spread of a limon-cello bottle, diamond-cut glassware, and a lemon torte on a crystal serving tray. The spread is surrounded by dozens of luscious lemons.*]

Brittasays　　✔Follow

New Jersey

Of course, Life is sometimes going to sense your success and hold up its hand and say, *Not so fast.* After all, it's not easy to transform your world, to demand that the universe sit up and pay attention to you. We've all heard, *when life hands you lemons, make lemonade.* But what if lemonade is too pedestrian for your tastes? Why don't those little philosophers ever suggest making lemon tortes, limoncello, lemon posset? *Because those recipes are harder.* It's up to you alone to stay true to your ultimate goals, to remain focused on what *you* truly want. Pivot with grace, yes, but also with intention. #Brittasays #risetothechallenge #empowerment #lifestyle #elegance

#clementine #SantoniniLimoncello #soiree #diningwithfriends #selfcare #wellness #wellbeing

"IT'S JUST RIDICULOUS," Britta whispers to Mabel, her eyes narrowing as she watches Padma—solo, Dev-less Padma—polish off her glass. "Dev must have known I wanted *him* here. How many times did I mention my Instagram feed to him at The Club, ask him about Clementine, connect the dots about our obvious corporate synergy? How could he think I wanted him to send the school's ex-secretary as his ambassador?"

Before Mabel can respond, Chef Romer's sommelier—Kat? Kate?—steps serenely toward the head of the table. Kat/Kate shakes her little dark pixie cut out of her eyes and brandishes a bottle of cava that the twenty-six-year-old "expert" insisted would pair better with Chef Romer's first course than would Britta's tried-and-true crowd-wow selection of champagne. Really, is this amateur hour? Did she really pay five grand for a thirty-year-old sous chef and a Gen Z sommelier?

Romer and Kat/Kate better be bringing their A game. Britta is so tired of incompetence.

"Welcome, welcome, to the Harris-Ches' Sunday Soiree. I'm Kat, head wine steward at Cash & Moreno, and boy, do we have a stellar list of wine and food pairings for you all this evening."

"Tom," Liz calls across the table.

Kat flashes Liz a nervous smile. "Our staff will be around momentarily with Chef Romer's *primer plato* of pan-seared squid and chorizo. You'll see that the light citrus notes of this Spanish sparkling wine highlight the dish's sultry flavors."

As Kat pours Frank's glass, Liz hiss-whispers again, "*Tom.*"

Britta clenches her jaw. What is the point of separating couples to mingle if people just shout at their spouses across the table?

Kat pours the tastings—Joel after Frank, then Spencer, then the *empty chair that was supposed to be Dev* . . .

Britta refocuses on Mabel as Chef Romer's staff serves the appetizers. "Speaking of misunderstandings, I'm so glad that our husbands worked out whatever silly beef was between them. Joel said they squalled about *poker*? Such a double faux pas, am I right? Two dads screaming in the school pickup line about gambling."

"Oh, I'm . . . not sure. Spencer didn't mention the fight to me." With a nod, Mabel accepts her glass from Kat.

"Well, thank goodness you canceled your plans and joined tonight," Britta murmurs. "If you weren't here, I swear I would've had a nervous breakdown by now."

Mabel nods again and swirls her glass of cava, a little golden whirlpool.

Britta lets out a nervous cackle. "Joel with his smug laugh and stupid bow tie and midlife crisis Westa. He was hiding out in the damn thing as the guests arrived. Did I tell you that?"

"I thought the Westa was in the shop."

Britta falters. She forgot that Mabel, daughter of a retired mechanic and self-professed "gearhead" herself, would pay attention to such inane details. "Oh. Just a little white lie, darling. Besides, did you *want* to see Frank Russo salivate on the hood?" She slings back a gulp of the admittedly delicious sparkling wine, then diverts. "But you know what *really* takes the cake? Joel knew all along that Dev wasn't coming. You saw him, yes, smiling while he drove in the knife?" She shakes her head. "Husbands can be such monstrous assholes."

Mabel clears her throat—a little *ahem*—as she twists her pearl necklace into a tight, complicated knot. "Maybe he forgot. Or maybe he thought he'd hurt you by telling you."

"I'm a big girl. I can handle it. Are *you* all right, by the way?"

Mabel's eyes widen. "Of course, why?"

"You're murdering those pearls."

Mabel lets go of her necklace.

Liz hisses across the table: "Tom, this is serious!"

When he doesn't answer, she pushes back her chair with a screech, drowning out Kat's little lecture on the Extremadura region, and darts straight out of the dining room.

Kat watches her, almost longingly, as if the young, lithe sommelier is also contemplating escape. No, there's no way this bright young thing is Cash & Moreno's "head wine steward." Which means Britta was bamboozled twice over: Moreno sans Cash, and a B-team sommelier.

Gwen leans across Liz's now-empty seat. "And just *what* was all that about?"

Padma says, with just the hint of a slur, "I was hoping you had the inside scoop, Mrs. Russo." She gives Gwen a theatrical, conspiratorial wink. "As always."

Kat stalls at the table head, looking around, smiling uneasily. "I . . . hope you can all taste the rich complexity that Codorníu is famous for? The lighter, evanescent bubbles pair expertly with the texture of the squid . . ."

"I should have listened to you," Britta murmurs to Mabel. "Liz is an obvious train wreck."

"No, that's not—I just think she's so *busy*. It's great that she volunteered for the PTA gala, but a little hard to pin down."

"I know you, darling, that's 'train wreck' in Mabel-speak." Britta pats Mabel's hand while Kat keeps blabbering. Britta really needs to sidebar her before the second course, tell her to nix the monologues: #NoOneCaresKat.

Mabel, though, recoils from her touch.

O-kayyy. Britta tosses her hair, deflecting, and pulls away. She's never had to play games with Mabel. Everyone else, yes, but Mabel?

Could Mabel be mad at Britta for something? Ridiculous, Mabel's never mad at anyone. Still, there's no denying she's . . . off. She has been for weeks now that Britta's thinking about it. Maybe something's going on with Spencer. Or, Christ, maybe

Gwen got to Mabel too . . . but that makes little sense; Mabel isn't petty, and their friendship is everything.

Liz's voice booms outside the gallery. "Laura, I can't hear you. Laura!" Then heavy footsteps, like Liz is sprinting through the foyer.

Sommelier Kat bows and steps back from the table. "Enjoy, everyone."

Britta raises her glass to refocus the crowd. "To good food, excellent wine, and even better company."

Liz: "Laura, *please*, can you hear me?"

Spencer, in his typical, merciless deadpan: "Tom, your wife all right out there? Sounds like she's in 'Nam."

Gwen peers around with hungry eyes. "Indeed, it's quite a spectacle."

Tom, at least, has the decency to look ashamed. "Liz is talking to her sister. Maybe something happened. Maybe I should check."

"She's fine," Britta snaps. "Creative types are naturally dramatic." Really, could this dinner party be more of a disaster? She slugs back her glass but has a sudden, overwhelming urge to scream. There must be a way to get Padma *home*, teleport Dev *here*—and doesn't Kat or a server or someone have the good sense to corral Liz back into the goddamned dining room?

As if summoned, Liz barrels back in, nearly taking out Chef Romer coming in from the kitchen.

Romer stutter-steps back, glancing at Britta. "I . . . hope the octopus is not making anyone run away?"

"Check your phones," Liz says breathlessly, peering around the table. "Though don't be surprised if your service is shit. This is serious."

"*Excuse me?*" Britta sputters. "Is this some kind of joke?"

"The air," Liz says, as if that explains anything. "They're saying the air's dangerously contaminated and to stay inside. I tried my sister, but the connection was awful. From what

I *could* hear, there's something going on at the airport, too. Something major."

"You're running through my gallery because of an *airport emergency*?"

Liz huffs at Tom. "I know I sound crazy, but it's all related. I feel it—the connection problems in the UK, the airport, the air warnings—"

Britta shakes her head. "*What?*"

Spencer mumbles too loudly to Joel, "She's that end-of-the-world author, right? What's that book called, *World Crushers*, or *Pulverizers*? *World Grinders*?"

Joel gives a small smirk. "Definitely not *World Grinders*."

Down the table, meanwhile, Tom rubs his temples.

"Tom, I mean it, check your news alerts!" Liz says. "Or your thousands of text chains, WhatsApps. Someone must be saying something about Newark. They're grounding flights apparently, and the air is . . . is poisoned? I knew we shouldn't have come."

Something inside Britta breaks in two. "Liz, calm down and take a seat."

Gwen says, with a small wave of her phone, "She's right about the service issues." Then she flashes Britta a little victorious smirk.

Mabel peers around Britta, down the table. "Spencer, should we call home to check in?" She pulls her own phone from her purse and begins tapping it, her delicate features soon collapsing into a frown. "Oh. I'm having service trouble too."

Britta squirms, freshly irked. "Liz, really. What are we freaking out about? The town posts these alarms all the time."

Liz says, "But the grounded flights—"

"They're spraying for mosquitos one day," Britta talks over her, "doing pesticide treatments the next. Paving the roads, watering the lawns." She pops a laugh. "A *stay inside* order isn't cause for running around someone's home screaming about conspiracy theories!"

The table falls silent.

Liz studies Britta with a look that Britta can't quite decipher.

Across the table, Padma holds up her phone. "She's also right about the airports. And it's not just grounded flights at Newark—"

Spencer interrupts, "How are you seeing anything? My service keeps stalling."

"HELLLOOOOO, MOMMY AND DADDY'S GUESTS!" sounds off from the front stairwell.

Britta pinches her eyes shut.

The kids. Of course. Their eight eleven PM show for Dev: Act II in Britta's clearly ill-conceived production, *Britta Is a Superwoman*. What awful stage timing.

The guests turn and peer through the dining room entry, as planned. Everyone has a perfect view of Britta and Joel's three children, lined up and smiling in brand-new PJs on the breezeway upstairs.

Avery gives young Marco a sharp elbow.

Marco startles, then fake-yawns. *"I'm so tired . . ."*

"Reid and Callie," Liz blurts. "Tom, what if they go outside with screen-free Sabina for whatever reason and this air contamination gets into their lungs? What if they don't even know to stay inside? What if they aren't safe?"

"My sweet Greg," Mabel whispers, choke-holding her pearls again.

Gwen leans back in her chair. "What an unfortunate soiree curveball."

Chef Romer, though, steps forward, commanding the table's attention. "You suburbanites love your TV, yes? American football? Netflix?" He looks pointedly at Britta. "Why don't we give these people what they want? Pause the dinner. Turn the television on. Figure out what's happening."

Down the table Joel stands, sending his herringbone china crashing into the silverware with a hollow *tinggg*. He finds Britta's eyes. "I'll take care of the kids. But Romer has a point. Just turn on the news. You can take everyone into the conservatory."

Joel's tone is hard and final, the last nail in a coffin he's been building all day. All year. Their entire fucking relationship, since that first night she met him, gorgeous and brooding, in Barcelona.

The guests all stare at her, waiting, increasingly anxious about this "town update" that Liz insists on spinning into a new disaster novel.

Britta pastes on a smile, trying to smother down her raging need to hear shattered glass, to scream until her throat is sore. *#Brittasays elegance, confidence, power, in that order. #Brittasays insist on lemon posset instead of lemonade.*

#Brittasays sit your asses down and eat this dinner that I just wasted two months planning for absolutely nothing!

She throws her cloth napkin beside Romer's octopus. "Fine."

Without another word, she clip-clops out of the dining room.

C H A P T E R

5

Padma

Today 7:15 PM

DEV

LOOK AT THIS GORGEOUS GIRL

> *[Texted picture of Baby Isobel, smiling and cooing on her changing table.]*

JUST LIKE HER MOM <3

Today 7:17 PM

DEV

PS, BURP CLOTHS? GENIUS. I SWEAR THIS WHOLE TIME I THOUGHT THEY WERE BABY SARONGS.

Today 7:31 PM

DEV

HOW'D BRITTA TAKE YOUR MINUS-ONE BTW?
HAS SHE RESORTED TO SELLING YOU ON #BRITTASAYS?

Today 7:32 PM

Me

IT'S SO OBVIOUS SHE WANTS YOU HERE AND NOT
ME!!!!

Today 7:33 PM

DEV

YOU JUST TAKE THAT TOKEN INVITE AND CASH IT IN, GIRL.

Today 7:34 PM

DEV

ENJOY TONIGHT, K? YOU DESERVE IT.

<3

T HAT'S IT. THAT'S the last time Padma heard from Dev. She hasn't even *thought* about him or the baby, other than as a defensive tactic, in the past hour; the Harris-Ches' "Sunday Soiree" proving ten times more rejuvenating than that CalmPro meditation app Dev tried to foist on her last week. She feels lighter, calmer, more herself than she has in months.

Guilt, hot and palpable, races through her, mixing with the alcohol in a heady, noxious rush. *I am such an asshole.*

Padma follows the party back into the gallery. Mrs. Russo (gah, *Gwen*, she must start calling these women by their first names) stays flanked beside her, lobbing murmured, persistent questions about Padma's take on the state of Britta and Joel's relationship ("Did you ever notice Joel was so domineering when you were working at the school? I mean, *Sleeping with the Enemy* much? And the *drinking*. I've always known they were too perfect . . .").

Liz, meanwhile, has broken away—sprinted in front of the group like a racehorse—and is now nipping at Britta's Louboutin heels.

"Can we hurry?" Liz asks. "My phone service still isn't working. The connection's glacial. Do you have a landline? Or maybe we should just go home—"

Britta hisses, "Just take a breath, Liz."

The crowd filters down the hall and into the conservatory. Mabel sits down primly next to her gloomy husband, Mr. Young (Spencer), on the couch, while Gwen slides into the nearest high-back wing chair.

Padma stands behind Gwen, watching as Gwen's husband, Frank, Mr. Brinkley (Tom), Sommelier Kat, Chef Romer, and the rest of the waitstaff trail in behind them.

Padma looks around. The conservatory is a sparkling gem of glass, filled with bookshelves, white furniture, and thoughtful bronze accents. The ceiling, hopscotched with skylights, showcases an expansive indigo tapestry of sky above.

She slides beside the massive fish tank on the room's opposite end, orange- and red-stained koi fish gliding through electric blue water. They stare dully at Padma with their wide, unblinking eyes.

She gets the strangest sensation that she's somehow trapped too. Submerged in a glass prison, and sinking.

Britta slides out a tablet from the console and points it at her TV. "You'll soon see that there is *nothing* to worry about." Light from the waking television glosses the glass walls of the conservatory in an unsettling, shimmery red. "A dropped call from Liz's sister at the airport? A local report on contaminated air? I mean, *really* not worthy of dismantling a seven-course . . ." Britta trails off.

On screen, the words *SPECIAL REPORT* are splashed across a TV news studio backdrop; a male reporter with caked-on foundation and thick blonde hair sits in the fore. Below him scroll a flurry of frantic headlines:

"GLIMMERING CLOUDS" REPORTED AT NEWARK INTERNATIONAL AIRPORT . . .
GROWING "MASS" SPOTTED IN BOSTON . . .
AIRPORTS QUARANTINED AMID GLIMMER-CLOUD PHENOMENON . . .

"Airports? Quarantined?" Gwen echoes hollowly. "Clouds?" As if breaking the words down separately will unlock their meaning. As if her stilted, chirpy parrot echo will suddenly infuse the room with understanding.

The reporter's voice booms through the conservatory: "Compounding the strangeness of these simultaneous reports of contamination is the fact that these airports are *not* responding to communication . . ."

"It's just like the UK, with the communication problems," Liz blurts. "Maybe that's why they're shutting down the airports. Maybe whatever is affecting the air *traveled*—"

"So bad air can travel?" Spencer grunts. "Did it fly first class?"

Beside Padma, Sommelier Kat smothers a snicker.

"Since when is it a crime to brainstorm?" Liz says. "I'm just trying to figure out what's going on."

Gwen whispers, "You ask me, and this is all feeling like a *Skyfall* episode."

"Liz used to work on that show too, you know," Tom says hollowly.

Gwen spins around in her chair, stares at Liz. "Are you serious? Liz, whyever did you *leave*? That show is killing it."

Spencer throws up his hands. "Can we just listen to the actual freaking news?"

The reporter's voice again consumes the room. ". . . are closing down the following airports due to these swiftly developing and hazardous phenomena. Again, that's Boston International Airport, Newark Airport, SFO, LAX . . ."

"Think about it. It makes sense," Liz sidebars Tom. "If something spread from the UK, it would start at the airports. That's why I could barely hear Laura. There was something wrong with the connection. And the sound . . . I don't know, it sounded like crickets, or wind chimes. Beyond strange. And the screams . . ."

Something cold and hard blooms inside Padma's chest. A frozen rose.

"I don't understand," Mabel says from the couch. "*What*, exactly, are these dangerous clouds?" She leans toward Spencer, clutching her pearls so tightly that she looks like she's going to strangle herself. Padma's never seen Mabel look so pale. Green, really. Crayola's "inchworm" color.

"They obviously don't know," Liz answers. "But the UK went entirely dark, no service, no cells, no internet. Which means in a few minutes, we might not even be able to order a Lyft. We've got to leave as soon as we can."

Tom, eyes still locked on the TV, gives an almost imperceptible nod.

Joel glides into the conservatory and scans the room for Britta. "The kids are in the gallery. I set them up with Candyland and took away their screens."

"*Screens?*" Britta chokes out an incredulous laugh.

Joel ignores her. "I didn't want them to see the news if it was scary. What are they saying about the air?"

Spencer mumbles, "Can't hear anything in here besides gossip and speculation."

The comment, Padma notices, turns Joel's face a checkerboard of red.

Joel takes the tablet from Britta and turns up the TV's volume:

". . . massive moving clouds unfurling from these airports, which experts say may be responsible for the rapidly shifting air quality and communication blackouts . . ."

"That's what I said!" Liz says.

The crowd shushes her.

". . . We're still unable to contact these locations, but we turn now to our on-the-ground Queens correspondent for more details on JFK."

A pause. The on-screen reporter grabs his ear. "Ron, are you there?"

Somewhere behind Padma, Chef Romer speaks up. "Perhaps another channel, Britta?"

Padma turns in time to spot Sommelier Kat leaning in close to the chef. Quite close. One might even say unprofessionally close.

"This doesn't look good," Kat murmurs. "Forget this, it's time to leave."

The chef keeps his eyes on the news. "We came here to do a job. We can't just up and run away; we need to think of the clients, the restaurant—"

Kat grits her teeth. "You need to stop being a Boy Scout."

Padma turns back to the screen, which now displays a blurry, glistening picture of a building complex. The entire image has been covered in an odd, grainy tinsel, looks a bit like a freeze frame from a staticky 1990s television set. It drudges up memories from long ago: Padma at seven, maybe eight, watching *Duck Tales* as her mom and Auntie Uma traded secrets in hushed Hindi in their little prefab kitchen.

The TV suddenly cuts out. Goes black. Everyone jumps.

Joel stabs the tablet with his finger. "Bloody Total Homes—"

Liz cries, "Wait, stop."

The wide-eyed reporter is back. ". . . UK has just telegraphed the Capitol with devastating news, mil—millions of deaths in London surrounds alone . . . widespread conjecture that these glimmering clouds are related to these casualties . . ."

Gwen's mouth falls open. "What on earth?"

"Millions . . . ?" Mabel whispers. "I don't . . . how is that . . ."

Liz waves her phone. "My phone's toast, Tom. Call a Lyft right now."

"Authorities are at a loss, but for now they instruct civilians to—"

"Tom!"

Tom jumps, as if waking from a dream, and fishes inside his pocket.

On screen, a flashing BREAKING NEWS graphic interrupts the reporter.

The screen cuts to a White House press conference; the president looks pale and dazed behind the microphone. His team of advisers are lined up behind him.

Padma grips the top of Gwen's high-back chair as the koi fish swim around her, oblivious. Millions of deaths? Is this a joke? What was in that old fashioned? What the hell is going on?

She closes her eyes and immediately pictures Dev at home in their den, watching the TV alone, an IPA in one hand, his other stress-channeling by mussing his hair. Or is he asleep? Still in Isobel's room, both adorably passed out together on the rocker, wiped from Isobel's eight PM breast milk bottle feeding? *You're the Hallmark Parent*, Padma always tells him whenever she catches him singing to Isobel in her swing in the morning, or snuggling with her in the carrier as he sorts through the mail. Padma can never bring herself to say what she really means—*You're the better parent. The real parent. The only one who's made for this*—because it's so devastatingly ironic. Padma's whole life has been about kids. Studying child psychology in college and graduate school, then teaching second grade for eight years before moving to the administration side—

"My fellow Americans," the president interrupts her spiraling thoughts. "We find ourselves in the throes of another grave emergency."

The president's address passes over Padma in a surreal fog. *Communication complications abroad delayed understanding . . . glimmering cloud deviations . . . learning more about this phenomenon but imperative for now that everyone finds shelter immediately, ideally in safe, sealed spaces . . .*

Tom says, "Liz, I can't get through to Lyft."

"Service issues, just like abroad." Liz turns to Padma. "Did you drive? Could you give us a ride home?"

Gwen stands up from the high-backed chair. "Frank, should we go?"

"Absolutely not." Britta steps forward. "They said to take shelter and that this 'air issue' is going to *pass*."

"Because that's what they always say at first!" Liz refocuses on Padma. "I know these situations, and there's a tiny window in which to leave and avoid serious disaster."

Britta sputters a laugh. "Just what do you mean by *you know these situations*?"

Tom mutters, "Easy with the Apocalypse CliffsNotes, Liz; you're scaring everyone."

Liz throws up her hands. "Did you just hear what they said about the UK? They should be scared!"

"They just admitted they don't know what's happened overseas," Britta says. "And they sure as hell haven't proven a connection to the air contamination here. Absent Garrison Cromwell's writer-for-hire, I think the rest of us can separate fact from conjecture, yes? There's no need to do something silly and rash like *leave*." Britta looks directly at Padma. "Or prevent your significant other from coming, as is applicable."

Liz blocks Padma's view of Britta, the TV, the world. "*Did. You. Drive?*"

Padma stutters, "N-no, I took a car service."

Liz turns. "Mabel, what about you?"

Before Mabel can answer, the secretary of defense takes questions from the press.

> "Could this 'glimmer phenomenon' be another strange
>   virus?"
> "Should individuals outside the home be wearing masks?"
> "Can you explain the nature of these millions of deaths?
>   Did they all happen in the span of the communication
>   blackout?"
> "Is climate change responsible?"
> "Biological warfare?"
> "Warfare from somewhere else?"

From across the room, Frank Russo blurts out, "And what the hell is this going to do to the markets?" He stands up from his chair with a yank of his pants.

The dozenth yank, Padma thinks numbly. *Why doesn't he wear smaller pants?*

"I gotta make some calls before tomorrow's open."

Britta tails Frank. "Gentlemen, ladies, please, let's just calm down . . ."

"Liz, maybe what's happening here *is* just some sort of pollution," Mabel says. "Maybe it's got nothing to do with what happened there, the millions . . ."

"And you're going to take that chance?" Liz moves to the center of the room, as if this is a hearing. Some surreal tribunal. *The People vs. Britta's Sunday Soiree.* "These are the facts: whatever these 'glimmering clouds' are, they're here now, and no one knows what they are, and the clouds were overseas and there have been countless deaths—"

"Daddy?"

Everyone turns to see the three Harris-Che children, in their adorable matching PJs, now standing in the conservatory doorway.

Joel pastes on a nervous smile. "Candyland done already?"

Avery tilts her head. "No, but Olivia's dad's out there now. He keeps screaming at his phone. I don't think it's working."

"Ah, don't mind Mr. Russo, he's just . . . dealing with the Sunday blues."

Joel's feeble joke, though, can't dispel the additional tension the kids have brought into the room: the tangible reminder of who his guests are missing.

Padma should be feeling it too. A sudden ache, a sharp pang of loss, the overwhelming need for her own child. But all she feels is her stomach bottom out. What would a Model Mom do right now? This is how she gets through most days with Isobel: *A Model Mom would go through the hassle of layering her baby, stuffing the diaper bag, and dragging the stroller out for a walk, as it's such a gorgeous spring day! A Model Mom would want to snuggle by the fire on a chilly April night, instead of joining a wine-tasting Zoom with her California cousins for vicarious happy hour.*

On the TV, the reporters keep shouting questions:

"If this phenomenon is some kind of coordinated attack, who could be behind it?"
"Is the secretary considering the 'glimmers' could be extraterrestrial?"

Avery looks up at Joel. "Wait, Dad, do they mean aliens?"

"Mabel," Liz tries to focus her. "We *need* to *leave*, for Reid, Callie, Gus—"

"Greg," Mabel says shakily.

Liz stares at her.

"My son's name is Greg. He and Reid are in the same homeroom—"

Liz throws up a hand, a clear attempt to quiet Mabel. Then she marches around the room fitfully, apparently now entering full-on commando mode.

Padma shrinks back. She's always gotten a kick out of this woman's intensity. Really, who has the nerve to typecast an entire community, to the elementary school secretary no less, on back-to-school night? But right now, Liz's "passion" is sort of terrifying. Does she really think that what's happened in the UK has somehow traveled *here*, all those deaths, that they . . . that they'll . . .

Padma can't even think it.

Liz stops pacing. "Do you hear that?"

Tom looks mortified. "Liz."

Spencer stands from the couch. "Joel, she's right, mute the TV."

Then Padma hears it too. They all do. An odd, tinny, mounting whistling coming from outside the glass walls. An eerie chorus of wind. Moaning crickets. Bells . . . no, not bells. Chimes. Unsettling, haunting chimes playing notes at pitches Padma has never heard before.

The Harris-Ches' youngest, Marco, wails, "Daddy, what is that? It's scary!"

Liz puts her hand to her mouth. "It's the same sound. The sound I heard through the phone—"

Britta says, "Liz, sit *down!*"

"—these glimmer clouds are *here*, and we need to go *now!*"

Joel grabs his children, pulls them out of the way, because the room has suddenly devolved into chaos: Frank Russo rushing in from the hall, waving his cell phone furiously, barking at Gwen that they need to leave so he can "*get on the phone ASAP with his PM!*" Mabel and Spencer jumping up, mumbling incredulous and gruff apologies, respectively, to Britta and Joel—as if they aren't fully in control. As if they're being driven by a force beyond themselves, the same primal, parental force driving Liz to single-handedly dismantle a dinner party.

Padma listens, but hears nothing but the absence of that force, a dank spacious silence, like the hollow of a tree. *A Model Mom would cry for her baby; a Model Mom would be consumed by her face, her tiny hands, her wild cries.* Just thinking the word *cry* makes Padma's breasts grow full, warm, and tingly, as if hot thread is unspooling inside her chest.

Damn it, Padma will never, *ever* get used to a milk letdown.

Liz rushes toward Joel. "The news mentioned wearing masks to stay safe outside."

"The news unequivocally told us to stay *inside*," Britta says.

"They might protect us," Liz says, "if you still have some COVID masks?"

Britta's gaze could burn a hole straight through Liz. But Joel untangles himself from his kids, leaves, and reemerges moments later with a container of mismatched surgical masks and KN95s.

Liz thrusts a plastic-wrapped mask into everyone's hands—Frank, Gwen, the Youngs, Padma, Tom. Liz grabs one for herself, then hands the box to Chef Romer, who's been watching the entire scene unfold with a permanently arched brow, as if he's equal parts perturbed and fascinated. He takes a mask, grabbing one for Kat as well, then passes the box to one of his black-clad servers.

"We should package up the food in case things get worse," he tells them, "and grab the supplies." He pulls a grudging Kat back into the kitchen.

The trio of servers, though, don't follow. Instead, they trail Liz, right along with Padma and the rest of the guests, into the foyer. The strange, disturbing song—that ghastly medley of dying crickets, chimes, whistling—is louder near the door. The unreality of the past ten minutes is bending, twisting, folding Padma, threatening to break her. She feels queasy. Like she might puke, retch right here in the middle of Britta's custom rug like some stomach-bugged first grader.

"Mabel, you live right near Padma, right?" Liz says. "You can drop me and Tom off first; we're right across Old Falls Road."

Mabel sputters, "But wait, I—"

"It'll be fast. My kids are with a stranger, a kid herself, please."

They all rush through the door.

Padma looks back, once, to the Harris-Ches still clustered near the conservatory: Britta holding the doorframe like she can't stand on her own. Joel, staring, staggered at the TV. The little ones gathered at their feet.

The oldest child, Avery, turns and meets Padma's gaze. Then she gives a little wave.

Maybe Padma's imagining it, searching for a sign, but she swears something passes between her and the second grader. An eerie message from the universe: a clandestine promise that Padma *will* be okay. That she's going to survive, not just tonight, but the eternity-devouring months of infancy ahead, the anguish of nursing, of sleeplessness. That she'll live to see her own eight-year-old daughter. Padma can almost picture Future Isobel sitting beside Avery: a ghost of who could be. A smart girl, spritely, funny, of course.

A girl who maybe even likes her mother.

Padma takes a fortifying breath, letting the notion of Future Isobel propel her through the foyer, out the door, down the steps, *home*.

She breaks into a trot before realizing that Liz has halted up ahead.

The group's self-appointed commander is audibly whimpering near the drive's island of azaleas.

6

Liz

"Liz?" Padma says, behind her.

Liz doesn't turn around, because, somehow, it's all worse than she imagined.

Everyone along Little Falls Road must have been watching the news. The street has swiftly, surreally devolved into total chaos. All down the road, cars are screeching out of drives. Across the cul-de-sac, a woman in her fifties attempts to wrangle a pair of teens inside as her husband juggles the trash cans and recycling bin off the curb. Two doors down, a quartet of young couples hurriedly packs up a corn hole set. Slammed doors. Screams. Revved engines. A shrieking car radio booming, then cut. That terrible, cloying noise she heard earlier on the phone with Laura now enveloping them like surround sound.

Liz shivers as a manic gust of wind billows, fluttering her thin blouse, goose-bumping her skin. She tries to focus on the warm, recycled air trapped inside her KN95. *In. Out. Get the hell out of here, get the hell home—*

"Wha . . . ," Padma whispers.

The thicket of trees beyond the homes begins to shiver and sway. In one roaring gust, birds and bats fly out from every branch and trunk, careening wildly across the night sky, bending and dipping and shrieking, an oncoming tornado of dark wings threaded with thousands, no, *millions* of strange, razor-thin strands of light. Bright white and searing yellow, pink, green. Rippling around the small animals, crackling across their wings.

"My God," Spencer whispers.

The manic onslaught plummets to the ground almost exactly as a hoard of squirrels and chipmunks flood the road, scrambling across the pavement in a grotesque, undulating brown sea. Possessed deer dart into the searing light of the cul-de-sac. Smashing into trash cans, parked vehicles, sprinting in front of moving cars. One careens into a transmitter at the end of the lane, and in a blink, half the street's lights pinch out.

"Armageddon." Spencer turns, shouts to Liz, "Go home with the Russos—they're closer!"

She sobers. "What? No, you promised!"

"Damn it, I still can't get through to my PM." Frank Russo waves his phone as he elbows past. "Gwen, we gotta rock!"

Gwen scurries after him, knocking squarely into Liz with a thud, sending Liz's own phone flying out of her hands. Her cartridge lands with a cringe-worthy smack on the cobblestone drive. "NO!"

"Move your ass, Gwen." Frank points his key fob at his Lexus like a weapon.

She teeters after him in her high heels, kicking Liz's phone.

"Gwen, what the hell!"

"Eek, so sorry, doll!"

Meanwhile, Spencer and Mabel are getting away.

Liz stands up, snatches her cracked phone, and races to catch the Youngs.

"This—this can't be real," Padma huffs behind Liz as she tries to keep stride.

Liz shakes her head and picks up her pace. Doesn't Padma understand that this moment may well be the realest of their lives? That their children, their reasons for living, their hearts, are beating without them on the other side of town? Didn't

Padma see what Liz just saw? "Spencer, don't you dare leave without us!"

Up ahead, past the Youngs, the Russos' Lexus suddenly roars to life, Frank at the wheel, still desperately trying to complete his call. Gwen fumbles with her seat belt beside him. Their car screeches past the drive. Down the curved road, the trio of black-clad servers piles into a parked white van. Did the young chef already leave too? With the sommelier?

Liz feels a sudden surprising ache for Britta. For the world of a half hour ago. For the privilege of mourning a dinner party.

Liz, Padma, Mabel, Spencer—they all reach the Youngs' car in uncoordinated unison. Mabel runs straight for the driver's seat, but Spencer nudges her aside. "Not this time."

Tom catches up, looks around at the thick collage of black wings splattering the yards, and the road, still clogged with scrambling vermin. "How the heck are you going to drive in this, buddy?"

Liz answers for him, "He'll find a way."

Spencer doesn't protest. As soon as he unlocks the doors, Liz begins climbing into the back seat. She pauses. "You still have a full car seat back here?"

Mabel slides into the front passenger side. "Of course."

Liz wrangles herself into the tiny contraption as Tom climbs in on the other side, Padma trailing. "But Gus is what, seven, eight?"

"*Greg's* pediatrician insisted," Mabel says. "Most do. Reid isn't safe with just a booster."

Spencer snaps, "Not the time, Mabes."

Liz grips his headrest as he swings the car around the drive's botanical island and out onto Little Falls Road's cul-de-sac.

The wind whips up again, knocking their car from all sides. It's so strong that their car veers into the curb.

Spencer says, "What the . . ."

It takes Liz a second to realize what he's looking at. She has to bend to see through the dashboard window. The sky is *glimmering*, twitching, as if it's covered in thin, living lightning. As if someone's adjusted it to an old TV station. Millions of glittering, multicolored threads writhe across the sky, rows of voltaic capillaries now undulating over the trees, The Falls' distant hills, pulsing and rippling across the nighttime.

She hears a distant battle cry, "TURN AROUND!"

But Liz can't take her eyes off the horizon.

Clouds. How could the news have called them *clouds*? Of all things, her old *Skyfall* showrunner's voice fills her mind. "*What does 'glimmering clouds' do for our SFX people? LAZY!*" And yet how do you describe unspooling light? Shimmering masses that look *alive*?

Liz retreats back into the narrow car seat. A swarm of living tinsel would have been more accurate. An army of zombie fireworks poised to devour the world.

"For God's sake, Spencer, please slow down," Mabel says, "and you should drop it into first gear—"

"I've got this!" Though Spencer slams on the brakes a split second before two deer dart in front of the car.

They all take a collective breath as Mabel whispers, "Probably not the time for an 'I told you so' either."

He ignores her, cautiously reaccelerating.

"I MEAN IT, YOU WON'T MAKE IT!" Britta, Liz realizes, is screaming from her driveway behind them.

Liz peers out the back of the car and finally spots Britta. Chiffon dress billowing, wide oak front door flapping behind her, like a stylish Wicked Witch of the West. "Listen to me, TURN AROUND!"

Liz leans forward. "Don't, Spencer, we have to go; we're nearly there."

A monstrous echo of shattered glass and torn metal drowns her out.

Spencer slams on the brakes again. The few cars in front of them—the others trying to flee the chaos of Little Falls Road—screech in time.

For a moment, Liz can only hear a dull, relentless drum between her ears.

"What was that?" Padma says. "What happened?"

Spencer eases his car a few feet forward.

Then Liz sees the wreck. A Jeep and a Lexus locked together as one unit in the middle of the street.

The Lexus.

Liz's hand crawls to her mouth again. It's the Russos' car; she recognizes it from the school's carline. But the car's so damaged it looks fake. A prop on the *Skyfall* television set. A sickly smear of red plasters Gwen's curls to the passenger window. Beside the Lexus, the Jeep lies on its side, back tire suspended and spinning.

"Oh my heavens," Mabel whispers. "Oh my goodness."

Spencer jumps out of the car. Tom and Padma, too.

"Wait." Liz tries to wrangle herself out of the car seat. "Look at that sky; we're running out of time!"

She flails outside as Tom and Spencer rush toward the accident.

Liz, her hips stiff from the car seat, trips over her feet as she dashes after them. "I mean it, look up, we need to get back in the car!"

The tinny, cloying surround sound of crickets, whistling, chimes is louder now, inescapable, even when she covers her ears. Like the noise is thrumming through her. "We need to figure another route out of here."

"*HEELLPPPPPP!*"

They all stop.

Liz turns and watches, disoriented, as Frank heaves himself through his Lexus's shattered window. His balding head, anguished eyes, the bottom half of his face still covered by a surgical mask, now smeared with thick, gory red. His dinner jacket is destroyed, and his high-waisted pants are ripped down one full leg. The rip exposes a crimson, wicked gash on his thigh.

Even from here, Frank's eyes look shiny, dazed. Somehow, he's still clutching that damn phone.

Frank stumbles, rights himself, dusts off his demolished jacket, stunned. He holds the phone up in surrender, slowly turning back to his car. "Gwen," he croaks. "Gwen, I need . . . I . . . need . . ."

Padma sobs, "Gwen."

"Wait, Padma—" Liz says, but Padma's already taken off, dashing around the car's broken body to see if Gwen survived.

The haunting, cricket crescendo feels like it's sinking into Liz's bones. As she tries to shake off the sensation, the sky above morphs before her eyes, and the countless threads of aerial tinsel tremble, vibrate, then plunge with a thin comet of lightning toward Frank and the Lexus.

The comet strikes, and Frank's skin bursts immediately into glimmering, tinsel-like hives, filaments of silver, gold, pale green weaving over and around his face, his shoulders, his torso like sizzling snakes. Frank stumble-steps, cries out, his limbs quaking and humming.

Liz gasps. Even from here, she can see his veins through his skin, glowing and pulsing with light, life, poison, she can't be sure—whatever was in those clouds now somehow worming and writhing right through him.

"Frank!" Mabel shrieks.

Spencer pulls her back. "Russo, don't come closer!"

Liz and Tom stumble back too. Frank looks inhuman. His skin sickly luminous, his face twisted grotesquely, his entire frame crawling with threads of electric color. He's trembling so badly he loses his balance, careening to the cement with a bone-shuddering crunch.

He moans, "I . . . need . . ."

Padma rushes around the car toward him. "Frank, ohmigod, are you—"

Liz says, "Stop, don't touch him, Padma!"

"What about Gwen?" Padma shuffles away. "I don't think she's . . ."

From the distance, Britta screams, "Get back, can't you see it's closing in?"

"She's right, we'll never make it." Spencer surveys Frank, body now still, head splayed on the asphalt, eyes unblinking. The road littered with vermin, deer corpses, the fauna still bursting forth from the trees in rolling waves. "Screw the car."

"No!" Liz shouts after him. "No, wait!" They need the car. They have to leave!

But Spencer and Mabel are dashing back toward the Harris-Ches' drive, toward Britta, a manic air traffic controller who's waving them inside.

Padma glances at Liz, shakes her head, and takes off after them.

Tom grabs Liz's arm to follow.

"We can't." She stumbles away. "If we go back to Britta's, we're stuck here, trapped. Don't you get it? Don't you see?"

"Liz, there's no option here. You just saw what happened to Frank." He tries to pull her into his sports jacket, but she wrangles free.

"I'll go alone, sprint across town if it gets me back—"

"Frank and Gwen are *dead*, dead as in gone, and I'm not losing you, Liz. Now come on!"

And then somehow, she and Tom are running down the cul-de-sac together. Under the sizzling sky, up the road, toward the Harris-Ches'. But they can't stay here. No, they can't, not with the kids home without them, not when she wasn't even supposed to be here!

There must be another answer, another way out of here, another way home.

As they scramble across the sidewalk, she sees it. A well-timed twist. A *Skyfall* cliffhanger. There it is, across the Harris-Ches' front lawn! A beacon of white parked in front of the adjacent home's garage. A white Nissan: the *Fords'* Nissan. It must be. Mrs. Ford said they're next-door neighbors to the Harris-Ches. Which means Sabina's mom is right next door with a getaway car.

Tom pulls Liz up the Harris-Ches' walkway, inside their home, but she's not staying. She can't. She's found their way back to Reid and Callie; she just needs to figure out how take it. Liz sees her solution so clearly now.

She'll get to the Fords.

Whatever it takes.

7

Mabel

[*Voice message, received from SPENCER YOUNG on April 3rd
at two twenty-two* PM
Mabel, it's me. Am I hallucinating? Did you just write Britta
and tell her we're coming tonight? Can you do me a favor? Can
you call me back and tell me just what the hell you're thinking? I thought we talked about this. I thought we agreed we
were . . . *backing away*, given everything. Cease-fire. Just. Call
me. Now.]

[*Voice message, received from THE FALLS PHARMACY on
April 3rd at four eleven* PM
Hello, Mrs. Young! This is Erin at The Falls Pharmacy calling
to let you know that both of your rush refill prescriptions are
ready! Please call us or come by to pick them up as soon as you
can. We're open until seven PM tonight. Thank youuu!]

[*Voice message, received from RACHEL DOWDEN on April 3rd
at five thirty-three* PM
Hi, Mrs. Young, this is Rachel, a catechist with Saint
Rose. I hope you're well. Father Patrick suggested I reach
out, considering everything that you and Spencer . . . just

given the circumstances. I'd love to talk . . . we missed you
tonight . . .]

* * *

A DOOR SLAMS BEHIND Mabel, like the last word. Loud as a
gavel. God's ruling. End of times. Is this hell? Is she still
breathing?

Spencer folds over beside her, huffing. "That sure as shit
wasn't 'contaminated air.'"

"Come," Britta says. "Everyone, move away from the door."

She places her hand on Mabel's back, steering her through
the black-and-white tiled foyer, which is swirling underneath
Mabel's feet like a horrific fun-house floor. She can't catch her
breath, and she's feeling that *pain* again. That heart attack
feeling, lightning fast. An acute ache radiating down her right
arm.

She looks around to find Spencer—because she's dying,
this time she must really be dying—but he's mumbling about
"the crazy sky" and "demon deer" and hurrying into the
kitchen without her. Mabel follows him, passing Chef Romer
and that pretty young sommelier, Kat, who are both tucked
into the foyer's corner. She catches bits of their conversation—
"Your sense of duty's going to kill us." "They shouldn't have left!"
"We owe these people nothing"—it sounds like they're arguing,
but Mabel isn't sure. She isn't sure of anything right now.

She and the rest of the dinner guests enter the kitchen,
where Britta's three children sit on a blanket, somber and
dazed, on the floor. Beyond disoriented herself, Mabel waves
at Avery, before remembering she's furious with the little girl
for how she's been treating Mabel's son these days. Greg's tiny
turncoat friend. *Second-grade Judas*, as Mabel's come to consider Avery.

Just thinking of her son again stabs Mabel from the inside.
Has Greg looked out the window? Has he seen the horrors that
she just witnessed? Is he beside himself worrying? Asleep? Safe?

Is he lost without her?

Mabel clutches her mouth and heaves. *God Almighty, do not let me get sick right now.*

"Mom? Where'd Dad go?" Avery asks Britta.

"Right here, baby."

On cue, Joel edges past Mabel, through the crowd, and around the breakfast nook toward his daughter.

He turns to address his guests. "The news is at a total loss. No one has any clue what's going on out there, what it is, and casualties are mounting. Service is jammed too, which means no one can get through to anyone. It's a mess—"

"And obviously *war*," Spencer says.

A weary-looking Chef Romer and Kat, her arms crossed across her chest, trail in.

"We don't know that," Chef Romer says quickly. "For all we know, it could be a natural phenomenon. A new storm pattern, perhaps, or a new microbial—"

"A micro what now?" Spencer shakes his head. "Come on, no natural storm looks like an exploded, murderous Christmas tree!"

"The chef's right; we can't make any assumptions," Liz says. "All we know is that it kills, near instantly—"

"I know warfare when I see it! That fucked-up glitter grew an *arm*, reached out and shook the life straight out of Frank!"

"Spencer, language, the kids," Mabel says. Dully, though, a reflex, no heat.

Still, Spencer glares at her. "Mark my words, those 'glimmer clouds' are weapons. Probably from another species, another planet."

Avery whimpers, "Dad, do you believe that?"

"Mabel's right, Spencer, let's . . ." Joel scrubs his face. "Put the theories aside. We need to focus on bunkering down, staying safe, at least until we can find out more."

Padma's voice rings hollow as a bell. "How is any of this happening? Gwen and Frank, all those deaths abroad, what about Dev, the baby, my parents, are we . . ."

"We're going to be all right." Joel cups Padma's shoulder. "Actionable steps, yes? Let's split up in teams, secure the house, since the security system's down."

Black stars race, screech, spin out across Mabel's vision. She grips the island, steadying herself.

". . . lock windows, doors, grab first aid," Joel keeps giving orders. "And take shelter downstairs. It's the safest place indoors." He paces. "Britta, Chef Romer, and Kat can pack the kitchen. I'll round up supplies. Spencer and Mabel, check the doors and windows in the upstairs wings—"

"Let me take the back hall."

Liz's "volunteer," a vaguely masked demand, slaps Mabel out of her stupor. Even now, Liz The Tyrant has the audacity, in Joel and Britta's home, to tell everyone how it's going to be. Completely self-focused, absorbed, even in the face of total chaos. Liz doesn't even wait for Joel's confirmation, just sprints down his dark, newly renovated corridor. But then Liz always does what she wants, no more, no less. Just look at how she handles her PTA duties; Mother of God, look how Liz *parents* that exclusive little nuisance Reid Brinkley.

Mabel swoons from the fervor of her mental condemnation.

She fights back her nausea. Perhaps she should stop throwing proverbial stones. Stones have gotten her into trouble as of late. And isn't Mabel the reason her own son is such a softie, as she's been told repeatedly? *Such an indoor cat*, her mother-in-law, Tammy, always coos in her pedantic little tone, as she watches Greg fiddle with Mabel's collection of scale model cars on the kitchen floor—as if Tammy's own macho man, Irish Catholic, crewmen star son Spence had no hand in raising Greg. *Maybe that's the problem, Tammy*, she's always wanted to scream, as Tammy just keeps driving in the knife. *A little old to be playing with toy cars, isn't he? Shouldn't he be playing sports? Spencer started rowing at seven. You're going to turn him weak. You're going to make him fragile . . .*

Oh Lord. Mabel just remembered Greg's inhaler refill is still stuffed inside her purse.

". . . take the billiards room and gallery. Padma, the dining and living room . . ." Joel keeps rattling off jobs, assigning every guest a chore. His voice, somehow, remains even, his face a pillar of admirable control.

Mabel looks around as the crowd disperses. Spencer, her naturally assigned partner in crime, has already run upstairs without her, no surprise. She hurries through the gallery alone, toward the front stairs.

As Mabel ascends, she spots Padma ducking into Britta's still beautifully set dining room. Mabel watches Padma fluff her long, dark hair from her shoulders, glance around guiltily, and then drain the entirety of her cava tasting. The adjacent glass too. Then she promptly folds over and sobs.

Mabel's heart twists. Poor thing, with a baby at home, and all she's going through to boot. Ordinarily, Mabel would shout words of comfort and support over the stairwell, but tonight has drained her dry, the anxiety wiping her mind clean as a windshield.

She bites her lip and climbs the steps. Seems like Dev was right, though, about his wife.

Up, up, up Mabel goes, past the full-length mirror at the top of the stairs, where a somber-looking, terrified ghost of a woman peers back at her. She ducks into the first door along the hall. *Lock the windows*, Joel had said. And he'd mentioned supplies. *Which* supplies?

She hurries into a room with lavender twin beds—Jane's room—slides onto the nearest one, and screams into a ruffled pillow. The sky is breaking in half and Greg is *there* and she is *here*, with Spencer *and* Joel, and she may well be having a fatal heart attack.

No, not a heart attack. She knows what panic feels like by now. But what can she possibly do about it? Her Klonopin prescription is still sitting at the pharmacy. There was no way she was going to let Spencer pick it up for her and let him know how bad her anxiety has gotten, seeing as he *refused* to let her park and go in herself.

The looming horizon glimmers sadistically outside the window. Billions of buzzing, tiny threads of light manically stitched across the sky. Festering, twitching, terrorizing The Falls. Terrorizing the *world*, if the reporters are right, though she can't wrap her head around that now. She can't even process what happened outside on Little Falls Road. She closes her eyes and sees Frank sprawled again in the street. Gwen's face plastered against the widow. The animal carcasses.

She wipes her eyes as Father Patrick's words echo through her. *"If we confess our sins, He will cleanse us from all unrighteousness."*

Mabel sniffs. She has so much to confess, she doesn't know where to start.

She trains her gaze on the room's trio of windows, and imagines her dad—safe, alive, his trademark calm—somewhere out there instead. *You can fix anything, sweetie, you just need to pick up the tools.* The mechanic's mantra—wise advice.

She ignores her rocketing pulse, those dizzying black stars revving across her vision. Then she methodically checks each window frame, making sure it's locked.

Mabel stumbles out of Jane's room, back into the hall, and spots, down the corridor, a shadowy form crouched in front of the linen closet. She hears the stale *beep-beep-CLICK!* of a safe.

Instinctively, she takes a step closer. "Joel?"

The man stands and spins around, shaken.

"*Spencer?* What are you . . ."

"Just leave it." Her husband stuffs something she can't make out into his back pocket and slams the closet door shut.

Holy Mother, does Spencer look disheveled. As disheveled as her husband gets, anyway. Oxford untucked, khakis wrinkled, close-cut silver hair on end. For a single, ludicrous, out-of-time second, Mabel aches for him to run to her, to throw his arms around her waist and erase the shattering world.

"Are you ransacking their linens?"

"I said forget it, Mabes. *Go*, do your job." He hurries down the back stairwell without another word.

Incensed, she bursts into the next room across the hall. Avery's room. With its horned pillows and wallpaper unicorns slurping up rainbow puddles on the walls. *Do you think she has a unicorn in her closet?* Greg had asked Mabel, years ago, during their first playdate at the Harris-Ches'. Her son's little voice thunders through her now, shaking her frame, pounding her skull.

She checks Avery's windows, then Marco's, then hurries toward the front stairs, where Joel is wearily ascending.

Joel stops short when he sees Mabel. His entire face softens. "Mabel. I've wanted to . . . are you . . ." He takes a few steps closer. "You look so pale—"

She backs up. "Don't."

"Is it another panic attack?" he says as he moves toward her tentatively, carefully. He reaches to put his arm around her shoulders, then must think better of it. "I hope you're finally seeing a therapist for them?"

"Yes." She sniffs. Not that it's any of his concern anymore. "But I don't have my medication."

"Oh, Mabel. I'm . . ." Joel's eyes pinch. "I know how ridiculous this sounds, but try to stay calm, or it's just going to make everything worse."

He's so close now. He smells the way he always does: that musky French cologne with just a hint of floral. The faint trace of aftershave and the mousse he uses in his hair. They were friends once, before everything. Before Mabel was even friends with Britta. The "dangerous duo" of the PTA: Joel, with his refreshing stay-at-home-dad perspective; his seemingly limitless resources; his grand ideas for field trips and unique enrichment activities. Mabel, with her keen eye for detail and chumminess with the school's administration.

Greg, she reminds herself. *Greg is more important than Joel and Britta and me and Spencer. Do not be meek. Do not be a softie.*

"We need to get back to our son," she says.

Joel searches her face, his bright eyes haunted. "I know. Mabel, I know, but right now, it's far too dangerous to leave."

"You're going to help me," she forces the words out. "You're going to find a way."

"Mabel, I—"

But she pushes away from him, stumbling back in her heels, grabbing the banister for purchase. Her heart now thrumming with one steady, singular beat.

Greg. Greg. Greg.

"Because if you don't, I'm telling everyone," she says. "Starting with Britta."

8

Britta

No Service   Verizon

<Britta's Notes>   [Done]
-Life Will Rise to the Challenge even under terrifying circumstances
 (too wordy)
-Life, Interrupted, Will Rise to the Challenge (???)
-Life Will Rise Above Uncertainty (YES!)—#Brittasays triumphs in the
 face of catastrophe
-must get pics of Little Falls, street chaos, weird lights over nature
 preserve
-get sound bites from guests (tricky)
-showcase reno and how it's helping us survive (#RenoWithForesight
 #AlwaysAnticipateTheUnexpected)
-three posts to tell the story → 1) world chaos 2) #Brittasays put into
 action 3) Life Rising Above Uncertainty
-Cache content and send posts from cellar
-posh survival feed = countless collabs
-COMEBACK

_____

CHAPTER

9

Liz

LIZ CAREENS THROUGH the kitchen, past Britta, who keeps fumbling with her phone. What is Insta-Britta doing? Is she actually checking *social media* right now?

She tries to slide past Romer and Kat, but the sidestep proves impossible. The two have created a clusterfuck around the island. Romer, speaking in hushed tones as he cleaves off pieces of Saran Wrap; Kat, gritting her teeth as she shoves a dozen wine bottles into perforated boxes.

Kat hisses, "You know we're catering our own funeral right now."

"We're being prudent," Romer whispers. "Safe, helpful, as we wait for this to pass."

"Don't give me that bullshit," Kat says. "I know you, and this is *not* time for playing hero, for unhinged client loyalty . . ."

Liz sneaks past them, past Spencer too, as he hurries down the back stairwell. She finally reaches her intended destination, the home's shadowed back hall. Tom's already off in the billiards room, intent on following Joel's orders like a good soldier. But she has other plans. Crucial plans. Plans that will save her and Tom, in the undeniably truest sense. Because there's a difference between *staying alive*—running around checking locks, gathering flashlights, burrowing like little suburban moles into the swank of the Harris-Che residence—and *saving your life*, the very essence of your existence, purpose, being.

Liz swears on hers, on God, the universe, on every word she's ever written, they're getting back to Reid and Callie. Whatever it takes.

She can still hear that horrible sound outside, the strange cacophony of crickets, wind, haunting, tinny notes—the same noise she heard magnified through her phone with Laura's garbled screams. The sound is mockingly, relentlessly unsettling. Unnatural. A perpetual reminder that everything, *everything*, about tonight is wrong.

If these clouds came from the UK, the phenomena reached their town in less than a couple of days. What does that mean for the next twenty-four hours?

Millions of deaths. *Millions.*

Liz swallows down the achy pull in her throat and keeps moving—no time to cry—past the sprawling family room with its low-slung leather couch and plushy rockers, and into the playroom they toured earlier that night—the kids' displayed artwork, now shadowed and sinister looking. She'd been able to see the Harris-Ches' backyard from these windows, the neighboring house too, if she remembers, which makes it a perfect spot to attempt to garner the Fords' attention now.

Liz crosses the room, pressing her nose to the glass. But from this angle, she can only see the Harris-Ches' lawn and the wall of rocks dividing the two properties.

Wait, she passed another room, didn't she? Another door along this same hall? Maybe she can better see the Fords' place from there.

Before leaving the playroom, Liz grabs some construction paper and a handful of markers from the nearby table caddy, then stuffs the materials into her tote bag.

She doubles back down the hall and twists the doorknob to the other room. But it doesn't budge. She presses all her weight against it. No dice.

Liz fumbles inside her tote for her thick, overstuffed lump of a wallet. She pulls out a credit card and jams it into the latch. She pushes the card in deeper, angling it up, and then jiggling the handle, as if wringing the knob's little haughty silver neck.

Finally, a click of release.

Liz flings open the door to a pitch-dark room, hurries inside—

Only to trip and go flying over a shadowed mass on the floor.

"Ow, *sh*—" She bites back the rest of her yelp.

Standing up, she rubs her arm and pinches her eyes shut to adjust to the dark. Forms begin to emerge. A bed. An open closet door. A tripping hazard of workout equipment across the floor. Free weights, push-up stands, yoga blocks, and . . . dirty clothes? Gross, who's staying in here, the *chef*? She wasn't entirely listening when Joel was introducing him, but maybe he's like a cook equivalent of an au pair or something. That feels very Britta. Besides, Liz sensed a familiarity earlier, something more even, between them.

Liz untangles a long red workout band from her tote handle and finally locates the windows.

The room's thick blackout shades are all pulled down. No wonder the room's such a black hole. Liz sidesteps the mess, grabs the drapes' chain, and yanks the window treatments up.

"Oh my God."

She edges up to the glass. That's it, the Fords' home no more than thirty feet away. The white Nissan that arrived at her own home a few hours ago is still parked in the house's sunken, curved drive below. There's a large bay window, dimly lit, on the first floor right above the garage.

Liz gropes the nearby walls, finds the room's lighting panel, and turns the lights on. She shivers, remembering the spooked deer that slammed into the transmitter down the road. Thank God the Ches have power.

The room she's in comes into full focus. The haphazardly made bed. The gadgets on the end tables. She closes the door and frantically flips the lights to get the Fords' attention . . .

Wait, no, there's a better way to do this.

Random tinder from *World Breakers* research ignites in her mind. The father in her book series, James, knew Morse code from his war days; Garrison Cromwell *insisted* that the father be a World War II hero, even though the timing made absolutely no sense. Liz had to Google the SOS sign in copyedits to make the scene feel more "authentic."

She turns back to the lights. *SOS.* Three short flashes. Three longer flashes. Three short flashes. *Stop.* Then again: three short beats. Three long. Three short again. *Stop.*

A hot ripple of panic courses through her. No one's coming to the Ford's first floor window. Maybe they're asleep. Or maybe they left. Perhaps they're bunkered down in the basement or being flayed by the glimmer, dying on Little Falls Road like Gwen and Frank.

Three long. Three short—

A light from deep inside the house blinks on across the way.

Liz keeps punching the panel, near-demented now with hope. Three short flips. Three long. Three short. *Stop.*

The room above the garage grows brighter.

Liz watches as a thin, chic woman hurries around the room's dining table and toward the window. Taupe jogging suit, fresh lob blowout.

Liz's breath catches. That's Mrs. Ford; she's positive. The woman who dropped Sabina off.

Liz sprints to the window as Mrs. Ford hurries toward her own. Liz wildly waves her hands and opens her mouth to scream across the properties (pointless), then moves to open the window (possibly suicidal).

Across the way, Mrs. Ford raises her hand to her ear, thumb and pinkie extended like a phone—*call me?*

Liz shakes her head. To drive her message home, she dislodges her phone from her tote and wrings it with frustration.

Mrs. Ford nods with a frown. Then gives a "thumbs down." Does that mean *bummer*, or that the Fords are also having service problems? Unclear. Maybe the whole neighborhood is out from the glimmer. The state. The world.

Liz remembers her gathered writing supplies and tips her large tote bag over, dumping the markers and construction paper onto the bed, the moonlight casting the bonfire of art materials in a ghostly sheen. She scrawls her most burning question in big, block blue letters across a yellow sheet.

> ### *HAVE YOU SPOKEN TO SABINA?*

Liz slaps the paper against the window.

Mrs. Ford leans forward, pressing her hands against her own window. The woman sadly shakes her head.

Damn it.

Liz scrawls another block-letter note on a pink sheet of paper:

> ### *DO U HAVE ANOTHER WAY TO*
> ### *CALL OUT? A LANDLINE?*

Mrs. Ford's face crumbles as she wipes her eyes. She shakes her head again.

Liz hears voices outside the bedroom now, louder than before. Tenser, if that's possible. It sounds like an argument, but she can't discern between who.

She pauses. Hears the chef squabbling about the best ways to preserve hallacas. A female voice responding. Then a slammed door. Maybe they're looking for Liz? She's running out of time.

Hard facts: cell service and Wi-Fi are jammed or dead and there's no way for Liz or Mrs. Ford to call out, or to field calls in. They may be able to get to Mrs. Ford's car unscathed, but who knows what they'd be driving into. Liz pictures Frank Russo again, that bolt of glimmering threads wrapping around him, crawling under his skin, into his veins. Who knows if they'd stand any chance of surviving the trip home. Hell, who knows if Sabina already tried to leave and come home herself.

Liz's stomach plunges to the cellar at the thought. It's the first time she's entertained the possibility that the eleven-year-old might have learned what's going on, panicked, ran, and left Reid and Callie alone.

Liz suddenly needs to squeeze a novel onto this construction paper. *What's your daughter like under pressure?*

Is Sabina a fighter?

Would she abandon my babies?

Look into a crystal ball, Mrs. Ford, and tell me, RIGHT NOW, what the hell's going on!

Mrs. Ford, though, is now buried in her dining room armoire. She pulls out several cloth napkins and scrawls in a frenzy across one of them. She presses the Sharpie-branded napkin against her window:

> ### *NEWS SAYS WE CANT LEAVE.*
> ### *TOO DANGEROUS.*

Seconds later, another napkin with dark, hurried scrawl:

> ### *BUT I WANT TO TRY.*
> ### *FALLS LANE IN BACK*
> ### *COULD WORK.*

Holy hell. Liz needs shotgun in that car.

She begins writing a flurry of responses across various sheets of white, green, and pink construction paper when a blood-curdling scream echoes from the front of the house.

Liz jumps, her papers flying around her like fallen leaves in a windstorm. "Crap!"

"Liz? Where are you!" Tom's flustered voice comes from down the hall. Then closer: "LIZ!"

Another voice: "NOW, find her, we need to move!"

Liz lunges for the papers, fumbling to reorganize her notes into a coherent dialogue. She reaches under the bed for an errant sheet . . . and sees something nestled in the middle of the workout equipment tangle.

Liz picks up the item. It's a Halloween mask.

Wait. No. It's a gas mask, with a full facepiece respirator, one that looks like a relic from World War II. Canvas with a plastic face covering, protruding air ducts, a long black hose. The only cue that it's a replica, and not an actual artifact, is the small insignia printed along the bottom of its air duct: *ROGUE TRAINING*.

She studies the pile again.

There's another mask lodged inside the nest of workout bands. She grabs that too; this one's got a half-face respirator, black with white air valves. A sporty logo, *ALTITUDE XTREME*, is stitched across its band.

The news had called the glimmering clouds "air contamination," at least at first, though Spencer's right—whatever they just witnessed outside is worlds away from pollution. Liz closes her eyes and pictures Frank Russo again, his COVID mask glazed in thick, red gore. His KN95 obviously didn't protect him. But still, maybe masks like these could be actual means of protection from the terrors outside, even if they're meant for sadistic workout training. And there are *two* of them, one for her and one for Tom. They only need a few seconds, after all, just enough time to run across the yard to Mrs. Ford's.

"Liz, answer me," Tom bellows from the hall.

She shoves the masks into her tote bag, scrambles to the window, and begins displaying her flipbook of notes to a stricken Mrs. Ford:

> ### THERE'S A SAFE ROOM IN OUR BASEMENT

> ### KIDS COULD BE SAFE

> ### LET'S GO

"This thing is on our doorstep!" Tom's voice comes straight through the door.

She needs to talk with him. Now. Liz stuffs her other notes into her tote bag, then scrawls another hasty message:

> ### DON'T MOVE BRB

Liz hopscotches around the room's mess, out the door, and into the hall. But Tom isn't there anymore. The kitchen is brightly lit, but empty too—the marble island a deserted sprawl of appetizer trays and a prepped second course long gone cold.

A ripple of screams sounds from the entry.

Liz sprints toward the gallery and collides with Tom.

"Thank God." He pulls her into a manic hug. "Where have you been? Everyone's looking for you."

"With their neighbor. We have to go back. I have a plan—"

A long, anguished wail drowns her out. Followed by Joel's voice: "No, Romer!"

"She said she wouldn't leave!" Romer, from the front of the house. "How could she? She promised—"

The rest of the chef's words are interrupted by another chorus of screams.

Joel: "Everyone, away from the door, downstairs!"

Liz wrangles out of Tom's hold and rushes into the foyer to see what's going on. But the crowd is roaring toward her like a wave, pushing past her, threatening to pull her along with them. She fights against their current and reaches Romer, who's standing in the foyer alone, anguished, staring out the door's sidelight windows.

Liz gasps.

Outside, it—she doesn't look of this world.

Down the Harris-Ches' cobblestone walk, twenty feet away, a luminous, hunched, slow-moving form writhes and lurches toward the house. A specter from a movie. A monster. A brilliant ghost. It takes Liz a few seconds to realize it's *Kat*. Her slim figure, limbs, face, little pixie cut are covered in thin, pulsing, tangled strands of crackling light—sheens of eerie green, gold, silver. Her veins glowing with submerged lightning.

Just like Frank.

Liz stumbles back. Whatever this glimmer is, wherever it came from, why, *how*, it's now on the other side of this door.

Outside, Kat lets out a shrieking wail, careening forward, her body encased in that web of sizzling light. Her hand is waving something Liz can't make out. "I can't . . . ," Kat says. "Y-you . . . can't . . ."

Romer shoves past Liz. "Let me go, I have to help her—!"

Before he can open the door, Joel and Tom are beside him, yanking him and Liz out of the entry.

They hurry into the kitchen, which, in just the past few minutes, has been transformed into a prepper base. Spencer stacking and grabbing the wrapped trays of Romer's food to bring downstairs; Mabel loading twin buckets of flashlights and soup cans. The Harris-Che kids are halfway down the steps already, Padma on their heels, Britta behind her, still buried in her stupid phone.

"Britta, turn that thing off," Spencer shouts. "Frank and the sommelier both just died with their phones in their hands!"

"A coincidence," Joel says, but Spencer's clearly unmoved.

"They say the glimmer causes service issues, but who knows, maybe phones cause the glimmer!"

Joel sighs. "All right, everyone, smartphones off, at least for now!"

The rest of the crowd funnels into the stairwell.

"Mrs. Ford," Liz says, shaking out of her stupor, grabbing her husband's arm. "Tom, we need to talk. I found another way to reach the kids."

"Joel said he has ethernet in the cellar." Tom waves her toward the basement door.

"No, that's not what I . . . there's another—"

"We can try the kids from the landline downstairs, come on."

"Wait, Tom, stop!" She tries to spin from his grasp, her massive tote bag smacking against her side, but Tom stays firm, escorting her forward like an unwanted guardian angel. But she can't let Mrs. Ford leave without them. These glimmering clouds are right outside; it could be hours, days, weeks, forever before it's safe to leave. They have no idea what's even out there, what they're dealing with!

"What if Reid and Callie opened a window?" Liz sputters. "What if Sabina opened the door?"

Tom says nothing as he hurries them into the stairwell. Maybe he thinks they did. Maybe *he* left a window open before they left. Maybe he saw their home's Nest cam footage earlier, before service went dead, and he *knows* they did and isn't sure how to tell her. The doubting, the questions, the not knowing . . . Liz can't stomach it. She needs to see them, talk to them, an aching hunger devouring her whole.

Somehow, they're down the steps and into the cellar's sconce-lit hall below.

Perhaps Padma was right. This *can't* be real.

Liz is halfway down the corridor when she realizes her fingers are tightly wound around a crumpled piece of pink construction paper. Her final note to Mrs. Ford.

> ***COMING NOW***
> ***WAIT FOR ME***

10

Britta

No Service   Verizon

< Britta's Notes >   [Done]
-wine cellar = haven
-how to *claim* authority in uncertainty
-sound bites from guests, #Brittasays as voice of reason/light in
 darkness
-interviews?????

"**M**OMMY," JANE WAILS. "No, the basement's creepy!" She leeches onto Britta's leg so tight that Britta's knees buckle. "MOMMY!"

"Give Mommy a second." Britta saves her "Draft notes" as they hurry past the home movie theater, then shoves her phone into the soft pocket of her chiffon dress. She moves to pat Jane's downy blonde head, but her daughter's already zigzagged through the crowd and attached herself to Joel. Marco, with his mussed dark hair and rosy cheeks, is full-on wailing like a fire engine, while Avery has shut down, her brown eyes now glazed and vacant. Out of all of them, Avery's probably the only one old enough to piece together that this is real, dangerous, far from a school fire drill. Britta should talk to her. *Nota bene: have a talk with her.*

Joel pulls Jane into a tight side bear hug, murmuring comforts to her, as he opens one of the wine cellar doors.

"What are we supposed to do?" Padma whispers behind Britta. "Stay here? Until when? How will we know when it's safe to go?"

"I don't know," Liz answers numbly. "But I can't just *wait*. Can't just sit here—"

"The glass is double-paned," Joel assures the crowd up ahead. "Special thermal, safest place in the house." He thrusts his foot against the door like a stopper and waves in the remains of her massacred party.

Stop that, Britta. No self-pity. Chaos equals opportunity.

She forces on a smile as she follows the crowd's wake—a tactful, sympathetic smile, like those doctors overseas who face all sorts of horrifying maladies and still manage to look graceful on their nonprofit websites. *I've got you*, this smile must say. *I'll help you every step of the way.* Because she's not going down without a fight. *This* will become her new opportunity. Really, what kind of lifestyle guru macro-influencer is she if she can't turn eight people fighting for their lives into a golden opportunity to showcase *Life Will Rise to the Challenge*?

Britta peers around at her guests shuffling into her wine cellar, past the wine towers and into the more spacious alcoves. These people need her wisdom, now more than ever, that much is obvious. Mabel's mumbling to herself—some kind of motivational gearhead mumbo-jumbo about big ends, little ends, firing on all pistons—while pacing in front of the rotating wine towers, her usually sculpted auburn bob now more closely resembling a vintage Halloween wig pulled out of storage. Liz, silk blouse blotted with sweat stains, drags a bewildered-looking Tom into an alcove off the cellar's main aisle. Padma's holding on with her chipped manicure for dear life to the granite counter of a nearby tasting table, appearing moments away from fainting.

Such a portrait of *overreaction*. Yes, Britta fell prey to it herself. It's shocking, obviously, horrific, about Frank and Gwen; she still can't fully process they've actually *died*. On her street, no less. And yet . . . they were tragedies, right, the first poor souls on the front lines, lessons for them all to pay heed, take shelter, be smart. This glimmering thing *will* pass. It must. It can't go on forever; the rule of all fads, trends, and troubles: nothing does. Which means she needs artful strategy, and to act now, ahead of the curve.

Joel closes the glass doors behind Britta, sealing them inside. "Romer's going to store his food in the wine fridges in case we need it. Who knows how long we'll be down here." He sighs, brow slick, bow tie undone, bright eyes sparkling with intensity. Christ, does she wish she could capture this cinematic #LifeInterrupted moment on film.

"I can handle the kids, spin it as an adventure for now, if you can get the ethernet up and running. Whatever this glimmer is, it's caused massive service issues. Can you hook up the tablet? Help people use the landline?"

Britta nods.

Apparently satisfied, Joel leaves her to help a distraught-looking Romer. The two grab the plastic-wrapped trays that have been momentarily precariously stacked onto the nearest tasting table. Some of the guests have begun hauling water jugs and supply buckets into the nearby alcoves. Britta's kids have siphoned off too—Jane, now skipping down the center of the cellar corridor, placated and happy again after Joel's doting; Marco, whining as he attempts to catch her. Avery, still floating like a confused ghost behind them both. Right, Britta must talk to Avery. Britta *will* talk to her.

But first, Britta slips her contraband phone out of her pocket.

Discreetly, she clicks her "camera" icon and swipes to video mode. She keeps the Wi-Fi off, given that Spencer's ever-evolving glimmer theory now involves sinister phones—though she wouldn't get service down here on a good day. She won't be intrusive or voyeuristic. No, she just needs evidence, a documentation of their struggles. A few clips, *short* ones. Shorts will be easier to upload via the ethernet anyway. She'll help her guests call their families afterward, of course she will. This will only take a second.

She glides down the aisle and stops in front of Mabel, Spencer, and Padma unpacking supplies.

RECORD:

INT. Wine cellar alcove, Bordeaux section. Mabel arranges cans of white beans, artichokes, and caviar on the granite-top tasting island. Spencer gruffly unloads flashlights and first-aid kits onto an armoire shelf behind her. Padma is folded over, one hand gripping a rotating wine rack, her fingers brushing a bottle of Chateau Branaire.

                    SPENCER
                   (to Mabel)
     I'm telling you, it's a war out there,
     I know what I saw. Chemicals, poi-
     son, maybe some kind of high-tech
     otherworldly weapon . . . wait, are
     you alphabetizing those cans?

                    MABEL
      (puts her head in her hands)
     Just a reflex.

Spencer moves closer, to touch Mabel's shoulder perhaps, but then thinks better of it. He looks up and catches Padma staring at them.

> SPENCER
> (warily)
> Everything okay?

> PADMA
> (sobering)
> Sorry. Just out of it.

Padma returns to shelving perishables in the wine fridge, but Spencer keeps watching her, brow furrowed. Thinking.

Britta presses **STOP**.

She hurries to the next alcove, stopping short of entering when she hears Liz and Tom arguing. Britta lingers, hiding behind the bordering wine racks.

RECORD:

INT. Wine cellar alcove, South American section. Liz and Tom stand shout-whispering at each other near an ambient-lit, built-in storage unit filled with Chilean Malbec (various labels and vintages).

> LIZ
> She's right next door with a car. We just need to reach her—

> TOM
> And I'm saying it's not safe.

                    LIZ
It will be. I have a plan, if you
just—

                    TOM
No, we need to bunker down, we're
all in this together—

                    LIZ
Are you insane? How the hell are we
"all in this together"?

Britta taps **STOP** again, slipping past the Brinkleys and hurrying farther down the corridor. The last thing she needs is a few seconds of Chef Romer footage so she can tag his restaurant, Cash & Moreno, to tap into the NYC feeds. And she must capture this clip of him and Joel *on the sly*. Joel would never understand. No, after tonight, it's obvious he's hell-bent on aggressively sabotaging her.

   She angles her camera through an open vantage point between two wine tower shelves, points the phone up, down, left . . . bingo, spot-on shot of Joel and Romer shoving the large foil catering trays into the double-access wine fridges. She zooms in till their faces are clear . . . perfect.

RECORD:

INT. Wine cellar. Joel and Chef Romer are
surrounded by Cash & Moreno's foil catering
trays near the double-access wine fridges,
the ones separating the main cellar corridor from its adjacent sitting room.

Joel extracts some wine bottles to make
room for the food, then shuts the fridge

door. He turns to find Chef Romer rubbing
his forehead, distressed.

                    JOEL
I really am so sorry, bro. About
Kat.

                    ROMER
Things weren't easy between us. But
I'd begged her to stay. That we owed
it to you, your friends, that it was
the safest move . . .
(He shakes his head.)
But maybe she was right. Maybe wait-
ing . . . maybe it killed her.

                    JOEL
I . . . I don't know what to say. She
seemed lovely, wonderf—

Romer spins around to face him.

                    ROMER
You have what you want, though.
The help at your beck and call.

                    JOEL
        (gently raises hands)
Come on, I'm on your side.

                    ROMER
On my side.
            (cold laugh)
You always get what you want, don't
you, Joel?

Romer brusquely grabs another tray.

> ROMER (CONT'D)
>Look at this place.
>I mean, look at your wife. Selling it
>all as picture-perfect while you're
>busy throwing it away. Does she have
>any clue why I'm here instead of Nico?

> JOEL
> (lowers voice)
>Don't.

> ROMER
>She has no idea, does she?
>Everything you're gambling . . .

> JOEL
>Who the hell do you think you are?
>I'm keeping you alive—

Joel stops, looks directly at Britta's camera, startled, as if noticing it for the
first time.

> JOEL (CONT'D)
>What are you doing?

Britta fumbles to press **STOP**.

She pastes on a smile, though her voice quivers. "Going to
the sitting room. For the landline."

She stomps away in her heels, ignoring her thrashing,
mutinous heart.

She has no idea, does she?

What the hell did that mean?

Joel catches up to her. "Were you filming us?"

Britta lifts her chin. "No, just . . . closing my apps. Phones off, as you said. You know."

She flings open a glass door to the sitting room, hoping for space, time to think—but Joel follows her. She needs a moment to process what she just heard. Romer meant their marital troubles, surely, yes? That they're on the rocks, sleeping in separate rooms, and, for whatever reason, he took it upon himself to point that out? She and Romer had that strange conversation at the beginning of the night, when it seemed he was fishing for information on her. Maybe he's a drama whore; maybe he's just curious. Or maybe he's one of those men who can't help but try to save women in distress?

Joel clambers in front of the coffee table, blocking her from the room's docked tablet. "I *saw you*, Britta. I saw you pointing that damn camera, and I know you. This is serious. There's an unprecedented threat outside our doors. People are dying and you're getting footage for Instagram?" He looks around and drops his voice. "Whatever you're planning, forget it, right now."

She attempts to push her worries aside, to compartmentalize, to assure Joel of her innocuous intentions, but . . . it just *can't* be their separate sleeping arrangements, can it? Because Romer would know that *Britta* would already know where Joel was sleeping.

She stares at the kaleidoscopic patterned woolen rug. She cannot stand being blindsided. Is it something horrendous? Did Joel squander more of his family money, like that ill-fated Bangkok bachelor party he threw for his cousin a few years ago? Or did he get wasted and make a scene at Cash & Moreno?

She nearly reaches out and grabs his bow tie, wrings his neck, forces him into telling her. The man is so devious, calculating, secretive. She's all alone, out in the dark, as always. He's locked her out for years.

"Or what?" Her hands are shaking now.

"Or I'll tell everyone," Joel says.

"Tell them what, exactly? That this soiree is a strategic move to solidify a once-in-a-lifetime opportunity? Because that was the plan all along, Joel. Until you decided to deliberately withhold key information from me and sabotage two months of work—"

"*Deliberately withhold—*"

"Dev, you moron! I'm talking about Dev and the fact that you knew all along he wasn't coming. You set me up like a fool!"

"Britta," Joel says, "that is . . . beyond unimportant . . ."

"So you're saying it wasn't deliberate?"

"We are *not* talking about this right now."

"Ah, maybe you just *tugged* that crucial piece of info right out of your brain and ejaculated it all over the Westa!"

Joel's eyes turn hard.

Wait.

Wait, that's it. She didn't fully process the whole mortifying "Westa scene" until this very moment, but there was a little mirror, wasn't there, a mirror dusted with white powder. Joel running after her, yelling *What did you see?*, and there was a little nose-tug, if she recalls, as he greeted their guests.

She has no idea, does she?

". . . need to grow up," Joel's still talking. "These past few years you've become so obsessed with image, 'perfection,' but your decisions tonight extend far beyond you and your disgusting social media accounts . . ."

Drugs. Yes, it all makes sense now. Joel coming home at all hours, looking like a strung-out zombie in the morning as he makes chocolate chip waffles for the kids. Joel, up late at night lifting weights, bench-pressing, then sprawled out on the couch, dead to the world, when she comes down for her kombucha break at two PM (#Calmbucha). Which means not only is Joel a cold and absent husband and a walking social liability, but now . . . now he's also a drug addict.

This is so off-brand, it's nauseating.

She grips the back of the nearby leather chair. Maybe Nico Cash, Romer's restaurant partner, is his dealer. *Everything you're gambling.* Maybe Joel's gambling too, to pay for the drugs. Is she really surprised, given how she met him, at a bar in Barcelona during his impetuous, splurge backpacking trip across Europe, after he hung up his hedge fund spurs *at twenty-nine*?

"If I catch you filming or scheming or doing anything else other than helping these poor people, Britta, I swear to God, I'll tell them—"

She blurts, "Then I'll tell your parents what I saw in the car."

Joel stops. Looks like he's been pummeled.

She adds mercilessly, "Oh yes, Joel. I saw the drugs. Not that you were making any real effort to hide them." Yes. Game, set, match, Britta.

But then Joel's face oddly twists into something resembling . . . relief.

"Are you trying to blackmail me?" He gives another cold laugh. "Not a very strategic move, Britta. You'd just be biting the hand that feeds you."

"Obviously I've been planning another meal. A meal prepared self-sufficiently, not that you'd know anything about that. And one that was nearly done, Joel—*macro status* was nearly mine—if you hadn't gone and ruined it all." She growls to hide the tremor in her voice. "So don't you dare even think of sabotaging my Plan B!"

The glass doors open with a little *whoosh*.

Liz, Tom, Mabel, Spencer, and Padma all stand there, speechless.

Oh, Christ. *What did they hear?*

Liz, at least, didn't catch any of Britta's self-incrimination, or else she's too focused to care. She hurries into the sitting room, scanning the couch, the bar, the room's corners. "Where's the landline? Does it work?"

Joel steps aside, waving the rest of the crowd in. Still, Britta's little trio manages to dart around the guests and enter first. Avery, still looking dazed and disaffected; Jane, now grumbling that she's hungry; little Marco following like a disgruntled caboose. "Christ, Mommy, I need my BED!"

Jane elbows him. "Don't curse."

"OW." Marco doubles over, staggering, as if Jane has put a bullet in his chest. "Mommy, she hurt me!"

"Am I really trapped down here with them?" Avery looks Britta dead in the eyes. "For how long?"

Britta glances nervously again at her audience, scrambling for some mommy words of assurance, some benign and calming wisdom, but on the spot, all she can think of is *when life hands you lemons, make limoncello.* Thankfully, Spencer saves her, stepping around Avery and into the sitting space with a loud and boisterous, "What if the landline is a death trap too?"

Mabel, Tom, and Padma trail in behind him.

"The *landline*?" Tom says uneasily.

"If the glimmer is affecting the phones, we could be playing right into the extraterrestrials' hands. Or . . . claws or probes, what have you."

Chef Romer, with a few balanced trays in his hands, slides past the crowd and toward the bar. "The jury is still out on the aliens," he says. "And the status of phones as death traps, for that matter."

"I told you, Kat and Frank were clutching *phones*—"

"Joel's landline doesn't run on cell service," Romer presses. "Besides, the landline and ethernet are the only way we can access the outside world."

"I *know that*," Spencer says. "Just check the line before any of us dial."

Britta bristles. "Romer is not our handyman."

Romer smirks, obviously less ruffled than she was by the comment, but Spencer glares at her, clearly furious over being chastened twice. She adds, "I just mean that we're all in this together, as Tom so pithily stated. The Harris-Che home is founded on *democracy*."

Tom, though, appears confused. Damn it, Britta's quoting a private conversation between him and Liz that she eavesdropped upon, isn't she? "So why don't we put it to a vote?" Britta blurts. "All in favor of using the landline to call out, despite the proffered risks?"

Every adult but Spencer raises their hand.

"Then it's settled." Joel points to their vintage bronze rotary telephone, tucked behind the cordials tray on the bar. "Please, by all means—"

"Oooh!" Britta stumbles back, because Mabel and Liz have both begun all-out sprinting across the room. Britta watches in mild horror as Mabel topples into an armchair, which enables Liz to reach the bar a second sooner. Liz's hand wraps around the phone's handle as Mabel's hand wraps around Liz's.

"Mabel, back up," Liz says.

Mabel, to her credit, doesn't let go. "You shoved me out of the way!"

Liz's teeth bare. "Wha—you're full of crap, Mabel. I did not—you tripped!"

Joel hurries to sandwich himself between them. "I know we're all beside ourselves, but we'll all get a turn and this *won't help*." He exchanges a look with Mabel that Britta catches but can't decode. Then he adds quietly, "And really, Liz, there's never a need to resort to violence."

Liz's mouth falls open. "What the—I didn't touch her!"

Tom moves toward Liz, pries her from the phone. "Sorry, everyone, she's just beside herself; we both are."

Liz shrugs him off.

Mabel, meanwhile, is already whipping her fingers around the dial. Britta aches to pull out her cell again. Mama bears battling over the landline? This is priceless, pre-Brittasays-to-the-rescue footage . . .

Her eyes fall on the tablet docked across the room. "I'm going to connect to the ethernet. See if I can load the news. Find out more."

As Britta connects the tablet into the cable jack, both of her daughters lunge for the same spot on the couch.

"Get *off*!" Avery cries savagely.

"I was here first," Jane retorts.

Joel says, "Girls, please, that's enough."

Britta discreetly loads the iPad's camera and angles it toward Mabel and Liz.

Jane says, "I need to eat something, or I'm going to eat Avery."

"Leave me alone," Avery says. "Everyone leave me alone!"

"Avery, baby, stop, come away from the doors, you can't leave," Joel says. "Britta, seriously, help me—girls, stop, *no one* can leave—"

Britta murmurs, "*Un momento.*"

RECORD:

INT. Wine cellar sitting room. Mabel has the telephone cradled between her ear and shoulder, her other hand visibly shaking as she uses the rotary dial. Liz keeps manically pacing behind her.

> MABEL
> Quiet, please, it's ringing!

> JOEL
> (leaves kids, rushes to Mabel's side)
> Oh, thank goodness.

> MABEL
> (freezes)
> Wait. Ugh, no, no, now I have a busy signal . . .

Mabel puts down the receiver, then starts to dial again.

> MABEL
> I'll try your dad.

> LIZ
> Trying another cell phone is point-
> less, lines have been jammed for
> hours.

Mabel tries anyway. Liz, not so tactfully,
edges Mabel out of the way, taking the
handle from her.

> MABEL
> We have to reach Greg somehow. He
> must be so terrified being alone—

> SPENCER
> What are my parents, chopped liver?
> He's *not* alone, Mabes.

> MABEL
> Well, your mother has a real talent
> for making everything worse.

> SPENCER
> What did you just say?

> LIZ
> I was quiet for you two, seriously,
> stop.

The room falls silent. Seconds pass. Liz
dials again.

> LIZ (CON'T)
> Why aren't Reid and Callie answering?!

                    TOM
Maybe that's a good thing. Maybe
Sabina took them to the safe room
and they can't hear the phone.

                    PADMA
                (tiny voice)
You have a safe room?

                    LIZ
It's a box compared to this.
(She refocuses on Tom.)
Maybe you're right. Or maybe it
means they *left*, you ever think of
that?
(sniffs)
Sabina's just a kid. What if she
panicked? What if she led them outside? We don't know what's going on
out there, and the news is saying—

                    JOEL
Britta, what *is* the news saying?

Britta startles. Comes back to earth. Fumbles to **STOP**.

"I—yes, just . . ." She clicks on an old bookmark
for the *New York Times* to load a page as cover. *Please,
#GoddessofTechnology, hear my cries!*

Thankfully the *Times* begins to load . . . then freezes.

"It's . . . really overwhelming," she stalls. "Just so much to
process—"

"Enough," Joel says. "Let me see for myself."

She thinks about darting away from him, holding
the tablet up high, like keep-away. Maybe she would if
she didn't have an audience. Instead, Britta tips the tablet

inward to hide it. *COME ON!* The screen is still shock white, "thinking," transforming into corroborating evidence so, so slowly.

Joel extends his hand. When she doesn't move, he raises an eyebrow, his dark, piercing eyes carrying just the faintest hints of doubt, concern, accusation—

Yes, yes, yes!

She pastes on her most assured #Brittasays smile and slaps the loaded tablet into her snake of a husband's palm.

* * *

THE NEW YORK TIMES

Glimmer Is Not Air Contamination, Experts Say

The terrorizing "glimmer" phenomenon is as lethal as it is hard to classify. "The swift movement of these cloud patterns, their strange lifelike agility, makes it extremely unlikely that we're dealing with a form of pollution," said Brianna Hult, EPA National Program Director . . .

nj.com

True Jersey

"Glimmer" Terrorizes NJ; Death Rate Immeasurable, Governor Says

While actual numbers are "impossible to calculate at this juncture," the governor's office says, estimates are in the "millions" across the state. Murphy urged in a press conference from his home, "We *must* stay inside, underground, until we learn more about this catastrophic anomaly . . ."

THE WALL STREET JOURNAL

White House Considers Aerial Counterattacks to Glimmer

Drastic measures are required to combat the phenomenon that is sending individuals into near-immediate shock, seizures, and cardiac arrest. "We've yet to rule out that these 'glimmering cloud' aberrations are the product of a purposeful design," said Andres Cadet of the U.S. Department of Defense in tonight's press conference. "And thus, may need to be dealt with accordingly . . ."

CHAPTER

11

Padma

"*THE PRODUCT OF purposeful design.* Hah!"
Padma watches, wearily, as Spencer rounds the bar
and helps himself to a glass of Scotch, his hands shaking as he
pours from the Harris-Ches' decanter. He takes a long pull
from the glass, adding, "If that isn't gov-code for *ET invasion*,
I don't know what is."

Padma shifts her legs out from under her, stretching them
long under the sitting room coffee table. The others have been
dissecting the news, putting the headlines under a microscope,
probing, prodding. Hoping the disparate facts and theories
will eventually arrange into a cohesive picture. The trouble is,
just like in sixth grade biology, everyone's convinced they're
seeing something different.

Romer lifts the glass that Spencer's slapped onto the bar
and slides a thin leather coaster underneath it. "*Purposeful
design* does not necessarily mean aliens," he says slowly. "It
could be designed by humans. Some sort of chemical or bio-
logical warfare. Or a design of nature, a new kind of natural
catastrophe, as I was saying before. A carbon or methane fallout, a result of the climate crisis—"

Spencer snaps, "So, what, you're telling me the clouds are cow farts?"

Across the room, Liz flops back against the couch with a groan. "And all we can do is sit here debating while they're home alone."

Tom places his hand on her knee, tentatively though, as if he's dealing with a caged, angry animal. "We've been through this already, Liz. There's no possible way to get to them. But they're okay. I feel it. I know it. They're smart kids. They'll know to stay in the safe room."

Padma can't watch them anymore. Especially Tom, just boldly lying like that—watch anyone feign such absurd and baseless confidence after what's just happened. Maybe he's just trying to calm Liz down, placate her. Who knows, maybe Dev would be the exact same way.

If he were here.

She turns back to her plate, picking at the remains of Chef Romer's mole chicken-skin empanadas, which are fantastic, even ice cold. Padma's still famished—stomach growling, head swimmy from so much cava on an empty tank—but everyone else appears to have lost their appetite, so probably best to follow suit; a Model Mom obviously couldn't stomach food right now. A half hour ago, Chef Romer pulled a few trays from the dual-access fridges and began to "plate" this second course—she wonders if there's some restaurant world mock prize for longest *culinary intermezzo*; Romer would skewer the competition, pun intended. Thank goodness he's still here, seeing as the rest of his staff ran for cover as soon as they had the chance. Though she's curious how long he can tolerate playing caterer, especially to this crowd.

After they'd scoured the internet for information on the glimmer phenomenon and all tried their loved ones countless times—when it became undeniably obvious that they were going to have to eat their next meal down here—everyone relented and sat. They now sprawl across every surface: the pair of armchairs, the sofa, the barstools, the floor, crowding the room that had looked so enviably spacious on their earlier tour.

Thankfully, at least, the little Harris-Che kids are no longer climbing all over the furniture. Jane and Marco complained ad nauseam about having to eat Romer's "gross tacos," but Jane, at least, finally had a few bites, then they both passed out in a tangle of blankets behind the couch. The oldest, Avery, is still awake, even though it must be at least midnight by now, and is curled into a little ball on one of the chairs. The girl hasn't said a word, just stares, dumbfounded, at the dual-access fridges, as if there's a movie playing inside that only she can see. Out of everything going on right now—their crowded quarters, the blistering, unbelievable news, Spencer's absurd extraterrestrial theories—the spritely second grader's resigned, eerie calm might be the most disconcerting.

Britta breaks the silence. "Do we want to try the police again?"

Spencer grunts, "Pointless. You saw. There must be hundreds of people across town with landlines, all trying the same number. It's useless."

"What about your loved ones once more?" Britta turns to Padma. "Dev, maybe?"

Padma shakes her head. "It's just making me more anxious, calling and not reaching him."

Britta sinks back in her chair, oddly serene, Padma notes, given the circumstances. "Well, I'm here, a pillar of strength to lean on, should you need anything."

Padma manages a weak, "Thanks."

"Of course. We must all be accountable to each other, cling to our best selves, if we're ever to best this catastrophe and *rise above it.*"

Padma doesn't respond. Britta's been sharing these weird, stilted little nuggets of "wisdom" ever since they've taken up residence in the sitting room. Maybe it's a host thing, this need to assuage her guests. Or it could be a coping mechanism, a reversion into Britta's online persona, *Brittasays*; which, PS, is one of the most showy, pedantic, and over-the-top voices Padma has *ever* encountered on Instagram. Dev was right; she's totally wrong for Clementine. Either way, it's like watching a motivational speaker walk into the wrong conference room and insist on giving their presentation anyway. "How to Teach Your Spouse Cooperation" to a room full of single mothers. Or "Tips in Goth Glamour" to a Falls PTA meeting.

For a moment, Padma wonders what would have happened if Dev had come instead, like Britta had obviously intended. Or, hell, if they'd been able to land a sitter, and he and Padma had come to this soiree together. It's impossible that he'd just be another body cowering in this wine cellar. Maybe he would have listened to Liz right away, would have run out to their car and driven home at the first signs of alarm. Or maybe he could have saved Frank and Gwen.

Padma closes her eyes. She sees Frank again, his writhing, tortured, luminous body sprawled on the road; Gwen's sickly smear of blood-soaked curls painted across the window.

It's unsettling how *no one* is talking about them. Somehow, Padma can still feel them in the room. She's even caught herself rolling her eyes, anticipating what Gwen will say in response to a news article or a Liz suggestion or one of Britta's increasingly out-of-touch retorts—only to remember that Gwen's body is crushed inside an upside-down car on Little Falls Road.

"I can't believe they're thinking of mounting air raids," Joel mumbles to the tablet, his fine features crinkling with concentration. "Do they think the raids will neutralize the clouds?"

Chef Romer paces behind him. "How American. Let's blow things up and see what happens."

"Might *need* an air raid," Spencer says. "The glimmer's obviously sophisticated warfare. It killed Frank and that little sommelier in minutes."

There's clearly a hole in Spencer's logic, just ask any fifth grade science student worth their salt. Two case studies hardly amount to "scientific fact." Yes, Frank and Kat were killed almost instantly—like the news was saying, they must have fallen victim to some kind of glimmer-induced seizure, maybe cardiac arrest. But maybe they're only beginning to witness what the glimmer is capable of.

Padma shudders. What if it can seep through floors? Walls? Lie in wait? What if it's somehow invaded the house? Why is nobody mentioning those possibilities? Has no one else thought about them, or are they all just ignoring the same morbid notions—just hoping for the best and pretending for one another?

At least that's something Padma is good at: pretending.

"We can't just wait down here like sitting ducks." Liz stands up. "We need to do something. Roundtable, come up with a plan." She crosses the room and grabs a custom Harris-Che Wine Notes notepad resting on the bar top. She flops back down, dislodges a pen from her tote, and fiendishly begins scribbling.

"We know more than we think," Liz mumbles, "between Frank's death, Kat, the news. Maybe we can figure this out."

Britta flashes her a pedantic smile. "Liz. The EPA, CDC, and Department of Defense are all at a loss. But yes, of course, a round of *writerly brainstorming* may indeed crack the code."

Liz ignores the dig. And really, maybe they should give Liz the floor. If they'd listened to her sooner, perhaps they'd all be home with their loved ones, safe across town.

"When we were outside, the clouds looked like lightning to me, or a bad channel on a TV." Liz frowns at her paper, then looks up. "And what about the noise?"

Joel shakes his head. "The noise?"

"Don't tell me you didn't hear it," Liz says incredulously. "The weird, tinny chirping. The wind tunnel sound—"

"And chimes." Padma nods. "I heard it too."

Romer says, "It continued the entire time we were upstairs."

"He's right," Britta adds.

Joel gives a mirthless laugh. "No news source has any theory on the noise."

Liz keeps studying her chicken-scrawl list, as if some careful rearranging, rewriting, reordering, might break this night wide open, unlock all its secrets. "There have to be rules to this thing." She leans on her forearms, begins visibly gnawing the side of her cheek. "There are always rules."

But that doesn't sit right with Padma. Just because there are "rules" doesn't mean things suddenly, beautifully click into place. Hell, look at motherhood. She follows all the rules, doesn't she? She does everything right. On the surface, she's a Model Mom.

"Any more word on The Falls in particular?" Tom asks.

As Joel turns back to the tablet, Padma's gaze drifts again to the pair of sleeping Harris-Che kids. She hasn't thought of Future Isobel since the made-up apparition propelled her out of Britta's house and onto the road. What would Future Isobel be doing right now, she wonders? Definitely not sleeping, Future Isobel wouldn't miss a trick. No, she'd be hovering by Joel's side, scouring the news herself, debating creative-though-still-scientifically-possible theories about these glimmering clouds.

Padma must be going crazy because she somehow *misses* this intelligent, spritely little figment . . . this future projection of her oft-writhing, furious, screaming, real-world baby.

Baby.

Padma's chest wells up at the word. This time, the milk letdown takes her breath away. There's no room in there. There's. No. More. Room.

Joel says, "Doesn't look like there's been any statement or updates from the town." He glances at Avery, then drops his voice an octave. "You saw outside, though. Who knows who's left at Town Hall."

"Wait, what about the Neighborhood Watch?" Tom says.

Everyone stares at him.

"Damon Campbell runs the Old Falls District's chat board," Tom adds, turning to Joel. "He's got a bunker."

Spencer comes around the bar. "Yes. Yes! Hell, if anyone's got the inside scoop on the glimmer situation, it's Campbell."

As Joel loads the Watch page, Tom beams like a first grader.

"It will be comforting, too," Britta says demurely, "to connect with other neighbors right now. In times like these, we think we're alone, but our experiences are so universal."

"I don't think there's anything 'universal' about a man with a mansion-sized bunker who spends forty hours a week lobbying for private stop signs." Liz looks around. "Or a twelve-hundred-square-foot wine cellar, for that matter."

"*Regardless.* There's so much we can learn from each other," Britta chirps. "Just look around, at how ingenious we've been in surviving!"

Padma takes a few deep, shaky breaths as the rest of the group debates Damon's "contributions" to the neighborhood. What the hell was she thinking, not bringing her pump? "*Your boobs are spoiled,*" Dev always jokes whenever Padma opts to pack her hospital-grade pump for even a twelve-hour visit to Mama's. But what Dev doesn't understand is Padma doesn't have a choice. It's *work* for her body to nurse, so much so that she doesn't keep more than a six-pack of Similac formula in the house, or else she'd be too tempted to throw in the towel altogether. Her body demands every modern tool to assist her, as her sleep cycles are slow to adjust, her mind is groggy, and her moods are a freaking roller-coaster ride. That terrible voice that whispers at three AM in Isobel's nursery is so *loud* now—loud enough to drown out the cellar, the other guests, sanity. *You are not made for this. You are not good at this.*

Joel lets out a frustrated sigh. "Do you have a Neighborhood Watch account, Tom? The site's password protected."

Tom slides off the couch to help. Padma's head, meanwhile, is spinning from the pain. Her chest feels like it's been set on fire. She needs to figure out a way to hand express, a means to relief. First step: escaping this suffocating room.

She stumbles to a stand.

Mabel appraises her with worried eyes. "You all right, Padma?"

What an asinine question. "Just light-headed."

Mabel bites her lip. "From all the champagne?"

Mabel's husband, Spencer, gives Padma a long, slow, evaluative look. These people, seriously.

Padma flashes the Youngs the tight-lipped smile she once reserved for The Falls Elementary's highest echelon of PITA parents. "It's . . . not the champagne, trust me." She forces out a dismissive little laugh. "Now, please excuse me."

Padma shoves her way through the sitting room's doors and back into the long storage space. She's never felt so alone in all her life. Yes, technically she's surrounded, crowded, by people, but none of them care. None of them know her, and she doesn't know them. Who are they really, parents who used to pretend to like her because of her daily access to their children? Insta-ladies who see Padma's family as a strategic business opportunity? Irreverent authors she's had a few drinks with, a few laughs with at others' expense?

The air in the storage corridor feels better, safer, cooler. Padma crosses the aisle and grabs two Ziploc bags from the mound of kitchen supplies that someone placed near the dual-access fridges. Chef Romer, no doubt. She chooses an alcove with a granite-topped tasting island in the middle. Oenophile camouflage.

As she ducks behind and slides to the floor, she tries to recall the advice of her nursing coach, Mandi ("*with an I, not a Y*"), at Prenatal to Cradle. Padma swears Mandi gave a lesson on hand expression, though those sessions are now a total blur, a haze of sleep deprivation and unbounded panic.

Maybe she just needs to close her eyes. Focus.

Padma takes off her feathered bolero, lifts her shirt, and unclips her nursing bra. Then angles her fuller left breast into the plastic bag. Wait, now she remembers; she needs to massage the area first. Mandi's voice finally comes to her, all trilly and superior, more suited to teaching ballroom dancing than "best breast" tactics. *"Mah-sahge, ladies! Mah-sahge!"*

Padma balances the bag, tries to massage the milk out. One drip. Another. Two more down the plastic bag, like errant rain on a windowpane. GOD! It's like she's right back in Overlook Hospital in her nubby blue gown, trying to position Isobel to nurse in a way that won't break her as the five other glowing new moms master *the football hold* and *the clutch position.*

You are not made for this. You are not good at this.

"Mah-sahge, ladies! Mah-sahge!" she croaks absurdly.

It's no use. Nothing. She tries again. And again. And then . . . oh. The stimulation—no, no, her chest is *tingling* now, throbbing, blooming with that distinct and overwhelming sensation of fullness, another letdown, and still nothing's coming out—

No, no, no, fucking no!

Padma thrusts her shirt down, grabs her bolero, presses it to her face, and screams.

↓ **NeighborhoodWATCH**

Old Falls District

Threads

Mentions & reactions

More . . .

↓ Channels

 # general

complaints

petition-ideas

stop-sign

mall-car-robbery

falls-elementary

+ Add channels

→ Direct Messages

(42 members)

SUNDAY, APRIL 3RD

Damon Campbell 5:35 PM
Well we need to force it on the agenda. I propose a street meeting about the stop sign next Sunday. Gotta coach soccer practice at 10 (GO FALLS BLUE!) but let's say noon.

Sean Zhao 6:13 PM
Hear hear

Damon Campbell 6:15 PM
You'd think with all the taxes we pay, they'd be clamoring for our town punch list.

Tom Brinkley 6:42 PM
Lol "town punch list"! Great idea about the meeting. I'll be there!

Damon Campbell 9:05 PM
Holy shit. Troops, you there? Everyone all right?

Colson Evanoff 9:37 PM
F*cking unreal man. Me and the fam are locked in the man cave downstairs. I funneled ethernet in . . . can't believe it's working. Cell service and Wi-Fi are a lost cause.

Damon Campbell 9:39 PM
You think this is a state conspiracy? A government trick?

Sean Zhao 10:06 PM
Don't think so. Worldwide chaos. Glad to hear you gents are safe BTW.

Damon Campbell 10:34 PM
I tell you, if this is an invasion, I'm cracking out the artillery.

Barry Elders 10:46 PM
Don't do anything rash, Damon. You step outside, it's over.

Sean Zhao 10:55 PM
Barry's alive! *fist pump* Does anyone know if they're really dropping air bombs? Trying to reach the county office. Hope Ruiz is still standing. MILLIONS of deaths??? How's that possible?

Barry Elders 10:59 PM
We're locked inside, praying it doesn't come in.

Damon Campbell 11:04 PM
Mistake. We need to go on the offensive. I'm planning to take the Hummer, patrol the streets. Someone's got to defend the neighborhood.

Barry Elders 11:25 PM
DON'T DO THAT DAMON

Damon Campbell 11:54 PM
Anyone see that footage from DC with the National Guard on the roads? Sure, they're in tanks and gas masks and hazmat suits but they're out there. ALIVE. Time to separate the men from the mice, boys.

I've got 100+ firearms in my bunker and I'm just itching for a little green-men target practice.

CHAPTER

12

Liz

L IZ PACES AS Tom keeps reading the Neighborhood Watch comments aloud.

Romer, now perched on the barstool next to Tom, gives a noticeable eye roll. "I really do not think your gun-wielding neighbor is a reliable source."

The chef is obviously right. These Watch dudes are absurd and dumb and reckless. *"Green-men target practice?" Really?* But Damon's also confirmed Liz's hunches about what it might take to survive on the streets—at least long enough to drive the two miles home.

"Should we write them back?" Tom says. "Ask Sean what he found out from the county executive's office?"

Joel leans over Tom's shoulder. "Worth a shot."

As Tom taps away, he mumbles, "Liz, I'm sending notes to Blake Derrier and Gus Mongi too, to see if they've got a clear view of our house, what might be going on inside. They'll tell us if power went out on the street, too."

"Great," she says tightly. She has no clue who Blake and Gus are, and now she's worried about the kids fumbling their way through pitch-black darkness.

Mabel slides off her barstool to peer at Joel's screen. "What did Barry mean that he's praying it *doesn't come in*? Is he implying that we—that Greg—isn't safe inside?"

Liz tries to tune Mabel out. More baseless speculation won't help. No, this handful of soiree survivors, at this point, are more distractions than anything else. They're already resigned to their fate—it felt like pulling teeth to even get them to collaborate, brainstorm, search for a solution—which means if Liz is getting home, it's going to be because she's resourceful, thinks through this on her own, connects the dots. That's what she's good at: threading patterns together. Constructing a cohesive narrative. *Gas masks, hazmat suits, tanks*—that's what Damon said. That the National Guard is outside and still *alive*, patrolling the streets in heavy-duty protection. Lo and behold, she's found two gas masks (fine, yes, *workout* gas masks, but they look legit; they must be legit) that are wedged inside her over-stuffed tote bag right now. Maybe she and Tom can take them, run to Mrs. Ford's after all, get in the Fords' car and across town.

Joel says, "I know the news is far from comprehensive right now . . . but for what this is worth, there haven't been any reports on the glimmer getting indoors, or affecting people inside."

Mabel sniffs. "I just can't believe God would let this happen. Greg is at home, without us, as millions die and air bombs rain down?" She fitfully shakes her disheveled bob. "What if the bombs make things worse? In what world does adding poison to poison *stop* poison?"

Liz paces away from the crowd, toward the door for some space, to better concentrate. Could she and Tom put on the masks and just run *home*? It's only two miles, after all. But that's putting a lot of faith in Joel's workout masks—and if air raids are coming soon, it's too dangerous to be on foot anyway. The quick jaunt to the Fords' car is a much safer bet. She wishes she could see that actual National Guard footage that Damon Campbell was talking about. "Can you ask Damon to share his sources?" she says. "See where he's getting this information from?"

Joel says, "Go on, Tom."

"Stroke his ego a little, too," Spencer adds. "Tell him how much we need him. Campbell can be cagey unless he knows he's appreciated."

Joel flashes Spencer a discreet little smirk as Liz gets back to pacing around the sitting room. What is it with these people, enemies one day, all chummy the next?

She pictures Ben Schreck cursing her out right now: *Damn it, Liz, stay focused on PLOT, not character.* Ben would be right; her old showrunner was always right, as much as she hated to admit it. If what Damon said about the National Guard is true—if she can find out for sure—there's genuine hope for breaking out of this bougie prison.

Chef Romer is now the only one left at the bar. He hops off his stool and begins aggressively wrapping his leftovers with Saran Wrap, giving a disapproving *tsk* as he does so. "You are all acting like this is a puzzle to be cracked," he says. "A game where you just need to learn the instructions, and all will be okay. Life is rarely so simple. Death is even more complicated. Believe me, I saw it. In her eyes."

Romer's eerie words crawl under Liz's skin, temporarily stopping her pacing. "What are you talking about?"

The chef fixes his intense gaze on Liz. "Have you ever considered that we are entering a new age of humanity, one where our illusions of control are gone? One where we are truly at the mercy of the elements, the unknown? Believe me, there is something powerful out there knocking at our doors. You didn't see Kat as she was—" He stops, collecting himself, his dark eyebrows stitching together. "She was . . . haunted by something. Something inhuman. Something older, more powerful, bigger than human—"

A blood-curdling scream echoes from outside the doors.

Britta's oldest daughter, Reid's friend, Avery, shoots up from her chair with a whimper while the other two, impossibly, keep dozing.

Liz quickly scans the room. Oh God, what? Or *who*? Who's missing?

Her eyes find Britta's.

"Padma," she and Britta say simultaneously.

Liz grabs her tote bag and flings the sitting-room doors open.

"Padma?" Britta's voice ricochets down the cellar.

"PADMA?" Liz's tone is louder and more frantic than she intended.

Padma finally answers in a small voice, "Back here, but— don't come closer!"

Britta and Liz both stop walking.

Britta cuts Liz a wary glance. "Darling, we just want to make sure you're not hurt!"

"I just need a minute alone!"

Mabel, too, has joined this potentially misguided search party. She sidles up beside Liz, her bob swishing. "I hate to say it," she whispers. "But Padma's been off all night. Something else is wrong; I can feel it. We really should be Good Samaritans. Check on her, offer help, despite what she says."

Good Samaritans.

Liz grits her teeth. Mabel may fool some feeble-minded women with her docile little patron saint act, but not her. Mabel Young is obviously *way* more calculating than she lets on. Case in point, Liz didn't lay a finger on her in the sitting room. That was some serious bullshit about the phones; why did Joel take her side? And Mabel's been poking at Padma all night about her "excessive drinking," sticking her nose where it doesn't belong.

That kind of *help* is why Liz breaks into hives before PTA meetings; always has a "deadline" when Tom pleads for some inane Delmonico's double-date with a "Club couple;" has culled her list of "Call-Back Worthies" to her mom, sister, and literary agent, Lila Strom. And The Falls is chock full of women like Mabel and Britta. Judgy little soul-suckers who just want to *help*.

Liz adds, "I promise, Padma, no judgment. We just want to talk."

Almost a full ten seconds later: "Whatever, fine, the South American section. I'm in the alcove near the front."

They find Padma sitting on the floor behind the tasting island, her feathered bolero strung across her lap like a carcass.

Padma peers up with watery eyes. "I . . . didn't pump before I left. I thought I was going to get home with plenty of time." She holds up an empty Ziploc bag like a white flag of surrender. "And now I don't know what to do."

Britta's eyes go wide.

Liz swallows. "Shit."

Mabel clip-clops around the bar in her increasingly impractical heels and kneels in front of Padma. "Did you try to hand express?"

"Yeah, of course." Padma rubs her eyes. "It's not working."

Mabel pastes on a smile as sickly sweet as bad medicine. "Well, maybe you're doing it wrong. It takes a lot of concentration. And patience."

Liz can't help but blurt, "Mabel, cut the shame stoning— it doesn't help."

Mabel presses her lips into a thin line. "I just meant that I know it's difficult." She glares up at Liz. "I've struggled with it too. I can help, though. Once I thought about becoming a midwife, if you can believe it. I took a lot of the classes. I'm almost certified."

Liz looks away to disguise an eye roll. Of course she can believe it.

"Well, I'm a lost cause," Padma says. "My body doesn't work the right way. It's taken an army of experts and like nuclear-powered pumps to even breastfeed, and now I'm here without my baby, without a pump, and I'm fucked . . ." Padma cradles her face in her hands. Her shoulders begin to tremble.

"No. You are *never* fucked until you give up trying, do you hear me?" Britta steps around Liz until she's directly in front of Padma, straight posture, a manic brightness to her eyes, like a chiffon-clad platoon leader. "What men don't understand is that we sweat and bleed for our children every day. We try, we fail, we reinvent ourselves because we have no choice." She squats down toward Padma. "That's what #Brittasays is all about: taking control of life's impossibilities and owning them, empowering ourselves, and saying, I can do this and *will* do this in style. I never thought I'd be nursing Marco until he was almost three, but the doctor urged for nutrition, and, given his allergies . . . I mean, it was hell on me exhaustion-wise, sex drive-wise, but I rose to th—"

"Wait, so you stopped nursing recently?" Liz says.

Britta blinks, visibly annoyed at having her back-door brag-fest interrupted. "That's what I said, yes."

"So then you still have your pump."

Padma lifts her head.

Britta straightens quickly. "Well, let me—ah. I guess I—"

"Padma could get some relief, you know," Liz says, "if we can get that pump for her."

Britta looks at Liz as if she's grown a third eye.

Mabel lets out an uneasy laugh.

But this could be Liz's big chance, the excuse that lets her and Tom escape upstairs, across the yard and to the Fords. "If you know where it is, Britta, Tom and I can search upstairs and bring it back to help Padma."

Padma studies Britta with wide, hopeful doe eyes.

Britta gives an awkward *tsk*. "Um . . . *Liz*. As much as I place the comfort and well-being of my guests above all else, you heard the news. We need to stay underground, in a safe, *sealed* environment. I mean, what if upstairs isn't even safe?"

She has a point.

Liz quickly runs through all she knows for sure about the glimmer, assessing the situation as rationally as she can. To choose logic instead of succumbing to fear. If the glimmer is some kind of purposefully designed aerial poison, the masks should still protect her and Tom. If it's "contamination" instead, the masks would safeguard them.

But if it's something else, something extraterrestrial that seeps through the skin, their pores, their minds, well, aren't they all doomed, anyway? If Spencer was right, if these glimmering clouds are alien, then hiding down here only delays the inevitable. Which makes Liz's next move, in any scenario, exactly the same.

Her heart thrashes around like a caught fish. "I'm willing to take the risk. Especially with these." She fumbles through her bag and dislodges the two gas masks. "I can wear one as protection. Tom can wear the other and come with me." *And get home together*, she amends mentally.

"Did you find those things here?" Britta's pale face is now blanched white. "In my house? Wait, where—"

"I forgot about them until just now. I needed a better angle to the . . . to outside, to see what was going on, so I—"

"But that room was locked," Britta says tightly.

Liz pauses, disoriented for a moment by why Britta would possibly care about "which room" she found the masks in. Liz mentally reconstructs the space where she found them. That shadowy mess of men's belongings. The tangle of workout equipment. Rumpled clothes, personal items . . .

Whoa. Wait. They were *Joel's* things, weren't they? Joel's things stashed in a locked bedroom.

Oh, this all makes sense now. Britta and Joel obviously took great care to hide that room. Can't have evidence on the "grand tour" that The Falls' golden couple isn't on sleeping terms. Liz tries to recall the couple's previous interactions tonight. There wasn't anything egregious . . . but they weren't ever really *together* either, were they? Are they just fighting, or officially separated?

Either way, Insta-Britta clearly doesn't want people to know, which might prove another opportune fact right now.

Liz recalibrates, "I don't think so. I swear I went into the kids' playroom for a better view. Then found the masks, strangely, in the closet across the hall."

Britta studies Liz carefully.

"You heard what Damon said about the National Guard," Liz presses onward. "If they're outside, on the streets, safe in gas masks, then maybe these things are enough to protect *us*, at least inside, upstairs. And given Padma's in such dire straits, I could be fast and grab your pump, Britta, assuming you know where it is. I've had trouble with nursing before, Padma, I get it."

Britta still doesn't say a word.

"Plus, if I'm successful, it might prove that upstairs is safe, that we can leave the cellar from time to time, use the rest of the house if needed. Maybe it even means the masks could save us outside—"

"I'll go with you," Mabel says.

What?

"Oh, Mabel, I'd feel more comfortable with Tom, you know, just in case anything happens."

Britta holds up her hands. "The jury is still far from decided on this and, besides, if *anyone* is rummaging through my house, it's me. We need to think long and hard about this."

"But, Britta, your kids are here," Liz presses. "You're really going to leave them when I'm willing to go?"

Britta's bottom lip quivers. She steals a look at Padma, who's still watching, sapped and defeated, from the floor.

"I'm not even sure where the pump's stored," Britta says. "It could be in the laundry room, my closet—"

Liz says, "So draw me a map of all the options."

"I should go," Padma croaks. "This is my fault, after all."

"This is no one's 'fault,'" Mabel says before Liz can. "Padma, you're dealing with enough right now. And I know Britta's house almost as well as my own."

Liz opens her mouth to protest again, but Mabel drowns her out. "Assuming Britta's on board with us going."

Us. Liz bites back a scream. How is Mabel turning this into some sort of collaborative PTA initiative? The best case: going with Tom. Next best: going alone, or hell, even with Padma. At least Liz could level with Padma, who's sensible. She'd understand that these are circumstances that call for drastic action. The two of them could take the masks and run for the Fords' together—Liz to her kids; Padma to her baby and Dev.

But Mabel? No way she'd dare do anything that one might construe as "selfish," that might compromise her soul's pristine docket. And even if she did, it sure as hell wouldn't be with Liz. Liz gets the distinct sense that Mabel can't stand her, that Liz doesn't meet Mabel's absurd qualifications for serving on the PTA. Whatever, isn't volunteering supposed to be voluntary? You do what you can, when you can? Liz can tell when she's being judged by other women, it happens a lot—the sidelong glances, the carefully worded slights—and Patron Saint, with her self-declared endorsement from God, is no different.

"Mabel, it's been a terrifying night, and I'd really like Tom by my side. No offense."

Britta nods. "You're right, we should round up with the husbands. This is strategy, the use of collective resources, and, really, who knows how long we're going to be down here. Best to make decisions like this together."

Oh shit, maybe Liz didn't fully think her last comment through—the more people involved, the more chance for disagreement. Spencer with his alien conspiracy theories, Romer with his subtext about climate change-driven ghosts . . . the men will debate this ad nauseam, maybe even stop them—and being saddled with Mabel is better than not going at all.

Liz steps forward, drops her voice. "Britta, I hate to say it, but look at Padma. She's fading. If we're going to do this, we need to go now."

"But the Harris-Che home is a pillar and exemplar of *democracy*—"

"That doesn't mean you can't make an executive decision." Then Liz pulls out the big guns. "As you always say, 'rise to the challenge.'"

Britta falters.

Padma, meanwhile, looks up again with weary fatigue. "I'm sorry to be such a pain in the ass."

Now Britta is the one visibly recalibrating. "Oh, I—no. Never a . . . pain, Padma, anything for you and Dev. Honestly, I can't imagine being apart from an infant. Of course, we must do what we can to help."

Britta turns to Liz with tempered resolve. "All right. Executive decision. Take the masks, get the pump," she says. "And perhaps . . . you could even do some recon while you're up there. You know, get a lay of the neighborhood, snap some pictures, so we better understand what we're dealing with."

Liz swallows a growl. Her phone is cracked, on 22 percent, and all her extra "recon" needs to be geared toward fleeing for the Fords'.

Then again, if ever there was a time for artistic license. "Good idea."

Before Britta can change her mind, Liz hands the Altitude Xtreme mask to Mabel—her hands won't stop shaking, will they?—and hangs onto the World War II–looking contraption.

Little Falls Road could be a wasteland, aerial bombs could be dropping from the sky, Sabina could be opening their front door, ushering her kids outside, into darkness, devastation, at any moment.

Stop, this is an excellent development.

A step in the right direction.

One step at a time to the Fords' and then all the way home.

"All right." Liz huffs as she untangles the mask's air tubes. "Where could this pump be?"

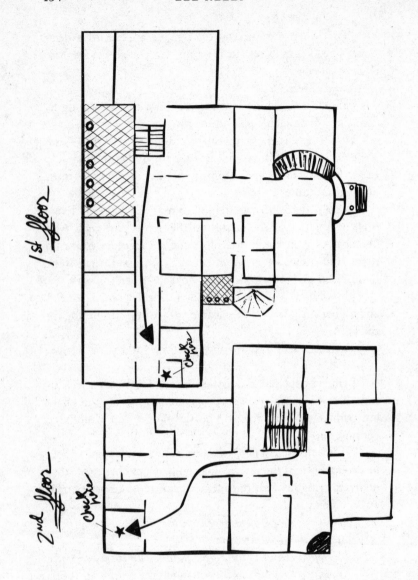

CHAPTER

13

Mabel

M ABEL WATCHES AS Liz yanks on her mask, a scary-
looking contrivance with tubes and a full canvas head
covering. The Altitude Xtreme mask in Mabel's hands looks
ridiculously wimpy in comparison, like she's getting ready
for an afternoon of breezy, oxygen-assisted skiing. What on
God's green earth does Joel have these for anyway? Suffocating
himself on an elliptical? Penance by fitness? Not that Mabel
believes she's ever really understood Joel—or herself, for that
matter.

Why, again, is she going *upstairs*?

Her chest throbs, as if her heart is knocking around for
an exit, threatening insurrection. Possibly threatening to quit
altogether.

Britta walks toward Mabel and adjusts her mask for her,
pulling the back strap tighter, then brushes Mabel's hair off her
shoulders. "There." Britta looks over her shoulder at Liz, who's
leaning against the front doors, studying Britta's house sketch
like a treasure map. She leans in conspiratorially. "There's no
need to be a hero right now, you know that, right, darling? Liz
said she and Tom could go upstairs instead. There's still time
to change your mind."

Mabel shakes her head, resisting the urge to shake her friend instead. *Britta, you need to wake up*, she longs to tell her. *Liz is more than just a train wreck.* Because she's positive now that Liz Brinkley is a bigger bully than her son is. Barking orders, bossing everyone around, stealing even, if it suits her. Honestly, Mabel's never seen Liz suggest or perform *one* truly altruistic action in the year and a half since she's met her; and really, who gets figurehead status on the PTA?

No, Liz doesn't just wear a questionably effective gas mask to locate a pump for another woman out of the goodness of her heart. She's up to something. And if Mabel's learning anything tonight, it's that she needs to put aside all pretenses about this being a "land of Good Samaritans," and bring on the wrath, go full "Old Testament." Just look how Liz pushed her out of the way for the telephone. Just look how Mabel had to all-out threaten Joel—*Joel*—with social ruin to force his hand into helping her.

Mabel ignores the pain rippling down her arm, her head swimmy with the promise of oncoming panic. Lord, how she wishes she'd told Spencer to shut it, that she'd parked at the pharmacy, ran in herself, and grabbed those pills. She attempts a breathing exercise instead. *How does adding poison to poison stop poison?* she'd asked the group earlier.

Well, she's going to have to find out. Father Patrick forgive her. If she ever wants to see Greg again, she may just have to step up and become lethal.

"Seriously, darling, you all right?" Britta says.

"Yes. Don't worry. This is the right move." Mabel pastes on a smile, then realizes it's for naught with the mask. So she gives a little Jackie-O wave, then nods to Padma, who's seated in the South American section. Mabel won't even risk a glance at the sitting room. Spencer would fight, tooth and nail, to prevent her from going upstairs. Not because he cares about her welfare, but because he's become obsessed with this alien theory of his; he's been the same way ever since she's known him, since college, his fixations masked as "assertiveness" and "tenacity."

If she's gleaned *any* takeaways from the nearly two decades of being forced to watch his dumb B-list movies, it's that aliens always find the group by torturing the lone specimen.

Spencer would never let anyone become a lone specimen.

"You ready?" Liz calls out, voice muffled. In her mask, she looks like a lazy teen on Halloween, hungry for candy, too "cool" for a costume.

"Be careful," Britta whispers. She grabs Mabel's hand and squeezes. "And don't forget the footage, yes? It can only help."

Mabel nods and joins Liz, who quickly opens one of the glass doors.

Then the two of them are floating outside the cellar, without an anchor, Liz leading the charge, Mabel trailing behind her.

Mabel can hear her own hot, ragged breath echoing through her mask as they head down the sconce-lit corridor. She remembers how Tom assured Liz that their kids were smart enough to hide in their basement safe room. Mabel has far less confidence in her in-laws. Would Tammy have the common sense to take Greg to their own basement? Would she move from the family room couch, shut off the TV?

As they pass the Harris-Ches' theater room, Liz says, "It's admirable that you came, but you didn't need to put yourself at risk."

Lie.

"Well, I wanted to help," Mabel says.

Another lie.

Liz nods. "If you know the house as well as you say, then you can take the top floor, search Britta's closet, her room. I'll search the laundry room."

Mabel balks, "Wait, why are we splitting up?"

"Too time-consuming to stay together. We need to be quick."

She remembers again those horrid scenes from Spencer's alien movies, the sole astronaut checking the rocket's thrust chamber. "Quick *and* safe," she says.

"Well, if we're going to go everywhere together, I may as well go alone."

Mabel bristles as she tries to keep pace. "You say that now, but you're going to want me when you're up there."

"I'm not scared. You should stay back if you are."

"Now we know who Reid takes after."

Liz stops. "Excuse me?"

Holy mother. Did Mabel just say that out loud? When she's about to enter an abandoned, potentially infected house? To possibly face the glimmer with this bona fide she-wolf?

"Nothing," she says, "clearing my throat. Fine. Splitting up is fine."

Liz lingers, as if ready to rumble in the middle of the hall, but Mabel stays moving, brushing past her, face burning as she heads toward the stairs. Horrendous idea to get into anything involving the kids right now. She lumbers up the steps and into the darkness of the Harris-Ches' kitchen.

She stops. One second. Two.

Liz emerges beside her and shuts the door.

They stare at each other. Waiting, Mabel guesses, for the other to erupt into lightning.

Mabel wraps her arms protectively around herself as she takes in Britta's shadowy kitchen. The space is so disorganized, so uncharacteristically Britta, that it's downright creepy—as if some hoarder alien or angry supernatural did decide to squat inside the abandoned mansion. Dirty plates piled on the marble counters. Leftovers splayed across the marble tub sink. The wide-mouthed orchids that, in the moonlight, transform the island into a grotesque, floating garden.

The odd noise they heard outside when they first saw the glimmer is just barely audible—perhaps a good sign. Still, the sound manages to creep under her skin, sing through her. The others thought it sounded like crickets and chimes. To Mabel, though, it sounds like a screaming chorus of all the lost souls in the world.

"Well. We're still standing." Liz huffs into her mask. "Let's clock that as a win. Come and get me in the laundry room if you find the pump first? If I do, I'll call up the stairs."

She turns and runs down the back hall, not waiting for any acknowledgment or confirmation.

Mabel thinks about following her.

Liz was right, though, loath as Mabel is to admit it. It's a waste of precious time to search together. Padma is a new mom without her infant and husband, a woman on the brink—at least that's how Dev made it sound. *Padma* is counting on Mabel. She'll search Britta's closet first and then loop back to figure out what Liz is really up to on this field trip.

The home's lights are all off on the second floor, save for the lamp in the upstairs hallway, which creeps like a shimmery specter across the top of the steps. Mabel hurries past the large mirror—she doesn't want to see herself again, meek, rumpled, terrified, peering out—and down the hall. Past the kids' rooms, toward the hallway closet where she found her husband suspiciously rooting through Britta's linens.

This night is unfolding like a strange, disjointed hymn, a dilated melody, entire lives held prisoner inside of verses. The ride across town, the stop at The Falls Pharmacy, feels like a lifetime ago. Someone could tell her that outside this mansion, real life carries on at a normal clip—that Greg has aged into a teenager as she's been trapped, pacing grooves in the Harris-Ches' slate floors—and she might believe it.

She pictures her gorgeous son now, in their home across town. Asleep, hopefully, in the little den in the basement. Mouth hanging open, floppy brown helmet of hair, the smattering of freckles across his nose. *"Painted with a flick of God's mighty paintbrush,"* as she always tells him. His face propels her down the hall.

She turns right at the closet and enters Britta and Joel's bedroom. Their marble fireplace, the drawn velvet indigo curtains, the mahogany floors. Her friend's life really looks so enviable from the outside. When she'd first seen these decadent quarters, Mabel told Britta that it felt cut from another world, another time. Quarters in Versailles or a movie about Marie Antoinette or Hearst Castle.

She closes her eyes, and Britta's hand-drawn map, still in Liz's pocket, appears: *CHECK HERE.*

Mabel hastens into her friend's massive walk-in closet and flicks on the lights. They're still working, thank God. She shudders, remembering the grotesque wave of animals racing across the road. Slamming into cars, homes, telephone poles. *How much of the town is dark?* she wonders. *How much of the town is* left?

She refocuses on Britta's colorful array of dresses and blouses. On the far closet wall are organized shelves of booties and heels in every shade of the rainbow—and toward the back, a matrix of storage containers.

Mabel hurries toward the containers and pulls down several trunks. She snaps the first open—older clothes, mainly spandex and stretchy fabric. Maybe they're pregnancy clothes? Then grabs another off the shelf full of sarongs, bikinis, bathing suits.

She heaves a third trunk onto the floor and snaps it open to reveal a collection of personalized burp cloths monogrammed *MARCO*, with a border of blue-and-green plaid. Baby stuff. Good sign. She fumbles through the clothes . . .

"Mother of God, yes."

Mabel scoops the pump to her chest—the octopus of an engine, tubes, suction cups—and hugs it like a long-lost friend. She sifts through the trunk a bit more. There are extra milk bottles, cleaning supplies, and wipes, a true bounty!

She stuffs everything back inside and snaps the trunk closed—she'll bring it all—and grabs the prize to go. As she does, she finally notices the empty carousel near the door.

Three empty carousels, to be exact.

Mabel looks around.

Wait. Where are *Joel's* clothes? The oxfords, ties, T-shirts, jeans, countless loafers?

She swallows, the closet shifting and swirling around her like a kaleidoscope. Her pulse mounts again, roaring now through her torso, rattling between her temples.

Did Britta kick Joel out of this room?

So does she know?

No, impossible, Mabel would have sensed it. *Wouldn't she?*

She doesn't have the time or mental capacity to worry about this now.

Mabel leaves the closet, the bedroom, and hurries into the hall. She passes the linen closet, the earlier image of Spencer lingering inside it like a ghost. That way he looked at her, the hatred, condemnation, bottled fury—

GO.

She dashes past the kids' rooms, the mirror, Britta's trunk thumping against her legs—*bu-rumm bu-rumm*—as the glimmer keeps playing its haunting song outside. Is it louder now? She swears it's louder. Closer. She nearly trips down the stairs. *Liz, find Liz.*

She flies into the foyer, toward the gallery. She can almost feel her secrets, her sins, taking corporeal form behind her. They're gaining on her. Breathing down her neck. Lurching, teeth bared, for her heels.

As she careens into the kitchen, something catches her eye outside in the Harris-Ches' expansive terrace. A flash of bright, unexpected color. Like a headlight or multicolored spotlight, or no—

Like a cascade of moving lightning.

Mabel stops. Transfixed, she inches toward the French doors leading outside.

"Oh God."

The lightning shape stops moving, as if it can feel Mabel's gaze. And then it turns. Like it *sees* her. Maybe it does, because it's not lightning at all, but an embodiment, a walking angel, glimmering, sparkling, moving now at full throttle toward the house, the doors, *her*—

Mabel stumbles back, trips, falls.

On the opposite side of the glass, the illuminated form opens its mouth.

Mabel, though, only hears her own screams.

14

Britta

#AnticipatetheUnexpected

Bʀɪᴛᴛᴀ ʀᴜʙs Pᴀᴅᴍᴀ's back (#Forcedintimacy or #Comforting? So hard to gauge) as they wait in the South American alcove.

"It's going to be all right. Mabel and Liz will find the pump, we'll get you relief, and you *will* get home to Dev and Isobel."

Padma offers a weak smile. "I feel really light-headed."

"Of course. It's been quite a night," Britta says. "But we're going to take care of you."

Padma shivers, then drapes her bolero around her shoulders. "Everyone's been trying to take care of me," she says. "Dev's the same way. But this is *my* job. I should be better at it."

"At *nursing*? Oh, darling, I wasn't aware it was like karate, with ranking belts and the like."

When Padma's face remains stony, Britta fakes a laugh. "Truly, Padma, I love her like a sister, but you can't listen to Mabel; she's a Madonna with baby care—"

"I mean all of it." Padma's eyes have a new shine to them.

Oh Christ. Britta wasn't expecting a "moment."

"I've been working with kids my entire life." Padma sniffs and adjusts her bolero. "You'd think it would've prepared me to have my own. I just thought it would feel how it looks, you know? From the outside. Like I'd give birth and everything would come to me, naturally, hard-wired, but it's so freaking hard. And then tonight, tonight . . ." Padma's voice breaks.

Britta doesn't know what to say. Of all things, her thoughts drift toward Joel. The first time they met, their hot, steamy weekend in Spain: Joel on one leg of his soul-searching world tour; Britta on a weekend holiday from her stint in Ogilvy's London office. Then her missed periods, her anxious debating over what to do, whether to tell him. The hastily planned wedding eight and a half years ago, courtesy of a huge, magnanimous check from Joel's parents. Young Britta rocking that Monique Lhuillier princess dress, her baby bump undetectable—even her eagle-eye grandmother told her she looked "*like a rail*." Joel, with his dazzling smile. The gorgeous crystal chandelier that cast the Waldorf's lobby entrance in a glittery, golden sheen, as if you were viewing the entire world from the bottom of a champagne glass. Britta had wanted to bottle that night, that palpable, delicious tonic of adventure, of invincibility, and save it for a rainy day. Hell, sip on it for the rest of her life.

It ran out so quickly, though. Nothing left for those blurry days of convincing the internet that she didn't forfeit her life, that she's still young, beautiful, and relevant. Nothing left for those nights when she lies awake, murder flowing through her veins, Joel who knows where, muted *Emily in Paris* episodes playing into the dull, blunt hours of the early morning.

"It never feels how it looks," she whispers.

Padma studies her curiously.

Britta sobers. This is Padma Khare. Not "new-mom" Padma. Not "ex-school secretary" Padma, but *Dev's wife*, de facto gatekeeper to Clementine.

"Rather, it never feels how it looks until you *claim* it," Britta adds brightly. "The first step is realizing that you are worthy of the new challenge, and then you must rise, Padma, embrace your new reality. It will all come together, it always does, but you must believe it will first."

Before losing her nerve, Britta gently cups Padma's shoulder, pinning her in place near the alcove's armoire. "Such a tragedy that Dev isn't here tonight. I mean, a blessing he's home with the baby. Still. It would have been so much easier for you. For all of us. I've long had this inkling that we'd work quite well together, and this horrific night would prove no exception."

Padma stares. Then she nods, a slow, singular nod that Britta clocks as a green light.

"We never had the chance to discuss my platform when you were working at the elementary school." Britta chirps a laugh. "All about the kids, right? But I've built up quite a following. These past few years, especially. Nearly macro status. A unique partnership opportunity for innovative, forward-thinking, lifestyle brands like Clementine."

"So I've seen." Padma's eyes slide away. She's tensed under Britta's grip, too. Okay, yes, this is clearly an ill-timed, awkward sales pitch, but when the hell else is Britta going to do this? And it's not as if she's bribing or blackmailing Padma. No, this is merely a *conversation* following an extension of goodwill. A conversation that must be had, one two months in the making. "I don't mean to put you on the spot, darling, but after tonight, it's quite clear that I have something to offer."

"Of course. And I'll put in a good word!" Padma laughs— one snap, hard and manic, like a clap of thunder—as she wipes her sweaty hair out of her eyes. "We should be so lucky to see a Clementine-Brittasays synergy. It means we survived, right?"

Britta sinks into her own laugh of relief.

"Okay. Well, great." Padma backs up against the alcove's built-in island.

Britta's entire body exhales. *Okay. Well, great.*

"Listen, Britta, would you mind giving me a minute?" Padma dabs her forehand with her bolero sleeve again. "I'm just feeling out of it."

"Right. Of course."

Britta straightens her spine as she walks down the cellar's hallway toward the sitting room. Why, exactly, doesn't this feel like an actual victory?

She smooths the ruffled mess of her chiffon hem. Perhaps she's just in shock. This is the culmination of months of strategizing, after all. As well as sabotage from her inner ranks. A night of unprecedented catastrophes, one after another. Maybe she just can't believe this devastating storm of a night can have an actual silver lining. Who can blame her?

She lifts her chin to a triumphant tilt—always helps to embrace the part—and turns her walk into a saunter. *A Clementine-Brittasays synergy.*

Britta tries her new status on like the first splurge purchase of the season. *Macro status.* It suits her. She just needs to settle into the victory, follow her own advice, and #ClaimIt.

Through the glass doors, she sees that no one's moved since the women left. Tom's on the sitting room couch; Joel's in an armchair; Spencer and Romer are both circling the bar. Avery must have finally relented to sleep and joined Jane and Marco, because all three kids are tangled together like an odd but adorable multilimbed monster in the corner.

The men all look up as Britta slips inside, the door shutting behind her.

"Where were you?" The sharpness of Joel's tone punctures her *macro-status* balloon.

Spencer looks around. "And where the hell's Mabel?"

"And Liz?" Tom adds.

"Yes, ah, right. Well, Padma was feeling . . ." Britta trails off. Because through the glass doors, she sees Padma approaching them now. Walking down the cellar's hall toward them with small, timid, cautious steps.

It strangely looks like she might fall over.

"What's her problem?" Spencer glares at Britta. "Is she sick?"

"No, goodness," Britta says. "At least not in the traditional sense. She's just separated from her baby and needs relief."

But Spencer swiftly steps in front of Britta, grabbing the double doors' handles and holding them closed before Padma can step inside and join them.

"Britta?" Joel says coolly. "Can you please freaking explain?"

Tom stands from the couch. Romer, too, rounds the bar. As if they're all advancing on her.

"All the women are fine, perfectly safe!" Britta holds up her hands. "They just went upstairs to help Padma."

Tom's voice cracks. "*What?*"

No one says anything else. The men are clearly waiting for her to elaborate, though for once, Britta doesn't want the floor. She locks eyes with Padma through the glass. Oh, can't these Neanderthals see her too, with her sad eyes, her clammy skin, that bedraggled bolero? Britta made a perfectly reasonable call! Her guest was in need, the women had protective masks and were willing to take the risk.

Britta delivers the facts without adornment, like rattling off the grocery list to her housekeeper Maria.

"They won't be long," she concludes. "Should be back any moment with the pump."

Joel stares at her, dumbfounded. "*Excuse me?*"

Britta stammers, "I-I-I said, I drew a map—"

"Let me get this straight," Joel says. "Liz and Mabel are upstairs right now?"

Britta swallows. "Yes, but they'll be all right!"

"Could I come in?" Padma knocks lightly on the glass door. "I'd love to lie down if that's okay . . ."

Spencer gives her a pedantic *one moment* finger.

"What if those masks don't work, Britta?" Tom says. "How do you know? How do you know the glimmer didn't get inside and infect upstairs?"

"I didn't think I had an option! A guest is suffering. Clearly I had to be a good host—"

"*A good host.*" Joel's laugh is hard and cold. "I warned you, I told you, these are people's lives you're playing with."

"I was doing the right thing!" Britta says, "Look at her: Padma was, *is*, in serious discomfort. And Liz and Mabel volunteered, it only made sense—"

Spencer: "It makes *no* sense. There's a deadly alien pathogen on the loose!"

Joel: "Really, Britta, how could you make this call without talking to me?"

"I understand, you are in a tough position, but you might have consulted us," Romer says, studying her. "As you said, aren't we all in this together?"

Britta withers under his wide-eyed, searing gaze. "Yes. I just, I needed to . . ."

But Romer's right, anything she says now sounds completely hypocritical. Obviously they aren't in this together, not entirely, not when Romer is still serving his seven courses in her cellar. Not when she prioritizes the wife of a strategic business partner over the safety of her other guests.

"What if they don't survive?" Tom says. "What if they don't come back?"

Spencer cuts in, "And how do you know she's even sick from her boobs!"

On the other side of the glass, Padma snaps out a sharp laugh. "Trust me, I know my body." She presses against the doors, but they don't budge, given that Spencer is still firmly gripping the handles.

"I'm telling you, Joel, I saw her," Spencer presses. "I told you I saw her—"

Joel raises his hand.

Spencer promptly cuts off.

Suddenly, Britta gets a horrible, sinking sensation. The feeling of missing something.

"Joel?" she says coolly. "Let Padma in."

Joel straightens. "Spencer's right," he says flatly. "They think the glimmer might actually be a pathogen. We've been talking to Damon Campbell."

"Yeah, well, Mr. Campbell's a maniac," Padma says.

"It's all over the news, too—the news we can get, anyway. Recent reports of how it may kill, how it might disseminate," Joel says. "Experts say the time between glimmer impact and death is so short it's impossible to know for sure, but—"

"One story's gone viral," Spencer huffs, grimly. "Someone in Florida ran into a homeless shelter. Must have carried it in. The glimmer killed over a hundred people inside."

"Another spread's happening inside the Javits Center," Joel says. "This thing's obviously airborne, but it's somehow being passed from person to person, or being transmitted through other means, they just don't know—"

"And I saw her." Spencer points through the glass at Padma, who stares at him, stunned, with her wide, glassy eyes. "Outside, when the accident happened. We all got out of the car to see what was going on, and *she's* the one who touched *Gwen*."

Padma shakes her head vehemently. "No." She looks to Britta for backup. "No, that's not true. I never touched her."

"She touched Gwen and probably got infected." Spencer's voice keeps rising. "And that's why she's sick!"

The room keeps spinning, rearranging, morphing on Britta, a shifting, sadistic set. She looks around for a modicum of rationality, for someone with sense to pipe up—and there's only one qualified candidate in this crew. "Romer, if Padma was infected, we'd know by now!"

Romer sadly shakes his head. "Are you sure?"

Britta swallows, cheeks burning under the oppressive lights. Joel and Spencer keep staring at her, seething, while Tom looks like he's stumbled upon a monster in a horror flick.

"No, please, *think*. We've been with her all night," Britta presses. "If Padma has it, *we'd* have it by now—"

"Says who?" Spencer demands. "How do you know?"

"Britta, I swear," Padma pleads. "All of you, I swear on my life. I just need some relief. I'm not sick . . . I just . . ."

But she chooses that precise moment to turn away from the doors and fall to the floor.

15

Liz

WHERE THE HELL is Mrs. Ford?

Liz has been running back and forth between Joel's new bedroom, the playroom, the mudroom, manically waving her hands, flicking the lights, even banging on the glass, but there's no sign of Sabina's mom in the house across the way. The Fords' dining room is empty, the side windows dark. Where's the Nissan? If Mrs. Ford left and went without her, Liz will never forgive her. Or herself.

Liz tears into the playroom again, begins fiendishly flicking the lights once more, off and on, off and on—

A shriek, ferocious and raw, booms from down the hall.

Mabel sobs, "LIZ!"

No, no, she's not ready for Mabel; she needs more time.

"Holy mother, Liz, come quick, come NOW!"

Liz sighs and hurries into the corridor.

She finds Mabel on the kitchen floor, frozen in place, pointing outside.

"Are you all right? Did you fall?" Liz rushes toward her. Before reaching Mabel, though, Liz spots what has overwhelmed the woman.

In the Harris-Ches' yard, a tall, lithe, luminous form careens toward them. Threaded, sizzling lines of multicolored light crawl over, across, and around the form, a raging current of tinsel, gold, green, pink, silver. It's a *woman . . .* or the remnants of a woman.

One who, Liz realizes with increasing horror, she recognizes.

Long blonde lob under the pulsing light. Fit form. Taupe jogging suit.

Holy hell. Holy fucking hell.

"Is it an angel?"

Liz grabs Mabel's forearm and yanks her to standing. "It's Mrs. Ford."

"*Who?* Wait, Britta's *neighbor?*"

Mabel's sudden movement from the floor must send Mrs. Ford into some kind of panicked advance, because the afflicted woman starts sprinting toward the house's French doors full throttle. Eyes shining and haunted, face contorted into an expression so pained, it's unhuman. Her luminous limbs are quaking from the rippling light, trembling with resistance.

Liz pales. How anyone could think the glimmer is "air contamination," she doesn't know. Whatever this thing is, it's under Mrs. Ford's *skin*, visibly worming inside her, fighting her, and Mrs. Ford is losing fast.

Mabel sobs. "This can't be happening."

Mrs. Ford smacks into the French doors with a hollow crunch.

"We need to move," Liz says. "Right now, come on!"

She drags Mabel away, yanking her to standing.

Mrs. Ford bangs, loudly, incessantly, on the glass.

"Holy mother!" Mabel shrieks. "Why is she here?! What's she doing?"

She's here for me, Liz thinks, the guilt a bitter tang on her tongue. Mrs. Ford really had waited for her. She was coming to help, to take Liz home to Reid and Callie. And what does she get as gratitude? An agonizing death alone in the Harris-Ches' yard.

"Wait," Mabel moans. "What's in her hand?"

Liz stops, angling for a better look. Mabel's right, there's a small object in her hand, almost like a . . .

"Crap, she has a key."

"Meaning like a neighborly key?!" Mabel says. "A key to *this house*?"

"Maybe? She could be in shock, still trying to get inside—"

"So what do we do?!"

Liz's thoughts are a torrent. "Make sure all the doors are deadbolted. Quick, move!"

Mabel runs for the mudroom as Liz lurches for the French doors. She snaps the extra lock on the top of the doorframe while Mrs. Ford stutter-steps outside, quaking still, covered head to toe in multicolored lightning.

Liz tries not to meet Mrs. Ford's gaze as Liz turns and sprints for the foyer. When she passes the entrance to the dining room, she notices, out of her peripheral vision, that Mrs. Ford is on the move, too, tracking Liz like a haunting ghoul, following her from window to window.

Liz puts her head down, not stopping until she's through the gallery, into the foyer and at the front door.

She checks it's locked, peers out the door's sidelight windows, and stops.

Mrs. Ford has parked her car in the Harris-Ches' drive.

Liz's ride home is *steps away*, right outside the front door.

"Wait, Mabel," Liz shouts. "Mabel, she brought her car, there's a car—!"

A startling crack, then a pounding booms from the dining room.

"She's still trying to get inside," Mabel screams from deeper within the house. "I've got the pump. We need to go!"

From somewhere outside, Mrs. Ford wails, "I can't . . . you can't . . ."

"Liz, please, she could break a window," Mabel says. "It's not safe up here!"

Liz studies the car again. There's a chance that Mrs. Ford left the car running, isn't there? A chance that the keys are in the car? Should she risk it? Run for the car, her life, her kids? Should Liz open this door as Mrs. Ford, writhing in pain from the glimmer, maddeningly encircles the house?

Fuck.

Fuck, fuck, fuck!

"Liz, I swear . . ."

Liz lets out a strangled sob of defeat and turns to find Mabel standing in the gallery. They take off, passing the dining room together, where its windows still display a luminous, contorted Mrs. Ford.

They burst through the door to the cellar. Liz slams it behind them as Mabel flails down the steps. She trips on the last stair and goes sprawling onto the floor. The "pump trunk" flies out of her hand and smacks into the glass wall of the movie theater.

Mabel, sprawled across the floor, drops her head in her hands. "I can't do this. I can't take the not knowing. What if Greg stepped outside? What if that happened to him? What if he's gone?"

"Don't do this to yourself, not now. Keep moving."

Liz heaves Mabel off the ground, grabs the trunk, and yanks her down the hall. The sconces flicker, swelling Liz's vision as she drags Mabel by the arm toward the wine cellar. Mabel's feral sobs are so loud that Liz can almost convince herself this is all a bad dream, a nightmare, and she just needs to wake up. If she tries, she can nearly imagine Reid and Callie crawling over her and Tom in their bed, a tangle of sheets, the kids giggling and asking for Lucky Charms for breakfast. Wake up.

WAKE UP.

As Liz reaches the wine cellar's entrance doors, she spots Padma sitting cross-legged in the storage corridor. Padma stands up suddenly and waves her hands—waving them off? Screaming at them? Liz can't hear her, but they'll find out soon enough. Her momentum propels them forward like a freight train. As she hurries Mabel inside, the doors seal behind them with a *whoosh*. Liz doesn't turn around. She's too terrified of seeing Mrs. Ford still on their heels, her radiant, shivering form following them into a different sort of hell.

Liz pushes up her mask on her forehead and takes a huge, centering breath.

Padma inches away. "Ladies, I—"

"The Harris-Ches' neighbor," Mabel blurts. "She was on the lawn, infected by the glimmer—she was coming for us!"

Wide-eyed, Padma looks back and forth between them. "That's . . . I . . . listen—"

But there's no time, they need to reconvene. "She's right, the glimmer's right outside; we saw it up close. We all need to talk—"

Padma blurts, "Liz, please stop, the three of us first . . ."

Liz angles straight for the doors to the sitting room, Britta's cumbersome trunk banging against her thigh. She's aching, thrumming, with the need to see Tom, regardless of any petty sparring tonight. For him to pull her in, console her, comfort her, in a way she hasn't needed, or admitted to have needed, in years. For him to swear to her, even if it's bullshit, that they *are* getting back to the kids.

When Liz tries to open the sitting room's doors, though, they don't budge.

She steps back, confused.

She notices that one of the sitting area's armchairs is now propped under the door handles.

Liz shakes her head, painfully disoriented. A fine-mesh strainer from the bar, too, has been fashioned into some type of lock, threaded around the handles in some ingenious way that bolts them closed.

She backs up again. Blinks.

Joel, Spencer, and Romer watch her warily from the bar. Britta sits in the far corner near her sleeping kids. Liz finally locates Tom. He's perched on the other leather chair, his hair standing on end, eyes wide and peering back at her through the glass. He looks like he's aged about a hundred years since she left.

Padma sidles beside her. "Liz, this is what I was trying to tell you."

"What the hell? Why are the doors locked?"

When no one moves, Liz shouts, "I said why'd you lock the doors?"

"It's not forever," Joel says hastily. "Just for a moment so we can *think*, regroup, as we find out more—"

"This is nuts." Tom steps forward. "We've *all* been with Padma, all night, and we just opened the doors for Britta."

"That was before we knew about Padma," Spencer snaps. "We need to mitigate risk going forward; we're dealing with life and death!"

"*Padma?*" Liz blurts, looking at the woman beside her. "What do they mean, what—"

"They think I'm sick," Padma says softly. "Listen, I'm so sorry, I never thought . . ."

Liz instinctively releases the handles.

Shit. Padma really does look ill. Tired. Washed out. She's sweating around her temples.

Padma carefully takes the trunk from Liz's hands. Liz resists the sudden urge to shrink away. "I think I'm hungover, or tired, or maybe it was the empanadas," Padma says quickly. "I wasn't infected with the glimmer. We know what that looks like, right? I'm fine."

Liz peers back through the glass, beyond mystified. "Tom?"

Her husband lets out a long, low breath, a train losing steam. "I want to go out there."

"Who cares what you want?" Spencer growls. "We're not opening the doors until we know they're not contagious!"

"How can we be contagious?" Liz shakes her head fitfully. "None of you are making sense. You were outside, you saw this thing, how it kills, it's not some new virus!"

"That is exactly what authorities are saying now," Chef Romer says softly.

Liz balks, momentarily silenced.

"The glimmer is far more complicated than anyone initially suspected," Romer adds. "A sophisticated threat that may be spreading in ways we've yet to fully understand."

"But those clouds, the lightning, that's imposs . . ." Liz trails off. What does she really know about this phenomenon? What do *any* of them know? Wasn't she thinking the same gory, terrifying possibility when she was upstairs, when Mrs. Ford lunged at them, writhing in agony? That if she managed to break inside, she'd somehow bring the glimmer with her?

"Liz is right, Joel, please." Mabel presses her hands against the glass doors. "It's obvious Padma's not lit up, flailing, stumbling around like Mrs. Ford—"

"Mrs. Ford?" Britta's hand flies to her mouth.

"She's got it? Where?" Spencer demands. "Upstairs? *In the house?*"

"Outside," Liz admits. "Sabina's mom, Tom."

"What was she doing outside *our* house?" Britta says.

Spencer scrubs his silver hair. "The cellar, the house, the yard, it's all been compromised! And you and my wife thought it was a good idea to waltz upstairs and gallivant around?"

Liz's thoughts whirl as she glares at the bolted doors. There's no way she's surviving down here, last Brinkley standing, separated from Tom. She whips off her mask, feeling cornered, claustrophobic.

"Wait a minute," Joel says, his face going slack as he studies her. "Is that . . . *mine*? Did you steal my workout equipment, Liz?"

She blinks, startling like a doe. "No, I-I found these earlier and thought they could be useful."

"No one's *stealing* anything; we're in this together!" Tom lets out a tight laugh. "Can't we all calm down and talk about this neighbor to neighbor?"

"Stakes are too high for that, Brinkley," Spencer says.

"So what's the alternative, locking us out, forgetting about us?" Mabel asks, incredulous. "Maybe it's not as easy for him as it is for you, Spencer."

"Oh, don't you dare," Spencer says. "You're as selfish as they fucking come, Mabes, so don't you pull your martyr routine on me!"

"What's going on?" Avery says from the room's corner. She sits up and rubs her eyes.

Avery. *Reid's* Avery.

"Avery, honey." Liz rushes closer to the glass, appealing to her. "You know me, right? Reid's mom? Reid's so scared without me there—"

"Stop it, Liz," Joel cuts her off. "That's not fair."

It's true: Avery's lips are quivering, as if she's going to burst into tears, but Liz has fallen so far, she's reached a new level of desperation. "Listen, sweetheart, now your parents are keeping me and Reid's dad apart—"

"Enough," Joel says. "Don't involve the kids!"

"But you promised, Joel," Mabel says, wiping her tears. "You promised me, and I meant what I said. I swear it, don't push me."

"Mabel, *please*." Joel steps closer, his words little clouds of mist against the glass. "I know you're smart. I *know* you can be rational. If you were me, would you open this door, given everything we know? Everything we don't?"

Mabel doesn't answer. Maybe because she doesn't need to. Maybe because Liz can't even argue with Joel's logic, his calm pragmatism.

"We need to keep as many people safe as we can," Joel adds. "Just give me time—"

"And speaking of, those masks you found are similar to the kind the Guard's using," Spencer says. "There are eight of us and three of you. Best to put them in the fridge in case we need them later."

Chef Romer shakes his head ruefully, his dark hair flopping across his forehead. "He is right, unfortunately. We can't risk you making another decision that affects everyone single-handedly."

Liz feels like she's free-falling.

"Those belong to the Ches," Spencer says. "Go on, do it."

Something inside her snaps in two. "No." Liz backs away, gripping her mask tightly. "This is the only thing I've got that resembles a shred of hope for getting back to them."

"Now," Spencer shouts.

"Open the door and take them yourself, or stand down, you stony-hearted motherfucker!"

Spencer storms over to the dual-access fridges, yanks a door open, and pulls out an object that Liz can't see.

He spins and trains a small gun right at Tom.

A scream rips from Liz's throat as Britta cries, "What are you doing?!"

Tom raises his hands like it's a stickup. "What the hell, Spence!" His entire body shrinks, a turtle into its shell.

"Tom," Liz croaks.

"Sorry," Spencer mutters. "Truly am." He finds Liz's eyes. "Do it. *Now.*"

"Easy, friend, this isn't wise." Romer edges away. "We should talk this out, put the gun down."

Britta's already grabbed Avery's hand and pulled her behind the sofa's side, hissing. "Spencer, how dare you bring that into my house."

"I didn't." Spencer cocks the pistol. "This is Joel's."

Britta's mouth falls open. "What the hell are you doing with a *gun?*"

Joel sputters, "I keep it in the linen closet just for protection, in case of intruders—"

"*Intruders?*"

"There's been carjackings near the mall!" he blurts. "And not the real issue here! What the hell? Is everyone ransacking our house, stealing our stuff?"

Britta lets out a little sob as she melts against the sofa.

She has no right to fall apart. Just look at her: *she's* the one with her daughter right beside her. The meddling psycho who forced Liz and Tom to leave their own with an eleven-year-old and locked them in her renovated cellar.

"This is *your* fault," Liz snaps before she can stop herself. "Your fault we're even here!"

"What?" Britta whips her head up. "Getting the pump, leaving, that was all your idea."

"I mean Sabina!"

Britta snaps a disbelieving little laugh.

"You didn't even want us here, admit it," Liz says, her fury, grief, utter and infuriating sense of helplessness now aimed toward one singular bull's-eye. "We were *third-tier invites*, as poor Gwen so graciously informed me. So, what, did you have a quota to fill the dining room? A roster? Because you just stole our lives."

"Climb down from your high horse. You want someone to blame? Blame him." Britta points at Tom, who still has his hands up, brow slick and pasty under the sitting room lights. "He knew who he was getting all along, so don't pin Sabina on my hosting pragmatism!"

Liz opens her mouth to holler, retort—but nothing comes out.

Britta's obviously lying. Tom couldn't possibly have known that Sabina was just a kid when he signed on, not when he knew Liz would be furious.

She blinks, her mind scrambling back to earlier that night, to her and Tom bickering in their basement, to her complaining about Britta.

Tom told Liz he'd thought Sabina was in college. Meaning they were in this together. Right? They were *both* duped.

Liz looks up and meets Tom's gaze.

His face right now. Those puppy dog eyes, that frile.

Oh God, Britta's right. He knew all along, didn't he? And boldface lied to her.

"Enough." Spencer presses the gun to Tom's temple. "I said put the masks in the fridges."

Tom winces. "Liz."

"I can't believe you," she whispers.

Tom raises his hands higher. "Liz, please, this all got so out of control. I'm sorry."

She stares at the mask in her hand. It's blurry, shifting like a mirage.

Joel steps between Spencer and Liz, placing one hand on Spencer's shoulder and his other against the glass.

"This *isn't* forever," he says carefully. "Just until we know more. Until we can be sure that Padma, that everyone, is okay." He huffs. "I know how incredibly fucked tonight has become, but Romer's right; we need to calm down, mitigate the risks. Pool our resources." Joel drops his hands and looks at Liz with pleading eyes. "Right now, unfortunately."

"Liz." Tom snaps out a flat, desperate squawk of a laugh as he raises his hands higher. "Come on. Please."

She wipes her eyes as she walks over to one of the empty fridges and opens its door.

She throws her mask inside. Mabel slides beside her. Without a word, without a glance, she tosses hers in as well.

Liz closes the fridge.

Spencer immediately lowers the gun. He backs away from Tom. "No hard feelings," he mumbles.

But Tom only has eyes for her. "Liz, please, I've been a mess too. I've been psychotically spamming Neighborhood Watch to see if we can find out more about the kids . . ."

She turns away.

"Maybe we can find another way to reach them?" he shouts after her. "Liz? Liz, come on, wait, talk to me!"

But she stumbles farther down the hall. Away from him. Away from everyone, until Tom's pleas fade to white noise behind her. Padma's already settled into a wine alcove across the way to pump. Possibly afflicted. Possibly contagious.

Liz edges away, desperate for a corner all her own. A quiet place. For the world to open its jaws and swallow her whole.

She ducks inside another empty alcove and slides to the floor.

She closes her eyes. Waking nightmares immediately accost her. Reid and Callie, Sabina. Alone. Terrified. Hungry. Hurt. Crying. Without her. Across town. How. No. These soul-sucking people. How could they? How could *she*?

Liz presses her face into her hands.

For a second, she swears she hears that tinny, haunting sound, all the way down here, in the full belly of this monstrous house. The hungry chirp of crickets, hollow wind, chimes ringing, ushering in a new dawn. A bleak, inevitable, merciless tomorrow.

But it's not the glimmer.

It's the taunting purr of Padma's pump.

↓ NeighborhoodWATCH
Old Falls District

Threads

Mentions & reactions

More : . .

↓ Channels

general

complaints

petition-ideas

stop-sign

mall-car-robbery

falls-elementary

+ Add channels

→ Direct Messages

(42 members)

MONDAY, APRIL 4TH

Tom Brinkley 1:17 AM
Good to know you're out there and safe.
We're at the Harris-Ches. Trying to figure out how to get home to our kids.

Sean Zhao 1:35 AM
Dude you're OUT?
Shit man. Condolences. Say hi to J.C. would ya?

Tom Brinkley 1:42 AM
Been trying to message neighbors through the system.
No one's answering.

Damon Campbell 2:02 AM
What's your home address again man?

Tom Brinkley 2:04 AM
We're at 15 Orchard
Are you in contact with the Derriers at 8 Orchard by chance? The Mongis at 20?

Damon Campbell 2:21 AM
Got a separate chain going with Blake D. Will check in w Barry to see if he can get through to Mongis.

Tom Brinkley 2:13 AM
Thank you so much Damon. Please keep me posted.

Tom Brinkley 3:03 AM
Just checking in, any word?

Tom Brinkley 3:23 AM
Damon, you there? Any word from neighbors?

Tom Brinkley 3:53 AM
Damon please, are you there?

Damon Campbell 4:05 AM
Here
Yeah sorry man, no answer. Think Blake's gone.
And Barry says he can see what's left of Gus Mongi's body out on his lawn.

CHAPTER

16

Britta

#TotalDisasterTerritory
#OutrightSpectacle

FORGET CLEMENTINE. BRITTA'S husband and friends just voted Padma off the sitting-room island, confining her to the cold floors of the wine storage area for who knows how long.

Liz and Mabel, too, after their heroic efforts to help, are now separated from their husbands and left to fend for themselves.

Is this really the right thing, impulsively dividing the group based on intermittent news stories? *For how long?*

Christ, does Britta loathe not knowing the next frame, the next move. *No one* could have predicted tonight's twists and turns, but she clearly underestimated the glimmer's holding power. Even more devastating, more unforgivable, is that Britta has completely lost control of this narrative.

How has everything spun so massively off-script?

She keeps pacing the far corner of the sitting area.

A gun.

Really, Britta thought she knew the full contours of Joel. She didn't like who she knew, and most definitively sometimes hated who she knew. But she thought she understood his parameters, his limits. Jacking off in a car minutes before their guests arrive? Yes, that was surprising, but not out of character. Joel is a master at performing self-care with almost perfunctory efficiency; she's seen him squeeze in a round of bicep reps while he waits on hold with a Verizon operator. His new but apparent abuse of stimulants? Nope, doesn't rise to the level of shocking, not when she considers his new angsty, vampirish persona. Even the gambling . . . Joel can be impetuous, as well as competitive.

But a weapon? What's Joel doing *with a gun*?

"How could you go through my things?" Joel hisses at Spencer. He grabs the pistol from Spencer and stuffs it into his pocket.

Spencer responds in his low, deadpan tone. "Because I don't trust these people, and if I hadn't—"

"You stole from me."

Spencer shrugs. "Desperate times call for desperate measures."

Joel leans in, so close it looks like he's going to head-butt Spencer. "Don't give me that crap. You know the pressure I'm under . . ."

Britta shivers and looks away, though her mind's wheels keep turning. *Pressure.* Meaning Joel keeps a gun because of his gambling debts? Are loan sharks after him? Is *Spencer* his loan shark?

It's gross, really, how Britta needs to piece together the truth from these whispers, just like some cheesy hard-boiled sleuth, some Instagram compendium of Daniel Craig in *Knives Out*. What she knows for sure: Joel and Spencer have a history of fighting about gambling. She'd confronted Joel about their fight a few weeks ago, right after Britta's friend Ainsley told her she'd caught the two of them all-out sparring in the school drop-off line. Joel had said it was about poker, specifically.

Or is "poker" just a code word for drugs?

Britta fitfully rubs her temples.

Maybe she should get some shut-eye. What is it, five AM? Marco and Jane, tucked into the room's far corner, have somehow slept through all the drama—not entirely surprising, Britta supposes, as they've slept through tripped alarms when Joel takes the trash out and forgets that their security system's on. Avery, though, has yet to turn back. She's curled into a little ball next to her sleeping siblings. Biting her nails, hugging her knees into her chest.

Poor kid. Avery has always been so much more sensitive, so much more attuned than the others. She's old enough to realize how much is wrong with tonight. That the world she's eventually, hopefully, going to see again has been altered fundamentally—and that there may be no going back to the world of before.

Britta should talk to her. She's been meaning to all night, but there's been one catastrophe after the next.

As Britta rounds the couch, she nearly trips over Tom on the floor, propped up against the couch's back.

"Sorry," Britta startles. "I didn't see you there."

Tom looks up at her with bloodshot eyes. "Why?"

"Because I was walking in heels with my gaze straight ahead—"

"Why did you tell Liz about Sabina?" Then he pauses, as if waiting for an actual answer, staring at her with this strange, flat expression that makes it look like he's just eaten bad Camembert.

Britta lets out a bitter laugh. Is he serious?

"Oh, Tom, my friend, grow up," she says evenly. "You wanted a solution, and I gave you one. The hell if it's my fault that Sabina didn't meet Liz's standards. I didn't make you use her, and I most certainly didn't hold you hostage to come." She winces at her regrettable turn of phrase, softening. "I really hope you're not too shaken up, by the way. That was despicable of Spencer."

Tom shakes his head. "You're right, though. We're only here because of me. Because I lied to Liz." Tom's bottom lip trembles. "This really . . . this really is all my fault."

He folds over his knees. For a second, Britta thinks he's spontaneously dozed off. But then his back begins to shake, almost as if he's . . .

Oh hell.

Now she's gone and made a grown man cry.

Knee-jerk, strategic, initial thought: this is priceless, pre-#Brittasays footage.

But no, Tom blubbering is just too raw. Raw and sad.

Second thought, strangely enough: taking her phone and crushing it with her Louboutin heel. How did she think her Instagram platform could rewrite this epic disaster into a comeback story? The gall. No, the *delusion*. She can't even land a big-time corporate sponsor like Clementine without resorting to undue influence. Did she really believe *#Brittasays* was an appropriate solution to a potential world apocalypse?

Britta blinks away her own tears, which have come on without permission. She moves to rub her eyes, then remembers her Shiseido mascara.

Stay on brand. Stay strong. Be the voice of reason.

She sinks down beside him. "Tom, darling, you need to look around. There's an unprecedented disaster raging on outside our doors. None of this is anyone's 'fault.' Dare I suggest that some sleep might help the cause?"

Tom sniffs. "You've got a point."

Maybe so. Maybe she still has something to offer. Something to say. She's still an influencer, after all. A pillar of wisdom for almost a hundred thousand followers. Which reminds her . . . her own daughter needs some wisdom right now. "Tom, if you'll excuse me . . ."

As she stands, though, she realizes that Romer's slid onto the nearby armchair, right behind her. How long has he been there? Was he watching her? Waiting for her?

She perches on the couch's arm beside him. "I'm sorry," she tells him straight away. "For Kat. And for you being stuck here. And my slip in judgment." She shakes her head. "You were right. I claimed my house was a democracy, and then I acted like a dictator, making unilateral calls as I saw fit."

Romer smirks. "'Dictator' is not a term to use lightly."

"No, of course." She blushes. "I just meant—anyway, for what it's worth, I agreed with Liz's plan to go upstairs because I was trying to help someone else." She pauses. "I just can't believe this. Splitting the crowd. Padma, possibly afflicted. Mrs. Ford . . . and Joel's gun? What is he *doing* with that?" She lets out a bitter laugh. "Because of carjackings at the mall. What a ridiculously overreactive purchase."

Romer studies the floor.

"Unless . . . unless I'm wrong about that."

He lets out a small, uncomfortable laugh. "I think Nico mentioned that Joel got mugged. One night he was heading home late to the train, a few months back." Romer rakes a hand through his thick, dark hair. "I guess he bought it as protection."

A sudden shiver crawls down her spine. Joel never said anything about a mugging.

"Don't worry. I took the bullets out of it," Romer whispers. "When Spencer first placed it on the bar. Seemed like the wisest move all around."

She nods. Thank God for this chef, truly.

She glances back at Joel and Spencer now. They're still locked in heated conversation. In their own combative world.

If there was ever a chance to find out more.

"You know, I've never actually heard the full story of how you and Nico met Joel," she says quietly. "I just spotted him on the restaurant's Instagram. It was Pilates, right, at a studio class in the city?"

"I don't do Pilates," Romer says huskily. As if "Pilates" is code for something more complicated, something possibly more sinister.

Romer can't be right. She remembers Joel met the lauded culinary duo Cash & Moreno through exercise circles; her husband had told her and confirmed the story countless times. He even gave her the name of the studio.

"Guess I just assumed," she tosses off, still deep in thought, "as you obviously have the body for it."

Heat immediately floods her face as Romer clears his throat, smothering a grin.

Really, Britta? That's *your stall tactic?*

She closes her eyes. "Sorry, so how do you know my husband? He told me—"

"He and Nico met at the studio, yes," Romer says, but he chooses his words carefully again, almost artfully. As if daring her to note that they're fragile, glossed over, and maybe even find the cracks. His earlier words come back to her now. *She has no idea, does she?*

"So then Nico is Joel's original friend."

"Indeed."

"And you met Joel through Nico . . . at the restaurant."

Romer nods.

"So then why are you here and not him?"

Romer squares his shoulders, facing her directly now, like a book cracking its spine and opening to reveal its secrets. Is he going to level with her? He leans forward. To confide in her . . . or maybe kiss her, he's that close. Not that she would want that. Or not that she would *assume* that. "Britta . . ."

Joel plops down on the opposite armchair, startling them both.

"Lord," Spencer says right on Joel's heels. He slides onto the couch, adding, "What a night."

Britta's still holding her breath, she realizes. She sits up straighter, inching away from Romer, trying to regroup. She studies her husband. Are he and Spencer *drinking* right now? Spencer holds a wine bottle by the neck, while Joel is nursing a full glass of red.

"Sorry, everyone, for the earlier drama," Spencer says. "Given the stakes, sometimes you need to pull out the big guns."

He takes a monstrous swig from the bottle. Out of habit, Britta reads the label, the old paper gleaming under the sitting room's ambient lights. A dated vintage of Penfolds Hermitage.

A pit blooms in the base of her belly.

Their fifteenth-anniversary bottle. Or at least, it was supposed to be. The bottle was part of her parents' wedding gift. "*White at five, red at fifteen, port at twenty-five!*" her mother had cooed as she kissed Britta's cheek at the Ches' lavish wedding after-party. Her mom had told her *entire* knitting club that Britta was marrying Singaporean royalty. Britta had priced her parents' bottles afterward: they were shockingly expensive, artfully picked, and her parents didn't know wine (they were self-declared "Malibu Bay Breeze people"). They'd been dying to impress the Ches with their fancy gifts, Mom's new dress, Dad's uncomfortable shoes, as their only daughter got her happily ever after. Britta's struck with a sudden ache for them now, her well-meaning, thoughtful parents. They're safe, aren't they? She hasn't had a moment to process, but they will—they *must*—survive this.

Oblivious, Joel wipes his lip on his form-fitted oxford. She has to stop herself from reaching out, grabbing his wine and throwing it into his smug face.

"How mature of you," she says, unable to help herself. "Getting hammered while we hold our guests hostage in the basement."

Joel downs half his glass. "I told you a thousand times I didn't want this party. Now people have died and we've got *blood* on our hands."

"Poor baby," she blurts. "Why stop at wine? Why not go do a line?"

Spencer stares at Joel.

Joel's neck flushes immediately. "Why not go take a selfie?"

She blinks. "I want you out of here."

"Well. That's not happening." Her rat of a husband finishes his glass and lets out a cartoonish, self-satisfied *ackhhhh*. "You want that separation you've been threatening? There's the door."

"That is enough," Romer says. "We just agreed that the doors stay sealed. No one comes in. No one leaves."

Joel shrugs and holds his glass out to Spencer for more.

"I mean it. This will not work for much longer if we cannot get along—"

"Perhaps you should confine your commentary to the empanadas, *Chef Romer*," Spencer mutters.

"Oh, get a fucking clue," Britta snaps, far more sharply than intended.

"*Me?*" Spencer smirks. "Sure, Britta. Will do."

Britta falters. Her head is now pounding so acutely that she sees shimmering spots. Maybe the glimmer's gotten her. Maybe this is how it starts, the feeling of liquid fury pulsing through her veins. Like her heart could shoot her to the moon. She hasn't realized it so precisely until right now, but she's been living someone else's life, hasn't she? Clueless to its full shape and story, and moreover, she's been *documenting* it all, all the carefully constructed lies and denials, advertising it actually, every day, even now, even as the world runs down.

Is there anything more pathetic?

"Do you know what bottle you're drinking, Joel?"

Her husband makes a big production of looking at his now-full glass. "Not a clue." He shrugs. "Though it's not very good."

She can't tell if he's putting on a show for her. But no. He really doesn't remember. As if their wedding has been willfully erased from his mind. Maybe that makes it easier to run away, by purging the memories of what you're leaving behind.

"That's our anniversary bottle."

For a moment, a flash of shock, regret, flashes across Joel's face. Quick, like summer lightning.

"Sorry," he whispers. Then he adds with a little shrug, "Guess I was just trying to be *a good host*."

"Why isn't Nico Cash here tonight?"

The self-satisfied grin slides off Joel's face. He glances at Spencer again. "I told you, he's busy. And that certainly isn't important now."

Spencer asks, "Who's Nico?"

"Is he your dealer, Joel?" Britta presses. "Your loan shark? Your pimp?"

Joel's eyes scan over her head, to their kids in the corner. "That's enough, Britta." He stands, but Britta follows him.

"I know you're keeping secrets," she says. "I know you're a filthy liar."

He spins around, hissing viciously. "Damn it, Avery's awake. Later, that's enough!"

She rounds the couch after him. "Don't use the kids as armor against me. Avery's a big girl. She can handle the truth, like I can. Tell me, who the hell is Nico Cash!?"

As soon as Britta's gaze falls on her daughter, though, she feels viscerally ill.

Avery is far from a big girl.

Avery is *eight*. Avery has been needing Britta all night, and now she's crying and consoling herself quietly in the corner.

"Oh, darling," Britta whispers. She swallows around the lump in her throat. "Darling, come here—"

"It's fine, I've got her," Joel says. "As always."

"Daddy," Avery pleads, arms extended.

Before Britta can protest, Joel scoops their daughter up. Their eight-year-old wraps her entire body around him, arms and legs, just like she did when she was just a toddler. *My little monkey*, Joel used to call her. *My wild monkey*. And Avery would hoot and scream and holler with delight.

As Joel carries Avery toward the bar, Britta catches another glimpse of her face. Splotchy. Contorted. Lost. Britta feels each one of her daughter's sobs, the slow twisting of a dozen knives.

"I don't understand why we can't leave," Avery mumbles into Joel's shoulder. "Please, Daddy, let us leave . . ."

"Shhhhh. It's okay," Joel coos. "I'm right here. You're safe. It's all going to be okay."

As he sits on the barstool, he finds Britta's eyes. "Nice," he mouths to her. "Well done."

Britta stumbles back so abruptly that she smacks into the coffee table. She has a sudden, desperate need to have someone hold *her*. How is cagey, lying, erratic Joel the "good parent" between the two of them? It's so unfair it's laughable. *She's* the one who's been holding everything up as he's all but disappeared—the family home, their well-being, their image and place in the community, all strapped to her back, her muscles quivering, her stress levels rocketing as she attempts to keep it all looking strong and as expected. For the past couple of years, she's been Luisa in fucking *Encanto*, for Christ's sake.

Britta leans against the couch back again, fuming and dazed. Romer and Spencer at least have the decency to scram for the bar and give her some space.

Though does roadkill need space on the side of the highway?

"It's the same for me," Tom whispers from the floor.

Britta looks down to find him staring at her with a look of strange recognition. She honestly forgot he was here, curled on the rug like a kicked dog.

Tom glances around the couch, to the storage area beyond. Trying to locate Liz, no doubt, who's likely hiding from him. Liz, Padma, and Mabel have all scattered. For a deranged second, Britta imagines they're playing a doomed game of hide-and-seek, folding themselves into the drawers of the wine armoires. Shutting them closed. Disappearing.

"It doesn't matter what they do, does it?" Tom adds. "If they're the favorite parent, you're always wrong."

Britta's mind is scrambling into response mode, trying to reframe the past few minutes, make them more palatable. Add that "high-impact sparkle." Of course her daughter doesn't prefer Britta's lying cad of a husband. Of course Britta is a good parent . . . she's just tired, all the time. So damn tired. She used to believe that everything could be recast with the right editing, lighting, caption, artfully shared introspection.

#Brittasays "fault" is the road to a more honest life!

#Brittasays compassion is the most stylish accessory!

#Brittasays admits that sometimes the camera needs to be turned around . . .

She studies Joel and Avery again, snuggling now on a barstool across the room. Speaking in soft, comforting tones to each other.

There's no repackaging, tagging, or revising this feeling.

No, for once, there's just nothing to say.

Township of THE FALLS

New Jersey

Emergency Alert → Glimmer News Hub

GLIMMER NEWS UPDATES

- BREAKING: Townships will initiate aerial release of combatants by drones in accordance with <u>Executive Order</u> at 12:00 PM Monday, April 4th, in cooperation with the federal government and National Guard. All residents are ordered to remain indoors and underground. More on glimmer safety measures <u>here</u>.
- Governor Murphy's emergency <u>press briefing.</u>
- See <u>Executive Order</u> from the federal government.

    . . .

17

Padma

Today 7:34 PM

DEV

ENJOY TONIGHT, K? YOU DESERVE IT.

<3

. . .

Tuesday, March 29 5:15 PM

DEV

TOOK THE EARLY TRAIN HOME.

DINNER FOR THREE, CHE DEV KHARE?

TACO TIME MAMA!

. . .

Monday, March 28 8:35 PM

DEV

SHE'S . . . ALLLLLLMOOOOOOST. . . . . ASLEEEEEEPPPPPPPPP. . . . .

ANNNNND. . . . SSSSSSSSSSSSOOOOOOO . . .

AMMMMMM. . , . . I. . . . .

. . .

Friday, March 25 6:15 PM

DEV

SURPRISE! FALLS CLUB IS COMING TO US—

MITCH BRINGING DINNER BY AT 6:30

WHO NEEDS A SITTER RIGHT ☺ POP A BOTTLE MAMA

YOU DESERVE THE WORLD. LOVE YA

. . .

P ADMA STOPS SCROLLING backward, wipes her eyes, and listens to the faint buzz of Britta's borrowed pump. Maybe
she should be saving her phone's juice in case she needs it later.
But reading these old texts feels imperative right now. Lifesav-
ing. Even if she can't hear Dev's voice, she still has his words.
If she tries hard enough, these texts may even convince her
she's not alone. That the two of them are huddled against
this armoire together. If she tries harder, she may transport
herself entirely. Maybe they're at some wine cellar restaurant
in Aspen. Or no, they've jet-setted to a renovated castle in
France. That's why she's pumping, because Isobel isn't with
them. They finally took the vacation that Padma's been dropping hints about since she left the hospital.

*Just the two of us. A long weekend away. Somewhere that
reminds us of who we are. We can't lose ourselves to the baby.*

Dev's face—she sees it so clearly now—after she gave that
little speech one too many times. His hurt. Or rather . . . his
disappointment. As if she was set to the wrong channel and
he'd been expecting a different show all along.

You are not made for this. You are not good at this.

From somewhere in the cellar, she hears Liz: ". . . now they
have all the supplies, the telephone, the tablet . . ."

"This isn't solitary confinement, Liz. They'll keep us
posted," Mabel says.

"Right. I'm sure it's their top priority." Liz pauses. "Do
you really think it's possible she has it?"

They're talking about her, of course. And they're trying
to whisper, Padma can tell, but between the women's panicky

escalation and the echoes off the floor tiles, she hears them both near perfectly.

Mabel: "Maybe. What do we really know about the glimmer? I mean, look at their neighbor."

Liz: "Terrifying."

Mabel: "It's possible she'd been infected hours before, right?"

Liz: "Anything's possible. Up close . . . it looked like lightning, rippling *inside* her skin. What kind of pathogen does that?"

Mabel: "We should keep our distance."

Liz: "But if Padma's afflicted, we would be too by now . . ."

The pump stops pulling at Padma, its engine dropping into a lower gear, then stopping altogether. She tries to tune out the women as she unhooks the suction cups, then takes the small plastic bottles halfway full of milk and dumps them both into a little numbered plastic bag.

Liquid gold, as she tells Dev. *Forget to put one of these babies in the fridge and there will be hell to pay.*

She holds the bag up to the light. Six ounces. Not her mode, to borrow from fifth grade math class, but definitely her mean. After particularly stressful days, she yields four or five ounces. On nights she's pumping during a show or rom-com, she can get almost seven. She's tried to build up her freezer stash—still pumping right before bed, even though Isobel no longer wakes up before midnight—and by her last calculation, she had forty ounces.

Padma closes her eyes and finally faces what she's been avoiding. The hard and cold facts.

Six Similac bottles of eight ounces each equals forty-eight ounces—assuming Isobel will even take formula—plus forty ounces of breast milk . . .

Is less than one hundred ounces total. Or about three days of food.

Three days.

Not to mention, Dev's probably torn through some of it already.

With shaking hands, Padma opens one of the alcove's storage fridges. She'll save tonight's milk. Hopefully the alcohol is out of her system. Hopefully she'll have the privilege of one day debating the milk's viability with Dev. She tucks the milk bag behind a bottle of wine called God's Hill. It will be impossible to forget that label. Tonight better not be the hill that God's chosen to die on.

As she shuts the door, she's hit by a wave of dizzying stars.

Damn it. Something's still wrong. The ache in her chest hasn't gone away, even after twenty minutes of being "milked." Plus, this strange nausea, light-headedness, and the headache . . .

Could she actually be sick-sick?

Sick like *afflicted*?

"Padma?" Mabel calls from somewhere beyond the alcove. "Everything okay?"

Padma presses her forehead against the cold glass of the fridge.

She's being paranoid, succumbing to worst case scenarios, mindless "spinning out." Worst case? She's still hungover because, despite what Spencer and Joel claimed they saw online, there's no way the same horrific force that struck Frank in the street and the young sommelier on the Harris-Ches' drive could somehow also be giving her flu symptoms. It defies science, common sense, reason. These people are typical Falls parent-neurotics. She can't let them get in her head.

"Padma, please, can you assure us you're all right?" Mabel says. "But stay where you are."

Her fellow inmates have turned on her, Padma can no longer deny it. Could she be double, no *triple*, quarantined? What would that even involve, being stuffed in a wine fridge?

Her head is searing now. She manages, "I'm still wrapping up—everything's fine!"

Fighting against her dizziness, Padma bends down and stuffs the pump parts back into Britta's trunk. She pictures Future Isobel sitting on the alcove island, hovering above her, dangling her little legs, smiling at Padma like she's the strongest, bravest woman in the world. Convincing her mother that she can keep doing this.

She has to keep doing this.

Sniffing, she closes the trunk and walks into the cellar's open corridor.

Down the hall, Liz stops pacing.

Mabel emerges from behind a wine rack and stands stiffly next to Liz. "Do you feel any better?"

Padma tries to remember what it feels like to smile. "I do."

Mabel and Liz exchange a long glance.

"Gotta say, you look awful," Liz says.

Padma forces a laugh. "You know, I worried that the bolero really didn't work for my skin tone."

Neither one of them cracks a smile.

Padma studies the floor. Option one: continue lying, show no weakness, pretend everything is fine and hope she doesn't faint again . . . although, with this option, she runs the risk of getting caught in a lie, and liars never fare well, at least in disaster movies.

Option two: come clean.

"Well. I guess I still feel off."

Liz tilts her head while Mabel takes another absolutely-not-discreet step backward.

"I had a bunch to drink earlier," Padma adds quickly. "It's probably just catching up with me."

Mabel says tightly, "Yes, that was hard to miss."

Liz shoots Mabel a reprimanding glare. "Describe your symptoms to us," she says. "I mean, how you're feeling. What's wrong."

"My head hurts." Padma swallows. "Throat and stomach are both kind of wonky. And I feel hot all around."

"Oh my Lord, it's starting," Mabel whispers.

Liz holds up her hand. "Easy, let's . . . get the emergency kit from the others. See what we're actually dealing with."

Padma moves to follow.

Both women take another abrupt step back.

"Given the risks," Liz says, "maybe it's best if you do keep some distance."

Padma nods, watching as the women head down the corridor for the doors to the sitting room. They tap on the glass, speaking to Britta in muffled voices, and then wait as Britta rummages around. Lingering, like inmates for their prison dinner, or those little addicts at pill time in *The Queen's Gambit* orphanage.

In moments, Liz and Mabel return with a small, red duffel bag.

They stop at an alcove about ten feet down the hall. Liz digs through the red CVS Emergency Kit, and dislodges a forehead thermometer. "We'll let you do the honors," she says. "There's some Advil in here too, which might help with the pain." Then the women float away and leave Padma to it.

Once she reaches the alcove, Padma grabs the thermometer and lifts her bangs off her forehead.

Beep-beep-beep.

Shit.

A fever isn't terribly surprising, she supposes. She's been practically hallucinating. But maybe she was wrong. Lightning makes you hot; is Mabel right? *Is this how the glimmer starts?*

"Padma?" Liz calls.

She admits, "One-oh-two."

Padma turns to find both women watching her from several paces away.

"Do us a favor," Liz says. "Can you take off your bolero?"

"What?"

"Just do it."

Padma doesn't have the strength or fortitude to protest. She slinks out of the garment, its soft feathers tickling her skin.

For a while, Liz and Mabel stare at her.

Mabel puts her hand across her mouth. "Of course. Why didn't I think of it?"

Padma forces out another laugh. "Why are you two eyeing me like a courtesan?"

Liz nods her chin toward her. "Because you've got a dark triangle above your left boob."

Padma looks down.

Random facts and tidbits swirl through her muddled mind. Nurse Mandi's vague warnings about "*improper technique.*" Those Prenatal to Cradle "Best Practices" pamphlets. The nurse at Overlook Hospital droning on about complications during those bizarre "group feeds," where the hospital's new moms would all graze together in the lounge and accelerate the process of feeling inadequate.

"No, but." Padma shakes her head. "Mastitis can't happen this fast—"

"Depends," Liz says. "I got a nasty case when I went out to a book signing one night and forgot to pump when I came home. Passed out. Woke up in chills. When's the last time you nursed or pumped, before now?"

"Right before I left the house."

But wait, that's not exactly true. Padma had wanted to pregame with Dev ("*just a glass, loosen me up for the PTA wolves*") before taking an Uber to Britta and Joel's. She'd nursed Isobel at four to give herself plenty of time . . . and the feeding had been a rush job. Isobel had been so fussy the whole time. Latching, then pulling off, wailing. Padma had only fed her on her right side. When had she last nursed on her left side?

"What time is it?"

"A bit past six AM," Mabel whispers.

Somehow, they've been captive in this house for eleven hours.

Padma's head spins like a carousel. Numbers fly through her head again. Eleven hours likely means three bottle feedings, which equates to twelve ounces of milk.

Meaning seventy-six ounces left.

"We should think of mastitis as a good thing," Liz breathes. "Considering the alternatives. Assuming we can get you antibiotics eventually."

"I'm sorry, though. I know mastitis can be painful." Mabel takes a hesitant step forward. "I've never had it myself, of course. Greg had such a consistent feeding schedule. Start taking Advil regularly and keep pumping to drain the breast."

Suddenly, Padma's head feels boiling hot. *The power of suggestion*, she used to tell the fifth grade girls at school, when, without fail, one or two from the class would come to her office claiming they "started having obsessive-compulsive disorder" after watching *Your Mind, Your Life* in Health. Everyone does it: you become what you hear. Did Padma feel exactly like this a minute ago, her head this warm, her body this frigid? Or is her subconscious wrapping itself around the word *mastitis*, filling in the gaps with aches and chills, with the sensation of the world sloughing off and sliding sideways?

". . . and hot compresses would help," Mabel's still talking to Liz. "I've heard cabbage, too."

"I doubt Romer's top-shelf menu features *cabbage*, so we're out of luck on both." Liz glares at the sitting room. "Though I'm sure there's means to hot water in the first-class accommodations."

Mabel purses her lips. "That's the type of thinking that got us into trouble."

"*That type of thinking?*" Liz says. "What the hell does that mean?"

Mabel shrugs. "I'm only reminding you that this isn't a war."

"Wasn't *your* husband the one who stole a gun and held my husband up to make a point?"

Mabel twists her necklace again. Padma's hallucinations must be reaching fever pitch, pun intended, because she's feeling bad for the piece of jewelry. She pictures all those tiny pearls crying out in simultaneous terror over Mabel's hovering hand. "Just remember that everyone's doing the best they can in this horrible situation," Mabel says. "It's less than ideal that the three of us are separated—"

"You mean banished," Liz interjects. "I notice *Britta* is inside."

"Only because they realized Padma was sick after Britta joined them—if the glimmer is contagious, it was the right call to make!"

Padma grabs her head, the pain between her temples searing now. She tries on the word again. *Mastitis.* Liz said she needs antibiotics? Can she get them?

"I can't believe you're defending them," Liz scoffs.

"I'm just saying the group was honest and transparent, and we could stand to act accordingly," Mabel says tightly.

"Cut the PC bullshit. Is that Catholic code for calling me a liar?"

Dev probably has something at home, some old prescription; he saves everything.

"I think you went upstairs under false pretenses, yes," Mabel says.

Liz snaps a disbelieving laugh. "I was trying to find the pump, same as you."

"Tell me there wasn't another reason."

"Excuse me?"

Mabel squares her shoulders. "I've 'worked with you' now on the PTA for over a year, and for such a prolific author, your contributions are nonexistent, not to mention your parenting style is clearly *dog-eats-dog*, so yes, I find it impossible to believe that you went upstairs solely for Padma's pump."

Padma glances around, suddenly more claustrophobic, if that's possible. She blinks. Are the wine towers *moving* right now? Inching in?

"All right, Detective Mabel, you really want to know?" Liz narrows her eyes. "Besides trying to stave off Padma's mastitis, *yes*, I went upstairs to contact Mrs. Ford—you know, the woman writhing and dying in Britta's yard?— because her daughter is watching my kids, and she's all of eleven years old and they're probably scared out of their minds right now!"

Their voices pound Padma's skull. "Ladies, please."

"Hell, maybe we shouldn't be trusting *you*, Mabel," Liz adds. "What did Spencer say? Oh right, that you're as *selfish as they fucking come*—'"

"That's enough," Mabel snaps.

"Big accusations from a man of God. Probably feels like a vacation for him, being in that sitting room without you—"

"I said that's enough!"

Padma resists the urge to place her hand across Mabel's mouth, shut her up, calm them down, lie down, have Dev tuck her in. *The baby*, he whispers to her now. *She's down. Asleep. Come here, Mama.*

Across the island, Mabel steps forward. She and Liz now stand face to face, like the start of some deranged mom brawl. "Don't talk about my family."

"Then don't pretend you're not playing just as scrappy down here, trying to get home, reach your kid any way you can. You literally hip-checked me getting to the telephone!"

Padma covers her ears. Her hands are scalding, too. "Please stop," she squeaks out.

"I *nudged* you out of the way because you're a tyrant," Mabel says to Liz. "You've been ordering me around all night, and I'm done with it, Liz, with you *and* your bully of a son, and if you think you're gaming this mess and leaving the rest of us rotting down here, you've got another thing coming—"

"You're such a hypocrite, pulling Reid into this! He's the furthest thing from a bully—"

"Then you're clueless too! If we ever get out of here, teach him how to treat mine like a human being; he's been picking on Greg all year! Like mother, like son—"

"Seriously, *just stop*!" Padma shouts. "If it's anyone's fault, it's mine for not bringing my pump, because I would have stayed out all damn night if I did! I'm sick and I'm tired and I left my baby with dwindling food, so both of you do me a favor and SHUT THE HELL UP!" She slinks to the floor, her back smacking against the island's side. Her arms have erupted in goose bumps, strange lace all up and down her skin. What she would give to be Dorothy in *The Wizard of Oz*. Click her heels. *No place like home.*

Imprisoned.

Mastitis.

So far away.

Mabel slides down on the floor beside her.

Padma huffs out a labored groan. There's no escaping even these two lunatics, is there?

There's. No. Escape.

"Apologies, Padma." Mabel bats her blue eyes. "The stress you must be under. You're going to get back to her, to Dev, you need to believe it." Mabel looks up at Liz, clearly pleading for a co-signatory. "We're all getting back to them."

"We must." Liz grudgingly sits down too.

Padma scrubs her face. "I swear, I just wanted *one night* alone. And what do I get for seeking reprieve? Punishment." She lets out a bitter laugh. "The worst thing is, I deserve it."

"Oh, Padma, none of us deserves this. Please." Mabel folds her legs underneath her peacock-patterned skirt. "I know the drinking's gotten bad, but you need to be kind to yourself."

"Why do you keep saying that?" Padma finally asks.

"What?"

"About the drinking."

Mabel fluffs her long lob—a futile gesture. Mrs. Young looks ten times more unkempt than Padma has ever seen her. Her auburn hair is now dull and disheveled. Her absurdly preppy dress is wrinkled, like she's just woken up from a nap. She's also got that old-lady lipstick thing going on, where only the edges of her lips carry the stain.

Still.

There's an uncanny resilience about Mabel Young. A brightness underneath the filth, like a storybook princess who's just gone on a Vegas weekend bender. Even in this moment, even as the world falls apart, as she's locked away from her husband, friends, as Liz tears her a new one, she's unflappable.

It's admirable, in a way.

Admirable and infuriating.

"Well. Your husband told me," Mabel says. "He's worried about you."

Padma sways as those words sink in. She looks up at Liz, demanding her reaction to this stinking, whopping lie.

Liz just shrugs. "I obviously wouldn't know."

Dev? *Dev* talked to busybody Mabel about *her*? When would they have even crossed paths, on a walk around the block with Isobel? In what world would Dev have flagged down this woman with a mild *"Finally some warm weather, right?"* and then launched into a monologue about Padma's drinking habits?

"Dev would never. What the hell? When would he have ever confided in *you*?"

"During one of Spencer's poker nights," Mabel says. "About a week ago."

Oh.

Shit, Dev had gone to a neighborhood card game a few nights back. Padma remembered she'd been begging him to attend since it was the same night that Padma's old sorority sisters had organized a "Friday Flip Cup Zoom," and she'd wanted no judgment. He'd walked out with a big smile and a *"Don't worry, I'll know when to fold 'em."*

Soon as the door was closed, she'd promptly nursed Isobel to sleep, then had taken the baby monitor out to their garage and drank and flipped three Solo cups' worth of IPA on their folding table.

"I guess Dev had lost a hand," Mabel continues. "He came out to the porch, saying he needed a break. Spencer had put some cigars out, and I was refilling the snacks. I kept waiting for someone else to join him. I was just trying to be a good host. Ask about the baby, work, you."

"How gracious of you."

If Mabel registers Padma's sarcasm, she doesn't let on. "He immediately started bragging about you, Padma. He lit up, really. You can tell he's very much in love with you." Mabel says the last line carefully, though, as if the words are extensions of herself, extra appendages, and she's pressing each one to the edge of a very sharp knife. "I'll admit, I've always been curious about you. In your position at the school, you always seemed so, I don't know . . . serene. In possession of yourself. I think of you as part of Greg's world, and that comforts me and, well, I suppose I was a little mad at you for leaving The Falls Elementary. Isn't that silly?" Mabel pulls on a strand of her lob. "So, yes, I was prying. Forgive me."

Padma doesn't say a word.

"He said you were happy you left your job, but . . . overwhelmed. I might have pressed. He might have said that you seemed happier before. That you'd been drinking more. Earlier in the day. That you seemed frazzled when he had texted to check in, and that's why he stepped outside. He asked if that was normal, to feel so frazzled with a baby. If I struggled my first few months."

The heat coursing through Padma has slowed and hardened. One sharp, burning little gem of hatred now, lodged right in the pit of her throat. *Don't shoot the messenger*, Shona, her vice principal, used to joke whenever she'd tell Padma and the staff that there was a scheduled teacher's conference on a vacation day. As if "messenger status" allows you to declaim all liability for suffering.

"I assured him it was normal—the anxiety, restlessness, difficulties—because it is, Padma. It's all normal."

Padma swallows around the gem. "So then, why have you been watching me like a hawk all night?"

"Because I felt responsible, I guess. I involved myself."

"You're incapable of minding your own business, aren't you?"

"No." Mabel's lip quivers. "I was raised to fix things, to take care of people. It's what I do best. It's really the only thing—"

Padma leans forward. "I'm not a car, Mabel. I don't need anyone to fix me!"

Mabel's head shakes, a confused little bird.

Padma shivers. Maybe it was better before when they thought she was contagious. "Can you two just leave me alone?"

Mabel doesn't move, only studies her with this doting, curious look. Liz, too, just freaking sits there.

Unbelievable. It's like Padma didn't even ask. Though is she really surprised? The women of this town are so enveloped in their own little lives and dramas that they can't see out of their silk thread count cocoons. Even now, apparently, stuck together in hell.

She scrambles to her feet. "No worries, I'll find another corner to cry in."

Mabel says, "Wait, Padma—"

But Padma's already stumbled out of the alcove.

She rushes down the corridor, resisting the urge to grab a bottle on the myriad wine towers bordering the storage hall, crack it open, start swigging. Or else smash it on the floor.

She really thought she was hiding her struggles better. She honestly thought Dev didn't realize. Never in a *million years* would she have imagined him—her darling, loving, open-book husband—confiding in some nosy, holier-than-thou, self-declared Mother of the Year like Mabel Young.

Padma ducks behind a row of wine shelves down the way, body shuddering, head aching, insides now cut open and exposed to the world. They know. Everyone knows.

She is not made for this.

She is not good at this.

She wraps her arms around herself, starts walking in tight circles around the granite-topped tasting island. A lab rat wearing grooves into her fancy cage.

The longer she paces, though, the more Padma swears she hears someone on her heels. Not Mabel or Liz. Someone quieter. Delicate, even. Not fully formed. A shadow, maybe, or a ghost. Future Isobel, perhaps, trying to catch up, assure Padma she's going to be okay. She can hear them whimpering, or whispering, or . . .

Ringing.

Padma spins around.

Yes.

Ringing.

18

Britta

B RITTA ALMOST DOESN'T hear it at first.

"Mac and cheese!" Marco, face flushed, PJs askew, belly exposed, is awake and howling in her ear. He has been for minutes. No interim setting, just Sleep and Insufferable. "I'm starving. I need to eat right now!"

Of course he won't listen to reason. *Sorry, darling, soiree cuisine doesn't feature "mac and cheese."* *Sweetie, it's six thirty in the morning. Wouldn't a granola bar be more appropriate?*

She's been eyeing Joel for help. If he gets billed as the "better parent," he should sure as hell pull his weight and earn the title—but he's still at the bar comforting Avery.

Marco's going to wake up Jane soon, with all this shrieking. Then Britta will be double-teamed. With no mac and cheese placations, no kids' iPads available as distractions, and no answers.

"Good God, can you shut him up?" Spencer mumbles, his words soft and slung together. Mabel's husband is all-out wasted; that much became clear when he took off his shoes and draped himself across the sitting room couch, his oxford unbuttoned, his gray hair mussed. Wasted off her and Joel's fifteenth-anniversary bottle no less, but never mind that, there are bigger mac and cheese bites to fry right now.

"Darling, please, for the last time . . ." Britta trails off as Romer, thankfully, bends down beside her and meets Marco eye to eye.

"I understand that I will never reach the heels of Kraft macaroni," Romer says. "But I may surprise you, if you give me a chance."

Marco whines, "All your food is gross."

"Because the adults *demanded* gross." Romer's eyes gleam with feigned (adorable) emphasis. "I can do better for a young discerning connoisseur." He reaches his hand out. "Come."

By some strange miracle, Marco takes the chef's hand. Britta tries to muster a thank you, or even a smile, when she hears a hollow, almost ostentatiously quaint *drrrrr-ing drrrrrrring* fill the blissful, momentary silence.

She freezes.

Looks around.

Everyone else has stopped talking. Stunned by the puncturing *d-d-d-dddddrrring* . . .

Joel slides Avery off his lap. "Am I dreaming?"

D-d-ddddrrrrrrring . . .

Marco: "Who is it, Mommy?"

Tom: "Oh my God."

Spencer sits up. "Just answer it, damn it!"

Joel's only steps away from the phone, but given that Avery's still clinging to him, Britta gets up to answer. She picks up the receiver, white-knuckled. "Hello?"

Silence.

"Hello?"

Nerves crawl up her arms, spine, neck like vines as she peers around. Padma, Liz, and Mabel clearly heard the ring from the cellar space too, because the trio of women now stands outside the glass, watching her.

"Hello?" she asks wildly. "Hell—"

The buzzing white noise of a prerecorded message kicks in:

"Hello . . . this is County Executive Ana Ruiz. Over the past twelve hours, a devastating phenomenon known as 'the glimmer' has spread across the globe. Scientists, experts, and government officials alike are working together—"

Spencer: "Who is it?"
Britta shushes him.

"—the means to keep our citizenry safe. As we continue to discover more about this phenomenon, we're understanding additional ways we may help keep you and your families protected—"

Spencer: "Put it on speaker!"
Joel: "It's a vintage collectible, there is no speaker."
Britta waves her hand again, quieting them.

"—transmission of this threat may be possible through surfaces, water sources, and potentially even power lines. Out of an abundance of caution, Somerson County will shut down all water, electricity, and sewage in the area starting this morning, Monday, April 4th, at eight AM to combat the rapid spread of the glimmer. Again, all water, electricity, and sewage systems in the county area will shut down at eight AM as an emergency measure and for the foreseeable future, until more information on this threat becomes available. Please keep safe and indoors during this time, and thank you for your cooperation."

* * *

That's it. The line goes dead. Still, Britta holds the receiver close to her ear, as if there's a chance that a real human being jumps on, starts laughing, confesses that this is all a very elaborate experiment designed to test her fortitude. Devised by Clementine scouts perhaps. Wacky Instagram followers. God.

She puts down the receiver.

"Who was it?" Joel asks.

"The town," she says evenly. "They're shutting off water, electricity, and sewage."

On cue, Marco promptly begins crying.

Romer steps forward. "Wait, why?"

She swallows, the magnitude of what she just heard settling in. This sitting room already feels insanely claustrophobic. What will it be like with no lights? No heat? No invisible arms of the ethernet reaching out to the wider world? "They think the glimmer clouds might be transmitted through surfaces, other means, other channels. Like you said, there's been cases of it spreading indoors. They don't know *how*, so they're shutting down everything."

Spencer sits up with a groan. "Who can even think in here with all this wailing?"

"When's this shutdown happening?" Romer says.

She pulls her smartphone from the pocket of her massacred dress. "In . . . about an hour."

Tom scrambles off the floor. "*An hour?*"

Joel, Romer, and Tom all simultaneously begin pacing. The strange, coordinated dance must signal the situation's severity to the kids, because Avery slides off the barstool and joins Jane and Marco, finally silent now, watching from the floor.

"I knew it. This thing was designed for invasion," Spencer slurs, looking to Joel. "Where are the candles, the flashlights? We need to prepare—"

"Britta." Liz bangs on the glass for her attention. "Why so soon? And what about calling home?!"

"Wait, we have a generator," Joel says. "It'll kick on when the power goes out."

"Indeed," Britta adds absently, mind still churning from all the recent developments. "It's always important to anticipate the unexpected." But her knee-jerk #Brittasays plug silences the room.

Tom looks around uneasily. "A generator is a *good* thing, right?"

Joel says, "Well, of course, yes . . ."

"But if they are shutting down power because it may transmit the glimmer," Romer says, "then a generator could be dangerous. Depending."

"Didn't the experts say they thought the glimmer was a pathogen?" Tom says. "A disease?"

Joel shakes his head. "I think it's quite clear that they have no clue what we're dealing with."

"Hell, I can believe the power lines are part of the problem," Spencer says thickly. "Remember Frank and that sommelier? Both looked like they stuck their fingers in a socket."

Chef Romer shoots him a glare, but Spencer's too drunk, or too oblivious, to register he's being tactless.

"We must think long and hard about this. A generator produces electric charges," Romer says. "Do they think the issue is the lines? Or electricity itself?"

Liz taps the glass again. "If they cut the power and we shut off the generator, that's it, we'll lose the landline."

"Our only way to reach our families," Mabel adds, "and the police."

"You saw, we can't reach them anyway." Spencer shrugs. "I think we need to shut it down, or risk exposure."

Britta squirms. Ordinarily, she'd be jockeying for control of this narrative, for a window to insert her own opinion on the matter. But right now, there aren't any solutions that can be tied up neatly with a catchphrase or a tag.

"So we either lose the internet, phones, lights," she summarizes slowly, "and the fridges, though things should stay cold for days . . . or we keep the generator on and take the risk that it transmits whatever 'glimmer' is out there . . . down here?"

Liz pipes up again, "The glimmer has been on your doorstep for a while. It struck Kat right outside."

"Mrs. Ford, too," Mabel adds.

Joel nods, processing. "And all the while we've been using the landline, the lights, the fridges. If power were a problem, wouldn't we have known it by now?"

"Perhaps a dangerous assumption," Romer says quietly. "Given the stakes."

"Well, if the Harris-Che residence is a democracy," Britta says, "we should put it to a vote."

"A *full* vote," Liz calls out. "And I think it's time to open these doors. Padma's not suffering from the glimmer. She has mastitis."

Spencer turns. "Mast what now?"

Britta can't help but roll her eyes. No wonder Mabel only had one child.

"It's not contagious," Padma assures them. "It's a sickness that comes on from inconsistent nursing—"

"But there's still the issue of Mabel and Liz," Spencer says evenly.

Liz spits out a laugh. "Oh, come on. This is ridiculous. We're not afflicted. We weren't even outside!"

"But you were upstairs, rooting around as their glimmer-infected neighbor was trying to get in," Spencer insists. "That's why we're quarantining the masks in the fridges. If it's transmissible through skin, clothes, surfaces—*you two* could be the problem."

"I think that's enough spinning out," Tom says. "The chances of that are so small, they're almost nonexistent."

"Says who? Who's your source on that? *Liz?*"

Tom and Spencer keep debating the prudence of letting their wives into the sitting room, while Joel and Romer step aside, discussing the risks of the generator in muted tones. Britta catches snippets, though: *Generator online . . . control it via the ethernet-connected tablet before power goes out . . . what does he think . . . vote could be political . . .* Outside the glass the ladies huddle up, huffing frustrations. It's a three-ring circus, prime #Brittasays footage, there's no denying that.

Her eyes slide again to the tablet. It's currently resting on the seat of an empty leather chair.

"Tom, we can't lose the telephone," Liz says.

Mabel adds, "And you need to stop punishing me, Spencer."

At that, Spencer stops conferring with Tom and abruptly turns toward the glass. "What did you just say?"

Britta slips away, past Romer and Joel, to grab the iPad on the chair. Any self-respecting influencer would nab this footage, capture this moment. She knows that. Still, it feels . . . wrong right now. Almost a chore. She tries to muster her rebooted vision from earlier—of a post-apocalyptic, cinematic, #Brittasays-branded success story—and clicks on the camera icon.

Behind her, Spencer's voice booms through the sitting room, loud, raw, and clearly inebriated. "And what about *you*? Are you done knitting that scarlet letter yet? Maybe I can wear it down here."

Mabel snaps back, "Grow up."

Britta hesitates before pressing **RECORD**. Instead, she flips through the quick clips she's already taken. The shots of Joel and Romer surveying their food spread. Christ, they're both so handsome, like a glossy ad for some private survival fitness gym. The videos of Liz and Mabel duking it out for the phone . . .

"Well, you've got the whole parish wrapped around your little finger." Spencer keeps up the insults. "Why should this sadistic soiree be any different?"

Britta bristles at *sadistic soiree*, but tunes him out again and flips to the next picture. Tom alone crying in the sitting room corner. Then the next few: a montage of selfies, Britta artfully arranging Romer's leftovers into tasteful "bunker cuisine," silhouettes of the kids huddling together in the corner.

Joel was right all along. This is nauseating. Ridiculous. Especially when she sees all the footage in rapid succession.

She should delete the photos, the videos. They were half-baked, ill-conceived. A rash, last-ditch effort to salvage something that was supposed to save her, something that would make her worth saving—

But Joel and Romer approach her before she gets the chance. She scrambles to close the photos, hide the screen.

"We're shutting the generator down," Joel tells her, "ASAP."

"Wait, what about the vote?" Britta says.

Behind them, Spencer shouts at Mabel, "You brought me here to destroy me. Admit it!"

"Spencer's wasted," Joel whispers. "He and Tom can't see clearly with their families at home. We need to be prudent, to trust the town's doing the right thing."

"What about what the women think?"

Behind her, Mabel squawks back, "Are you serious right now?"

"It's for everyone's safety," Joel hisses at Britta. "The decision is made."

Britta looks to Romer. "And you agree?"

"It's your house," the chef says tightly. "And, as I've been told by some before, perhaps best not to weigh in."

"By who?" Britta pops a laugh. "It's pretty obvious you're the only clear-eyed person here."

As if proving her point, Spencer shouts, "Dead-ah-fucking ah-serious!"

Joel pinches his eyes shut. "We're almost out of time." He yanks the tablet from her before she can formulate a challenge. "Grab some flashlights, candles. Get ready, we're talking less than an hour before lights out."

"Wait," Tom says.

She, Joel, and Romer spin around.

"Please, you can't shut anything down before Liz and I try our neighbors once more. I'm still trying to reach someone on our street through the Watch app."

"Always something." Joel huffs, collecting himself. He tosses Tom the tablet. "Fine. You've got one minute."

Romer waves Britta to follow him toward the buckets of supplies stacked behind the bar. They promptly begin sorting flashlights, lighters, matches, candles. Romer pushes one bucket aside.

Britta raises her eyebrows, questioning.

"For the women," he says.

"Ah. Thoughtful. *For the women*," she mumbles. "How very 'Puritan settlement' the soiree vibe has become."

Romer hands her the bucket with a smirk. She carries the supplies over to one of the dual-access fridges.

"I'm done, Spencer," Mabel's still shouting. "Let us in, or I have nothing left to lose. I'll tell everyone—"

"And maybe the truth shall set you free." Spencer throws his arms out dramatically. "Go on. I dare you. Go right ahead!"

"Unbelievable," Romer mutters. He steps around the bar, putting himself between Spencer and Mabel. "I would say that is *enough*!"

The room falls quiet.

"The power will be out before we know it," Romer continues. "Which means we need to focus. Prepare. Now end this pettiness and start acting, helping. All of you. Come on."

His admonition must have done the trick, because Mabel and Spencer finally stop bickering. Together with Liz, Mabel grabs the bucket that Britta left them, and they hurry away to prep the storage area with Padma.

Britta turns away. She doesn't want to watch them—her victims, the fallout of her "*sadistic soiree*"—any longer, because she's been *petty* too. Guilting her best friend, Mabel, into attending with Spencer when the two are obviously amid a marital spat of Britta-and-Joel proportions. Sabotaging Liz's vehement efforts to leave the party during the first course. And Padma . . . pumping her up with her ridiculous #Brittasays nonsense and Clementine synergy. Offering vague and completely spineless promises *to take care of her*.

It's becoming increasingly obvious that Britta can't take care of anyone.

Just look at her wailing son.

Her daughters.

Her failed marriage.

Herself.

No, perhaps this image of Britta "*holding everything up*" has all been a ridiculous self-delusion too.

That, when it really matters, #Brittasays just topples like a house of cards.

CHAPTER

19

Liz

Liz places Britta's charity package—the small bucket of candles, flashlights, a lighter, an extra water jug—on the nearby island counter. Her mind's still racing from the news. The town is shutting down modern life. *Electricity. Sewage. Water.* She pictures Reid and Callie huddled with Sabina in total darkness. Will Sabina have any clue what to do? How the hell have they handled going to the bathroom? Do they have enough to drink? To eat?

Liz may throw up from anxiety.

Beside her, Padma whispers again, "I'm sorry, so sorry about all of this."

Liz sighs. "It's not your fault." She's about to tell Padma to prep a washing station or a makeshift bathroom, to go be useful, but the words die in her throat. Party Principal Padma looks so defeated—her gorgeous brown skin pallid, the hair around her temples caked in sweat. Her thin frame's visibly shaking now too, every inch of her quivering with shivers.

The Advil's obviously not helping. Padma's going to need medicine. *Real* medicine.

As if she can hear Liz's thoughts, Padma adds, "I'm freezing."

"Britta?" Liz calls through the glass. "We need one of your dozens of blankets. There's a shivering woman out here." She pulls a small flashlight out of the bucket and hands it to Padma. "Hang in there. One step at a time, okay?"

Padma nods unconvincingly.

Liz forces herself to move on, to consider this moment a crucial turning point. Time's ticking. The choices they make in these next few moments, with the lights on, could determine the course of the next few days.

She flags down Mabel. "Take these candles." Liz thrusts the bucket at her. "Be strategic about placing them around the cellar, choose opportune spots. I'll handle setting up a bathroom and hand-washing station."

Mabel fishes out the candles and lighter without a word. She doesn't even meet Liz's eyes. Maybe she thinks Liz is being a bully again, ordering her around, taking control.

Whatever. There's too much else to worry about. The chef was right. Who has time for petty bullshit right now? Besides, Liz doesn't care what Mabel thinks, never has and never will. And honestly, what a hypocrite, calling Liz a selfish liar while Mabel's own husband tells the whole cellar she's as bad as they come.

Liz hurries down the hall, searching the alcoves until she finds one with a working sink. "Working sink" being an understatement. It's a full-on water basin. Huge, sleek, porcelain, complete with accessories and a floating cutting board.

She works fast, plugging the drain, filling the basin, and then a decanter with fresh water for rinsing. Still, she can't stop mulling over Mabel's accusations. As if Liz's subconscious is desperate for something else to chew on besides her family's fate.

Dog-eats-dog parenting.
A liar.
A bully.

This is ridiculous. Liz needs to focus. Who cares about being "liked" when you're fighting for your life?

Liz pours liquid soap into the sink, swirling it around, making a good lather.

Anyway, it's obvious Mabel's, like, insane. A *bully*. *Bully* implies social power and standing, and Liz has neither. She's the outsider at this psychotic dinner party, same as Reid when he started at The Falls Elementary. What a tight-knit, cliquey little school. Not a *single* kid had bothered to welcome him, so Liz told him he had to make space for himself. Her whole life, she's had to do the same thing, because Liz has always been the outsider. The girl who showed up in seventh grade homeroom to find all her friends had decided that summer that she no longer "fit the crew." The only roommate in her Manhattan apartment who'd come home to an empty pad every Friday— talk about Unhappy Hour. The "new kid" in the writing room who Showrunner Schreck made an "example of," who never got a credit, who was dismissed out of turn. The weird genre writer other moms whisper about, who doesn't wear the right clothes, doesn't belong to the right clubs, doesn't know the right people.

Tom's dig from a few nights ago floats back to her. *Isn't it exhausting? Liz Brinkley against the world?*

Tom doesn't see it, though. *She's* not the one waging the war.

Liz turns the water off and sets to placing the "potty bucket" and accompanying flashlight behind the island.

Whatever. At least Tom tried to fight for her tonight . . . in his own socially acceptable, nonconfrontational way. She knows, at least, that *he* wanted to open those doors. Spencer, the drunken oaf, was near crazed with excitement at the chance to keep Mabel locked out.

Satisfied with the makeshift bathroom, Liz heads down the corridor, bucking an inconvenient reflex to feel sorry for Mabel.

Abruptly, Liz stops in the middle of the hall.

Tom.

Tom, on the other side of the glass, is manically waving to get her attention. He's alone, leaning against the leather armchair blockading the doors. Everyone else in the sitting room is busy running around, prepping for the town's imminent shutdown.

Tom's shoulders square off, his body pressed tightly against the glass. In his hand are a few pieces of paper. He gives the pile a few fitful shakes, as if willing her to focus on them.

Liz blinks. The entire scene is so disconcerting that at first she doesn't realize that he's trying to signal to her, *Love Actually* style, through the glass.

She looks around to see if Padma and Mabel are watching him too, but no—Padma's curled up with a blanket near the wall of dual-access fridges, and Mabel's busy lighting candles in an alcove across the hall.

Realizing he's gotten her attention, he flips through the notes in rapid succession.

> *Harris-Che Wine Notes*
>
> ~
>
> *Wine Notes:*
>
> *I need to tell u some things.*
>
> *They can't hear this way.*

Liz inches closer.

> *Harris-Che Wine Notes*
>
> ~
>
> *Wine Notes:*
>
> *You and kids are most important things,*
>
> *Believe me PLEASE!*

> *Harris-Che Wine Notes*
>
> ~
>
> *Wine Notes:*
>
> I love you.

The third note takes her by surprise. A tightness pinches the back of her throat. Really, ever since they moved to the suburbs, it's felt like there's been a wall of glass between them. An invisible but undeniable divide.

She's about to tell him she loves him too, but his next note comes fast:

> *Harris-Che Wine Notes*
>
> ~
>
> *Wine Notes:*
>
> And you were right.
>
> We can't trust these people.

> *Harris-Che Wine Notes*
>
> ~
>
> *Wine Notes:*
>
> Spencer holding me hostage
>
> The Ches locking you out

Harris-Che Wine Notes

~

Wine Notes:

And Britta's been filming it all

I saw video clips of us on the iPad. Scaveng-
ing. Crying. Fighting.

We're nothing to them.

Liz stares at Tom's last note.

What the hell does he mean, *Britta's filming us*? She's been
recording videos and pictures, what, for evidence? To *post*?
That conniving little . . .

Liz will kill her.

In fact, they better not open that door, because right now,
Liz could absolutely murder Britta if this is true, squeeze the
fucking life out of her.

Harris-Che Wine Notes

~

Wine Notes:

Gloves are off.

Do whatever the hell you can to get us home.

20

Padma

I T'S LIKE A parasite, the chill, growing inside her. Bigger, stronger, hungrier every time Padma takes a breath. At first, the shaking was confined to just her hands. Then the shivers moved up her arms, her shoulders, her chest. Now her whole body's convulsing. As if she's been overtaken. Or possessed.

She grips the blanket tighter around her shoulders. It's only going to get worse when the lights and heat go off. How much time do they have left? The emergency kits have no antibiotics—Liz already checked—so how long can Padma manage without them?

How long can Isobel manage without her?

Padma closes her eyes, thinking of her baby and Dev across town. Maybe her husband is thinking of her right now too, like a strange mind-meld across time. Space and time have lost all meaning in this cellar. Padma's thoughts have been looping, helixing, folding in on themselves ever since the town called. A swirling constellation of worries and hallucinations, set to the soundtrack of her chattering teeth. It's so loud inside her skull that she can barely hear Mabel puttering about, staying busy, asking, from time to time, if she's "okay."

Padma is light-years from "okay."

As if on cue, a cool hand presses against her forehead now. Mabel, of course. Again.

"Apologies for startling you." Mabel sniffs. "Just monitoring that temperature."

Padma peers up at her. Mabel might look as awful as Padma feels. Her smeared makeup, the circles and splotches around her eyes. She's been crying; Padma can see it plainly on Mabel's face. Not surprising, Padma supposes, seeing as Spencer ripped Mabel a new one, and in front of everyone no less.

Padma leans back against the wall of fridges for fortitude. She pushes each word out, like a series of births. "That wa-wa-wasn't fair . . . of Spencer."

"Well." Mabel lets out a soft laugh. "I guess not every husband is a gem like yours."

Mabel bends down beside Padma. She looks as if she wants to say more. Instead, Mabel tucks a strand of Padma's long, dark, sweaty hair behind her ears.

"You feel the least bit cooler," she finally says. "Hopefully the Advil is helping?"

"Cooler as in f-f-frigid," Padma shivers. She tries for a smile. "By the way . . . y-you and Dev would be p-proud. When I took Britta's b-blanket out of the f-fridge, I left the c-c-cabernet."

Mabel frowns. "Lord, I really have been awful tonight, haven't I?"

"P-p-pretty sure you've been trying to help." Padma breathes under her blanket, letting the puffs of warm air give her momentary relief. "But now I'm not sure y-you're okay."

Mabel wipes her eyes. "Oh, goodness, yes, I've been called far worse." She pauses. "I just don't understand how Spencer can be so cut-and-dried, so pragmatic, in making such difficult decisions. He's always been this way. Ever since I've known him."

Padma would choose a different word than "pragmatic" to describe Mr. Young tonight. *Belligerent*, maybe. Or *asshole*. Or *three sheets to the wind.* But playing Taboo with Mabel probably isn't the best use of her dwindling energy.

"I just keep picturing Greg's face," Mabel whispers. "You know, you're really so lucky that . . ." Her voice cracks down the middle, like fine chinaware slipping and shattering. "I mean, none of us are *lucky.* It's fortunate, though, that Dev is with Isobel right now. How I wish one of us were home." Mabel's eyes go blurry with tears. "Greg's just so fragile. I have his inhaler refill in my purse, if you can believe it, like a fool. Though it's not just the asthma I'm worried about. He's sensitive, just so sensitive . . ." Mabel trails off.

"S-since misery loves company," Padma whispers, "Isobel's m-milk stash is probably going to run out in . . . I don't know, T-T-T minus three days?"

Mabel's face falls. "You're serious?"

"As the g-glimmer." Padma gives a hollow laugh. "And I know your s-son, Mabel. I s-s-saw him every day before I left for maternity leave. He is s-s-sensitive, s-shy, but . . ." Padma steals a breath. "A few months back, his classmate Sara W-Willis fell off the slide when s-some kids were horsing around. Greg brought her to my office and stayed with her. All of r-recess. Holding her hand. T-t-telling her she was brave."

Padma looks into Mabel's warm, welling eyes. "You r-raised him well. He's a wonderful l-l-little boy. Strong. Like his mother."

Mabel wipes away her tears. "He feels like all I have left anymore."

Padma's aching to press on that. In fact, she's been wondering for hours how someone as righteous and just altruistically omnipresent as PTA President Mabel Young could do anything that would prompt her partner to call her as *"selfish as they fucking come."* But it feels like kicking a good dog when it's down.

She changes tack. "H-h-harder than it looks—parenting."

"Isn't that the truth," Mabel says.

"T-told you, I thought I'd learn it through osmosis, b-b-being around kids all day. I have a m-master's in child education. But I don't have a clue. I'm horrible."

"That's absolutely untrue." Mabel sniffs. "And I promise, it gets easier. Or maybe not easier, per se, but more second nature."

"I'm not sure. S-sometimes I . . ." Padma burrows deeper into her blanket. "I've been picturing her here, you know. Isobel. Not my actual b-baby, though. My daughter when she's . . . older. This probably sounds insane, but I have to pretend she likes me. I'm not sure she will. I'm more . . ." She hesitates to say the word, but is too tired to fish for anything else. "More selfish, I guess, than I thought I would be. I w-want my time."

"Padma. That's natural."

Padma tucks her chin into the blanket again. For a moment, she closes her eyes, tries to imagine being transported into a scalding shower, hot water wrapping around her limbs, the steam so heavy it fogs the glass. "I g-get angry with the baby. When she needs things. I sleep through her cries. Dev tries the bottle with her before he rouses me from b-b-bear-worthy hibernation."

"But all of us have felt that way at one point or another," Mabel whispers. "I don't know why moms don't talk about it more. Shame? We go through it alone—the nursing, sleep deprivation, hormones, lack of self, of self-care . . . they shouldn't be dirty secrets or things to confess."

"One night, the b-baby was crying so much, I w-w-walked out the door. Thank goodness for Dev. Had to be three AM. I took a canister of tea and bundled up and walked. *Hours*, M-Mabel. Don't tell me you ever did that. I w-won't believe you. You're not the person who walks away."

Mabel's face grows unexpectedly hard at that.

"No," she says. "But"—she leans in with a bitter laugh—"sometimes walking away is the sanest thing to do."

Her steely, world-weary tone takes Padma by surprise. But before she can figure out how to respond, Liz reappears with a dangling bucket in hand.

"Hey," Liz says, breathless. "We need to talk."

"Well, Padma needs to rest," Mabel says.

"After. It's important, for both of you," Liz says. "For all of us, and we have little time. I'm not trying to be a boss, just . . . please."

Mabel finally relents. She stands and helps Padma up from the floor.

The two of them follow Liz into another alcove down the way. As soon as they're past the wine towers, hidden from the sitting room, Liz launches in. "Tom saw footage on the tablet. Of us, he said. Tonight."

Padma doesn't understand. "F-footage?"

"Britta that Insta-psychotic has been *filming* us down here, ever since the glimmer started. Like we're part of some gross reality show."

Mabel shoots Padma a strange look. "That's impossible. Britta would never."

Liz snaps a laugh. "Tom said there are clips of us flailing around, gathering supplies and food. Fighting amongst the ranks. Footage of us sobbing—"

"Well, there has to be some rational explanation," Mabel says.

"There is. Instagram." Liz shakes her head in disbelief. "I knew the woman was self-absorbed, but never, *never* in all my life would I believe she'd have the gall to use tonight to boost her platform."

"I w-would," Padma says. Damn it, these shivers really won't go away. "I think she'd do anything to prove her value to the world. She tried to p-parlay using her pump into a c-collaboration with my husband."

"That's disgusting," Liz says.

Mabel, though, stays silent.

"This is *all* disgusting," Liz adds. "The exploitation, the separation, the quarantining—"

"Everyone's just trying to do the best they can," Mabel whispers.

But Padma doesn't quite buy it anymore. Mabel's knee-jerk Pollyanna response now sounds hollow as a reed in the wind.

"Why do you keep taking their side?" Liz says. "We all heard Spencer, his shaming. He's literally locking you out. It feels personal, like he's punishing us, and your answer is to just sit and take it, to be a victim in Britta's maniacal production?"

"No, that's not—"

"Even Jesus would say that *turn the other cheek* doesn't apply tonight," Liz says. "We've got to stop sitting here, praying, and actually *do* something!"

"L-like what?" Padma says. "I mean, I'm p-pissed, furious, too, but what the hell can we do? W-we can't leave; we can't kn-knock down the door—"

"Maybe we can force them out."

Liz takes her bucket, filled with a few leftover candles and matches, and shoves it under the women's noses. "We can use these," she says, "and start a fire."

Mabel lets out a strangled laugh. "That's a morbid joke."

But Liz doesn't fold. "Just a small one. Strategically placed to set off an alarm."

Mabel's smile slides off her face.

"The power's going out, right? This could be our last chance to reach the authorities, an SOS to the police. The town called *us*, so someone at least is out there, and the window to reach them is closing!"

"You want us to attempt contact by starting a fire in a locked box?" Mabel says.

Padma suddenly feels sicker, if that's possible. "She's right, Liz, that's a t-t-terrible idea."

"Why?" Liz demands. "Because it's not a nice thing? Because it's not *fair*? Well, none of this is fair! Especially Britta, sitting in her warm, cozy sitting room with her kids and her gas masks, touting 'democracy' while she locks her guests out in the cold and the dark!"

Mabel's lips are quivering as badly as Padma's now. "No way. This is bananas. Far too dangerous. It could get out of control."

"Please, you really think the Harris-Ches are going to watch their wine empire burn to the ground?" Liz lets out a flat laugh. "No, they'll open the doors when they see the fire, and we put an end to this second-class bullshit."

"And w-what does that accomplish?"

"How about access to the telephone before power goes out?" Liz says. "Access to the rest of the supplies, the food, the masks, without begging for them? Access to our husbands, if we—"

"It's too risky," Mabel says.

"It's a *play*," Liz says, "a means to *try*, to take a step closer toward home, versus just sitting here, resigned!"

Padma says nothing. Because this is insane.

This is insane, right?

"We don't have much time," Liz says. "The town is shutting everything down at eight." She reaches into her jeans' back pocket and dislodges her phone.

The screen, set to airplane mode, reads 7:38 AM.

"You know Spencer would do this if the roles were reversed," Liz tells Mabel. "You don't owe him anything."

Mabel doesn't argue with that. Instead, she rakes her hands through her ratty bob. "Holy Mother, Liz. I just don't know . . ."

"And what about you?" Liz sets her fervent gaze on Padma. "You know you need proper medicine. If the police come, by some miracle, we could get you home. Or we could take the masks back, you know, and run home ourselves—"

"C-can you stop u-using me as your mutiny p-poster child?"

Liz heaves out a breath. "Listen. I *am* sorry. I know I've come on . . . a little intense tonight. I used you, Padma. Bossed Mabel around. Took things that weren't mine. But I'm scared, wrecked about the kids. And if I'm not fighting for them, I'm imagining the worst, the two of them alone or hurt or—" Liz's voice pinches. "I obviously didn't mean to be a *bully*."

Padma glances at Mabel. Because someone needs to remain the voice of reason, and it can't be Padma, not tonight, not now, not when she's half deranged with fever. They can't set fire to a friend's wine cellar, it's arson, and Mabel's right, what if it rages beyond control? Who'll save them then? *Who sets fire to their own sanctuary?*

And yet something's changed in Mabel's face. She's not really contemplating this, is she?

Padma opens her mouth to protest . . .

But nothing comes out.

Maybe Liz makes a case, after all. After everything they've been through tonight, perhaps she, Mabel, and Liz shouldn't be the ones bound up by decency.

Padma's been used *all night*. And not just by Liz. Ever since she arrived at the Harris-Ches' front door, Britta's made it clear that Padma's just a pawn in her social media game, and a second-choice pawn to Dev at that. Padma's been locked in Britta's basement, then thrown out again, all the while apparently being filmed like a tortured reality TV star, and for what, *sport*? Evidence that Britta's ridiculous #Brittasays platform applies to disaster scenarios? How about some evidence that Britta is a real human being, with some actual freaking compassion, or empathy?

"Time's ticking," Liz whispers.

"I'm-m in."

Liz lets out a slow, shaky exhale. "Mabel?"

Mabel's silent for a few moments. "I suppose what options do we have left?"

Liz beams. "All right." She glances at her phone once more before pocketing it. "We've got about twenty minutes now—"

"Though do me a favor and nix the *Skyfall*-like countdowns?" Mabel says. "My anxiety can't take it."

Liz nods, scrambling to her feet, and offers a hand to Mabel and Padma, her grip strong and warm as a compress. Padma resists the urge to press Liz's hand to her cheek.

"Padma, you sit guard," Liz says. "If the others ask where we are, just tell them we're prepping for the outage. Mabel and I will take care of the rest."

Padma lugs her blanket into the hall, and then finds a lookout spot in front of a centrally located wine tower. She watches as Mabel and Liz hurry back into the alcove, backs hunched, eyes darting around, like some bad *SNL* skit of suburban moms playing at *Mission Impossible*.

She closes her eyes.

It doesn't take long to imagine the flames. The familiar orange flickers of a campfire, its warmth, the flood of comfort it would flush into her cheeks and around her shoulders. She can't help but bask in the glow of her illusion.

But even in Padma's imagination, the fire grows. Flames transform into roaring, uncontainable beasts. Molten snakes that slither up the wine towers, race across the armoires, the islands. Transforming into walls, a cage, until all that's left is ash.

She blinks her eyes open.

Just a vivid waking dream. A hallucination from the fever. She's sick, of course, half delusional.

But then again, to do this, they must all be delusional.

Padma borrows a page from Mabel's book and, for the first time in her life, prays.

CHAPTER

21

Britta

Artful Adaptability

> [*Instagram post displays the Harris-Che children—Avery, Jane, and Marco—huddled together in a makeshift blanket fort.*]

Brittasays   ✔ Follow

New Jersey

Surviving.
Barely.
But we are still here.
#Brittasays #risetothechallenge #empowerment #survival #NJ
#glimmer #HanginThere

SHE WASN'T SURE about the post. She still isn't, but too late now. This could be #Brittasays' ultimate word for quite a while, she knew that, and yet wasn't sure what her final manifesto could or should say. There was no time for careful rearranging of flashlights and candles, no point to a shoppable post. She lost the stomach for baseless bravado hours ago.

No, in the end, Britta finally settled on the truth.

The posting process itself was dicey, given that it had to be clandestine, the whole thing shot, arranged, and posted via the ethernet in the two minutes between the time that Tom finally relinquished his quest to reach his neighbors and Joel's demand for the tablet.

Joel has the iPad in hand now, his brow furrowed as he and Spencer huddle around it, figuring out how to shut down the generator from Joel's online account. Ordinarily, Britta basks in the afterglow of a post for minutes, sometimes hours, depending on the extent and excitement of her followers' reactions. But not tonight. No, tonight she's just sending a message in a virtual bottle, a shout into the void. Without any angled branding or coherent message, her little post feels . . . a bit directionless. Lost.

Romer steps into her line of sight.

She sobers, blinking away tears she hadn't felt come on.

He perches on the armrest of the sofa, beside her. "Are you all right?"

From their shared vantage point, they can both see through the glass doors, into the corridor of the storage area, where Padma sits, shivering and wrapped in one of the kids' nubby blankets.

"Given what everyone else is going through, I probably have nothing to complain about."

"I don't know." Romer shrugs. "I'd say you are in a tough position, being host at a time like this. It is difficult, with so many people, so much fear, with everyone believing and wanting something different."

She nods, studying the bodies clustered on this side of the glass. Joel and Spencer, together with the iPad, nearer to the bar. Tom, giving her a strange, evil stink-eye from the corner. Her kids, huddled in the opposite nook, their blankets still piled like a sad, makeshift fortress. The three of them are watching Joel with such absent stares that Britta finds her eyes watering once more. Christ, even *Marco* has fallen silent.

It's not good.

"I understand, in a way," Romer adds, carefully. "How hard it is to keep up the appearance of control when everything is secretly falling apart." He swallows. "It's why I've been intrigued by you from the start."

Britta blushes, oddly uncomfortable from that loaded compliment. It almost sounds as if Romer's referring to myriad secret catastrophes that extend far beyond tonight. She stalls, debating whether she should try and press him again, tease out some real information about Joel—but finds herself too exhausted for strategery now.

"You asked me what I wanted," she whispers. "At the beginning of this cursed soiree. Do you remember?"

"Of course."

"I think . . . I just wanted to show that I was okay," she says. "Even to myself. Especially to myself. That I must be happy, that life must be perfect if it *looked* so perfect and beautiful." She looks at Romer. "You must think I'm so ridiculous."

She notices he's closer than he was a moment ago, hovering over her with his cut-glass jaw, and those big, brown eyes.

"Far from ridiculous, Britta," he says. "In fact, I empathize."

The sound of her name on his lips sends a tingling, unexpected cascade across her shoulders. Almost as if he'd reached out and touched her (#Pathetic #Lonelymuch?).

She sniffs, looking back at her kids. "Well, *I* think I'm a fool. And I certainly have no business pretending I can tell people '*what they want*.' Maybe I never did, but my antics tonight?" She shivers. "I've gone beyond arrogance. It's despicable."

"Maybe you've only been trying to tell a better story," Romer says. "I lived that way for a long time." A small laugh escapes him. "Not so publicly, though. But being the glue—it can be a lot of pressure."

The glue. So pedestrian. So simple. She's never thought of herself like that, though she kind of likes it.

Romer pauses, as if debating over whether, and how much, to share. "You know, when I was younger, my father left," he says finally. "My family still needed to eat, so my mother took on two jobs. A day shift, a night shift. As the oldest son, I quickly became the man of the house."

She blushes, surprised by his honesty. A swift wave of shame washes over her again. Here she is complaining about her loveless marriage to her rags-to-Michelin star chef in her world-class wine cellar.

"I-I'm so sorry, Romer."

"Nothing to say sorry for," he says. "But I was my sisters' babysitter. The homework helper. The family cook. I worried, all the time, about my mother, my sisters, the future. Nothing I ever did felt right. Nothing ever felt like it was going to work out. I was very careful, though, to show the world who I wanted them to see. A tough guy, confident, in control. Someone you wouldn't mess with. Someone you'd never dare call *pelabola*." He looks at her. "If I showed them, I thought maybe I'd believe the lie, too."

Britta studies him. His perfect, olive complexion, his rose and peacock feather tattoos rippling across his forearms. This close, she'd bet that he's younger than her by at least five years, if not ten. And yet it sounds like he's already lived a few lifetimes.

"That must have been so hard." She swallows. "So much pressure."

Romer shrugs. "It helped that my mother told me every day how proud she was. That I was her lifeline. That I was enough," he says. "Sometimes it is the simplest things, easily given, that keep us all afloat."

"I never feel like I'm enough," Britta laughs. But the flippant admission dredges up something deep—insecurities she thought she murdered, buried, long ago. She's mortified when her throat goes tight again.

Romer places a firm hand on her shoulder. "I think it is easy to forget these days," he whispers, "but we are all enough, Britta."

Christ, it's been such a long time since anyone comforted her. She almost melts under his touch. She nearly reaches for his hand to squeeze it.

But then he's letting go—reluctantly?—and standing up with a sigh. "I should probably see if Joel needs anything."

Then he's gone.

Britta turns around, her gaze falling on the kids again, who are all wide awake but still quiet, almost chillingly so, as if Avery's mute, glum detachment turned contagious.

We are all enough. Romer's words suddenly feel imperative to share. Not that Avery, Jane, and Marco have ever wanted for anything. On paper at least, their childhoods are worlds away from Romer's, from her own for that matter, growing up with her parents, both practical, hardworking teachers in central Jersey. Her kids have an overstuffed toy room, massive bedrooms, and premier Jersey schools. They have their dozens of after-school activities and near-acre-sized yard. And though Joel withdrew from Britta years ago, he is a phenomenal father and treats their trio like gold. No one can deny that; she certainly wouldn't.

She watches Avery, who's now staring dully at the glass doors as if pondering escape, absently twisting the ends of her hair. Britta's cheeks turn hot again. She honestly can't remember the last time she told her daughter that she was proud of her. The last time she's mentally regarded her children as anything other than a prop . . . or a nuisance . . . or an item on a to-do list. Even tonight. Especially tonight.

Do they know they're enough for her? That everything she's doing has been, in some messed-up, misguided way, to prove that she's worthy? That she's enough for them?

The kids all glance up as Britta approaches, Jane staring warily with her wide brown eyes. Marco, with his little chin resting on his knees. He never really ate, did he? He simply gave up wailing for mac and cheese.

Avery, though, won't look at Britta.

"Mommy?" Jane whispers. "When are the lights going out?"

"In a few minutes," Britta says, as brightly as she can muster. "Which still leaves time for a picnic."

She takes a blanket that's been shoved into a ball near their feet, and briskly shakes it out, laying it flat across the floor.

"I don't want the yucky food," Marco whimpers.

"So defeatist, darling. Give Mommy *un momento*."

She sidesteps the kids on her way to the bar, pointedly ignoring Avery's suspicious glare, trying not to let the men's preparations, the drama, pull Britta into their orbit.

She analyzes the remnants of Romer's appetizers and second course scattered across the bar top, then gathers three plates and a knife. Britta works briskly, gutting three mole empanadas, until all that's left is the fried dough. She swipes some of the raspberry jam from the leftover brie appetizers and plugs it inside each pocket. Finally, the box of Peanut Butter Cap'n Crunch Joel brought down from the pantry.

"*Voilà.*" Britta plunks the three plates down. "Close your eyes and take a bite. It's crunchy PB&J, and I guarantee you'll want another."

Marco sucks his thumb. Avery keeps staring at her. Jane, though, her most fearless child, does as she's told and takes a huge bite.

Her eyes go wide. "This is awesome."

Marco lunges for his like a ravenous raccoon and sinks in deep. "Oh, Mommy," he says with a full mouth. "Mommy-mommy-mommy—"

Finally Avery dives in, too, swiping a chunk of jam from the corner of her lip. She says around mouthfuls, "So what do you need us to do?"

Britta falters. "What do you mean?"

"I mean, why are you giving us this?"

"Oh." Britta swallows. "This isn't a bribe. I . . . just wanted to make sure you ate . . . with the lights on."

Marco takes another bite. "I'm afraid of the dark."

Jane shudders. "Me too."

"I understand. But there are good things about the dark, too."

Avery rolls her eyes. "Nothing about tonight is good."

"I beg your pardon," Britta says, with mock offense. "That sandwich gets a *ten*, for creativity."

Avery shrugs and takes another bite.

Britta lowers her voice. "And I hate to brag with all these other parents around, but my shadow puppet productions are the best in the state."

"Sure," Avery says.

Britta looks at her with feigned shock. "You've never noticed the framed New Jersey Shadow Puppet Award in my bedroom?"

Jane and Marco both giggle.

"I'm actually quite hurt." Britta keeps up the act. "Well. I suppose we'll just have to sort it via puppet duel."

Avery bites her lip . . . to keep from smiling, Britta's nearly certain. A lightness flitters inside her chest, an errant butterfly.

"I'm too old for shadow puppets," Avery says.

Jane giggles again. "Maybe you're just scared Mom will beat you."

"Yeah, that Mom's alligator will eat your duck," Marco adds.

"I'm not scared, you weenies." Avery tries to roll her eyes again, but her mouth's corners keep twisting up. "Puppet duels aren't even a thing."

"They are in the dark underworld of shadow puppetry," Britta says gravely. "No more stalling, darling. Will you rise to the challenge?"

Avery meets Britta's eyes, finally looks about to laugh—

But a long, low wail comes out instead.

Avery startles. So does Britta.

"What was that?" Avery shouts, but Britta can barely hear her over the whiney roar. "Mom?"

WEEE-OOO, WEE-OOOO.

Britta hurries to stand. What's that noise, the glimmer? Are they safe? No, no it's—

"The fire alarm," she cries to Joel.

Spencer and Joel are already rushing around the room, searching for the source.

"Something must have set it off," Joel says wildly, "but I don't see any sparks or flames—"

"Could you have messed with it when you were shutting down the generator online?"

"What? No, I'm not an idiot, Britta!"

"It sounds like it's coming from outside the doors," Spencer says.

Britta turns to the kids. "Stay right here. Don't move."

Avery says, "But—"

"I mean it, darlings, finish those sandwiches."

Britta hurries to catch up with the men, who are now clustered at the doors, still fastened tight by Spencer's Boy Scout–worthy strainer-cum-security system. They all locate the source of the fire in unison. Outside the glass, halfway down the cellar's storage area, a thick, ropy trail of gray smoke loops toward the ceiling.

"Oh my goodness," she whispers. How did this happen? Where are Mabel and Padma and Liz? Are they safe? *Hurt?*

She can barely think over this screeching noise. "Ladies," she shouts into the glass, "are you all right?"

WEEE-OOOOO, WEEEEEE-OOOOOO.

Joel scrubs his thick, dark hair. "Screw it. I need to go out there."

Spencer stops him with a hand to the chest. "No way, you go out and the glimmer could come in!"

Britta's thoughts keep spiraling. There's a fire extinguisher down here somewhere, right, in the closet maybe? Or out in the storage area? Where are these women? And the wine, their nest egg, their liquid fortune—

"Get your hands off me," Joel snaps.

Britta takes a reflexive step back because Spencer hasn't moved. He's just staring at Joel with this strange, wild look that Britta has never quite seen before—though of course she's heard loads about Spencer's intensity through Mabel over the years, his almost clinical single-mindedness. Britta's witnessed his fanaticism tonight. She remembers afresh that story of Joel and Spencer's brawl in the school's carline . . . Christ, does that word feel so strange now, she thinks numbly. *Carline.* Like a relic from an ancient world.

"Here, help me move this." Tom's command slices through her thoughts. He starts shoving the armchair away from the doors.

WEEE-OOOOO, WEEEEEE-OOOOOO.

"I don't see Liz," he says. "What if they're hurt? Passed out from the smoke? What if—"

"I'll get the fire extinguisher." Joel brushes past Spencer with a shoulder check. "Romer, help Tom!" Joel rounds the bar, presses open a thin pocket door on the wall, and reveals a small glass cabinet with a slim red extinguisher inside. There it is.

"Wait," Spencer calls after him. "Wait, the ladies are okay. Stop. Look!"

Britta turns.

It's true. Mabel is all-out racing down the hall toward them. Her dress is ripped at the hem, her pockmarked pearl necklace now a smile with missing teeth, her makeup splotched in black clumps near her eyes. Britta pales. Mabel looks like a witch. Or a ghoul. And just like in a horror movie, right as she sprints toward them, the lights overhead all blink, blink, *blink*—

Out.

Behind Britta, the kids shriek as loud as they can.

"Don't move!" she orders. Britta thrusts her arms in front of her, feeling through the utter black. Joel must be holding a flashlight, because a searing beam of light immediately cuts through the darkness, spears the glass, sends blinding little orbs of light onto the walls.

Britta squints to adjust her vision.

She turns, blinks, finds the kids still huddled in the corner. "Everyone okay?"

They all nod, shaken.

"Help us," Mabel shouts behind her. "Please. The fire, it's getting out of control—"

"She's lying!" Spencer cuts her off. "I can tell. She's playing chicken again. I know her; I know it—"

"We're not taking any chances; you want to be burned alive?!" Joel shoves past him.

Romer and Tom finish cracking the strainer lock and fling open the doors. Extinguisher in hand, Joel gives them each a flashlight, and the trio hurries outside. As they follow Mabel down the hall, a waft of ash and the smell of burnt hair sails into the sitting room.

"Shut the doors." Spencer coughs. "The glimmer could be down here—"

"It's smoke," Britta says, hoping to assure the kids, "and nothing more."

"Mom?" Avery cries. "Is the basement going to burn down?"

All at once there comes a whooshing sound. An ear-piercing, waterfall-like roar. Britta watches as a cloud of white, frothy powder blooms into the cellar hall and dissipates into the air like a bomb of powdery snow.

The noise promptly stops.

She watches through the glass for movement, any signs of life, but the hall is silent, empty, just the swirling aftermath of the extinguisher, like a grainy, expanding pinwheel.

Then she hears a low chorus of coughs, hacks, sobs.

Britta peeks through the doors and calls out, "Is anyone hurt? What's the damage?"

No one answers.

"Hello?"

"Where is everyone?" Avery asks.

Britta shakes her head. Her own heartbeat is deafening.

The silence stretches so long and wide that she imagines the fire has burned a hole straight through the world, and they've all fallen through.

She hears the muffled sobs again.

"Stay here," she tells Avery. "You're in charge."

"I can't be in charge!"

Britta spins around. "I trust you," she says. "Completely, you're my lifeline. You hear me, darling? I'm so proud of you; of all of you."

Avery swallows, nodding.

Britta slips out the doors and shuts them behind her, keeping the kids sequestered inside. She walks down the hall, inspecting for signs of life and damage as she goes. She stops when she hears a faint voice down the way.

"They're not coming."

Liz's voice, she thinks. Liz is okay. She's alive. Britta's shoulders relax just an inch.

She clicks on her flashlight, pointing it forward. A knife slicing through the dark.

"Liz, n-no one is coming."

Padma's voice. Then Padma's all right, too. The three women, alive.

Britta almost cries out in relief.

"There's no p-police, no w-white knight, n-no one," Padma whispers—to Liz, or Britta, or to herself, Britta can't be sure. "W-we're all going to die down here."

22

Liz

Tom's dinner jacket–clad arm feels like a warm compress. Tangible proof that she isn't alone. With Tom here, if Liz shuts her eyes, she could actually believe that she's dreaming. That tonight has been one long, impossible nightmare.

Setting the fire was a mistake. An idea born of desperation. A reckless distress flare shot into a void.

Though there is one good thing. Without the fire, Tom wouldn't be right beside her. Liz chooses to think of that as a tiny, symbolic win. Something.

"We should get some pillows from the sitting room," he says. "Both take a rest. Look at this with fresh eyes."

"I don't think I can sleep."

Liz closes her eyes and sees the fire again. The little flame jumping from the makeshift bonfire they set up in the granite cigar ashtray; how they debated, and finally agreed to, lighting a shred of Mabel's dress's silk underskirt to coax the flame. How the fire spread so fast, so hungrily. They destroyed the island wholesale, not to mention ruined some supplies.

Their half-baked plan could have burned the entire cellar down. What were they thinking? What was *she* thinking?

She wasn't. She's been in survival mode for far too long to be held to something as shifty as "common sense." Away from Reid and Callie, locked in a cellar, separated from Tom, reduced to her worst and basest instincts.

"Still shaken up?" Tom shimmies out of his jacket and drapes it across Liz's shoulders. She's about to protest it's too warm down here now, too claustrophobic with the clouds from the extinguisher, the smell and taste of ash. As soon as the garment is around her, though, she feels better.

"It just got so out of control."

Liz peers around. The cellar is dark aside from the small islands of light strategically placed around the cellar, the cluster of flameless candles Joel placed on the sitting room's bar, the high-powered flashlight on its coffee table.

She can see almost everyone inside. Spencer is now passed out on the couch, sleeping, mouth open. He and Joel nearly came to blows after the fire, fighting about who can be trusted and where they should keep the supplies. Of course, Spencer suspected their foul play, though how's he going to prove it? Joel, grim-faced, perches on one of the armchairs, sipping on some amber-colored liquid. Britta's with her squadron of kids on the floor in the opposite corner, snuggling amid a mound of blankets. Cooing to them. Comforting them with damn shadow puppets.

It was a small fire, but it's out now. You are safe; you are loved, Britta kept telling the kids, over and over after Joel put out the fire.

What Liz would give to tell Reid and Callie that, just once tonight. *You are safe. You are loved.*

Liz watches Avery, Reid's best friend, grudgingly make her fist into a rabbit in front of the flashlight. Britta kisses her head, whispering something to her that Liz obviously can't hear.

Avery smiles.

Stupid, performative, voyeuristic Britta. Liz would bet money this new turn as "caring mommy" is all a show too, some sort of misguided attempt to woo her dwindling audience.

I hate her, Liz thinks. *I loathe her.*

But the reminder sounds canned, even to her. Like a scheduled ping from Grudge Headquarters, versus anything with true heat.

She's too exhausted for hate right now.

Her co-arsonists must be hiding somewhere amid the wine towers. Liz can't see them. They all scattered after the fire was doused, true to crime-gang form. Mabel and Padma must have claimed an alcove for themselves, like she and Tom have, because they're not in the sitting room. Maybe they can't stomach Britta and the others anymore, either. Or maybe it's Pavlovian, learned behavior.

Regardless, Liz wonders what Mabel and Padma are thinking. Do they think there's a remote chance that the one-minute fire alarm could have alerted the authorities . . . if there are even authorities left? That there's any possibility of ever stepping outside this cellar again? That there's still a compelling force beyond themselves in this universe, rooting for good, rooting for them—call it fate, love, heroic meta-narration—that won't just let them wither and die?

We're going to die down here.

Liz shivers.

"Hey. Come here." Tom pulls her into his chest. The warmth of him, the familiar scent of him, transports her, like a promise of home. "It's not over, Liz. You know that."

She sniffs. "I don't know that."

"Come on. You're not one to give up."

When she doesn't answer, he squeezes her tighter, adding, "Then I'll believe for the both of us."

"I tried." Her voice cracks like an egg in a pan. "Tom, I tried—"

"I know. It's okay," he whispers. "I know. You've been trying this whole time."

Tom must also suspect they set the fire on purpose. She can tell by the way he's dancing around the subject, the way he won't quite meet her eyes. He won't ask, though. Maybe he's appalled: the last vestiges of people-pleaser Suburban Tom, who refuses to dissolve even as they plunge to the bottom of the world. Or who knows, he could be secretly proud of her. Perhaps he expected Liz would do something so drastic after he told her that Britta was filming them for #Brittasays. Maybe he counts on her to be the one who takes up arms, who rushes outside in the face of disaster and dismantles a dinner party. Same as she counts on him to reel her back in.

"You're a wonderful mother," he whispers, "and partner. I know I don't say it enough."

He takes her hand and turns it over gently. "This honestly feels like a nightmare . . . a horror movie that we can't turn off."

Liz shakes her head. "Told you the 'burbs were worse than Zombieland."

He lets out a rueful laugh.

"I just keep praying that Sabina knew to go to the safe room," Liz says. "That she's smart. That she remembered it was the safest place. God, do you think she knew that?"

"Remember how prepared she was? Maybe the most over-prepared eleven-year-old I've ever met," Tom says. "Hell, remember what she was wearing? That bizarre little business suit."

Liz nods. "Like Melanie Griffith in *Working Girl*."

"Or a traveling salesman from the 1950s."

Liz croaks out a laugh, before remembering in a flash that Sabina's mom is gone. In the course of one stint of babysitting, the world has changed and turned on the little girl.

Liz starts crying again.

"Liz."

"I'm fine."

"Liz, hell, I'm sorry. I—I miss you. I miss you so much and you're right here."

She rubs her eyes.

"If we ever get out of here . . ." Tom trails off. He studies his lap. "Some things actually seem clearer down here, if that makes any sense."

"How do you mean?"

He shrugs. "Some things we talk about." Then smirks. "And fight about."

The silence stretches between them, long and wide, but it isn't uncomfortable. Liz is used to it. Tom's always been like this. Small talk, joking, lighter fare—that comes easily to him, especially compared to Liz. But the soul searching, the deeper conversations, those are her domain. When they were younger, she'd almost wanted to strangle his opinions out of him. He'd be so hesitant, so contemplative . . . but she's learned to give him the space and time to dive in.

"When I was a kid, our house was basically a commune. There were always at least ten friends from the neighborhood running around. Dads hanging with mine near the grill. Moms on our deck screaming for us all to slow down, to be careful."

As he leans his head against the armoire, Liz takes his hand.

"I just assumed . . . I just figured that was *life*," Tom continues. "What everyone wanted."

"Understandable, I guess," Liz says, thinking of her own parents, of how much of Liz's apparent "dog-eats-dog" parenting style can likely be traced back to her tough-as-nails mother. In fact, Liz's pep talk to Reid when he started at The Falls Elementary was ripped straight from her mother's parenting playbook, was more or less the same speech Liz heard when she herself was having friendship trouble in seventh grade. "Lots of people view the world through the lenses of their own childhood."

"But we never talked about it. I never asked if you wanted that. Honestly, I'm not even sure if *I* want that. I'm sorry if I . . ." His Adam's apple bobs like a boat on a river. "I don't know how we drifted so far apart out here. I want us, *you*, more than any of that. I need you to know that, if things ever . . . if we ever . . ."

"Get another chance."

She looks back toward the sitting room, at her neighbors, the Harris-Ches in particular, the parents of her son's dearest friend. Tom and Liz have lived in The Falls for over a year. Almost *two*, and the past twelve hours in this cellar are the closest Liz has come to actually "knowing" anyone here. Yes, there have been plenty of legitimate excuses: her deadlines; meetings with Cromwell; word counts and Zooms with other writers; catch-up quarterly trips and dinners with Laura and her mom.

But all the paltry excuses add up to the bigger truth: Liz is an island out here.

"I haven't made it easy either." She stares at the tips of her boots, scuffed and mud-streaked, still stained from their mad dash outside. "I know I've been holding on to this idea of the four of us against the world. Is it weird that I miss the crazy COVID quarantine years? I mean, home school, working together from home . . . I know it was all a mess, but . . ."—she swallows—"I guess it was *our* mess. Our little universe with the kids." She looks up at Tom. "For a while, we froze time. I know that sounds fucked up."

"It doesn't."

Liz presses her hands into her ragged indigo jeans. "And ever since, I've—I feel you've been pulling away, or that I just can't get back to real life. It's too big now, or hectic, or complicated. Maybe it's my fault. I just feel alone out here."

"You're not alone," Tom says. "We're still the four of us, the four of us against the world." His voice hitches, though, as if his words have snagged on a tear. His eyes are watering now, too. Liz can't remember the last time she saw him cry. When Callie was born? When Reid had that horrible case of foot and mouth and Tom was in LA, deranged with exhaustion from closing the Zeneca deal?

"What's even going to be left for our kids if we get back to them?" He shakes the dark thought away, clears his throat with purpose. "We really should sleep. We're no good to them comatose."

Liz doesn't answer.

"At some point, Liz, you need to sleep."

He's right, of course. If her calculations are right, she hasn't slept in a day and a half. Fifteen hours now of clawing, relentless, bone-shaking worrying—and she hasn't even processed her missing sister, or spun out on whether her mom, snug in her senior living community in Florida, is safe.

Liz thought she might have settled into some sort of morbid holding pattern by now, a stasis where she admitted their new reality. Not *accepted* it, never, but been able to drop into a second gear, heart pounding at less than fight mode. The parents of those missing kids kidnapped by strangers in the woods or in white vans, in TV shows and movies—they eventually fall asleep. They eat. They keep feeling their new hellscape pulse like poison in their veins, lock their heart in a vise—every minute, every second—but they go on living, despite it.

"There's no way I can sleep," she whispers.

Tom gives her that sad smile again. "Then lie down and stare at the wine."

He returns in minutes with a pair of pillows and a blanket from the sitting room. Then he fashions a makeshift bedroom for them inside their little cellar alcove, propping the pillows against the island, splaying out his suit jacket for Liz to lie on.

He shimmies down and reaches for her hand, so she gives it to him and lies down beside him.

"We're going to see them again," he says. "I promise you."

Apparently, Tom convinced himself with that unfounded promise, because he's asleep in minutes. The soft, familiar purr of his snore settles around her, a melody underscoring the mantra looping in her head. *Reid. Callie. Reid and Callie.*

Their names become her second heartbeat. Her mind swirls again with hundreds of what-if scenarios. She's surprised that she can close her eyes.

"Liz."

She startles.

She turns to find Mabel hovering above her in the darkness. "Oh Lord, I'm sorry. Were you really sleeping?"

Liz sits up. "No, just . . . pretending, I guess. For Tom."

Mabel's ratty hair and soot-stained skin come into better focus as Liz's vision adjusts. Mabel's eyes are wide as moons. She looks haunted, or . . . frantic, Liz can't be sure.

"Listen, Liz, can we talk?" Mabel whispers. "I think I might have remembered something very important."

CHAPTER

23

Mabel

"WHAT'S THIS ABOUT?"
Mabel doesn't answer, just waves Liz forward, down the storage area corridor and toward the cellar's main front doors. The group huddled in the sitting room all appeared to be sleeping when Mabel last checked—her inebriated husband ostensibly passed out cold—but she doesn't want to take any chances.

She stops in front of the wine cellar entrance, then ushers Liz to the left, into the narrow space between the door and first wall of floor-to-ceiling wine shelving. In a flash, Mabel remembers seeing this renovated cellar for the first time earlier that night, when they all took the walking tour down Britta and Joel's gleaming new sconce-lit hall. She remembers so many details of tonight now with startling, almost breathtaking clarity, as if some angel pinned her to death's threshold, flashed life's moments before her in a divine sort of Morse code. The cellar light shimmering across this Rioja section. The perpetual twist of smothered jealousy on Spencer's face as they viewed the TV room, the conservatory, the gigantic playroom. Frank and Gwen, all wide eyes and smiles as they craned their necks, taking in every inch.

But the most important detail of that tour . . . how could she have forgotten it until now?

Mabel follows Liz inside the narrow space.

"Hey," Padma whispers. She waves her pocket flashlight in hello, the beam of light bouncing around like a strobe light at a Christian rock concert. She's right where Mabel left her. Sweat-stained hairline, nearly blue lips, tucked into the corner and shivering with that ratty blanket still draped around her shoulders.

"Oh, man," Liz says. "Have you slept at all?"

"N-nah, can't get comfortable." Padma looks away. "Too much on my mind."

Liz turns around for Mabel's take, but Mabel only shrugs. Why deny the truth? Padma looks awful because she *feels* awful. This isn't sustainable. None of tonight is sustainable.

"I gave her more Advil," Mabel says. "But she needs antibiotics."

"Dev is a p-pack rat," Padma shivers. "There's s-some at home, I'd bet money on it."

"Liz, why don't you sit?"

For once, Liz does as she's told.

Mabel follows suit, wedging herself between the women on the floor. "I . . . think it's fair to say things have spun out of control."

Liz lets out a laugh. "Not sure we needed a convention to make that assessment."

"No one can see straight anymore, least of all me," Mabel says. "But what I *do* know is that Greg feels farther and farther away with each passing minute. And everyone's so panicked, they keep making terrible decisions."

Liz pauses. "I know the fire was a bad call."

"It was," Mabel says slowly. "But I'm not talking about the fire."

Liz pulls her knees to her chest. "Then . . . what's this about?"

Mabel yanks at her necklace again. She needs to end this tic, immediately—she's nearly ruined these pearls—but she can't seem to stop fiddling with them. They were grossly expensive, a gift from Spencer years ago. Back when he still cared enough to pay for forgiveness.

"That fire was also the first time I felt like I took matters into my own hands," Mabel whispers. "Where I accepted that we're honestly trapped down here. By no one's fault, but trapped all the same, and that no one's going to save us." She eyes Liz. "That's where you've been all along, isn't it? And I've been condemning you for it."

Liz stays silent.

"I've been running through tonight. Over and over. In the dark. Every inch of it. For anything I've missed, overlooked, any way to get out and get back to them." Mabel studies her hands. They look so old under the filmy light of Padma's flashlight, frail and vein-riddled. The hands of her grandmother. "Earlier tonight on the tour, Frank Russo asked to see Joel's new car in the garage. Do you remember that? Joel's new Westa."

"Yeah, sure," Liz says slowly. "But it was in the shop."

Mabel folds her ancient-looking hands. Another habit—reflexive prayer. *Please, God, give me the strength to know what is just here. What is right. Please, God, show me the way back to Greg.*

A numbing silence answers again. Mabel almost laughs. Where has God been tonight?

"It's not in the shop," she says.

"W-wait," Padma says, "Are you saying there's a Westa upstairs?"

"Are you sure?" Liz shakes her head. "Why would Joel and Britta lie about *that*? The house tour was before all this madness, before the glimmer even hit."

"I don't know. I think Joel was using the car before the party," Mabel says. "Maybe he left it in a state of disarray—"

"Is that code for whacking off or something?"

"Liz, I don't . . . Lord, I don't know! I just know that Britta was lying because she told me."

"They're such a sham." Liz snaps a laugh. "This whole night has been a *total* sham. Pretending to save us as they film us struggling. Showcasing their Insta-perfect marriage while they lock their separate rooms." Liz must note Mabel's shock, because she adds, "Don't bother defending her, Mabel, I found Joel's 'man quarters,' bolted up tight like a dirty secret."

Mabel feels her blood crystallizing, transforming into ice. So then Liz already knows about Britta and Joel.

Maybe it's only a matter of time before everyone knows why.

"They do seem perfect," Padma whispers. "Though I also can't say I'm s-surprised."

"The car," Liz refocuses them. "The Westa. On the tour, Frank said it's essentially a tank."

Mabel nods, recalling Joel's model. "Their model is top of the line, too. It even comes with a biodefense system. I've been excited to read the spec ever since Joel got it."

"Biodefense," Liz echoes. "Meaning it may actually get us out of here, across town?"

"We still need to think it through. Learn from Mrs. Ford, Frank, Gwen," Mabel says quickly. "We can't pretend that leaving wouldn't be a risk."

"And it's an EV, isn't it?" Liz says.

"Yes," Mabel says. "*Stored* energy. Even if power lines somehow do transmit the glimmer, why would batteries, a charged car, be a danger? Besides, we were using power all night. For the record, I never would have turned off the generator."

Liz says, "And if there were ever a time, a means, to take such a risk—"

"Isobel only has two more days of food," Padma whispers.

Mabel nods, swallowing. "I think we all agree 'now' is quite the opportune time here."

Liz lets out a long, shaky exhale. She looks over Mabel's head, toward the doors. "So, what, do we attempt to steal back the masks first?"

"We could definitely use those g-gas masks," Padma says. "We're going to have to l-leave the car, go outside at some point to get home."

"There's only two of them, remember," Liz says. "And we also need to figure out how to snag Joel's car keys—"

"Wait," Mabel says. "Just. Hold on. I meant we should *talk* to them, ask to borrow the car, not concoct a hair-brained heist."

"*Talk?*" Liz says. "You've gotta be kidding me, Mabel. You really think we're at a place right now where 'asking' is going to do anything?"

Mabel bites her lip. But this is what she expected from Liz, wasn't it? For the fury, the dissent, the final push Mabel needs to betray all of them.

"Mabel," Liz centers her. "The Harris-Ches are hiding down here because they *can*. Honestly, despite how much I've argued to the contrary, because they should. Joel and Britta's kids are safe in this cellar. And if I were them, I'd probably be making the same decisions, thinking of the majority, of keeping all their potential assets close—the food, the car, the masks."

"Who knows how long the glimmer's going to last," Padma adds numbly.

"Or if help and safety are a couple of blocks or a hundred miles away." Liz presses her hands to her temples. "If you ask them, if you *force* them to decide, they're going to say no."

Mabel squawks a bitter laugh. "So we just steal everything instead."

"Because for us, waiting is death!" Liz blurts. "We need those masks and that car to get home." She leans closer. "I know you want to do the right thing, always, and I get that, but there are a dozen 'right' things, depending on who you are and how you look at it."

"That's not true!"

Lord, her voice is shaking now, but Liz is pressing on a wound, on the sore truth that Mabel has been coming around to, slowly, especially after everything that's happened between her, Joel, and Spencer. And after tonight? Her old bifurcations of right and wrong, good and evil, are near obliterated. She used to imagine purgatory as a place where those kinds of things were sorted, where weak, wicked souls were tinkered into instruments worthy of a better place. Maybe purgatory is far more ambiguous than that. Perhaps limbo is just a grandiose wine cellar.

"I understand," Mabel tries again. "I hear what you're saying, but I can talk to Joel; he owes me."

"He owes you nothing. Are you listening to me? Not tonight." Liz shifts onto her heels. "The rules have changed— if there ever were rules—and diplomacy is dead down here. Just think of your own husband, of the choices he's made to keep himself safe, the shit he's been slinging at you—"

Padma chides, "L-Liz."

"I'm sorry, but it's true! This may be our only chance to get home alive to the kids and you're throwing it away because of Golden Rules and turning the other cheek—"

"*He owes me!*" Mabel's voice is too loud now, and as broken and jagged as a piece of glass. They don't understand. No one understands. *Because you keep it all locked up inside*, a small voice whispers. *Confess.* "There's more going on than you know," she says quickly, before losing the nerve, "for a long time, and Joel . . . Spencer and I are having problems, too, because . . ."

But she can't believe she's going to say the words.

She heaves a shaky breath. Then draws each word forward, blood from a stone. "Because Joel and Spencer were sleeping together," she whispers. "A couple of months ago. I don't know how it started. I'm not sure for how long."

"*What?*" Padma's mouth drops open in shock.

Liz reels back with a gasp. "Um. Holy shit."

Mabel closes her eyes, shutting them out, or she might not be able to go on. "I saw texts from Joel on Spencer's phone in February," she says quickly. "And he broke down and told me—that he didn't know what came over him, but that it was a mistake. That he'll never do it again. We've had similar fights in the past. He's had trysts once or twice before." She pictures younger Spencer now, after his first affair, during a Boston College service trip, for goodness' sake, spring break of their senior year. His tortured face as he confessed to her. His palpable helplessness. It was the vulnerability that did her in, the possibility that, behind his dogged faith, confidence, athleticism, Spencer Young might have been someone just as fragile as she was, someone who longed to be fixed.

Then it happened again, with a twenty-something from his office, a few months before their wedding. Then a young man he met on a solo golf trip to Ireland. A one-night stand after Greg was born, another before their tenth anniversary. Every time he'd come to her, confessing, bearing expensive gifts, indulgences for his infidelity, and then they'd be all right for a while, as if her forgiveness had baptized him anew.

"This time, it was just so thoughtless, hurtful," Mabel says now. "So close to home. Britta's *husband*. Something snapped. I screamed. Cried. Insisted on a divorce, but Spencer begged for counseling, pointed to our church, kept saying he really loved me, our life, our parish. That he wanted a second chance."

"B-big ask," Padma whispers. "Sounds like f-fifth or tenth chance."

"But he'd broken us. I hated him." Mabel pinches her eyes shut. "Hated Joel. I still do, and wanted to punish them."

"Mabel, I'm so sorry. I can't even—" Liz recalibrates. "Does *Britta* know? How, why are you even here tonight?"

Mabel lets out a mirthless laugh. "Optics?"

She closes her eyes and pictures that first morning she saw Britta, after Mabel read Joel's texts on Spencer's phone. Opening the front door to find her chirpy friend in Lycra yoga pants, her picture-perfect blonde ponytail and guileless smile. Mabel couldn't tell her, not then, not when it was so fresh, boiling, blazing under her skin. So she stayed silent during their entire Friday walk, letting Britta chatter on about her idea for a soiree, her plan to boost her influence, to solidify her platform. How very much she needed it.

"Britta doesn't know," Mabel says now. "I've tried to avoid her, dodged her for weeks about coffee, yoga, our Friday walks. You know her, though, she just kept pestering about this party, how 'crucial' it was that it be a success for—" Mabel glances guiltily at Padma. "Well, for Dev."

Padma lifts her chin. "Oh, Britta's made that abundantly clear."

"She's been going through a hard time herself," Mabel adds softly, slipping so easily back into protective mode. Playing the Good Samaritan. "Joel's been pulling away for years, and they got together under . . . tricky circumstances. It was fraught from the beginning. But it sounds like he's really gone off the rails since Spencer broke it off. Escaping into the city, partying, sleeping it off when the kids are at school. I guess Britta just assumes it's a midlife crisis." Mabel gives a rueful laugh. "She found a picture of Joel on Cash & Moreno's Instagram feed and was none the wiser, I suppose. Thought, *hey, a perfect soiree caterer*. I'm nearly positive Joel and their head chef, Nico Cash, are sleeping together. I just couldn't be the one to shatter what's left of her world. It's not fair."

"None of this is fair," Liz says softly.

"But I felt so guilty. *Feel* so guilty. She kept asking about tonight, and I caved and said we'd make an appearance." Mabel sniffs. "I hate myself for that."

Padma reaches for her hand. "Remember what you said to me? You're doing the best you can."

"I thought *I* had issues coming here." Liz shakes her head. "And Spencer's had the gall to be such a monstrous asshole to you tonight! I honestly don't know how you do it. You really are a saint."

Mabel doesn't answer. She could leave it like this, so neat, so tidy—with her as the martyr, and Spencer as the overbearing wrongdoer, the sadist. That's what she'd wanted, had intended, isn't it? For Spencer to be punished? And at the beginning of all of this, it *was* true.

But the rest of the story she's suppressed still scratches at her like a demon, cloying, begging to be let out. Who's she still pretending for anyway as the world falls apart? These women? Herself? *God?* She's kidding herself if she thinks He doesn't already know.

If He still exists.

Mabel lets the warm dark envelop her, imagines St. Rose's confessional box, its small bench, the wooden lattice, Father Patrick's soft words of assurance. Maybe Liz is right: what do "sins," right and wrong, matter anymore, with the real world stripped away, with the glimmer at their door?

Then again, maybe the truth is all that matters.

"No," Mabel whispers. "I'm far from a saint."

Padma squeezes her hand. "Oh, M-Mabel, don't—"

"I threatened to tell his illiberal parents if he didn't break it off with Joel," she adds, pulling away. "He'd begged me not to. So I told Father Patrick instead."

"Oh, well, that's . . ." Padma clears her throat. "Understandable. That's what Catholics do, right, share their secrets in confession?"

"Not in confession," Mabel whispers. "I told the entire Parish Council, embellishing where it suited me. And my Bible group. Spencer's Bible study leader too. I told them all he was a rampant, callous adulterer. There have been rumblings for his excommunication, banishment from his beloved church— the end of his cherished identity as a pious, devoted 'man of God.'" She collects her breath. "It was thoughtless revenge. Secrets like this one don't stay inside of stained-glass walls. It's only a matter of time before the truth ripples out and straight through The Falls. And I'll have to deal with the repercussions. *Greg* will have to deal with the repercussions."

Padma and Liz exchange a discreet, concerned look. Mabel shivers and turns away.

"I swear, I hate Spencer so much it consumes me," she says. "And the hatred has turned me spiteful. Reckless. I hate that I still love him and that tonight cost me my son and that I'm picturing my mother-in-law and wondering if that beastly woman is going to raise Greg for the rest of his life because I died attending the damned dinner party of my husband's param—" Mabel's voice catches, fat tears trail around her chin. Searing shame blooms at the base of her neck.

Did she really just confess all that?

She can't look at Liz or Padma anymore. Or see how they're looking at *her*. She waits for the familiar scratching, the itching, the clawing, but it doesn't come. No, she just feels hollow inside.

She finally glances up.

There's no judgment on their faces. Pity, yes. Sadness. Understanding, though maybe she's just seeing what she longs to see.

"I'm so sorry, Mabel," Padma whispers.

"I had no idea," Liz says. "About any of this. I'm sorry too, for you, for everything—"

"I'm sorry too."

The voice, startling but familiar, comes from behind them.

Mabel turns around slowly to see Britta standing at the threshold of the alcove, a dark flashlight dangling from her hand.

"I'm sorry for believing you were actually my friend."

CHAPTER

24

Britta

MABEL'S FACE TWISTS with shock. Then abject horror. "Oh my Lord." She hurries to stand. "Oh, Britta, did you—"

"Save it." Pressure tightens around Britta's throat, twitches behind her eyes, but she swallows it down, blinks it back, because Mabel doesn't get to see her cry. None of them do.

"Britta, please—"

"How could you keep this from me?"

Mabel sputters, "I didn't, I—"

"You're my best friend, and you knew about Spencer and Joel for *months* and said nothing?"

Mabel rushes for her. "Britta, I—"

"Don't touch me." Britta stumbles backward, gaze falling on Liz and Padma. "And you two. I've done everything I can to keep you alive, safe, and you scheme to set my house on fire and steal our *car?*"

Liz's face falls. "How long were you listening?"

"Long enough to know I'm done!" Britta snaps. "I don't care what you think of me or my house or my stupid efforts to impress, because obviously my life *is* a fucking sham!"

A hiccup of a sob escapes her, which prompts Mabel to lurch forward, reach for her again, but Britta knocks Mabel's hand away. She spins, sprinting barefoot down the corridor.

But where is there to run?

"Britta, wait," Mabel calls behind her. "Please, let's talk!"

Britta ignores her, passing the alcove, which Tom has set up like a make-do bedroom. She slides into the next space, ducking behind its tasting island, slinking into its dark shadows, heart thundering, head screaming.

And to think, she was coming to check on them, help them, *be a good host*, and walked straight into an ambush.

"Britta?" She hears Mabel and the others calling her name with increasing desperation from somewhere in the storage corridor. "Britta? Britta!"

She wrenches her hair, leaning against the armoire's side, curling herself into an insignificant little ball as thoughts keep frantically firing and colliding across her mind. Joel and Spencer. The Westa. Fighting in the carline. The Falls Club. *I hate you! You ruined my life!* Pilates. The city. Nico Cash.

She has no idea, does she?

She wants to howl at the moon.

How mortifying.

How wrong, traitorous, despicable, but the *mortification*. Hosting a soiree for your husband's former lover using his present lover's restaurant! It's . . . beyond pathetic. Unforgivably humiliating.

The women are still searching for Britta through the storage area. She can hear their exchanged whispers now: "She's not in the sitting room."

"Maybe she needs space."

"Well, we can't leave it like that, Mabel. If we do, it's all over."

Britta thrusts her head against the armoire. What a fool she's been. What a macro-status fool. She's not some master of the lifestyle game, she's a damn pawn. Expendable, the punch line of a joke, and apparently everyone knows it. Joel. Spencer. Romer. Liz and Padma. And Mabel. *Mabel*, all along.

When the hell did Britta convince herself that she had the courage, the gall, the privilege of "rising above" anything? When did she convince herself that she mattered at all?

The tears are coming, fast and furious now. She tries to catch her breath. The whispers of the women eventually die down. The staccato chorus of their flats and bare feet across the slate floor eventually stops altogether.

Part of her wishes she could just disappear. *POOF.* Swirl into the disintegration of the world, her little sob story insignificant, just a grain of sand in the hourglass.

And yet her fury.

The *rage.*

She peers around the island.

If she wants true revenge, she could throw down in the sitting room right now. Have it all out. What real-world consequences are there anymore? She could confront Joel and Spencer. Hell, even Romer too, for keeping this from her. He clearly knew what was going on with Joel and Nico—he hinted about it enough. He's probably here instead as some kind of "cover" for Joel. Justice must be rendered.

She picks herself up and slides silently down the hall . . . but stops before entering the sitting room.

So much for revenge. All three men—Joel, Spencer, and Romer—are dozing, or at least attempting to. Spencer's audibly snoring in the armchair. She can hear it through the glass. Joel lies face-down on a pillow, body draped across the couch, as if he fell down mid-battle. Romer is engaged in his own losing war to stay awake in the other armchair, eyes fluttering closed.

The kids, though, are all still wide awake, gathered under the bar right where she left them with their hoard of blankets and flashlights.

Britta steps closer to the glass. She can't quite make out the kids' whispers from here, but from what she can tell, Avery's attempting to give Jane and Marco a puppet tutorial on the wall. A bunny, maybe. No, a jackal. A wide-eyed crocodile.

The sharp lightning inside begins to quell. Britta can feel it tempering to a dull heat.

Maybe because the truth has finally hit her. She and Joel are done. Yes, there was a part of her that hoped they were salvageable, that might have even craved a real happy ending despite everything. With the truth, though, comes one small blessing. The catharsis of saying goodbye to a relationship that's been painfully dying.

Or maybe it's just because there's no room for revenge. Not with the kids here. Not tonight.

She softly presses her forehead against the sitting room's glass.

People had warned her. Right after she'd realized that Joel had gotten her pregnant, after she'd settled back into her fabulous life as a young consultant in London. Her friends called her crazy for thinking she could honestly raise a child with some debonair, trust-fund baby turned overworked financier turned wayward traveler, and one she'd met on vacation, to boot. *Kids transform your whole life*, her friends and colleagues had told her. *Marriage, children, are not a whim decision.*

How she had laughed them off, scoffed, rolled her eyes. Life was just one long adventure, and she wasn't about to get lost in it, despite taking an untrodden path. "Selfless" was an oxymoron of a word. Preposterous. A diagnosis for people— women in particular—who didn't have enough "self" to begin with.

When precisely had she let her adventure give way to image? Success? The appearance of stilted perfection?

She sighs and carefully, quietly, opens the doors.

Avery looks up instantly. "Oh. Hey, Mom. Did you talk to your friends?"

Britta tries for a smile. "I did."

She rounds the couch and sits beside them, sandwiching herself between the barstools.

Jane rubs her arms. Her middle child looks so tired, eyes now hollow sockets from the flashlight's shadows. "I really want to go upstairs, Mommy."

Britta can't help but nod. "Yeah, kiddo," she whispers. "Me too."

Avery stares at her, biting her lip. "Mom . . . did Reid's mom start that fire on purpose?"

Britta debates a litany of answers before finally settling on, "Yes. I think she did."

All three of the kids' mouths become perfect *O*s.

"Because she thought it was the right thing," Britta adds quickly. "Because she thought it could get her home."

Avery considers this. "You know Reid's always getting into trouble at school too," she says, finally. "I have to tell on him, like, all the time."

"I thought Reid was your best friend."

"He is." Avery shrugs. "It's kind of complicated."

Truer words have never been spoken. As Jane nestles into Britta's lap, Marco, never one to be left out, scoots over and grabs Britta's right arm tightly, like a lovey, staking his territory.

"Sounds like Reid is as tough as his mom," Britta adds, then promptly realizes that she doesn't know Reid at all, does she? In a lineup of second graders, she probably couldn't identify him. For over a year, her daughter's best friend has been a faceless blob, his name only taking on considerable importance these last couple of weeks when Britta realized Liz could be a last-minute, advantageous soiree substitute.

Christ. Britta really has been insufferable. Hasn't she?

"*Super* tough," Avery says, none the wiser. "I've never even seen him cry. Not once. Not even when Mrs. Spalding gets super angry when he goofs off in science and she screams and sends him to the principal's office." She leans against Britta's free arm. "His mom's right, though. He's probably crying now."

Britta's own eyes well up, but she wipes them before her daughter can see. She looks past the couch, her sleeping husband, past Spencer and Romer, into the darkness of the cellar's storage area. She pictures Liz, Padma, and Mabel again, hiding from her in the wine stacks. Trading secrets. Gossiping about her marriage troubles, her missteps. Scheming how to steal her things and leave Britta and the rest of them high and dry.

But that's not the real story. She knows that. As much as she's been trying to keep them safe, she's betrayed them. She's used them all too. Been busy "controlling the narrative," whatever the hell that means anymore. If tonight has shown her anything, it's that there's no such thing as control, no such thing even as fairness, and that whatever she's been dealing with down here, those three women all have it far, far worse. Padma, with mastitis, separated from her new baby, for Christ's sake. Liz's kids are with a stranger. And Mabel . . .

Britta still can't believe it. How could Mabel hold down such a secret, such world-altering information, without being eaten alive?

Britta grabs Avery's arm and squeezes, suddenly desperate to remind herself of how lucky she is, despite it all. That she's literally surrounded by love right now.

"Ow," Avery whispers.

"Sorry, darling." Britta pauses. "You know . . . I've been wanting to talk to you."

"You have?" Avery asks quietly.

"I've been running around, focused on taking care of the guests . . . but I also should have been taking care of *you*. This all must be so scary for you." A flurry of platitudes she could offer as a tag, as empty assurance, scroll through Britta's mind. *It'll be okay. It's all right, darling. Don't worry.* She resists them, forcing herself to give Avery an honest answer again. "It's scary for me, too. But we are *together*. And I will do whatever it takes to make sure that tomorrow, that every tomorrow, is a better day."

Avery nods, scooting closer. She burrows her head beside Jane's in Britta's lap and whispers, "Can you help me fall asleep?"

"Of course." Britta sniffs, then begins to gently rub Avery's temples. "I used to do this when you were little. Do you remember?"

"I think so," Avery says, her tone already thick.

As Britta comforts Avery, she can't help but wonder if Mabel, Liz, and Padma will ever sleep again. Compare that to the men, who look so restful, so peaceful right now. What is it about their gender that allows them to prioritize basic needs, to shut out and promptly forget the world to recharge?

Then it hits her.

Britta sits up so suddenly from her realization that she worries she's jostled the kids, but Avery is almost out cold, mouth open like a frozen angel, just like the others.

Britta waits a few minutes more, to be sure. But now that the notion has struck her, time feels relentless. Joel's new EV. His keys. The masks. The garage.

She shifts, carefully, trying not to wake her dozing children. Surveying the scene, as much as she can in the dark. Romer hasn't stirred. Joel, still immobile, splayed across the couch. Spencer's chest is rising and falling, his snore incessant, his neck lolled against the chair's back.

And directly behind Spencer's chair—the refrigerator with the masks.

From this angle, she can just about see the tangle of oxygen masks inside the fridge's glass door.

Her breath turns ragged, as if she's already decided. As if they've caught her red-handed. She's made so many mistakes tonight, so many slipups, but this burst of an idea feels right, essential even.

Britta reaches for a pillow. With her other hand, she lifts Jane's head a few inches, then performs a mom version of an *Indiana Jones* rock-for-idol swap. Once she's cradled Jane's head, she carefully angles Avery onto the pillow's other corner. Britta grabs a blanket off the mound, balls it up, and slips it under Marco.

She creeps toward Spencer. Liz was right, regardless of what she was scheming to steal. *Asking* for the masks, and for the car—there's no way Joel would put it to a democratic vote, no way he'd just give away their only means of leaving, of finding help. Maybe Britta's being absurd, naïve, thinking that handing the same over to the women will lead to anything other than them driving to their deaths—that helping them will amount to more than keeping Britta, her kids, and the rest of this motley crew trapped in this house forever.

But the kids, the men, herself, *are* safe down here. They are, indeed, together and alive. As for Mabel, Liz, Padma—there are so many meanings of the word "survival," aren't there? So many ways to keep on breathing and die inside. She knows that intimately.

Britta inches closer to the fridge, holding her breath as she leans around Spencer. She imagines him waking up, pulling Joel's gun from a cowboy holster, shooting her—until she remembers that Romer took the bullets out.

She takes another shaky breath, reaches out, and carefully cracks open the door. She fishes for the masks' straps, and once she has them wrapped around her wrist, she lifts the devices without a sound, and gently presses the fridge door closed.

Slinking toward the couch, Britta assesses Joel's long, taut, perfect backside. There's a bulge in his back pocket. The right one, where he always keeps his keys.

She glances at Spencer again. In the dark, his jaw appears slack. Dead to the world. Romer too . . . are his eyes fluttering? No. He's asleep. Though she wonders, now, if he'd be on board, even proud of her, for trying to help these women. For attempting to craft a better story.

She inches along the couch's length, positioning herself beside Joel. Watching his back rise and fall to the rhythm of his dreams. Her pulse is a hummingbird now between her ears. She hovers her hand over his pocket. Carefully, slowly, so slowly, she slides her fingers inside and wraps them around the keys. With a small tug, she frees the tangle from the pocket's fabric. Inches them out, so, so . . .

Free.

She grabs the keys with both hands, silencing their tinny jingle, and hurries around the couch.

"Wha . . ." She hears a dull voice.

Spencer.

Britta blinks but doesn't turn around.

"Hey," he says sleepily.

She has the sudden urge to spin and punch him in his fat mouth.

Instead, she heads for the doors.

"Hey, wait. What? Wait, are those—"

"Go back to sleep," she hisses, grabbing a door handle, flinging it open.

"Hey, wait, Britta, Joel, stop . . ."

Britta slips out of the sitting room, begins sprinting.

"Don't," Spencer shouts behind her. "Joel, she's . . . STOP!"

The commotion blooms behind her. Spencer tripping to stand. Joel waking. A fight, she can't be sure.

"Mabel?" she cries out, searching each alcove as she races down the corridor. "Mabel, please, answer me—!"

She spots the trio emerging from the wine racks ahead.

"Take them." Britta thrusts the keys into Liz's hands, the masks into Mabel's. "You need to go, right now, or you're never going to get the chance—"

Liz's eyes widen. "Oh my, oh crap—wait, Tom—"

"I'll tell him," Britta says firmly. "I promise, but it's now or never, seriously, GO!"

Mabel yanks her into a hug. Then Liz, Padma, and Mabel practically trip over one another on their way to the door.

"Thank you," Padma says over her shoulder. "I don't know how we'll ever thank you—"

"Go!"

They thrust open the cellar's main doors, fumbling with the keys, the masks. Britta hears the men behind her now, shouting, arguing, Spencer screaming. And Joel.

So many thoughts fly through her mind. *Was this the right move? Will they survive? There's going to be hell to pay* . . .

The worries fade as she watches her trio of guests making a break for it.

Perhaps she's more influential than she ever realized. All along.

CHAPTER

25

Liz

THEY FLY INTO the cellar corridor. Liz's head swimmy, her vision littered with stars. She's half convinced she fell asleep beside Tom, that she's trapped inside a lucid dream, but Mabel's sobs and Padma's shivering feel too real for dreams.

Reid. Callie. Home. Tom.

I'll tell him, I promise. What happens when Tom wakes up to find she's gone? Will he understand? Why she left? *Wouldn't he want her to go?*

The three women race past the Harris-Ches' shadowed Equinox-sized workout room, past the in-home movie theater. The cellar looks transformed, the earlier, glowing ambience of Britta's sconce-lit hallway now replaced with a long, pitch-back gangway. Only the narrow light from Padma's flashlight presses against the darkness like a second-rate lightsaber. When they reach the bottom of the steps, Liz stops. They need to regroup before going up there. Before going outside.

"Elephant in the room," she says quickly, "there're two masks and three of us." She peers over Mabel's shoulder, back down the hall. In the dark, it's impossible to tell if anyone's coming after them.

Padma says, "Meaning what? That we pass them round-robin style? Duck-duck-goose?"

"Honor system," Liz suggests quickly. "Count to fifty and then pass your mask to the person without it. Mabel to me, me to you, you to Mabel. Round and round all the way to the car." She hands a mask to each of them. "You two take them first. Let's go."

Mabel yanks Joel's Altitude Xtreme mask over her head without protest. Padma shudders as she pulls on the full-face, war movie–looking contraption, then shines her flashlight up the stairs.

When they reach the last step, Liz takes a huge breath and holds it. Though maybe she should have been holding her breath this whole time. Maybe the glimmer is in the house, lurking in the cellar, and it's only moments before her skin erupts into lightning.

Liz shakes off the ghastly thoughts as they push through the door and into the kitchen. She gets the sudden sensation of letting go, becoming caught in a current, and floating fast away from the shore.

Are Mabel and Padma still counting?

They pass the French doors where they first saw Mrs. Ford. Then into the back hall, past the family room, the playroom.

Liz's chest is burning now. She tries to imagine Callie's smile to distract her, Reid's eyes crinkling with mischief. The way the kids would tear into their bedroom on a Saturday and flop onto the bottom of the bed . . .

As they cross the mudroom's threshold, Mabel hands her the mask.

Liz thrusts it over her head. Then settles into a deep, shaky breath.

One, two, three . . .

They reach the door to the garage. Mabel holds up the keys. They never decided who's driving, did they? Is Mabel fast? Could Padma drive across a street of dead deer if she needed to?

Eight, nine, ten, eleven . . .

Mabel thrusts the keys into Liz's hand. Then she pushes open the door, with puffed-out, cartoonish cheeks—what an unnecessarily dramatic way to hold your breath, Liz thinks absently—into the dank air of the garage, which is at least twenty degrees cooler than the rest of the house.

Twenty, twenty-one, twenty-two . . .

Liz slinks into the garage, bracing for one of them to seize up, start convulsing. Waiting for the glimmer to come sizzling out of the crack underneath the garage door.

But no. They are all okay.

For now.

She points the key fob at the Westa and the car's headlights cheerily blink in response.

Thirty, thirty-one . . .

Liz slides into the driver's side, while Padma climbs into the back. Mabel, meanwhile, has manually heaved the Harris-Ches' garage door open and is now climbing into the car's front seat. She moves a dead iPad from the shotgun seat to the floor.

Forty-three, forty-four . . .

After they close the car doors, the inside becomes washed in glamorous, comforting tech-blue.

Padma leans forward, dusting off a strange constellation of blue-white dust on the console. She says, muffled through her mask, "What is this, baby powder?"

"That's fifty." Liz takes one last breath, pulls off her mask, and hands it to Mabel.

Mabel yanks it on as she fiddles with the dashboard buttons. "I know cars," she finally says to Liz, gesturing to the virtual gearshift. "My dad was a mechanic. I figured you'd drive while I manage the biodefense system."

Liz nods and puts the car in reverse.

As if this were just any old day. A carpool to a PTA meeting.

They are leaving.

They are actually *leaving* the Harris-Ches'.

Padma drops her mask into Liz's lap.

Liz tugs it on. In a nightmare, a movie, a *Skyfall* episode, all it would take is one tiny mistake to send the entire narrative off-course—a strange look, a wrongly dismantled bomb, a misdialed number. There's no bandwidth for that tonight. No room for error.

Liz cautiously, carefully eases the car out of the garage.

As she does, a whooshing sound, like a captured wind tunnel, overtakes the interior.

Mabel gives an endearingly cheesy thumbs-up. "Biodefense is on!"

Liz swings the car around the Harris-Ches' circular drive. Biodefense. Gas masks. Contaminated air. A contagious pathogen. Extraterrestrial. Electrical. Manufactured. Climate fallout. It's terrifying because they don't know what the glimmer is, no one does, maybe no one ever will. Liz has never felt it so palpably: maybe there is no guiding, goodwill "force." Maybe each of them, all of them, are expendable, a blink, just minuscule specks on an evolving rock hurtling through space, far from in control of anything. But that still doesn't change that everything in her being pounds the same names, screams in the same direction, pleads for just one more day with Reid and Callie, one moment, even just a goodbye. So imperatively simple now. She presses the car into drive and steers past Mrs. Ford's abandoned Nissan, still parked near the walkway, and around the Harris-Ches' lush traffic island of birch trees and flower beds.

Mabel passes her mask back to Padma, who tugs it on and leans forward, meeting Liz's eyes through the rearview mirror. "Do you see the glimmer?" Padma asks. "Any lightning? Or any 'murderous Christmas trees'?"

Liz shakes her head as the Westa's headlights roam the property, casting sallow, ghostly shadows across the front yard. The sky is tame in comparison to the last time they were outside, deep gray and bloated, even though it's midmorning. The car's clock reads 11:17 AM. It's quiet, Liz realizes. Almost too quiet. "The strange noise," Liz says. "The crickets, chimes. It's gone."

"Does that mean the glimmer's gone too? That we're safe?" Padma says, "I mean, as s-safe as possible, safe enough, to breathe, w-whatever. I can't stand this. The suspense is killing me." She takes a few calming, audible breaths . . . and then yanks off her mask.

Liz and Mabel both spin around.

"Padma!" Liz blurts out.

"I'm . . . I'm okay." Padma's face breaks into a slow smile. "Still ticking. At least for now."

Mabel cautiously lets out the air she's been holding onto. "This has to be a good sign, yes? This has to—"

But the rest of her words hiccup into a gasp as they round the drive.

Little Falls Road looks like a *Skyfall* set torn apart. Cars are everywhere: abandoned in the middle of the road, their doors flapping open like the entrances to haunted homes. Bodies litter the street. Human and animal. There are countless birds, deer, vermin, and dog carcasses splayed out across the concrete like a grotesque jigsaw puzzle.

Bile swims up her throat. There are no lights at all now, down the street. *Because the town shut off electricity*, Liz remembers, though she can't help but think it's more than that. The lack of movement and life feels as complete and absolute as a black hole.

"Look at the sky," Mabel says.

Liz cranes her neck, peering through the front window. She can't see and realizes she's still wearing the mask.

She rips it off fast as a Band-Aid, and the night takes on an immediate high-def quality. A horizon of paper-house cutouts. Dark, forested hills in the distance. The sky streaky, almost singed, with noticeable black, ashen lines staining the gray morning, like a film negative of an airplane advertising parade.

"Could this mean it's over?" Padma whispers.

"I think this is far from over," Liz says.

She inches the car forward again, trying to avoid the bodies in the street, angling around the other cars. Perverse hopscotch. But the Westa's tires moan and grate, then stop altogether.

She presses the gas harder, and the tires spin underneath, a gross, whizzing sound. *Are they even on the ground?*

The car comes crashing down in an instant. Then a crunching, creaking noise.

Liz flinches.

"Ohmigod." Padma gags. "W-was that what I think it was?"

Liz puts her hand over her mouth, takes a shuddering breath, then turns the wheels. She pumps the accelerator, but the tires don't budge.

Mabel grips her seat. "Do I want to know what we're stuck on?"

Liz throws the car into park and angles over the dashboard to see. She spots a pair of legs, denim, the edges of a floral top—

Liz sits down and dry heaves. "No."

"How are we going to drive home through this?" Padma says.

As Liz rests her head on the seat's back, the sidewalk comes into view, specifically Mrs. Ford's mailbox, and the little hill of grass between her property and the Harris-Ches' yard. The Fords' beautiful white Victorian looks abandoned, desolate, its long ornate windows somber as coffins. If she tries, she can imagine Mrs. Ford in one of those windows, last night, still flashing notes about leaving for their kids . . .

Liz sits up suddenly.

Mrs. Ford had said she wanted to drive "*out back.*"

That's right. Mrs. Ford had been planning to drive *through* Falls Lane—she'd said so in her notes, unequivocally. Which means that Mrs. Ford somehow believed she could drive *across* her yard.

"We can try Falls Lane."

"S-sure." Padma gives a disbelieving little laugh. "A car this pricey probably has a t-teleportation device—"

"No, Britta's neighbor, Mrs. Ford, before she died, I—" Liz collects herself. "We were . . . communicating when everything first went down. She'd mentioned that her yard backs up directly to Falls Lane. That we could drive across their lawn to get there, that it might be easier."

"We might crash the car doing that," Mabel says, "blow the tires."

Liz gestures down Little Falls Road. "Well, this isn't a road. It's an obstacle course."

Mabel glances at Padma in the back seat.

Padma squawks out another laugh. "What do we have to lose?"

Liz taps the accelerator once more, trying to edge around another deer carcass, the Westa's tires spinning and groaning as she angles toward the sidewalk. She steers around two trash cans lying on their sides, the mess of milk cartons, spoiled food, and newspaper spilling out of them like guts, then eases the car over a lumpy field of animal carnage that lies between the cans and the Fords' winding driveway. Liz can almost feel the wheels sigh, relax, as they hit the smooth cement.

"Okay," Padma exhales. "Okay, here we go."

Liz careens down the Fords' long drive, slinking around to a three-car garage tucked into the mansion's back pocket. The driveway abruptly dead ends into a wide, expansive, dark emerald yard bordered by thick fir trees that look like charcoal smudges against the gloomy gray daylight.

"How do you j-jump a curb," Padma says. "Fast or slow?"

"Theoretically, you come at the curb from the side," Mabel says. "But my real-life getaway car experience? Quite limited."

Liz rides the brakes for a moment, shutting her eyes, trying to envision her old *Skyfall* set—the special effects and stunts she'd catch when she'd get to watch filming, when she finally saw the magic of her words made manifest. Well, not *her* words, the *team's* words, watered down and swapped and layered so that they belonged to all of them and none of them. There was an episode in the second season, wasn't there, where the main characters Bo and Everly were in a car chase fleeing a pair of burning-rain mutants?

"You're right," Liz says, "and it needs to be fast."

No one disagrees. Liz reverses, angling the Westa so that its back tire is almost parallel to the side yard. Over the Westa's whirring biodefense system, Liz's heart roars louder than a freight train.

"Go for it," Padma whispers.

Liz presses drive, then slams on the accelerator and the car flies forward, straight for the corner of the Fords' home. As they approach the garage, Liz yanks the steering wheel right, and the car's tires screech. The Westa rumbles onto the grass, bumping and jostling and sending Liz smacking into the driver's seat window.

Mabel grips the dashboard. "Holy Mother, oh my Lord, you did it—"

"Yassss!" Padma gives Liz's head a congratulatory ruffle. "Go, go, fucking go!"

They bump over the grass, pass a shadowy swing set on the right, then a row of orderly flower beds lining the perimeter of the Fords' expansive yard. The back edge of the property, also lined with thick evergreens, looms closer. Liz still can't see a road behind it. But she has to believe their escape route is right behind that thicket of trees. Waiting for them, like a secret magic portal.

"Slow and steady now," Mabel says. "Can't risk a fast impact cracking or shattering the glass."

Liz eases up on the accelerator and spots a sliver of an opening between two trees. They'll wedge inside there. She grips the steering wheel tight as a talisman. Go. Go, go, go. As they steer into the evergreens, Liz drives even slower. There's a cloying, groaning sound as the branches slide against the

Westa's metal body, a tug-of-war as the car wrangles with the foliage. Then, finally, a release.

They're staring at a desolate, narrow road.

She tries to catch her breath as she looks around. Mabel's fine, clutching her pearls, yes, and looking a bit like she's about to have an aneurysm, but safe. Padma, too, is in one piece in the rearview, slick with sweat, mouth a wide *O*.

Liz slowly presses the pedal again, and they start down Falls Lane.

Mrs. Ford's escape plan did them a solid. Liz can see that now. If her sense of town direction is correct—which after nearly two years, is still a big "if"—this back road will eventually wind them down to the elementary school. Moreover, no one actually appears to *live* on Falls Lane. The street is a slew of large, open plots of land. On the left, cleared rolling hills; on the right, a half-acre of woods. Farther down the road, several smaller lots are marked with LAND FOR SALE signs. Only when they're halfway down the lane do the undeveloped plots of land give way to actual, fully finished homes—all of them cookie-cutters of one another—with slated roofs and copper finishes gleaming gold in the dark morning. *New builds.* The Falls is full of them, the town exploding in the past decade as its high school climbed to the top of Jersey's rankings. Hordes of city transplants came pouring in, particularly during and after the pandemic, Liz and Tom right along with the rest of them.

How quaint it all seems to her now, the "suburbs," with their rectangular lawns and model homes and social clubs. The experience of raising your kids alongside hundreds, thousands, of other people doing the exact same thing.

Is it possible for Liz to miss something she never really had?

Never even really wanted?

"Take a right on Prospect Road," Padma says from the back. "That'll take us around to the school. Then we can follow Hobart right out to Old Falls Road."

"Assuming those main roads are even drivable," Mabel says.

"They better be." Liz makes a right.

Prospect Road, though, quickly reveals itself to be a mess as well. The street is peppered with smashed cars, fallen victims, homes with open garages and front doors flapping in the wind. But Liz notices right away . . . there are no deer. No sea of vermin across the concrete, unlike Britta and Joel's road, which sits overlooking the town's natural reserve.

They wind around, toward the school. Liz spots the building's boxy silhouette, its large empty front parking lot. She can practically taste Old Falls Road in the distance. So close now, like a beacon, a shore calling to their makeshift little ship. She cries when the school's playground comes into view. Big, messy sobs. It feels so possible now, even inevitable: Liz is going home.

They approach the school's parking lot just as searing white headlights come flailing around the corner.

Liz shields her eyes. "What the—"

A roaring engine drowns her out. The shocking shriek of brakes.

Padma moans. "Those lights are giving me vertigo."

"Who on earth is on the road?" Mabel looks at Liz. "The police?"

Liz blinks furiously.

Her eyes adjust to find a dark green Hummer parked at an angle in the center of Prospect Road. Definitely not the police. In the front sit two men, by the appearance of their builds. The pair are donning serious-looking gas masks that make them look like a team of patrolling aliens. There's at least one more person in the back, holding some object that Liz can't quite make out.

Padma shields her eyes as she leans forward on the console. "That's Campbell's car."

"*Damon Campbell?*" Mabel says. "How can you be sure?"

"From carline. I'd know it anywhere." Padma points at the front window. "Look at the front vanity plate. MAJRDAD."

"Okay." Mabel relaxes. "But, wait . . . what are they doing riding around?"

Liz sinks back into her seat. This weird development should bring her some comfort. She knows Damon Campbell, his family—vaguely, but still.

Instead, a weary uneasiness creeps around her shoulders.

Damon's front passenger rolls down his window. The man sticks out a megaphone. "THE FALLS IS UNDER LOCKDOWN," he booms. "NO ONE'S ALLOWED ON THE STREETS. RETURN TO YOUR HOMES IMMEDIATELY."

Then Damon gives a flicker of his high beams for good measure.

No. No, not when they're so close. They don't have time for this macho-man garbage! Liz unbuckles her seat belt and climbs forward, pressing her face toward the window so they can see her better. She waves, pointing adamantly down the road, in the hopes that he gets the gist: *Going home; get out of our way.*

"BY THE ORDER OF TOWN, STATE, AND COUNTRY, TURN AROUND AND TAKE SANCTUARY."

"This is garbage," Padma says. "They don't have any authority to stop us!"

Mabel adds, "Liz, it's pretty dark. Cut the lights so they can see us better."

Liz does so, then repositions herself against the front window. She waves Mabel and Padma forward to join. It's obvious, isn't it? Three women, sans children and families, on the road after everything that's transpired—the story tells itself.

But these meatheads aren't understanding, or else aren't seeing them, don't want to, because the megaphone booms again. "THE GLIMMER IS AN INTERNATIONAL THREAT TO OUR CIVILIZATION. YOU ARE RISKING LIFE AND LIMB AND COMPROMISING

COVERT EFFORTS TO COMBAT THE THREAT BY BEING ON THE ROAD."

Mabel echoes, "Covert . . . efforts . . . ?"

"Campbell's such a m-megalomaniac," Padma mutters. "This isn't some government-blessed citizens' army. It's him and his dad friends playing cops and robbers." She wipes her glistening brow. "What I'd give for a megaphone to scream back."

"You're right," Liz says. "We just need to make him hear us, understand." She rifles through her tote until she finds what she's looking for—the remaining construction paper and markers she swiped from the Harris-Ches' playroom. Where to start? How does she distill tonight into micro-fiction?

She dashes the facts onto two pieces of paper, and climbs onto the dashboard again, shielding her eyes from the lights. She slaps her notes against the front window.

> We are moms from town.
> Separated from kids.

> Found safe way home.
> Please let us pass.

Liz waits, the moment breaking open, hatching an eternity. *Come on, you assholes.*

There's no cutting of the Hummer's lights. No acknowledgment from the megaphone.

Padma groans. "Shake the papers, Liz."

The Hummer's front passenger steps outside. His mask looks like a prop from a sci-fi film. Wide, dark goggle lenses, air chambers like black lungs on the sides. He raises the megaphone. "AERIAL COUNTERATTACKS ARE

PROCEEDING AT NOON BY DRONES. ALL STREETS MUST BE CLEARED. YOU ARE COMPROMISING THE SAFETY OF THE NEIGHBORHOOD."

Padma whispers, "The fuck?"

The third masked man climbs out from the back and slams his door.

Liz finally recognizes the object in his hand for what it is.

"Oh, Mother Mary," Mabel whispers.

But Liz has gone numb.

The third man raises the rifle.

"Drive," Padma pleads, "Liz, they're crazy, just drive!"

Liz presses the car into reverse, steps hard and screeches backward and into the school's parking lot.

"WAIT FOR US TO ESCORT YOU HOME. THE STREETS ARE NOT SAFE."

Liz turns the car on a hairpin and careens back down Prospect Road, retreating in the direction they came from. She glares at the rearview. Behind them, Megaphone-Dude and Rifle-Man are scrambling into Damon's Hummer, hopping in, slamming doors. The Hummer starts up and begins following them. Liz's ears roar like she's swallowed an ocean. "Obviously we need another cut-through," she says. "Do either of you know this area well? If they cut off Prospect, we need another way across town—"

Mabel glances over her shoulder. "And they're still behind us."

"I say stick with the plan. What are they going to do, *shoot us*?" Padma says. "They don't know where we live; we should just keep going—"

"And what happens when we get to my house?" Liz asks. "You think these delusional GI Joes are going to let you and Mabel carpool home in peace while they try to save the neighborhood?"

"*Your* house?" Padma asks.

Liz looks at her, confused.

Padma shrugs. "I didn't realize we'd decided your house was our first stop."

Liz's cheeks warm. "I . . . was just offering a hypothetical."

The megaphone booms: "MAINTAIN SPEED LIMITS."

Liz white-knuckles the wheel. "This isn't happening. I'm not going back to that cellar."

"Take a right!" Padma sputters.

"What—"

"Trust me, just do it, Liz!"

Liz does as she's told again.

"DRIVE SLOWLY!"

The Westa's wheels whine in protest as Liz makes a sharp turn onto an unfamiliar street lined with dark, manicured mansions, large plots. There are cars abandoned all down the way, vermin clumped under trees like grotesque puddles. But the street is still clearer than the Harris-Ches'. Cluttered, yes, but traversable.

Liz meets Padma's eyes through the rearview.

"This is Hobart," Padma says evenly. "It loops back down to the school, where there's a back lot that connects with the school's front drop-off lot."

"Meaning you think we can lose them?" Liz says, piecing it together.

Mabel looks back and forth between them. "*What?*"

Liz shifts her hands into ten-two position on the wheel, racecar driver style, heart all-out revving now.

She peeks back at Damon's car. "The car's silent. We might take them by surprise, if I drive fast enough . . ."

Mabel presses her back against the seat. "Oh, Lord."

Padma nods. "They won't hear us if we break away. And without the lights . . ."

Liz finishes, "They can't track us."

Mabel does a quick sign of the cross. "Just tell me when it's over."

Hobart Road is a minefield of obstacles, so Liz will need to stay alert, play it safe, keep to the center of the street. In a minute, though, the rows of homes give way to the empty expanse of the school's back parking lot. Just as Padma promised.

Behind them, Damon's car booms: "SLOW DOWN. STAY SAFE."

Liz's hands are shaking as they approach the elementary school, the white-hot light of Damon's headlights shimmering off her rearview. She takes a breath and, with a sudden jerk, turns the wheel, careening into the empty parking lot.

The megaphone: "I REPEAT, SLOW DOWN."

But Liz floors the accelerator. The Westa sails across the asphalt. She follows the dips and curves of the lot, past the empty windows of the school, until they are back around, facing Prospect.

The megaphone: "STOP!"

But Liz has tapped into another fuel source, pure adrenaline, a repository culled from B-movies, 1990s heroes, scraps of *Skyfall* script left on the cutting room floor. *Be the car chase.* She takes a sharp right. The Westa revs in response and sails forward, back down Prospect Road.

"Wait, why are we going back the way we came?" Mabel thrusts her hand onto the console to steady herself.

Liz says, "We can't outrun them. We need to *lose* them!"

The megaphone: "SLOW DOWN, OR YOU'LL FORCE US TO TAKE ADDITIONAL MEASURES!"

Liz steals another glance at the Hummer, its thick lights blinding, piercing against the glass. But she knows which areas to avoid now driving down Prospect this second time: the toppled trash cans on the right, the family of victims near the curb, down the road, on the left. They glide, soundless, toward the Prospect-Hobart intersection.

"You going for it this time?" Padma asks.

Liz nods. "Now or never."

Mabel throws her head back against the seat rest, holding her pearls like a rosary. "Holy Father and Son and all the saints, give us horsepower, give us strength . . ."

Liz cuts the wheel hard onto Hobart, then floors it.

The megaphone roars a series of flustered curses.

They fly straight down the middle of Hobart, toward the school's back lot. She nearly forgets to cut the lights.

"STOP, THAT'S AN ORDER!"

The first gunshot rips through the air like a crack of thunder.

Mabel whips her head around. "Oh my Lord, they actually are shooting at us!"

"Jesus, Mabel, duck, don't look back!" Liz cries. She slams harder on the accelerator. The speedometer jumps to sixty miles per hour. Seventy. Seventy-five.

Another hungry *POP* from the rifle. Another. The sound of the Hummer's screeching tires.

"Hold on!" Liz makes a hard, Formula One–worthy turn into the school back lot, but this time, instead of following the lot's curves around toward the right side of the school and the drop-off line area, she veers left. There's a tearing, ghastly sound of metal on metal as Liz wrenches the wheel and the car angrily bumps over the paved sidewalk, past the bike racks and playground. They fly over the curb and around the front of the school as shots keep ringing out—*POP, POP, POP!* Liz clutches the wheel as they head past the entrance, then makes a hard bumpy left onto Prospect Road.

"Go," Padma says from the back. "Go, Liz, just go!"

Liz speeds down Prospect Road, swerving around a family of fallen deer, bumping over dead squirrels, around cars. *Reid and Callie. Reid and Callie.*

She risks another look in the rearview mirror, but this time the Hummer's headlights aren't there.

They race across Old Falls Road, which is abandoned, dark, not a soul in sight. Liz imagines them gliding over dark water, into an uncharted sea, breaking out into the unknown. Freedom. She takes a hard left and then another right, sliding into a side street off Old Falls Road.

She bumps into the first empty driveway. Waiting. Watching. Listening for more shots.

"Do you hear anything?" Padma asks.

"No." Liz looks wildly to Mabel for confirmation. "You?" But a soft ping answers.

"What was that?" Mabel says. "The dashboard . . ."

Confused, Liz looks around until she finds its source too.

A small virtual replica of the car has blinked into existence on the right side of the car's tech board, along with pressure readings for the four wheels.

The top right tire gauge is free-falling.

39, 36, 33, 29 . . .

"No," she whispers.

"What is it?" Padma says. "Is it the air system?"

"The tire," Mabel says numbly. "We blew a tire."

Padma lets out a muffled sob. "Okay. Okay, we'll just have to change it." She angles around to fold down the back seat and to get at the trunk.

Liz slams her head against the headrest. This can't be happening. Not like this, not after everything they've been through at the Harris-Ches. Not when they are *sitting* in a car on Old Falls Road.

She opens her eyes to find Padma's weary gaze in the rearview.

Padma shakes her head. "There's no spare."

26

Mabel

L IZ FOLDS OVER the steering wheel and weeps.

Mabel—trying to breathe, trying not to fall apart—stares at the abandoned house at the top of the driveway. The panic is humming inside her, like an old friend by this point. It's crawling up her arms, her spine, rattling through her entire frame. Her heart's booming like a rifle inside her rib cage.

They are so close. Close enough that, any other day, Mabel could kick open her door and stroll the six blocks home, scoop Greg into her arms, have a good-natured laugh about the car trouble. *Nothing Mom and Grandpa can't fix, sweetheart.*

Liz wipes her eyes. "We can't sit here waiting for Damon to find us. We can drive on a flat tire."

"Not for long," Mabel says. "A mile tops, and that's a mile on a *flat* road, not, not . . . this."

Padma wilts as she peers out the side window. "This street might be as bad as Britta's."

"This is one of those rotary phone nightmares, the ones I'd have as a kid," Liz mumbles. "We just keep dialing, fingers fumbling, getting nowhere—"

"Wow." Padma stifles a sob. "What a well-timed, appropriate analogy."

Mabel turns. "Have to ask, are you a writer?"

"Because that's deep AF."

Liz lets out a stilted laugh. Then Padma laughs. And then Mabel can't help it. The night's iron hold on her heart loosens, just an inch, just enough for her to sink into the collective half-laughing, half-sobbing fit.

The little tire's air pressure on the dashboard keeps falling too.

Mabel rubs her eyes again. There must be another way. Six blocks home. There must be a fix—

"My garage," she blurts.

Liz looks up.

"There's a spare in our Acura," Mabel explains, "and I've changed plenty of tires before. My dad taught me when I was little. I hung around his shop all the time. I can do it. We can drive to my place. I'll wear the mask, change the tire, then you go on with Padma. She lives right down my road."

Mabel watches as Liz works it out in her head. "But . . ."

"Do either of *you* know how to change one?" Mabel says.

Padma snorts. "I don't even pump my own gas."

"So . . . we go to your house first," Liz repeats. "And wait as you, being a mere few feet away from your son, mercifully spend the time playing mechanic so that we can get home too?"

"Yes, that's what I said."

Liz studies the virtual car on the dashboard, biting her lip, as if debating. As if they have another choice.

"You still don't trust me, do you?" Mabel says incredulously.

"It's not that." Liz sighs. "I guess, well. I guess I don't really trust anyone. But maybe it's time to buck up."

Liz eases the car into reverse.

Mabel's heart keeps hammering, but with hope now, adrenaline, the allure of fixing things, of making things right. Her gorgeous, perfect Greg. The house. Her home. "Make the next right," she says. "Downton Lane. Then a left on Sulton. My house is third on the left."

Liz nods and gingerly steers the car around a BMW slammed into the curb.

Mabel glances at the passing driveway, the one right beyond the wreck. The Millers live there. She wonders if the car is theirs. Doug Miller could be sprawled out dead under the car, or on the sidewalk behind it for all she knows, just steps away from his door. This is her neighborhood, her safe place, reduced to ruin and rot. She and Spencer drove this very route to the pharmacy before going to the Harris-Ches—what, a day ago?—Spencer quietly seething at the wheel, calling her cruel, insisting that she was torturing him, that she was setting them up for *four hours* with Joel and Britta. "*If you hate me this much,*" he'd said so petulantly, "*then I guess it's over.*"

Of course it's over.

She wishes she could go back in time. Not to yesterday, or a year ago, but further, pre-Spencer days, discover who she used to be before she molded her identity around sacrifice. Around persecution. God's obviously not to blame for the decades she spent bending and shaping herself into a picture-perfect "saint." How much would she do differently, given the chance? What does she even enjoy besides taking care of people? Tinkering with engines? Cooking? Aren't those "pseudo-likes," adjacent hobbies that come with the territory of being a "helper"?

"Sulton?" Liz confirms.

"Indeed," she says absently.

A dizzying wave crashes over Mabel as they turn onto her road. The Chestons' house has five deer sprawled across their lawn. The Martins' car hugs their miniature-house-replica mailbox. Her own Cape Cod–inspired home is just moments away; she can see her red door, her curling front path, her blue shutters. Her heart leaps as she imagines Greg inside, tucked into his bed—no, *safe in the basement,* snuggled tight on their wrap-around couch, surrounded by all his favorite stuffies and blankets. Dreaming of her.

Her adrenaline has kicked into second gear now. This time she might well lift off.

"That's mine"—she points—"pull all the way down the drive."

Liz turns in.

Mabel half-expects to see ghosts in her windows. The reflection of Tammy in the kitchen, cleaning up. But there's no one on the first floor. *Good signs*, she reminds herself. *All good signs.*

Liz stops in front of Mabel's stand-alone two-car garage at the end of the drive.

"You two wait here." Mabel unclips her seat belt. "No power, remember? I'll open the garage manually. Once you pull inside, Liz, turn off the car and I'll change the tire."

As Liz nods, Mabel pulls the Rogue Training mask over her head. Like a reflex, she lapses into a prayer. She tries to make this one count, to choose the most important wish she's ever sent up to the heavens. *God, if you're out there, give me the strength to do this.*

Show me who I am.

As she reaches for the door, she turns around. "If something were to happen to me—"

"Mabel, don't you dare think like that," Padma says.

"We need to be pragmatic." Mabel sets her jaw. "I need you to swear on your life that you will both look after Greg. That you'll make sure he has everything he needs if we—if the world ever gets up after this."

Padma reaches across the console for her hand. "Friend. You're going to be fine."

Liz nods. "But you have our word."

Mabel wipes her tears, repositions her mask. Then, before she can doubt herself, second-guess, slow down, she kicks open the Westa's door and slams it behind her.

The April air is breath-stealingly brisk and immediately prickles her skin. She left her trench coat in Britta's foyer closet, didn't she? No matter. She'll get warm from the work.

She bends in front of the garage and slots her key into its lock. *Click, turn, release.* Then grabs the door and yanks the heavy gate upward, like a rumbling, widening monster's jaw.

Mabel can hear her own breath, shaky and amplified inside her mask, as Liz eases the Westa into their empty car spot.

She hurries across the garage and opens her Acura's driver-side door, then presses the button to release the trunk. Once open, she lifts the trunk's flap and reveals the small, sunken spare tire inside.

She grabs the tire with two hands, lifts it with a groan, and wheels it around to the Westa's front. She stops, scanning the garage's shelving for their spare tire kit.

There.

Once the red toolbox is in hand, she sets to work.

From this angle, the Westa's flat tire looks like love handles spilling over a waistline, bloated rubber oozing onto the garage floor.

She loosens the lug nuts. *Show me who I am.* Oddly, her prayers have been answered in a way, because this feels so familiar, kneeling in front of a tire, or over an engine, with her dad. Repairing things. She was always her father's best pupil. She has two older brothers, and yet Mabel was always the one at her dad's shop after school—his right-hand handywoman, his fixer.

Mabel groans as she cranks the jack.

Maybe Padma was right in that cellar. Maybe Mabel's the person who stays, who tries to repair things, who doesn't walk away because it's in her constitution, always has been.

She imagines her son again as she unscrews the lug nuts. She pictures Greg sitting beside her, watching her. How would she explain tonight? What would she teach him, if it were Greg and her here, just like she used to be with her dad?

She pulls the tire off, grease smearing across her dress's peacock pattern. As she lines up the spare's rim with the lug bolts, she listens to the absence of noise coming from the car, the loaded silence, Liz and Padma waiting, counting on her. She smiles at imaginary Greg, at him witnessing her attempts to save these women, to save their families. And, really, maybe she's been expecting too much from God. Maybe all he can do is give them tools. He was probably lonely at the beginning. Perhaps he designed a fix for himself, a deceptively simple universe. One where the only way to survive is to connect and hold on together.

She lowers the jack, groans as she pushes on the lug wrench, tightening the nuts.

She catches her distorted reflection in the hubcap.

If she ever gets another chance, she'll set about saving herself.

She sweeps the tools back into the kit, dropping the box onto the shelf where she found it. When she rounds the car and peers into Liz's window, Liz is holding her breath, looking up at Mabel, lips pressed thin and eyes wide.

"It's done," Mabel says.

Liz thrusts a celebratory fist into the air, then waves Mabel into the back.

Padma scoots over as Mabel slides inside. "It might be an uneven ride," she explains, "but it should work. At least to Padma's and your place, Liz."

"You're amazing," Padma says. "Go on, Liz, try it, turn it on."

Liz nods, giving a little squeal of relief when the dashboard tells a better story. "Thank you. I don't know how we'll ever thank you." She angles around her seat and grabs Mabel's hand. "Do you want us to wait here? Or drive you closer to the back door? We want to make sure you get inside—"

"That's unnecessary."

Liz squawks a laugh. Then her face falls when she sees Mabel's serious. "No more martyr stuff, Mabel. We're not just driving away and leaving you—"

"I'm not, I'm . . . I need to do this my way, all right?" She steals a breath. "The most important thing is getting

Greg his inhaler. The next steps I . . . I just need time to figure out."

She looks back to her house, her sprawling backyard, the colorful flower beds appearing almost neon under the gloomy sky, and adds softly, "If Greg knows I'm out here, he'll run outside; I know he will. If I sneak inside . . . who knows, maybe I somehow bring the glimmer in."

Mabel straightens. "Just stay until I make sure they're inside, okay?" She leans over the console and grabs her purse from the passenger well, fishing until her fingers wrap around Greg's prescription bag.

Liz and Padma exchange an unmissable "look" through the rearview, but they don't argue with her. Suddenly, Mabel's need for them to go feels imperious, intense, like an ache. Like another panic attack coming on, but she can't sit here in the Westa's back seat and weather the storm. No, she needs to get to that mail slot. Plus, she won't have Liz and Padma trapped here, taking care of *her*—she can't do that to them.

"I'm not changing my mind," Mabel says. "If you're trying to play chicken with me, we're going to crash."

Liz sighs. She turns and slowly, carefully, reverses.

Mabel's breath hitches. It's working. They're driving on the spare. The Westa inches backward down her drive and toward her front door, but her mind keeps revving, racing through all the twists and turns of tonight, the still upcoming course. "Liz, do you have any paper left?"

Mabel roots through the messy, overstuffed tote bag Liz hands her, finally finding what she needs as the car reaches her front walkway. "Here," Mabel says. "Right here is fine."

"We'll find you." Liz turns. "After everything . . . we'll find each other."

Mabel puts one hand on Liz's shoulder, and her other on Padma's, "I know," she says. "Now hold your breath."

Mabel adjusts her mask, then bursts out of the car, sprinting straight to her front porch, taking the stairs two at a time.

She opens the metal mail slot, jams Greg's asthma prescription inside the little door, and then turns and gives the women a manic thumbs up.

Mabel hurries around her side yard, looking for the basement's sunken windows. She dashes through her manicured tulip beds, daffodils, calla lilies, and stops when she spots the small window on the backside of the house.

She falls to her knees, crawls forward, and presses her masked face to the glass.

The basement looks so devastatingly dark. A deep pit. The path to perdition. Mabel's arms are full-on numb now. She scans the dark room wildly. Did Tammy do right by her?

Are they upstairs?

Could they be gone?

Then slowly, forms take shape out of the dark. Little life rafts emerging out of a shadowed, sunken sea. Two bodies strewn across a wrap-around couch, toe to toe.

Mabel blinks harder, looks closer.

Oh Lord, there they are, her father-in-law, snoring; she can see his belly rising and falling from here. Tammy's sprawled body, alone . . . no, *not* alone . . . wrapped around a smaller one. Greg, sleeping, curled around his old Lightning McQueen stuffie.

The relief, the elation, it explodes like fireworks inside her, exuberant, spectacular, almost blinding. Below, Greg shifts on the couch—*is he sleeping? Has he been up all night, worrying?*—and rubs his eyes, as if he can't quite believe what he's seeing in his dreams.

Alive.

He's alive.

She turns away from the window and crumbles. "Thank you. Just thank you."

Mabel dislodges Liz's paper and pen, and scrawls a quick series of notes, trying to fit everything she needs to say—a love letter to her son, the world, her gratitude—onto a single piece of construction paper.

> *It's Mabel (Mom)*
>
> *Greg's medicine in mail slot*
>
> *I love you Greg*
>
> *I hope to see you very soon*

She holds the sheet against the window, wedging the note flat against the glass, then secures the page with a few large stones from her flower beds.

She collapses back, beaming, crying, still euphoric. Then she remembers Liz and Padma. What is she thinking, not sending them off?

She runs around the side yard again, spots the Westa on the street and gives another thumbs up. Then, when the car doesn't move, an exaggerated wave goodbye. She's soon reduced to a flagman in a car race, shooing them away, gesticulating down the road.

The Westa's headlights finally disappear, leaving her yard an eerie field of gray in the strange morning light. She tries not to look back, to instead think through her next moves, step by step. Her side entrance opens to an enclosed breezeway. That's her safest bet. She can wait in there for a little while, make sure she isn't contaminated herself before going downstairs—

Mabel stops.

The skyline.

She blinks.

Something is moving on the horizon. No, the horizon *itself* is moving, like dark storm clouds. Black lightning. The glimmer. She can see the advancing darkness through the branches of the oak trees in her yard.

Mabel stumbles back, heart now rallying between her ears.

The darkness seems to shift and crystallize into tiny forms, hundreds of flying satellites. Strange, advancing predators. It doesn't look like the glimmer, at least the last time she saw it, out on Little Falls Road—that menacing light show of shimmering, explosive color—but it's coming for her all the same. Advancing. An ominous, hungry army.

Her pulse is a rocket now, her arms numb, heart crawling up her chest. The oak trees go hazy. The world slides out of focus . . .

She falls to her knees. Her chest can't contain the knocking, the pounding, and it's spreading down her arms. *Just panic*, a voice whispers, and she fumbles with her purse before remembering anew that she never got her medicine. Her mask is so fogged now, she can no longer see the sky.

Breathe. She stumbles forward, lands face first on her lawn, smells cut grass, and a faint undercurrent of something choking, cloying.

Just breathe.

But her chest keeps tightening. Like a noose, as if someone is pressing her inside a casket. So close, but so far. All of life's tiny moments flash before her again. Britta's cellar. The sconce lights shimmering across the wine bottles. The freckles on Greg's nose crinkling when he laughs, Spencer humming as he makes waffles in the kitchen. Mabel's father, hands smeared with oil, Phil Collins playing on low . . .

"Thank you," she whispers again, closing her eyes.

The world folds inward, collapsing, until she feels two rough hands, like those from a disgruntled angel, grabbing her by the armpits. *Hold on*, she thinks. *Hold on together.*

"Get up," a familiar voice shouts. "The air combatants, the drones, it's noon, come on, get up, get inside!"

27

Padma

PADMA WATCHES, ANXIOUS and freezing in the back seat, as Liz and Mabel hobble together across Mabel's lawn. Thank goodness. Thank freaking goodness. Liz was right; to hell with what Mabel wanted, they couldn't just leave her.

Padma slides onto the console for a better view, and sees Liz ushering Mabel toward her home's side door. They're arguing about something, both waving their hands. Then the women change positions, moving so that Padma can no longer see them . . . *did Mabel get inside*?

In moments, Liz is sprinting back toward the car.

Liz collapses into the driver's seat, tossing the other mask into Padma's lap.

"Wha—"

"Even during a panic attack in the backyard, Mabel insisted," Liz says. "Payback for 'saving her life.'" Liz shifts the car into drive. "She held her breath all the way into her breezeway. She's inside."

Liz screeches away from the curb.

The sky is littered now with a full-blown army, a field of small, advancing drones of combatants or chemicals or whatever the town believes may possibly end the glimmer.

Somehow, though, the drones make things feel bleaker. So, instead, Padma focuses on the road, the car, her own house, just a few doors away now. Dev and Isobel are so close. Impossibly close.

"Strange, isn't it?" Liz says tightly as they head down Mabel's street. "Driving with a spare. Like a boat tipped to one side."

"That's in your head," Padma says. "The perils of an active imagination."

In the rearview, a faint smirk ripples across Liz's face, like a fish in still water. "If you gave me a decade, I never could have imagined tonight."

Padma smiles. "Don't underestimate yourself."

The Westa's headlights flash across the street sign up ahead. *Parkview Lane*. Padma's street. Her head spins, dizzy with hope. "It's a left, here."

Liz flicks on her turning signal.

"Seriously?" Padma asks.

"Habit, I guess."

They pass the corner lot. Padma's gable metal roof shines in the distance. They're so close she can nearly hear Isobel's gurgles, that little hiccup-coo she makes in the middle of the night. So close she can almost see the shape, the shadow, of Future Isobel sprinting across her lawn.

"A part of me thought we were never getting out of that cellar." Padma shudders. The chills are coming on again, now that the last of Britta's Advil is wearing off. "A part of me really thought I deserved to be down there."

"Don't say that, Padma." Liz finds her eyes again through the mirror. "Listen. You're not guilty for missing something that's gone. For bucking change. It's not a crime to miss how your life was before the baby," she says. "It's too bad none of us ever want to show each other anything but having it all together."

Padma looks out the window, watching as the homes continue to slide past, as the horizon buzzes with advancing drones.

Liz is right. It started that first day in the hospital, didn't it? Hiding her terror, her anguish under cheap smiles and feigned mastery of the nursing "football hold." As soon as Isobel arrived, Padma bottled all her feelings of inadequacy; she hadn't even talked to her *mother* about it—her mother who'd taught her, shown her, her whole life that a good Indian wife keeps a spotless home, a happy family, with no complaints. Knowing Mama, she would have seen Padma's struggle as her *own* deficiency. What a different world it would be, could be, if she—if everyone—was taught to knock on each other's doors instead, asking for a little reprieve, or at least commiseration. What a different world if they expected the sharing of imperfections and mistakes. If people didn't curate out all the real stuff and allowed it to bind them together into something so much stronger.

Padma studies her hands. Should she be worried about opening her door? There's so much they still don't know, so many risks they could be taking without realizing. Until it's too late.

"When you found Mabel in the backyard," she ventures. "Was she scared about going inside? That she'd somehow let the glimmer in?"

"Maybe she was." Liz shakes her head. "But what are our alternatives? Waiting outside until this passes? What if it *never* passes?" She nods toward the car's front window, which showcases the drone-drenched sky. "Or what if, while we're waiting, we're poisoned by this 'solution'?"

"Isobel needs me."

"Just like *you* need medicine. Right now," Liz says. "You think you have some leftover antibiotics? Something you can take?"

"Told you, Dev's a pack rat. He throws nothing away. Though don't tell minimalist Clementine."

Two houses away. One. Liz steers around a crime scene of overturned garbage, a deer carcass splayed out like an offering in front.

"The next driveway," Padma whispers. "On the right."

Her chest is throbbing now. Expectation, longing, terror—a thick tangle sliding its way through her chest, up her throat.

Her house comes into full view. Padma's robin's egg–colored door, the dark windows. Her curved walkway bordered with the little pots of pansies she left for Dev to plant. Padma blinks, swearing she sees something else.

Someone. A shadow.

She blinks again. No. An apparition. Future Isobel, skirting around the hedges again . . . though the form suddenly looks different to her now, outside of the cellar.

More familiar.

Padma leans against the window as Liz pulls into the driveway. She watches the figment hurry around the yard and to her side door. Long dark hair, the slight build, sundress flapping in the wind . . .

The tangle lodges itself at the base of Padma's throat.

That isn't Future Isobel at all. Never was.

It's herself. Or how Padma used to be, younger, a girl. No, how she still *is*, buried somewhere, somehow. Confident, spritely, self-assured.

Padma rubs her eyes. Maybe all of them are seeing things tonight, unraveling, hallucinating. Or maybe there are truths in this world that can't be explained, that can't be neatly understood and analyzed. Maybe Padma's never been lost at all.

Or, like Liz said, maybe she's no more lost than anyone else.

She hugs Liz around the neck. "Find me when this is all over?"

Liz squeezes her arm. "I will."

Padma pulls on her mask, fingers shaking, shivering, her teeth chattering wildly now.

"Go," Liz says.

Padma kicks open the door, slides out, and runs, sprinting across the front yard and around to the side. Liz was right all along. What Padma would give for even the illusion of rules tonight. Black-and-white answers. Right and wrong.

She scans her yard and finds her figment self again, then follows the ghostly little girl, newly resolved.

The apparition won't steer her wrong. She feels it in her bones. The ghost's pull on her heart perhaps more fundamental, truer, than clear-cut answers.

She stops at the back door, meeting her reflection in the door's glass window.

Her long, dark, ragged hair curling at the bottom of her World War II–inspired mask. Her bedraggled, feathered bolero still draped across her shoulders.

Padma takes a deep, echoing breath.

She pulls her keys from her pocket and opens her door.

CHAPTER

28

Liz

PADMA SLIPS INSIDE the house.

Liz's turn. Reid. Callie.

Their names have been a compass, her North Stars, all night. Two little dreams. *Reid and Callie.*

She puts the car into reverse and slides back down Padma's driveway. The biodefense system keeps whooshing around her, so she takes off her mask to see better. The crowded sky comes into clearer focus, the advance of small black drones. She brushes the tears from her cheeks. *Stay calm.* She can't give in to the terror, the what-ifs, the worries. Not now. Not when she's this close.

She drives down Parkview, and around again to Mabel's road.

It's kind of terrifying, now, being alone, after having Padma and Mabel by her side for so long. She turns onto Downton Lane, steering around a flipped recycling bin in the middle of the street.

Finally, she reaches Old Falls Road.

For the first time on this mad dash, she allows herself to think about Tom. Britta will explain why she left, Liz believes that, but will he understand? Why she took the chance to run and didn't look back? Why she left without him? He told her to do whatever she could to get home, didn't he?

"If we survive this," she says aloud, pretending that he can hear her. "We're getting our second chance. We're going to be a team again." She swallows around the tightness in her throat and adds what she never got to say in the cellar, "Because I love you too."

So close now. Still so far. Liz slows the car as she approaches an ambulance tangled with an Audi on Old Falls' shoulder. There are forms inside the ambulance—victims maybe—but if she looks at the carnage, she might lose herself. If she looks, she might surrender.

"And I'm sorry," she tells Tom. "For doubting you. For everything."

Three blocks away, Mabel's spare tire is still holding strong. *Two.* Then Liz is turning onto her own road, edging down the well-worn path she's driven thousands of times without a second thought. The Khumurs' ancient oak tree twisting over the road like a future lawsuit. The Horaces' addition over the garage, mid-construction, an empty tractor still parked at the top of the drive. A smattering of cars docked along the road.

"*Please,*" she whispers. "*Please, please, please.*"

Her house emerges like a beacon. Dark and stately. Almost sinister in the day's gloomy glow. She swallows down her heart again and pulls into her driveway, lights off. The kids can't see the car approach. No, it would be a particular brand of torture to travel so far, battle the odds to get home, only to have Reid and Callie burst out the front door. If the glimmer is still here, simmering, waiting, around the horizon's bend.

Is it still here?

Liz pulls the car right up to the back door, her shaking hands jangling the keys from her tote.

She takes a huge, fortifying breath. Pulls on the mask. "Game time." She cuts the engine, kicks open the car door, and runs. No second-guessing. No overthinking. *Go.*

She unlocks her door, slipping inside, closing it soundlessly. She surveys their mudroom, the dark silence so thick it's suffocating. She flips the lights out of habit, then remembers the electricity's off. Did the glimmer follow her in? Is she carrying it on her clothes? All the theories, the news stories, accost her mind like a storm. *The glimmer might be contagious. The glimmer might travel by wire. By water. By air.*

Inside.

She starts moving again, refusing to let fear wind around her and pin her to the ground.

Liz slings her tote bag over her head and feels her way through the mudroom, into her kitchen, nerves singing, head so buzzy she's almost floating.

There's still no sign of the kids.

She heads toward the front entry and feels her way up the stairs. To the second floor. Into Reid's room. Preemptive grief grips her by the throat as she imagines him splayed out, tortured, dying, in his bed—

The room is empty.

She hurries across the hall to Callie's room, rummaging through her daughter's tousled covers, but she's mercifully not there.

Delirious hope crests over her shoulders, warm and thick as honey. *The basement. They must be downstairs.*

As she takes the steps down into the entry again, the other, far more terrifying possibility seizes her.

Unless they left.

Through the dining room's windows, she scans the backyard, the side grounds, but there's no sign of them outside; no coats are missing from the closet. She hurries through the basement door, panicked, electric, desperate to see them immediately, to process definitively if they're safe or gone, if she will live or break—

Liz's foot catches on something—a board game? A pile of clutter?—that someone placed on the first step.

The ground drops out. Liz is suddenly flailing, airborne, catapulting into the darkness. Her hip catches the edge of a stair, her elbow slams into something—the banister—her head against the steps. "Agghhhhh," she blurts. "No . . . !"

She crashes like a bowling ball into the stockpile of Amazon boxes at the bottom of the stairs.

As she tries to sit up, her hip throbs with cloying, searing pain. Liz shifts to take her weight off it. A deep shot of agony sparks down her leg.

"Hello?!" A voice, muffled, sounds through the dark. "Who's there!"

Liz freezes.

That voice.

Not Reid's or Callie's.

"I said, who's there!"

Liz lets out a whimper. *Sabina.* Alive. Sabina is alive!

"Sabina, it's Li—Mrs. Brinkley, but don't open the safe room door!"

"MOMMY!" Callie's voice, booming from the safe room, is a full-bodied hug. A cocoon. The best, brightest sound Liz has ever heard.

"Oh, baby, yes, I'm here," Liz chokes out. "I'm okay—"

"Mom!" Reid. Liz's tears churn the darkness into a thick current of black. Perfect, beautiful, devilish, wondrous Reid. "Mommy, please, Mom, we were so scared—"

"Oh, my babies, stay put, all right, I'm here. We're all right here."

They're alive. They are *right there*, behind the door. Liz crawls on her hands and knees toward the safe room, then collapses against it. "We're together, we are all together," she croaks. "And Daddy soon, so soon."

She closes her eyes and touches the safe room, imagining her hand passing straight through it, wrapping around them, pulling her children close. For one perfect, singular instant everything in the world is all right. Liz lets the moment unfold, surround her, fortify her. Until she's convinced that this sliver of a flash, right here, right now, will come to define her whole existence.

An unfamiliar sensation, gratitude, relief, peace, everything, all at once, flows through her. She hardly feels the pain in her hip anymore.

"I need to know you're all okay," she calls. "Do you have food, water—?"

"Yes," Sabina says. "We're down to snacks, but . . . I've tried so hard—I—" Sabina's voice cracks.

How Liz longs to reach through again, to pull the over-prepared little girl into her arms. Gather all of them. Is Sabina still wearing her business attire? What exactly have they eaten? How have they passed the time? How have they survived?

"I want to see you so badly," Liz says. "We just need to make sure it's safe. That the house stays safe—that I'm not a danger. Just a little while longer. But you've done so well. You all—you all are so, so very, *very* brave. I love you. More than anything. I love you so much."

Liz peers at the ceiling, so dark right now that it looks like it opens to space. Somewhere across this expanse there is someone, just like Liz, reuniting with their children. Somewhere else, someone's taking their last breath. In another corner of the world, someone balances on the razor's edge of a life-changing step. How could she not see it before? How did she not feel it, this connection, this looping, beautiful tethering across the world?

"I want you, Mommy," Callie cries.

"I know, baby. I love you. I need you too."

Sabina's voice is thin but strong as wire. "But we're okay, right, guys? We'll be all right. Made it this far, Mrs. Brinkley."

With sudden bone-shaking clarity, Liz remembers Mrs. Ford.

"Sabina, I can't—" She chokes on a sob. "I can't thank you enough. You've saved their lives. You've saved *my* life." Is *Mr.*

Ford alive, she wonders? What does the future hold for this resourceful little girl?

"Mom," Reid croaks. "I really can't wait to see you."

"Oh, my Reid." She turns and presses her face into the cold exterior of the safe room door. She closes her eyes and sings. Nonsensical at first, but then a song from long ago emerges from the drivel. From the days of nursing Callie, Reid beside her in Callie's big rocker, all of them drifting off to sleep. "*Love burns bright in the dark . . .*"

Her vision adjusts. The piles of her and Tom's Amazon shipments come into focus—the blankets, cots, the astronaut food pouches. Sabina has done some damage already. Good girl. Brilliant girl.

"*Like a beacon, like a beacon . . .*"

Liz decides, then and there, that she'll take care of her. She'll love Mrs. Ford's daughter as long as Sabina will let her. If she survives tonight.

Let them all survive tonight.

Liz curls her body around the door.

Britta

#Epilogue

G UIDE TO THE *End of the World*.
        Too on the nose.
    New World Playbook.
    Absolutely not, Christ, that sounds like some diabolical football coach's guide.
    "Mom!" Avery calls from downstairs. "Mom, I need you!"
    Britta looks down at the mound of items she's been tasked with hand-washing. Old habits die hard, apparently. How long has she been playing this silly game, just staring into her half-filled iron clawfoot tub, brainstorming titles for an *Insta* post-apoc comeback banner? The water they took the care to boil must be lukewarm by now.
    "MOM!"
    "I'm coming!"
    Britta drops the still-soiled laundry back into a basket near the tub. As she passes the bathroom's mirror, she barely recognizes the haggard woman staring back. Ugh, her *roots*. Is she honestly wearing sweatpants? There's just been so much to do—a never-ending list of daily tasks, cleaning, helping with

the cooking, planning, outreach, communication. The glimmer quarantine order lifted, what, four weeks ago, after sightings and casualties finally, slowly dwindled, and then stopped altogether. Yet Spencer Young and Romer Moreno have essentially made this their permanent residence . . . not to mention the countless grieving friends, from The Club, that she's taken in for a night or two, just until they have the strength to face their new reality. So many lives lost. So many families dismantled. She could walk down any block in The Falls and rattle off a dozen casualties, which leaves Britta Harris-Che running the world's most luxe commune.

Oddly, though, she doesn't mind her new situation. Being busy is so much better than being lonely.

Britta's been thinking a lot about "necessities" these past few weeks. For as much as she sometimes pretends that she's planning the rebranding event of the century, she's also been . . . secretly . . . content? To just worry about the next meal, the next move . . . to scheme *with* others (instead of, say, against them).

She heads down the hall, past Marco's room, slowing when she hears Joel reading to him inside.

"*But there is only one hat, and two of us . . .*"

Jon Klassen's *We Found a Hat*. Marco's favorite.

"I still don't get it," Marco says as Britta steps inside the room. "Why don't they just share it?"

Her ex looks up, smiling when he realizes she's watching. And *ex* being a less-than-formal term, though they've come to a mutually agreed-upon arrangement. They've become civil since the power came back on intermittently and they've been able to leave the cellar. She had some things to apologize for, of course. That fateful soiree. How she treated Joel near the end of their marriage. How she used denial as a sword and a shield.

But he owed her a whopping apology too.

"Oh," Marco says. "Hey, Mom."

Britta leans against the doorframe. "You two want some lunch? Romer should be back soon from the Gardens."

"What do you say, kiddo?" Joel gives Marco a hug as he meets her eyes. His are kind again, like they were long ago, warm and forgiving. That's what she remembers most from the beginning: Joel's kindness. When she'd found out about the pregnancy, she'd told Joel he could be as present or as absent as he wanted. His answer had been to move halfway across the world, back to where Britta grew up, to make an "honest life" with her, whatever that meant. To be a real parent to his daughter. They both had changed the entire trajectory of their lives because of Avery, because of *one weekend* ten years ago.

Neither regrets the decision. But as he's tried to explain, during their late-night chats when the rest of the house is asleep and the two of them sit reminiscing and chipping away at their wine stash, Joel changed the course of who he was becoming too.

"Lunch!" Marco agrees giddily as Joel tickles him into another bear hug. "Lunch, lunch, lunch!"

Britta laughs. "Twenty minutes?"

Joel winks. "Sounds perfect."

She turns for the hall. She'll always love Joel on some level, there's no getting around that, but they've been through enough, haven't they? Joel shouldn't need to, say, hide in the garage and masturbate to man porn. She *wants* him to be happy, surprisingly. And if brutish Spencer actually makes him so, then hurrah, hurrah, *#Rebootedmodernfamily*, etcetera.

Britta takes the stairs, pointedly ignoring the hallway mirror, too.

Mabel, on the other hand . . .

She's yet to even *visit*, refuses to even share space with Spencer, which means she hasn't seen Britta since she ran out of the wine cellar. And Britta's positive that Liz and Padma see Mabel and Greg all the time—Britta knows from Liz's regular calls checking in.

Whatever, Britta can't take Mabel's preferences personally. Obviously, her house comes with serious baggage . . .

But yes, of course, she's hurt.

As Britta enters her kitchen, she finds Avery sitting at their table, surrounded by a flurry of papers, drawings, and sketches. The pile surprises Britta, seeing as it's late May and there have been no signs at all of returning to school—to any real semblance of their old life—at least for the foreseeable future. The idea of a working Falls infrastructure is laughable, really, a pipe dream, as it seems to be everywhere else. Locally, they've got rationed power, thanks to a slim, tireless staff working in shifts to give the county access to electricity for cooking and other essential uses. But who knows when other modern conveniences—industry, distribution, education—are coming back. Romer has been feeding them and their neighbors through makeshift backyard crops and new "gardens" in the town park, for goodness' sake.

Still, they're so damn lucky. Britta knows that. So much luckier than most.

Avery visibly relaxes when she sees her. "I want to show you something."

Britta leans over her daughter's shoulder.

"I've been trying to figure out how we can spread important messages, you know?" Avery says. "Now that service is so spotty and the TVs still aren't running."

Avery arranges three pieces of paper in an orderly row. Her drawings are crude, but they're labeled, and it only takes Britta a moment to realize that they display their Falls neighborhood. She's sketched out all the main roads and intersections: Hobart Lane, Prospect Road, Sulton Street. Old Falls Road runs down the center of town like a spine. Moreover, Avery has drawn a map of arrows, from house to house, with little labels like *"Pass message"* and *"share news."* The map is cursory, of course, but the arrows extend accurately across The Falls, an economic system of passing information through the community. Like a modern-day Paul Revere's ride.

"My goodness," Britta whispers. Because this makes sense. There is *vision* here, cohesion, a fundamental understanding of how information is disseminated. Christ, her daughter is a natural. #PotentialCollab? #LikeMotherLikeDaughter?

No, her Insta-days are behind her. For the most part.

"This is good," Britta murmurs. "Actually, this . . . this is brilliant, Avery."

Her daughter blushes, then beams.

"I'm so proud of you. We've really got to show your fath—"

"Britta?"

Britta turns to find Romer leaning against the kitchen entrance, staring at them.

"A word?"

Her heart gives that strange flutter, as it always does whenever she hears her name on Romer's lips. *Briii-ttha*. No one else has ever said her name like that before. Like a lullaby, or a prayer.

"Ah yes, of course."

Romer waits for her to follow.

She trails him into the back hallway and up their second set of stairs. She's not sure what she's so nervous about. That he's overworked? Unappreciated? She's shared her home with him, after all, despite how most of the neighborhood now calls it "Romer's," like some pop-up, end-of-the-world chic café. And fine, she can't pretend he hasn't near single-handedly given them hope, breathed new life and purpose into The Falls. Romer spends most days at the Gardens and most nights locked in her cupboard, analyzing its contents, running inventory of their stash of canned goods and supplies. Trying to cook up ingenious new recipes for the community (now there's an idea if the internet ever really gets powered up and going again—*Post-Apocalyptic Chic: Pantry to Table*).

Romer finally stops at the end of her hall, then turns and walks straight through her bedroom door.

She follows him inside.

"We need to talk," he murmurs. "About my place here."

How fast she turns cold. Is he about to tell her that he's going to *leave*? Does he want to go back to New York? *Why?*

The cities were hit even harder—entire apartment buildings, city blocks, subway systems, gone—indeed the news (that they get) says the glimmer's casualties could be almost a *billion*. The entire world is in a state of repair. And yes, comparatively, her home can feel a little crowded, overwhelmed, but they're making a new collective life here—why leave and venture into the unknown, especially when the unknown is clearly in shambles?

Unless he's miserable.

"Well, we were in a time of transition," she says, as diplomatically as she can muster. "It was good of you, saintly really, to stay and help as long as you have. But of course you have your own life to make. Can't expect you to cook avant-garde feasts for what's left of the neighborhood forever, right?" She laughs uncomfortably, then takes a cautious step closer. "But truly . . . thank you . . . for everything you've done. Who you are. Really, I couldn't have survived this without you. We've loved having . . . I've loved—please rest assured—*ooooh*!"

Before she realizes what's happening, Romer's gone and swept her, tango-style, into her walk-in closet.

Then he steps back, as if assessing her reaction; Romer, now the one looking nervous.

"Britta, I don't want to go anywhere." He reaches for her hand, turns her wrist. "That is . . . if you want me to stay."

Her heartbeat bleats inside her throat.

He slowly, carefully, wraps his decadent arms around her waist. "I've asked you before and I'll dare ask you again," he whispers. "What do you want?"

She can't contain her smile. Unbounded, joyful, she answers him with her body, her entire frame reacting to his spontaneously, unscripted. Standing on her tiptoes, back arching, a sudden, thrilling warmth spreading down her spine (#SteamyChefinResidence? #PostApocRomance?).

"Does this answer your question?" she whispers.

She kisses him first.

30

Liz

"ALIENS," REID SAYS as Liz scrubs her face over the bucket of tepid water.

"Aliens?" Liz echoes, then laughs. "You really think aliens are going to spot this mess of a planet on their way to some galactic convention and say, *Hey, you know what, let's be Good Samaritans, make a pit stop and save these sorry sacks?*"

Reid smiles a toothy grin and shrugs. "Maybe."

Liz twists her hair's excess water out over the bucket. She has to admit, she's quite taken with Reid's faith in such a beneficent universe. That, despite everything that's happened over the past month or so, her son can still *believe* in such a universe. Liz has spent most of these last few weeks teaching him, Callie, and Sabina (and Greg, as much as Mabel will let her) all the "survival basics" she picked up from her *World Breakers* research in their backyard. How to distinguish edible mushrooms. How to hunt squirrels with a homemade bow and arrow set—though that one doesn't translate as easily to real life, unfortunately. How to build and light a fire with friction. The Falls' pantries will probably last until the new park community gardens are fully up and running, thanks to Chef

Romer and good fortune, but it's never a bad idea to learn potentially necessary life skills.

"Liz?" Tom calls upstairs. "You ready?"

"Coming!"

"Time to hop, kiddo." She rumples Reid's shaggy, overgrown hair. "And clean this mop already—"

"Aw, can't I just do it tomorrow?"

"The water's already warm and soapy," she says. Besides, there's no way she wants to get into the habit of going to the town reservoir every day. Most folks are making the effort to get their water directly from the source when they can, versus relying on the water main, as staffing's slim everywhere. *Is the faucet water* really *clean? Can they be sure anymore?* Anyway, they need to conserve—it's the community's only true freshwater resource—but she resists the urge to share this little speech with Reid. *Again.*

Her son groans, but finally does as she asks, and holds his nose, dunking the top of his head into the bucket. For like *two seconds*, but Liz bites her tongue again. He flips his head up, grinning at himself in the mirror, then slicks the wet thicket of hair into a serious mohawk. "I'll meet you down there."

Liz rolls her eyes and laughs.

Right as she steps into the hall, Callie bursts out of her room. Her daughter monster-tackles her legs before she can descend the stairs.

"It's okay, sweetheart," Liz whispers. "I'm not going anywhere."

But she lifts Callie up anyway and carries her down the steps.

Tom and Sabina look up from the entryway, watching them.

"Where's Reid?" Sabina says.

Liz smirks. "Still primping."

They're making the trek over to Mabel's house, a near-daily excursion ever since Tom arrived home. The walk is two miles. Once upon a time, a trek down Old Falls Road and into the Park section would have felt unfathomable, but now, it's nothing more than a morning jaunt. Pack travel. Communities stitched together through well-worn routes.

Liz assumes most of the world looks as primitive as The Falls does these days, and she'd be lying if she said this simplified life didn't suit her. But she'd also be lying if she said she never wakes up at night sobbing for what they've lost. For *who* they've lost. Laura. Tom's parents. Padma's father; Mabel's brother. Kat, Gwen, and Frank. Mrs. Ford—maybe Mr. Ford too, unless he's still out there, somewhere; they won't stop searching for Sabina's sake. And, Liz recently heard through neighbors, Damon Campbell. Someone said he never returned home from his patrolling that night back in April—maybe all that "green-men target practice" cost him in the end.

Not to mention, of course, the hundreds of millions of others.

"Reid, buddy, it's just a walk!" Tom calls up.

"All right, all right!"

And then they're out the door.

Reid immediately skips ahead down the sidewalk. But Sabina takes Callie's hand. "Just because there's no cars doesn't mean you don't need to be careful." She throws a discreet wink to Liz. "Now, come on. No stepping on cracks."

"Why not?" Callie says.

"Because . . . because you'll have a panic attack."

Callie giggles.

Tom raises Liz an eyebrow.

"I'll have a talk with her," Liz whispers.

Tom calls ahead to Reid, "Hey, buddy, not too far."

Reid groans. "I know, I know."

Tom and Liz fall into lockstep as they walk through the remains of the neighborhood. So many abandoned cars, empty homes. Trash cans and recycling bins still lie like carcasses along the roadside. The town's trying to pick up the pieces, like everywhere else in the world, but there's only so many left, and so much to do.

"I got word from the Harris-Ches the other day," Tom says.

Liz perks up at that. "Oh, yeah?"

"Joel called when you and Reid were at the Gardens. I was thinking of riding the bike over, making a visit."

"Maybe we should all go, together," Liz says. "I owe Britta a visit, too."

Tom nods. "Let's make it happen."

It's been just about a month since Tom left the Harris-Ches' basement and came home. As soon as Tom heard the remaining news sources claim the air was "safe enough" to breathe, he made the journey back. Which had been exactly ten days *after* Liz had burst through their home's front door and taken up permanent residence beside the safe room. The longest days of Liz's life.

Tom mentioned it was hard to glean an accurate picture of what was going on, as there were so many conflicting sources and information. These days, the few reporters at the *Times* say casualties have mounted to a point where counting is impossible. The skeleton staff at *The Guardian* keeps dropping the number "a billion." But Liz doesn't need the internet to confirm their new reality. She sees it every day.

In The Falls, at least, lots of people worry that the glimmer is still loaded in the air, despite experts' declarations that the threat is gone. That the phenomenon could be lingering, waiting for the perfect conditions to mount and wreak havoc again. It's made people cautious. Superstitious, even. Wi-Fi is still a mess, and logging onto the internet a distant dream—but many of their neighbors claim they're never going to use devices again, at least until they find out what caused the glimmer. The popular theory right now is that it was man-made, designed to travel and infect through communication systems. Others say it was an ancient pathogen released from the ice—one somehow able to spread through energy waves.

Spencer, though, still swears up and down to anyone who will listen that it's aliens.

"Reid!" Greg bursts out the front door when they're still halfway down the block. He nearly tackles Liz's son with a bear hug. "I've got the troops cornered in the treehouse, but I can't handle them myself. Come on!"

Reid cackles and trails Greg into his backyard. Liz watches, a gear in her heart clicking into place. Mabel once called her son a bully, but now, nothing could be further from the truth. The boys are thick as thieves. Not that Reid chats about anything emotional ("*feelings, ew gross*") but their friendship is one of the best things that came out of this mess.

Liz's friendships, too.

She and Tom follow the boys into Mabel's slightly overgrown backyard, the tulips sprouting, bright and beautiful, in front of the shrubs, the weeds bursting from the roots. The undeniable disorder makes Liz's heart swell. Finally, Mabel has slowed down, is taking care of her own needs, prioritizing her rest and health.

Mabel comes to the back door now and opens her screen door. She smiles. "I wasn't expecting company today." Which is what Mabel always says—a running joke, by this point.

So Liz responds with her own well-worn lines: "We're not company. Now come out. Sit down."

Mabel sighs, but does as she's told, taking a seat in one of the clustered patio chairs. Liz slides onto the one beside her.

On cue, Padma and Dev walk around the Youngs' side yard. Dev holds what appears to be some sort of prepared appetizer. Probably an old Clementine recipe. Padma's beside him, looking radiant, wearing Isobel on her chest in a carrier.

"Ladies," Padma says brightly, then curtseys, as if for a pair of queens.

"Morning," Dev adds, following Padma up the short set of stairs, setting his dish on the patio table.

Padma slips into the empty chair on Liz's other side, peering up at Dev. "Want to pull another one over, hun?"

"And interrupt this trio?" Dev smirks. "I think I know better." He winks and crosses the yard to join Tom.

Padma smiles. "I've trained him well."

"Which is good, because I only brought three." Liz reaches into her weathered tote bag and pulls out her surprise: a few White Claws, old-world contraband and warm as hell.

Still, Mabel and Padma simultaneously gasp with delight.

"What's the occasion?" Mabel says.

Liz shrugs with a smile. "You're looking at it."

"Oooh, put mine on ice. *Proverbial* ice." Padma leans down and murmurs to Isobel, "Your libations come first."

As Padma arranges Isobel to nurse, Liz cracks the cans open and passes them around. Then she takes a long, warm, satisfying sip.

They all watch as Sabina leads Callie into Greg's sandbox to play. Tom and Dev, laughing, linger nearby, offering tips for how to avoid crumbling the castles. Reid and Greg, meanwhile, keep racing around the yard, calling out nonsensical commands as they thrust their finger-guns in the air.

"By the way, Mabel, Britta keeps asking about you," Liz says, aiming for casual.

Padma gives a knowing little laugh. "Here we go."

Mabel waggles her can. "You're trying to get me buzzed, aren't you? Have me impulsively agree to a reunion?"

Liz shrugs. "Is it such a crime to get a dinner on the calendar?"

Mabel and Padma both burst out laughing. It's a lovely sound, loud and free and unexpected.

"Of course I miss her." Mabel tips her head back against her chair. "But I'm just not ready. To see Spencer, to go over there and get into it. And . . . I think it's probably my job to extend the olive branch after everything."

"You know how sensitive Britta is, is all," Liz says.

"Sensitive, sadistic. Potato, pohtahto," Padma says—then rolls her eyes when Liz shoots her an admonishing glare. "Come on, you both know I'm *joking*. I swear, I'm over her shenanigans."

"And, anyway, you don't have to go over there," Liz says. "I think Britta would hop on Joel's Schwinn in a heartbeat if she thought you wanted to see her."

Mabel stays silent.

"In fact, I . . . could set something up," Liz says carefully, "if you'd be open to it. For all of us. Like a real get-together. Maybe at my house." But she feels strange, almost giddy, as soon as the words sail out.

Mabel takes a long sip, considering her.

"Okay, Liz," she says finally. "Go ahead, work your peace-making magic."

Padma lets out a feigned gasp. "Do my ears deceive . . . or is *Liz Brinkley* our new social coordinator?" She tucks Isobel back into the carrier, finally picks up her White Claw, and clinks it against Liz's in approval.

Liz bites back a smile, making a mental note to tell Britta about this development in person. Liz can't wait to see her face. Yes, it's a small win, she supposes, building a bridge between people she's grown to care about, people she may even love. But the realization that she, of all people, is making connections—bringing people together instead of polarizing them—fills Liz with a glittering, unexpected burst of hope, like impromptu fireworks on a random summer night.

She sinks back in her patio chair, enjoying the tangy fizz of the drink on her tongue, the sounds of Tom and her children's laughter, the warm, early summer dew on her skin. She wishes she could bottle this all, stop time somehow, tell Mabel and Padma that this moment matters, that *they* matter. That the universe may go on expanding, spinning, cold, oblivious, without any of them, but that Liz's world will never be the same.

Liz gives a playful shrug. "No promises," she says, "but I'll rise to that challenge."

ACKNOWLEDGMENTS

THIS STORY IS ultimately a story about family and community, so I'd like to start by thanking mine. I am beyond blessed to have the support and endless love of my parents, Linda and Joe Appicello, who fostered my love of writing, reading, and life itself: your joy and dedication to our family made me want to be a parent, and it's been the greatest gift. A huge thanks to my confidantes and life partners-in-crime, my sisters Jill and Bridget; to my ever-encouraging and enthusiastic husband Jeff, who makes every day better by being in it; to my children, Penn and Summer, the world's best cheerleaders—you never let me give up, and you make me want to make you proud.

Thanks to my family "in law" and in heart: Alice, Paul, Jon, Mike, Susan, Peter, Alicia, Kevin, Jon, Laura, and Will (the last two who get extra thanks for lending their names to recent stories). Lots of love, too, to my SHC community (especially the paddle girls!) and my OKS moms' crew. You are the best support network a parent could ask for (though I'm so grateful I didn't have to survive the horrific experiences in this book to find you all ;).

Huge thanks to Toni Kirkpatrick, my wonderful, savvy, supportive editor and warm welcomer to the Crooked Lane fold; Yezanira Venecia, whose keen editorial insight and feedback crystallized the book's twists and themes; Rebecca Nelson, my excellent and dedicated production editor; and Sarah Brody, the talented designer of this book's fabulous cover. Many thanks too to Madeline Rathle, Dulce Botello, Thai Perez, Stephanie Manova, and the rest of the remarkable Crooked Lane team.

A million thanks to my brilliant and tireless agent, Katelyn Detweiler, who believed in this story from the very beginning and who brought new insight and fresh excitement to all its iterations. Your support is boundless, and I am simply the luckiest to have you in my corner. Lots of gratitude as well to Denise Page, Sam Farkas, and the rest of the all-star crew at JGLM, and to my dynamite film agent, Debbie Deuble Hill.

I'd also like to express gratitude to early readers Melissa Frain, Jennifer Thorne, Lori Goldstein, Lindsey Leavitt Brown, and Nicky Lovick—you are all story gurus and phenomenal human beings—and to my community of writers who make the author life so much more fun: my Freshman Fifteens, Fearless Fifteeners, Princeton-Yardley lunch group, VCFA family, *mediabistro* crew, and last but certainly not least, my Alliterati cohort. You are all found family at its finest. Thank you for your continued support, friendship, and camaraderie over these many years.

Finally, a heartfelt thanks to every reader, bookseller, librarian, BookToker, bookstagrammer, and book blogger who picked up this genre-blending novel and spread the word about it. This story was a very different and difficult one for me, and there were many days where I assumed its final home might be my laptop. I am so thrilled and grateful that *With Regrets* found its way into your hands.